Incorruption

By the same author

Fiction titles:

The Knowledge Stone (Piquant)

Non-Fiction titles

A Small Piece of Pure Gold (Highland)

Climate Change Apocalypse (Highland)

Divine Weather (Highland)

Incorruption

Jack McGinnigle

First published in 2017 by Highland Books Ltd,
2 High Pines, Knoll Road, Godalming, Surrey, GU7 2EP.

ISBN-13: 978-1897913-94-9

ISBN-10: 1-897913-94-x

e-edition ISBN: 978-1909690-94-3

Printed in Great Britain by CPI Limited, Croydon

Contents

Dedication

In memory of my friend
John Nodding

Part One

Mayn

1

Day 1

The man inside the escape pod said nothing, almost thought nothing, as he felt the gentle bump that announced his arrival on the asteroid. However, just for an instant, he felt a pang of admiration for the sophistication of the vehicle that contained him, able to transport the Space traveller so safely, so comfortably on their chosen journey; able to save them from harm when danger threatened. And this man knew that this was precisely the purpose for which this vehicle had been designed.

Unfortunately, this particular journey had not been to rescue, nor even to transport pleasantly and conveniently. This journey was different, exceptional in so many ways. It had not taken long, no more than half a day, so vast distances of Space had not been traversed. Nevertheless, the man inside recognised he had been cut off from his previous life. Effectively excised from it, in fact.

It had all started so casually. Part of an ordinary day. Admittedly, he had thought it was an unusual request. It had been many years since he was asked to investigate a problem in a GTN67UV Escape Pod. This vehicle was standard equipment on the large Space Survey Platform (SSP) Yggdrasil, his home for the last five years. The Platform had a great many of this type of escape pod, each one primed for any emergency;

indeed, all large Space vehicles in the Command were similarly equipped so the routine service technicians were well used to dealing with these small but essential vehicles. On the other hand, the man had told himself, it must be a very unusual problem – so unusual that the technicians were seeking advice from the very designer of the vehicle himself. He remembered smiling: 'That's the trouble with calling it a GTN – it reminds people that it's Gorton-designed!'

In fact, Scientist-Commander Dr Maynard Gorton (Mayn to his friends) had been very much in the forefront of Space vehicle design for more than a decade. In his early twenties, his all-round brilliance had been recognised by Command and very soon he had held an important research and design position. In subsequent years, he had been personally responsible for the conception and design of many of the Space vehicles that were used routinely across all Regions. Because of this, he was very well known across the whole Command; famous, in fact. On SSP Yggdrasil, the largest and most complex of the Space Survey Platforms, he was now the highest ranking Space research and design engineer on board despite his young age, just in his early thirties. Invariably, his expertise was sought when intractable problems baffled the scientific and technical teams.

In addition to these extremely important scientific and technical qualities, Maynard Gorton was recognised to be a wonderful influence on the Platform. Everyone from the Chief Commanding Officer (CCO1) downwards consulted him when serious difficulties developed in any aspect of the Platform's operations. Although many of these problems were apparently not within Mayn's area of expertise, somehow he was always able to help. Almost mysteriously, he brought peace to situations of tension or conflict, resolution to human or organisational disharmony and perfect solutions to apparently insoluble problems.

People would shake their heads in admiration and speak in tones of wonder. 'I really don't know how he does it! He makes it look so simple. Time and again we have a situation that cannot be solved, a situation that's getting worse and worse and then – we take it to him and he makes everything

OK. He comes up with the perfect solution. And we scratch our heads and say: "Why didn't we think of that!" Why, I've even seen him sort people out after the Meds have given up on them! Not the physical stuff – they have machines to sort that out – I'm talking about the really difficult cases, the psychological breakdowns and the like. He can sort those out. Can you believe that? Maynard Gorton is a wonderful guy. We're so very lucky to have him on the Platform.'

Because of all these amazing feats, Mayn had acquired a nickname that was well-known throughout the Platform. In recent years, he had become "The Yggdrasil Healer", a name invariably spoken with awe and respect. If Mayn knew about his nickname, he never gave any sign.

Consulting the brief message for assistance on his communicator, Mayn now climbed aboard his personal transporter buggy and gave the location of the GTN pod to the vehicle's control system. Because the pod was located in a very remote part of the Platform, at the farthest end of one of the huge trailing arms, it was almost half an hour before he arrived at the spacious docking area, after travelling along several kilometres of deserted metal corridors. Parking the buggy by the side of the docking area, he crossed the decking and approached the familiar shape of the escape pod, held securely in its launch mountings.

Through the open hatch of the pod, he could see bright engineering lights burning inside. 'Let's hope whoever is in there can explain to me exactly what the problem is,' he thought, 'I have a meeting at 1400 and I don't want to be late.' He climbed the steps to the open hatch and stuck his head inside, calling out:

'Hello! Commander Gorton responding to your call. Technical Team, respond, where are you?'

Silence, apart from the low hum of powered-up equipment. 'Perhaps they're in the engineering area of the dock,' he thought, 'I'll go and check there.'

Returning to deck level, he made his way to the inner part of the docking area where there were work benches and a large range of electronic and mechanical equipment, everything brightly lit and powered-up. However, there was still no sign of any technicians.

'Hello,' he called again, 'anyone here?' Silence. No movement. No response. Just winking equipment lights. 'This is becoming a bit of a mystery,' he told himself, 'I'll have one last check in the pod and, if I can't find anyone, I'll just instigate a broadcast query and return to my office.'

This time, Mayn climbed through the hatch into the interior of the GTN67UV. He smiled as he looked around, remembering how he had worked for many months on the design of the vehicle, working out with precision where all the equipment should be fitted and building an inspired ergonomic control system for those who would travel in it.

'Hello!' He shouted this loudly in case the technicians were unable to hear his normal voice level over the noise of the whirring systems. 'It's Commander Gorton. You called for my help!' Still no response. He swept his eyes around the Control Cabin, noting that some of the equipment casings were unlocked and propped open. 'Looks like problems with the control systems,' he murmured, 'I wonder what it is?'

Mayn swung himself into the seat at Control Position P1 and scanned the dials and screens for clues. As he did so, he heard a familiar sound – the unmistakable "swoosh" of the hatch closing. As he looked around, he could see the inner handle rotating to "Full Lock". 'That's funny,' he thought, 'I certainly didn't do that, because the hatch controls are operated from Control P2.' He slid across to Control P2 and reviewed the switch settings there. Sure enough, the hatch control was switched to "Close" and "Full Lock".

'Maybe this is the fault they were calling me about,' he mused. 'I've certainly never heard about any problem with this part of the system. It's perfectly straightforward and normally gives no trouble. It's very much a standard vehicle fitment.' As he thought these words, he clicked the switches to "Unlock" and "Open". Nothing happened. He clicked the switches back and forward several times to no avail. Puzzled, he released the catches on the panel and lifted it up on its hinges to study the connections below. 'Nothing abnormal here,' he commented under his breath.

Rising to his feet, he walked to a small storage recess nearby and collected an Engineer's Kit. Returning to position P2, he lifted the panel again and checked the connections with a sensitive meter, noting that the various readings were precisely as expected.

'Vehicle on standard countdown for transit. Minutes ten and counting.' The voice was loud and strident. This was a deliberate design feature to guarantee that everyone on board was aware of the impending departure. Mayn sighed and sat down at Control P1, clicking a switch to transmit.

'Register command: Origin Commander Maynard Gorton aboard GTN67UV Serial GTN36716XT: Abort countdown immediately. Acknowledge.'

{The response was immediate}

"Command not accepted. Vehicle under special control. Minutes nine and counting."

'Repeat register command: Origin Commander Maynard Gorton aboard GTN67UV Serial GTN36716XT: Abort countdown immediately. Acknowledge.'

"Repeat command not accepted. Vehicle under special control. Minutes eight and counting."

With a tongue click of annoyance, the man clicked the transmit switch to open once more.

'Register Condition Red Command. I repeat Condition Red Command. Disconnect all external control this vehicle. Return control to internal. This is a Condition Red Command. Acknowledge.'

There was a full minute of silence. Then the voice blared out:

"Condition Red command rejected. Special situation obtains. Minutes six and counting."

For the first time, Mayn felt that solid, heavy pang of fear low in his stomach. His mind whirled. What was happening here? How could Central Control ignore a Condition Red Command? This was totally illogical, impossible, even. Condition Red Commands were an early safeguard introduced when Space travel first became widespread. It was the ultimate guarantee that the human controller could always take over any situation. Mayn's head started to pulse with tension. He racked his brains. Surely he could do something? Surely this couldn't possibly happen?

> "Vehicle on standard countdown for flight."

The emotionless mechanical voice was harsh and strident.

> "Four minutes and counting. All personnel secure themselves for departure."

Mayn rose to his feet and strode to the closed hatch. He would unlock the hatch manually and he knew that this would shut the departure sequence down. He seized the handle and tried to turn it to the "Unlock" position. The handle would not move. He applied all his strength to no avail.

Mayn now returned to Control P1. He had just remembered the Emergency Power Down Control, fitted to every vehicle. This was a "Fail Safe" control designed for dire emergencies. He would operate this and all would be well! The large red knob was located on a separate control panel with a stout hinged cover protecting it from inadvertent operation. Mayn flipped back the cover and punched the knob, knowing that he would immediately hear the distinctive clicking of many electrical relays as their electrical contacts were broken followed by a strange wailing harmony of descending tones as all the pumps, generators and electric motors powered down. Of course, he also knew that all the lights in the vehicle would be extinguished at the same time. 'Good test for the backup illumination,' he muttered.

Nothing happened. No clicks. No wails. No darkness. Astonished, he punched the red emergency knob again and again. No response.

"Two minutes and counting."

The voice blared through speakers in all parts of the vehicle, causing him to start.

"All personnel secure themselves for departure."

Suddenly, a revelation! His PAC (Personal Advisor Communicator)! How could he have forgotten that? He could initiate a Platform-wide emergency call from that. Yes, he accepted it was probably too late to prevent the vehicle from undocking but the Duty Central Controller would soon take over manual control of the vehicle and turn it around to execute a re-dock back at the Platform. As he took out his PAC from a pocket, he thought: 'This malfunction will certainly be an interesting one to sort out! I look forward to that!' (This surprising thought flitted through the consciousness of his fright.) PAC in hand, he activated its emergency control. Nothing happened. He looked at the device with surprise, seeing immediately that the power indicator showed "Zero". 'How can it be discharged? These are always on auto power charge!' He was dumbfounded as these instant thoughts flashed through his mind.

Then he felt it. A vibration spreading through the vehicle. Mayn knew exactly what this was. The engines were powering up. The departure sequence was underway. He heard the rumble of releasing external clamps and knew the vehicle was now free to leave the dock. As the designer of this vehicle, he knew the exact sequence of everything that was about to happen.

"Twenty seconds and counting."

The relentless metallic voice.

"All personnel make secure."

The vibration increased. The roar of the engines could be heard.

> "Vehicle departing. Ten, nine,
> eight, seven, six, five, four,
> three, two, one, ZERO."

The pressure of acceleration. The intense brightness outside. The vehicle efficiently stabilising itself, adjusting its course. The Platform diminishing in size on the screen. Mayn screaming, wrestling with flaccid, disconnected controls, his hands setting and resetting switches and control levers. Nothing worked. Internal control was totally inoperative. The small vehicle now set a purposeful course and its speed increased to a maximum. Soon, the Platform became a spot on the visual screen before it finally disappeared.

Mayn sat at Control P1, totally bewildered. How can this have happened to him? How could it happen to anyone? He shook his head and spoke out loud: 'I conceived and designed this vehicle to be a saviour. Every system is carefully structured to look after those who travel in it. All the safety features are carefully thought out. Everything is ergonomic. And, above all, the crew are always in control, whatever happens. Yes, it is fitted with the most sophisticated auto-flight systems but these must be switched on and programmed by the crew. Of course it is possible for the vehicle to be controlled from the Platform – every Space vehicle can be flown remotely – but fundamental control is never taken away from the crew. It's impossible. It just cannot happen.' He looked around and then added, 'but it just has happened.'

Suddenly, totally exhausted by fear and bewilderment, Mayn slumped back in his seat and entered a semi-dream world, a defence mechanism switched on by his body to allow him to recover to some degree. His dream state transferred him to the world of his earliest memories, the time he lived on Planet Earth. As a little child, he had been happy there. And happy memories were exactly what he needed at this moment to help to overcome the severe shocks he had just experienced.

Four years old. He remembered being four. Something unusual had happened when he was four, hadn't it? That's probably why he remembered it, he thought. He remembered the happy time, out with his father and mother in their little family transporter. He remembered the journey into the mountains, the fresh, cool air, the green of the trees and the soft grass under his feet. He remembered playing games with his father, games with a ball and a bat; thrilling chasing games, too. Running, being caught, being hugged. He remembered the lovely food and drinks that they had when they sat down beside a broad stream; the warm sunshine, glinting upon the sparkling water as it produced ever-changing, fascinating patterns of ripples as it flowed past. He remembered delight, pleasure and the happiness of love.

But then something was wrong. He felt it. The chill of it wrapped around him like a clammy blanket, changing the day from warm, comfortable, safe pleasure to a darkening feeling of worry and concern, a trembling feeling of fear, happiness cruelly banished. He looked around. Nothing had changed, had it? The sun still shone down, the stream flowed on as before; they were still there, the three of them, serene, comfortable and fulfilled, weren't they?

Then he looked at his parents and at that moment, he knew. There was no serenity there, no happiness, no reassuring smiles. They both looked lost and bewildered, grim and serious. For some reason, his father was standing in the river with his hand and arm deep in the water. His mother was crouching on the river bank, whispering to him. The young Mayn leapt to his feet, ran to his mother and, sobbing with fear, threw himself into her arms.

His mother's loving arms tightened around him. 'It's OK, Mayn. There's nothing for you to worry about. Don't cry. It's just that we have a bit of a problem. Not a big problem but it's going to be a bit awkward for us.' Mayn was only four but already he was a very bright little boy, well advanced for his years. 'What is the problem?' he asked through his tears.

'Well,' said his mother, trying to sound reassuring, 'your father was taking his coat off and his keycard case has fallen into the river. That's why he has gone into the water. He's hoping he can find it.'

The man lifted dripping arms from the water and straightened up, his face dark with worry and concern. 'It's no use,' he said, 'I've searched the river bottom all around here and haven't found anything. The current is quite strong, so I think the keycard case has already been swept away. It could be anywhere downstream on the riverbed or it could still be floating towards the sea. Whichever, it's gone for good.' The man stepped back on to the river bank and sat down despondently, holding his head in his hands. 'I don't know what to do. It's a real disaster.'

Mayn knew this was serious. His parents had told him all about keycards and how important they were. He knew that all adults had special government-issued keycards to lock and unlock all the things they needed to keep secure. He knew also that it was against the Law to lose any cards and exceptionally difficult to replace them. This was a government security regulation and it was always strictly applied and invariably prosecuted.

'Don't you have your keycards with you?' Mayn asked his mother.

'I don't, Mayn. I didn't think I needed to bring them. They're back at the house. Anyway, most of my keycards are different from your father's.' She turned to address her husband. 'Listen, Darling, which keycards have you lost?'

He looked up, his expression horror-stricken. 'All of them. Every one. All the house cards. All the office cards, doors, desk, cabinets, safe. All the security and status cards. All the money cards.' Then his jaw dropped. 'Oh no,' he said, faintly.

'What is it?' A note of rising panic in his wife's voice.

'The transporter card is gone. How do we get home from here?' He looked wildly around at the deserted mountain and then at the sun sinking lower in the sky. At that moment, all three felt a sudden frightening chill in the air, the harbinger of a very cold night to come.

Strangely, the little boy had now stopped crying and he disengaged himself from his mother's arms. Going over to his father, he put his arms around him and said: 'Don't worry, Daddy, I'll help you.' The man was overcome. 'Thank you, Mayn, you're a lovely, very clever boy but I'm afraid there nothing you can do about this. All my keycards are gone. It's my fault. I was careless. But you don't need to worry, because I'll solve this somehow.'

As he said this, the man was overcome by the emptiness of deep despair. At that moment he couldn't imagine how he was going to solve the immediate problem of getting his family home again, or indeed how they would be able to enter their house when they finally got there. He knew also that the authorities would be totally unsympathetic and unhelpful. Losing your keycards was a serious misdemeanour and the authorities would make your life extremely awkward for a considerable period. The family of the perpetrator of the "crime" would also suffer.

They all sat in a silence of bleak contemplation for a few moments. Then his father, haggard and drawn, said: 'Mayn, could you just play by yourself for a few minutes while I speak to your mother.' The man and the woman sat down beside each other on a grassy bank and began to speak to each other in low tones, their heads close together, trying desperately to work out a strategy to deal with this catastrophic situation. They were so deeply absorbed in this conversation that they did not see their little son go a few metres downstream and reach down to trail a small hand in the flowing water. Minutes passed. The man and woman were staring into the abyss of no progress.

'Daddy...'

'Not now, Mayn, Darling. I'm talking to Mummy.'

The little boy said nothing as he placed a dripping keycard case in his father's hand. The man looked at the case in absolute disbelief. After a long pause he regained some semblance of speech.

'Mayn! How did you... What... How...' His voice faded as his mind blanked. He looked at this beautiful child with incredulous wonder and awe – his child, his flesh and blood – this child who had just produced the most wonderful, impossible solution to their insoluble problem.

The child was grave, looking steadily into the eyes of the man. He knew the question his father was trying to ask him. 'I just knew where to find it, Daddy,' he said quietly.

That was the first time.

Aboard the escape pod, Mayn surfaced through layers of unconsciousness and felt much calmer. 'This whole scenario needs to be studied carefully,' he told himself. 'Obviously I don't know where I'm going and how long I'm going to be in transit. Maybe I'm going nowhere. Maybe this vehicle is programmed to keep flying on a constant course until it runs out of energy.'

As the designer, Mayn knew that this would take a long time, years, in fact. The vehicle made its own energy from electromagnetic radiations in Space, using radiation sources from the millions of stars in the universes. However, knowing the design of the vehicle, he did not think it likely that it would have been programmed in that way because this would be a violation of the vehicle's own protection systems. 'It's much more likely to have a programmed destination,' he concluded. Then he added, 'not a destination that is populated – because I would then be able to report to Command what had happened to me on Yggdrasil. It's likely to be a small uninhabited body; a small planet or an asteroid.'

Satisfied that he had taken the logic of his flight circumstances as far as it could go, he now turned his attention to the question of taking control of the vehicle. 'I'll need to start right away and discover why I could not assume local control. Also why the emergency command systems did not work. With my detailed knowledge of this vehicle, hopefully, I can restore control. When I've discovered these things, I'll have to work out where I should go; not back to Yggdrasil, that's for sure! I should go to a medium or large-sized facility where I can make a full report to Command. Once I've set a course to that sort of facility, I can start to work out who might have done this to me and why. If I ever get out of this situation, I will report everything comprehensively to Command. They will investigate and act against the perpetrators of this crime. I would imagine they would send an investigation team.' He thought for a moment. 'I seem to remember that the Intergalactic Rescue and Salvage organisation (IRS) has a responsibility to do that sort of thing. One of their teams would probably be despatched to Yggdrasil to get to the bottom of it.' He rose to his feet. 'Now, time to get to work and find out why I have no control over this vehicle.' He said this out loud in a strong, determined tone.

Taking an engineering kit in hand, Mayn now began to work on the control system of the vehicle, checking inside the many control panels and system cabinets. Working quickly and methodically, he soon established why he was unable to restore local control. Virtually all of the local control modules had not only been disconnected but removed totally from the vehicle! This also applied to most of the communications systems and also to the emergency alert system as well.

Now he understood why the Automatic Central Control system on Yggdrasil acted as it did. It would have attempted to carry out his commands to switch to local control but found that it could not do so. In these circumstances, the Platform's system is programmed to seek the reason for its failure to comply; however, because the escape pod had been disabled in so many ways, its investigation would fail and terminate. As a result, it would revert to a refusal and resume the sequence of commands which locked him in the vehicle and sent him off on this journey.

Mayn sat down to assess the full implication of the missing equipment. Although it should be possible to disengage the central command control of the escape pod (he thought he could do that), he knew that action would send his vehicle out of control, tumbling violently in Space. This would happen because he had no facilities to take control. Wisely, he judged that this would be a catastrophic move.

His lack of communication facilities was equally serious because this included all the distress channels. The removal of the Distress Signalling system meant that he could not switch on the powerful signal that would have alerted every vehicle nearby of his emergency situation. In addition, all IRS rescue vehicles anywhere in the Region would have received the signals and the nearest would head towards him immediately.

He looked around the cabin at all the empty racks and cabinets. 'A clean sweep! I'll obviously check the backup spares situation but I have a feeling that all the spares for these systems will have disappeared. I had better carry out that search right away.'

Mayn now made his way to the storage areas of the vehicle and began to examine the spares situation. While most of the routine spares packs were still racked in their appointed places, the bays in which all the spares relating to the control systems, the communication systems and the Distress Signal equipment were empty. Noting all he had seen, he returned to a seat in the Control Cabin, saying to himself: 'Whoever did all this had a very high degree of skill and knowledge. I reckon that narrows it down a bit. I'll need to think about this later. First I need to see whether there's anything I can construct to replace any part of these missing systems. This will certainly be a real challenge.'

As he thought this, he recognised that the vehicle had begun to decelerate. He looked at the forward visual screen and saw that the vehicle was heading for a large asteroid, tumbling languidly in Space. The screen identified the asteroid as AT56G7/89. About thirty minutes later, the escape pod approached the asteroid and hovered above it until it had measured the spin and tumble below.

'All personnel secure themselves for landing,' the loud metallic voice commanded and Mayn strapped himself securely into the seat at Control P1. The vehicle then sank down very slowly towards the rocky surface of the asteroid, choosing the smoothest surface it could find. This proved to be in a shallow fissure in the surface. It was not long before the escape pod touched down gently and automatically stabilised itself before hooking on to the rocky surface to guarantee that the vehicle would not drift in the weak gravity field of the asteroid. Then, with a clear sense of finality, the engines powered down and all became silent apart from the humming and whine of the cabin life systems.

2

Day 2

In the disturbing stillness that now pervaded the escape pod, the vehicle's time display showed him that the dreadful Day108 of UniverseYear5664 had just come to an end. After unstrapping from his seat, he had consulted various control panels to check upon the operation of the life support systems of the vehicle and found them all set correctly for automatic operation. Unsurprisingly, he felt very tired and decided to retire to the sleeping compartment of the pod. 'Tomorrow is another day,' he told himself with grim irony. 'Tomorrow I'll get to work and start to dig myself out of this hole I'm in. But tonight, I really need to rest and recover.'

So saying, he went to the sleeping compartment, washed and dried in the highly efficient autoshower, donned a light sleeping suit and strapped himself into one of the two comfortable bunks. Before long his body had succumbed to sleep and, in a relaxing and restoring dream, his mind took him back once again to his childhood on Planet Earth. This time, he was ten years old.

'What's wrong, Lucy? What has happened to make you cry?' Mayn had gone to the house of his friend and constant companion, Lucy, a slight girl just a little younger than him.

He had found her sitting on a garden bench, weeping quietly. They had been firm friends for years, ever since her family had moved into the house adjacent to Mayn's. He had been absolutely delighted to see a child moving in next door. Previously, there had been no children living in that house and Mayn's only regular contact with other children had been at College, where learning was taken so very seriously that there was never any time to play or establish friendships with the other children there.

'You are here to learn as much as you can as quickly as you can,' their tutors had told them severely, fixing them all with a fierce and unfriendly gaze, 'we do not waste time on childish activities here. We leave playing and the like to the two-year olds and younger.'

So all the students at College spent their whole time in study, with just a few short breaks from time to time for essential rest, food and drink. Even then, they were "strongly encouraged" to spend these times in deep thought about their studies rather than in conversation with the other students. Absolute silence was expected. There was always a tutor on hand to ensure that students on "rest-time" obeyed the College directives on leisure behaviour. Those who did not were reprimanded and given extra work to do.

Mayn was around seven years old when Lucy and her family moved into the vacant house next door. Mayn had been excited when the previous occupants moved out; he hoped that the incoming occupants would be a family with a boy around his age. Mayn resolved that he would do his best to make firm friends with this boy and then they could meet in the evening after College and play a whole range of wonderful games in each other's gardens! Ball games, running games, noisy games – and rough and tumble games, of course! Mayn was totally enchanted by the prospect!

Then came the day when the removal transporter's vehicles arrived with all the new family's possessions. The removers started to unload all the items into the house. After some hours, the family themselves arrived in their personal transporter. A pleasant-looking man and woman alighted from the transporter and, seeing Mayn watching them over the fence, walked over to speak to him. 'Hello. What's your name?' The man was very friendly and held out his hand.

Mayn had shaken his hand and replied. 'I'm Maynard Gorton but all my friends call me Mayn.' Then, after a pause, he added rather unnecessarily, 'I live here.'

'Yes,' the man had said with a smile, 'I guessed that. I'm very pleased to meet you. How old are you?'

'I'm seven,' Mayn had replied gravely.

'Ah, just a little older than ours.' The man smiled across at his wife.

Mayn was delighted. A boy around his age was coming to live next door! How absolutely wonderful! They would become friends and they could play all the favourite boy's games and have an absolutely marvellous time in each other's gardens!

'Come through the gate and meet our family – our family of just one, that is,' the man smiled.

Mayn joined them in their garden and they walked towards the personal transporter.

'Darling,' the man called, 'come and meet the boy from next door. His name is Mayn.'

Mayn was taken aback when a pretty little girl jumped out of the transporter. She held out a small, soft hand. 'Hello, Mayn. I'm pleased to meet you. I hope we'll be friends. I'm Lucy.'

Mayn was confused and embarrassed. He couldn't understand it – the boy next door was a girl! 'Ah, ah...' he spluttered, '... you're a girl,' he finally managed to say, faintly.

'Of course I am,' she said, 'I'm Lucy. Who were you expecting?' She sounded rather annoyed.

'I thought... I thought...' He stumbled. Then, collecting himself with great difficulty, took her hand in his and said. 'Sorry about that. I got confused. I really am pleased to meet you, Lucy.'

She looked at him doubtfully. However, he did look like quite a nice boy, she thought. 'Well, OK,' she said in a level tone, 'I hope you really mean that.'

He flushed bright red in embarrassment. 'I do, Lucy. I really do. I'm really sorry.'

So began a relationship which quickly became a very firm friendship. They played together on most days and Mayn found, to his great surprise, that Lucy was able to play all the boy's games as well as any of his friends who were boys. She knew some really interesting girl's games, too! 'I'm really lucky to have Lucy as my special friend,' Mayn thought, 'she's every bit as good as a boy!' A really striking admission indeed!

Now he was really worried about his friend. Why was she crying? She wasn't a girl who cried easily (like some girls he had met!), so he knew something very serious must have happened. He sat down beside her and took her hand, repeating his words: 'what's wrong, Lucy? What has happened to make you cry?'

'It's Freddy,' she sobbed. Of course, Mayn knew who Freddy was. Freddy was the family cat, a placid black animal with beautiful soft fur and a really sweet, loving nature. Freddy had been a member of the family for at least ten years. When Lucy was born, it was not long before the cat had made a special bond with her, often stretched out near her when she was a baby and a toddler. Then, later, Freddy was often to be found curled up contentedly in Lucy's lap, enjoying her gentle strokes.

'What about Freddy? What's happened to him?'

'We don't know what's happened,' Lucy said tearfully, 'last night he seemed to be very quiet and weak when he came back to the house. We all thought maybe he had been doing too much running about – you know – he's not a young cat any more. Then, this morning, he was very ill and now he's getting worse all the time!'

'Can't you take him to see the cat doctor? They're very good at curing cats with illnesses.'

'We've done that,' Lucy said, 'Daddy took Freddy to see the cat doctor this morning. He examined him thoroughly and did a lot of tests on him. Daddy won't tell me exactly what the doctor said but I think he told him that Freddy is dying.' Lucy burst into fresh tears. 'Please, Mayn, I don't want Freddy to die. He's always been my friend since I was little.'

Mayn wanted desperately to reassure his friend. 'Don't worry, Lucy. Cats are tough animals. Maybe he's just eaten something stupid, you know, something that was poisonous to him. Animals do that sort of thing sometimes – in fact, we all do it sometimes, don't we? I'm sure he'll recover. After all, he may not be young but he's in very good condition, isn't he? He's very fit and healthy.' He did his very best to sound convincing.

'Well, yes, I suppose so,' Lucy said disconsolately, 'I do hope you're right.'

'Where is Freddy now? Is he here at home?'

'Yes, Daddy brought him back in his basket after he'd seen the doctor.'

Mayn took her hand. 'Shouldn't we go in and see how he is getting along? Maybe he's starting to recover. Didn't the doctor give Freddy some medicine to take?'

'I don't think he did,' Lucy replied, 'Daddy didn't say anything about it when he came back.'

Lucy and Mayn rose from the garden seat and went to into the house. 'Freddy should be in his bed in the kitchen,' Lucy said. 'Let's go through.'

The kitchen door slid open as they approached and Lucy could see that her mother and father were deep in conversation, sitting at the large kitchen table. Lucy said nothing as she and Mayn went straight to Freddy's bed, anxious to see how he was progressing. As she approached the bed, she stopped so suddenly that Mayn bumped into her. 'Sorry, Lucy, your brakes were too good for me then!' A brave attempt at humour.

Lucy did not hear him. Her eyes widened as she looked into Freddy's bed. It was empty! The cat, her beautiful beloved cat, wasn't there. He had gone! Where had he gone? She looked around the kitchen wildly. Perhaps her mother or father was holding Freddy on their lap? (He would enjoy that.) She checked. Freddy was not on either lap. Both her father and mother were looking at her, saying nothing. They looked sad. As she registered all these facts, she felt a rush of absolute dread.

'What has happened to him? Where is he?' Her voice quiet and trembling.

Her father rose from his seat and knelt down before her, taking her slim body in his arms and kissing her gently before saying: 'He's gone, Lucy. He died just half an hour ago. The doctor said there was nothing he could do for him. He thought that Freddy had somehow been poisoned. It was only a matter of time before he died. I didn't want to tell you before. I didn't want to make you sad. I was hoping that maybe the doctor was wrong and that Freddy would recover. Unfortunately he didn't. Your mother and I are so sorry, Lucy. We know how very fond of him you were. We were fond of him, too.'

Lucy was silent. Rigid. Absolutely dumbfounded that such a terrible thing could happen. Finally, she spoke quietly. 'Where is he? What are you going to do with him?'

Her father was clearly uncomfortable. 'Well, Lucy, I have to take him, I mean his body, back to the animal medical facility. That's what the Law says we must do.'

Lucy was silent once more, thinking about what her father had said. Then she gulped: 'I want to see him. Where have you put him?'

Her father held her tight. 'Lucy, do you think that's a good idea? I mean, wouldn't it be better for you to remember him like he was when he was alive? He was always such a lovely cat.'

Lucy was resolute. 'No. I want to see him and I want Mayn to come with me too. He's my friend. What have you done with him?'

Again the man was reluctant. 'Well, Lucy, I put him in a strong cardboard box and it's on the bench in the storeroom. I am going to take him to the medical facility tomorrow.'

'Come with me, Mayn,' Lucy said, wriggling free from her father's arms.

'Do you want me to come, too?' Her father was anxious and concerned.

Lucy was grave and composed. 'No, thank you, Daddy. I just want Mayn to come. I just want to say goodbye to Freddy.'

The two children stood in the storeroom, the top of the cardboard box folded open. The body of the cat was stretched out on an old piece of towelling, totally inert as the dead always are, blank unseeing eyes half open.

'Poor Freddy.' Lucy stroked his soft fur, feeling the familiar slim, lean body strangely cold for the first time in her life, 'I wish you hadn't died. I always enjoyed you so much. I hope you're at peace, wherever you are.' Then she sat down on a chair and held her head, eyes closed, sobbing quietly, tears streaming down. Minutes passed.

'Lucy!' Mayn's voice penetrated her grief.

She lifted her head and smiled at him wanly. 'Yes, Mayn?'

'I just saw his tail twitch, Lucy. I don't think he's dead.'

Lucy jumped up and looked into the box. As she did so, the end of Freddy's tail twitched again. Astonished, she touched the tail. It was warm. She felt the cat's body. It, too, was warm and, incredibly, she saw the flank rising and falling with rapid breath. As she was about to speak, Freddy opened his eyes fully and made a tiny sound.

'Mayn.' Lucy's voice was an incredulous whisper. 'Run and fetch Daddy and Mummy, please. Tell them what has happened.'

'Freddy has come alive!' An excited Mayn had burst into the kitchen. 'Please come!'

The doctor was dumbfounded. 'You're telling me that cat you brought in here yesterday has survived? Not only survived but now completely fit and well? Well, I must say I certainly didn't expect that! The tests showed me that his insides were destroyed and he had only a short time to live.' He shook his head incredulously. 'But now you're telling me he died and then came alive again!' He smiled rather derisively at Lucy's father. 'You mean you thought he died! Animals who have died stay dead – take my word for it. I've been doing this job for twenty-five years and I've seen thousands of dead animals.

And of these thousands, not a single one ever came alive again. It just doesn't happen, Sir, believe me.' He finished these words with a knowing smirk.

'What's that, you disagree? You know what you experienced? And you know what you saw? Well, that's OK by me, Sir. You can have it your own way, of course. I'm only the animal doctor, here.' The man turned away, saying: 'Have you handed in the Animal Disposal Form I gave you? OK, thanks for that. Oh and thanks for the fairy story. I'll tell it at the next medical conference!'

Lucy's father smiled neutrally, shook the doctor's hand and left without speaking. The doctor watched him go with a serious expression. 'Came alive again!' He spoke softly. 'That's certainly a trick I have often wished I could do!'

Freddy the cat recovered fully and lived on in Lucy's family for many more years.

That was the fifth time.

Mayn found he was smiling as he woke up:

'Freddy the cat! I haven't thought about him for a long time. Lucy was so pleased when he came back.'

He checked the time. It was 0800. 'I'll have to establish a routine. I'll work on that this morning. This afternoon, I'll consider whether I should examine the outside of the vehicle. There are certain things that can only be checked properly from the outside. I'll have to see whether I have the right equipment to do what I may need to do outside.'

Mayn left the sleeping compartment and went to the rest area of the vehicle where he would eat his meals. 'This low gravity will take some time to get used to,' he smiled as he almost floated along, 'I'll need to make sure I use the special exercise kit in the vehicle to maintain my muscles.' All people who went Space-side were fully trained to deal with the effects of reduced gravity.

Arriving in the rest area, he knew that the vehicle would provide everything he needed for sustenance. This was a self-maintaining system that would last "indefinitely". The same philosophy was applied to the life support systems of the vehicle. However, "indefinitely" really meant "until there was a serious and irreparable failure in some fundamental part of the system." Mayn knew that most systems lasted several years, at the very least. Of course the GTN67UV Escape Pod was a vehicle designed for temporary occupation; it was assumed that anyone aboard this type of vehicle would be rescued as soon as possible, often within a very few days. 'So, in one way, I've got plenty of time to try to solve this predicament I'm in,' he mused, 'however, in another way, the "Sword of Damocles" is hanging over me. If any part of my support systems fails catastrophically, that will be the end of me. So my "plenty time" is totally unquantifiable!'

After eating his first meal (still called breakfast), Mayn started to analyse his situation. He worked with his PAC, whose power was now fully restored. This small but extremely powerful personal machine would record all his words and thoughts on any situation, analyse them and then enter a live discussion with him which would lead to a range of viable outcomes. He would examine these carefully so that he could make the very best decisions.

He started off by initiating an enquiry about the sudden loss of PAC power the day before. The reply was soon displayed:

```
PAC operational power was drained by a very
powerful pulsating magnetic field (parameters
defined and available) set up in the Platform
docking area around GTN67UV just before
departure yesterday. This was deliberate
sabotage of equipment causing temporary failure
of all circuits. No damage was sustained and
full power is now restored. Report recorded.
```

'That's an important piece of evidence,' Mayn mused, 'I'll make sure I retain that.' Then the man settled down to work intensively with the PAC for some hours. Later that morning, the best sequence of actions had been worked out.

The first task was to investigate how far he could restore local control to the rescue pod. If he could succeed in doing this, he could achieve his own rescue flight. The first action in the task was to investigate the exterior of the vehicle, because some essential modules of the control system could only be accessed from outside. This in turn meant that Mayn had to discover what facilities he had for working outside. 'Let's hope we have the normal range of working suits still stored in the vehicle, along with the external toolkits.'

He knew exactly where these items would be stored and went there immediately. He was pleased to find two complete suits of the latest design. Also, the external tool kits were stored in their correct locations. He removed one of the kits and found it to be complete. 'That's the first hurdle cleared,' he thought.

It took some time to prepare the suit and put it on. It was some time since he had donned a Space Survival Suit and he had to concentrate carefully as he did so. Then he was ready to plug the suit into various systems in the vehicle that would initiate a complex series of tests and checks. At last, the check reports advised that all his suit systems were primed and ready for action. At that, he clipped the external tool kit securely to the suit and made his way to the hatch airlock.

The airlock was inflated and the inner door slid open. Somewhat clumsily, he climbed in and operated the atmosphere venting system. When a green light showed, he was able to open the outer hatch and extend a light ladder to the surface of the asteroid. Seconds later, he was standing on the uneven rocky surface. In the low gravity, he was able to move with a minimum of effort. Once or twice, he bounced higher above the surface than he intended! However, practice soon showed him the best and most efficient way to move around on the asteroid's surface. Of course, there was absolutely nothing to see, just the endless barren, twisted black and grey rock. 'I doubt whether I'll be doing much exploring here,' Mayn said to himself, 'there's absolutely nothing to explore! Anyway, I'm going to be too busy to do much exploring.'

Turning back towards his vehicle, now towering above him, he decided it would be wise to check on its physical stability. From his initial Space training, he remembered that this was one of the problems that may occur when a vehicle lands in a low gravity environment. The strength of the force of gravity on the surface of any Space body is dependent on its size. Obviously, even a large asteroid like this one was still a very small body in Space, so its force of gravity was considerably less than Planet Earth. Because Space vehicles may land on many different sizes of Space bodies, all were fitted with clamping systems that they could deploy to dig into the surface and hold the vehicle securely to its chosen landing spot. Mayn knew that his vehicle had done that automatically when it touched down on the asteroid; however, it was best to double check this, because any subsequent movement of the vehicle by weightless drift had the potential to damage the landing supports. He examined each of the four feet carefully and was pleased to see that the clamping system had set his vehicle firmly and securely into the asteroid surface. 'This will stay put until I'm ready to leave,' he concluded.

Now he turned to the front of the vehicle and located the large panel that enclosed many of the modules concerned with local control of the vehicle. Using the external toolkit, it took a considerable time to release the large panel but, finally, he succeeded. He could not help uttering a gasp as he looked inside the large compartment. Most of the module racks were empty! And he noticed that many of the racks were now filled by non-standard modules that he did not recognise. Using a powerful portable light, he tried to identify the various purposes of these modules but the specification information given on their cases was unintelligible to him. 'I'll digitally scan all this equipment,' he thought, 'so that I know where all the connections are. After that, I'll remove the modules, one by one, take them into the vehicle and dismantle them to find out what they are and how they work. Then I'll see whether I can re-model them to become local control units that I can use for my purposes.'

Mayn set to work with his camera scanner and recorded every detail of the equipment he had found. At the end of that process, he noted that he been outside the vehicle for many hours and decided it was time to stop the work for that day. Replacing the external panel, he returned through the hatch and airlock to the inside of the vehicle. It took some time to divest himself of the suit and return it to its store where a sterilisation and restoration process would make it like new, ready for the next time he would go outside. Then he went to the rest area for food and refreshment while he communed with his PAC on the discoveries of the day.

'It's no wonder there was no local control in this vehicle. As far as I can see, all the modules which provided that control have been removed and the whole system replaced with something else – something, I imagine, that gives total control to a remote source. I'll know much more when I've dismantled all these unknown units. That will certainly take a long time, because I'll need to remove the units one by one and keep going until I understand exactly what has been done and how it all fits together. I might even find a clue or two about who might have done this, too.'

All the information was downloaded and fully discussed in a PAC seminar consultation – the highest level offered by the PAC system. Mayn was very tired when it finished and was glad to retire to his sleeping compartment where he spent the whole night in dreamless sleep.

3

Day 48

The weeks had flown past in a seamless blur. Early on, Mayn had recognised the importance of establishing himself on a fixed routine. He was convinced that this would be the most efficient way of applying himself to the considerable task of reconstruction. His time readout awoke him every morning at precisely 0800. After washing and dressing, he immediately went to the rest area and ate his breakfast while studying his work schedule for the day and checking out any new thoughts with his PAC. By 0930, he was in the Control Cabin, starting on the work designated for that day.

Many weeks before, when he had started his process of investigation, he had soon found out that progress was going to be very slow. It took many hours of work outside the vehicle to remove the parts of the unfamiliar control systems he had found installed in the external bays. Also, working in a suit was always very tiring and he often found that he needed to rest for some hours after he returned inside the vehicle.

Dismantling and examining the non-standard modules usually took several days; it seemed that these modules were not designed to be taken apart easily and he often needed to deploy special equipment or, indeed, develop completely new tools to tackle the job. Then, once inside, it took a considerable amount of time to understand the function and operation of the unit. Meanwhile, Mayn was always considering how he could modify each of these units so that it would perform a function that would begin to restore control to him. Consequently, he had to spend many hours in collaboration with his PAC to ensure that he was missing nothing as he worked.

Alongside all this technical work, Mayn also gave considerable time and thought to the possible reasons for his desperate situation. He found it useful to put his thoughts into words. 'Speaking it out means I have to discipline myself and follow absolute logic,' he thought, 'so it's worth going through the rather clumsy process of physical speech. Anyway, it probably does me good to hear my own voice. There's a certain reassurance about that. It helps to convince me that I'm still alive!' These "conversations" with himself usually took place either during his rest periods after exhausting hours outside the vehicle or during the hours before he retired to his bunk.

Quite often, they brought memories of specific incidents which he was able to consider carefully to see if they might have had any bearing on his current plight. 'I'm in absolutely no doubt that someone set all this up to get rid of me permanently. And because of the complexity involved, it seems to me that several people must have been involved. However, someone had to be the instigator. A detailed plan must have been worked on for an extended period and then there must have been a huge technical effort to redesign the control and communications systems of this vehicle. That would have taken considerable time and effort as well as a great deal of skill and knowledge.'

Mayn had worked on these analyses several times and had not been able to come to any conclusion. Recognising his lack of progress, he decided to think about motivation. 'Why would anyone want to kill me? I thought the people on Yggdrasil liked me. I thought that the senior people, including CCO1, thought I was an asset on the Platform. They never hesitated to use me as a sort of trouble-shooter when they came across an insoluble problem, did they? Of course, I was always pleased to help. I gave it my full attention and, on most occasions, found an answer that seemed to solve the problem. Everyone seemed very pleased.'

He pondered on this and then added: 'However, it couldn't have pleased absolutely everyone, could it? Someone, maybe a group of people, did not like what I had achieved. Did not like me enough to plan to get rid of me – to send me to a lonely death. Goodness! They must have hated me very much. But why?'

It was then he remembered what had happened when he was a teenager at college.

Mayn had been studying at the College for nine years and had developed into a tall scrawny thirteen-year-old who showed little talent for sports, especially those that were of a more violent nature. Despite this lack of talent, he had always been a popular boy who was invariably friendly, kind and supportive of the other students. Likewise, he was well regarded by all the tutors, who noted that he never failed or fell behind in his studies. In fact the tutoring staff rated Mayn very highly, knowing that he was extremely intelligent and very much of an original and inventive thinker. Over the years, special study programmes had been developed for him and, as a result, his knowledge and studies were far ahead of his contemporaries.

It is a fact that able, bright and inventive students like Mayn can be insular as they devote all their time and effort to their own progress and development. This is not necessarily because they are selfish and uncaring of others; rather it may be that their enthusiasm for the progression of their own particular interests becomes all-pervading and they are unable to see beyond this. Their world is a wonderful academic place of learning and research where they excel, while other students, especially those of lesser ability, achieve no visibility in such a world.

Mayn was never like this. Although incredibly bright and extremely focussed on his own work and development, he always kept a close eye on his fellow students and was quick to come to their aid if they required help or support. The College insisted on 100% success and any student falling behind was treated with increasing harshness by the tutoring staff, who applied the rules of the institution without pity or compassion. In the past, many intelligent but diffident students had been crushed underfoot by the uncompromising regime they found at the College; the statistics showed that there had been many expulsions over the years and, sometimes, even suicide attempts.

As already mentioned, the study regime at the College was draconian. This meant that social interaction between the students was minimal. Students were directed to continue their studies at all times, engaging in deep thought if it were not appropriate to read or write at that time. This applied even during the brief rest or meal periods. Nevertheless, Mayn covertly studied his fellow students and made note of any who were struggling. Then, after the College day had finished, he would approach them and offer to help by providing informal coaching sessions on the subject with which they were struggling. Throughout the years, a significant number of students had good reason to be extremely grateful for Mayn's kindness and compassion.

'You see that thin boy over there?' A student would point out Mayn to a newcomer. 'He may not look much but he's the brightest student in the College and he's the nicest guy you could ever meet. He'll always help anyone if they've got a problem with their studies – or, indeed, with anything else! Had it not been for him, I probably would have been kicked out of College a long time ago. He's a really wonderful guy!'

For his part, Mayn never thought his actions were special in any way. If anyone ever commented on his kindness, he would reply: 'Well, I just think it's natural to help others if you can. If I'm lucky enough to be able to understand most of the teaching I get here and I can see that some of my fellow students are not coping with it so well, why should I not help them if I can? After all, if the boot were on the other foot and I was floundering with some aspect of my life, I'm sure one of my friends would soon come and help me. It's just a matter of logic to me.'

So with his constant outward focus, the thirteen-year-old Mayn had observed that a very large, muscular boy called

Kurt was in trouble with his studies and, clearly, was sinking under the increasing bitter and sarcastic onslaught of his tutors. After the college day finished, Mayn had sought him out. 'Hi Kurt, I'm Mayn. We haven't talked much but we've been classmates for a couple of years. I could help you with your studies, if you want. You know, help you deal with the problems you're having with the tutors.'

Kurt was taken aback. No-one had ever offered to help him before. 'Why would you do that? What do you want?' he replied truculently.

'Listen, Kurt, I don't want anything. I just saw you're getting into trouble and, if you tell me what the problem is, I can probably help you.'

Kurt was still suspicious. He could not understand why Mayn should help him – for nothing! However, he was beginning to realise that Mayn may be throwing him a lifeline. He knew he was in deep trouble with the tutors and was probably heading for expulsion from the College. Of course he knew Mayn by reputation – everyone in the College knew Mayn for his outstanding abilities. Maybe such an "egghead" could give him chance? As all these unfamiliar thoughts whirled around in his head, he continued to glower at this thin, scrawny boy, who was smiling at him encouragingly. Eventually he growled: 'Well, OK, if you want to. We'll see how it goes.'

So began an association that lasted over a year. The two boys met several times a week and Mayn coached Kurt in all his deficiencies. He found that Kurt was far from bright and was probably below standard for the College. Mayn had to go back to first principles and build up Kurt's knowledge slowly. It was a tribute to his patience and skill that, in the end, he was successful. At last, he was able to say: 'OK, Kurt, I guess you're sorted now, aren't you? You can hold your own at College, can't you?'

'Yeah, OK, thanks,' Kurt muttered crossly, unused to giving anyone thanks for anything but fully aware that Mayn had saved him from expulsion.

The following year was one of notable success for Mayn. Now turned fifteen, he had done such excellent original work at the College that he was informed he was to be awarded a very special prize. This was a special award that was given only rarely. After dinner that night, he had informed his parents. 'I've got a bit of good news. I've been awarded the Einstein Prize.'

Of course his parents crowed with delight. 'The Einstein Prize?' His father had whistled in admiration. 'That's hardly ever given to anyone. Wasn't the last one twelve years ago?'

Mayn was rather embarrassed. 'Yeah, well, I think it was. Maybe I'm just a very lucky guy!'

His father embraced him warmly. 'Listen, Mayn, it's not because you're a lucky guy, it's because you are such a brilliant guy! I know the College. I went there myself many years ago – and I never got the Einstein Prize and neither did anyone else. That platinum and gold trophy just sat in its armoured glass case in the Assembly Hall. We all looked at it with awe – and that's as far as we got! But that was before we managed to get a brilliant son!'

Of course Mayn was very pleased. He knew that the award of the Einstein Prize was a very rare event and that he had got it for completely original work, far above the normal quality expected of a sixteen-year-old student at the college.

'Do they give you a trophy?' his father asked. 'I assume they don't give you the original!'

Mayn laughed. 'Hardly! The original is unique – and solid platinum and gold! I was told I would get a very fine glass replica. A beautiful piece of work and very valuable, they said.'

'You better not drop it, then,' his father joked, 'maybe we need to insure it before you touch it!'

'Well, I'll try not to drop it,' Mayn smiled back, 'but, if I do, I know you'll buy me another, won't you?' They all laughed.

Soon, the day of the college prize-giving came. As is normal on these occasions, the highest prize is given at the very end, an exciting culmination to the event. Of course, this was the award of the Einstein Prize.

'And finally we come to a very special award,' the Head Tutor intoned in his reedy voice. 'This is awarded only for work of the very highest original quality. This year, for the first time in twelve years, the Einstein Prize is awarded to Maynard Gorton for his original, excellent work on Spacecraft Control Systems. Would you please come forward and receive the award, Gorton, which we give as a fine glass replica of the original platinum and gold trophy that is retained in the College security cabinet in this Assembly Hall.'

Mayn, dressed for the occasion in the special blue and gold uniform of the College, came forward and mounted the platform.

'Here you are, Gorton. Congratulations. You are greatly honoured, you know!'

To thunderous applause, Mayn stood modestly, displaying the beautiful, multi-coloured glass award to an adoring audience. Meanwhile, his parents had tears of joy streaming down their faces as they regarded their son with awe and delight, their minds automatically racing through an amazingly-detailed life story that started with the miracle of a tiny new-born baby and ended with the scene before them. Such is the awesome power of the human mind.

Eventually, it was finished and a relieved Mayn came to his parents to be enclosed in the sort of all-enveloping, constricting hug that adoring mothers give their sons on such very special public occasions of triumph. 'Hey,' he laughed, 'Stop! You'll break me! But what is worse, you might break this!'

Releasing him, his mother asked, 'Would you like us to take charge of the Einstein Prize?'

Mayn shook his head. 'No, Mother, I'll just keep it with me for the moment. I think some of my friends may want to see it before we go home. I'll just go off and get changed out of this formal College uniform in the locker room upstairs. I'll be back soon, looking like a normal person, thank goodness!'

Mayn had displayed the Prize to a number of his friends as he made his way to the locker room, modestly receiving their admiring congratulations. A few more of his friends were changing out of their college uniforms in the locker room and they too asked to see the Einstein Prize. Mayn complied. 'I guess I'm just lucky, that's all,' he kept saying.

Soon he was alone and he quickly stripped off the formal college clothes, hanging them up carefully in his locker. As he reached inside the locker to retrieve his normal clothes, the full-length mirror mounted on the inside of the door suddenly showed him the stark reality of his near-naked self, a pale, exceptionally bony youth dressed only in baggy cotton underpants. As he ruefully observed this familiar image, he murmured: 'Good thing I have no ambition to be a sportsman! Look at me! Bones sticking out everywhere! Look at these ribs! You can see every one!'

To remove the offending image from his sight, Mayn pushed the locker door to a different angle. He was startled when the reflection in the mirror now revealed a large figure standing silent and motionless in the locker room doorway. Spinning around, he recognised the large muscular figure of Kurt, standing with a strange half-smile on his face.

'Goodness, Kurt. You certainly made me jump. I thought I was alone. How are you? Want a look at the Einstein? Come and have a look. I've got it just here.'

There was a heavy silence for a few moments. 'No I don't want to see it,' Kurt growled. 'That's the trouble with you clever little boys. Always wanting to display your intelligence. Always being superior to ordinary people. Well, I'm fed up with it and now I'm going to do something about it. Nice to see you're nearly prepared for what's about to happen.'

Mayn was perplexed. 'Prepared? Prepared how—prepared for what?'

'You're pretty well stripped down for the beating you're about to get. Saves us the bother of stripping your clothes off.'

Mayn was astonished. 'What do you mean, Kurt? Beating? You and I are friends, aren't we? We worked together for a long time and you became a good student. Are you having problems again? If you are, I can...'

'No, I'm not having problems, clever little boy,' Kurt rasped, 'I passed my year exams OK but I'm fed up with little clever boys like you being so superior, winning all the prizes and sucking up to the tutors.'

'Look, Kurt, you're really wrong about that. I don't suck up to anyone. I just try to help people if I see they've got troubles. What's the problem with that?'

'Shut up, little clever boy.' Kurt was now working himself up into a fury. 'I hate people like you and I hate you especially. And now I'm going to make you suffer just like all these tutors made me suffer.' He produced a heavy baseball bat from behind his back. 'I'm going to break every bone in your body, little clever boy who sucks up to the tutors.'

As he spoke, five more muscular boys sidled into the locker room, all carrying baseball bats.

'These are my real friends, little clever boy, my loyal gang,' Kurt snarled. 'We play sport together, something that your puny little body can't do. And, by the time we've finished with you, you certainly won't be able to play any sport. You won't be able to do anything at all because you'll be in hospital for years. Then you won't be able to be a little clever boy any more. We're going to see to that.'

Mayn was completely transfixed by the violence in Kurt's eyes. He felt the weakness of intense terror spreading though him, freezing his thought processes and almost causing his knees to give way. He was bewildered. He could not understand why Kurt wanted to hurt him like this. Hadn't he helped him with his studies? Hadn't he saved him from expulsion? Why was Kurt saying that he hated him? He was sure that Kurt meant everything he said and he and his friends seemed more than ready to hit him with these horrific baseball bats.

Now he looked with dread at the solid, heavy bats, each one held in large, powerful hands. He felt his skin crawling with terror as he pictured his pathetic, naked figure knocked violently to the floor as a baseball bat smashed into his ribcage, driving splintered, razor-sharp bone into the sensitive flesh within, while, simultaneously, another attacked spindly shins, instantly splitting taut flesh and shattering the tibias and fibulas within. What had Kurt had said? He would break *every* bone in his body! EVERY bone! Legs, feet, arms, hands, fingers, pelvis, ribs, spine, skull... It would take hundreds of blows to achieve that! And he would be completely and utterly destroyed at the end of it. Writhing in pure agony in a welter of blood on the locker room floor! His life finished. Either dead, or as good as dead. Terrified, he wrapped his thin arms around his body to protect its nakedness.

Then a vain hope! Maybe he could reason with Kurt? 'Kurt, please, don't do this. I'm your friend.' His voice a trembling squeak. 'I helped you for a long time. And, listen, Kurt, if you do this to me you'll destroy yourself. You'll be a criminal. You'll be sent to a prison planet. And the same will happen to all your friends here. You'll all be criminals. You'll be there for the rest of your lives.'

Kurt's face became purple with rage as he listened. 'You think we're stupid, little clever boy? No-one will ever know it was us that did it. Because you will either be dead or maybe you'll be brain-dead after we've finished with you. And if, by any chance, you ever recover enough to talk, you'll keep your mouth shut about us because, if you don't, we'll come and beat you to death, slowly – very slowly! Don't think we won't! Right now, we're going to start by beating you senseless, then we'll break all your bones. When we've finished, we'll just melt away. We've done it before to other clever little boys and we always get away with it. It has all been carefully planned. We know exactly what we're doing. What do you think of that, little clever boy?' He ended with a fearsome roar of cruel triumph.

It was true! Mayn had heard of other boys being severely beaten. Some did not survive. Although there had been extensive police investigations, the perpetrators had never been found. Now Mayn knew his situation was hopeless. He fell on his knees and started to plead for his life. 'Kurt, please don't hurt me,' he wailed piteously. 'I've done nothing bad to you. I helped you. Please let me go. I'm sorry if I've done anything to upset you. Please, I'll do anything. Look, here's the Einstein Prize, take it and break it into pieces, but please don't hurt me, Kurt. Please. I'll do anything! Tell me what you want me to do and I'll do it. For as long as you like. I'll be your slave. Please, don't hurt me!' His voice rising to become a thin scream.

Kurt's face now wore a very ugly smile. 'Listen, little clever boy, you'll do anything, eh? You'll do anything I want, eh? Well, the only thing I want is for you to be lying on that floor with every bone in your little puny body broken. And that's exactly what my friends and I are going to do now. I'm not interested in breaking that glass thing, what I really want to break is YOU, little clever boy.' He turned to the others. 'OK, boys, let's get on with it. It shouldn't take long.'

The large, powerful boy swung the baseball bat violently through the air with a loud swishing sound and started to move towards the whimpering Mayn, now kneeling on the floor with thin, pleading arms raised high in hopeless supplication...

Click! The noise was imperceptible but its effect on Mayn was intense. Suddenly, it was as if a dazzling light had been switched on in his brain. Suddenly, a mighty power surged through him like an explosive flame. Suddenly, everything was changed. Suddenly, he understood. Suddenly, he was completely calm. Icy calm.

Kurt and his companions were rooted to the spot with astonishment as they saw the thin, bony figure of Mayn dropping his arms, rising slowly to his feet and moving to his open locker. Totally ignoring all the menacing figures, he lifted his everyday clothes from the locker and calmly slipped on each garment until he was fully dressed. Then, he bent down, picked up the Einstein Prize and began to walk slowly and calmly towards the doorway of the locker room as if he was the only one present in the room.

His progress was soon brought to a halt. Kurt's large and powerful hand grasped his arm tightly as he prepared to walk past the bigger boy. Mayn turned slowly and directed his eyes straight into Kurt's ferocious gaze. For several minutes, the locker room was a "still life" picture; nothing moved, nobody breathed. Then, slowly, almost imperceptibly, Kurt's grasp slackened and eventually his arm fell back to his side. Mayn disengaged his eyes from Kurt's and moved forward again towards the doorway, only to be grasped in a similar manner by one of Kurt's friends. The scene was repeated with an exactly similar result; and again... and again. Finally, as if an invisible wedge had been driven between them, the last two boys blocking the doorway parted at Mayn's approach and, totally unimpeded, he walked softly from the locker room.

A calm and assured Mayn rejoined his parents in the Assembly Hall.

'We thought you had got lost,' his mother said.

Mayn smiled gently. 'A lot of my friends wanted to see the Einstein Prize,' he said quietly. 'It took me a while to get changed.'

That was the eleventh time. After that, he stopped counting.

'I did learn something from that. Something very important.' Mayn had returned from his vivid journey into the past and was once again relaxing in the escape pod. Now he tried to rationalise his thoughts. 'It's impossible to fathom the exact operation of another person's brain. Maybe Kurt was envious of my knowledge and ability. But I couldn't have helped him if I had not had that knowledge and ability. On the other hand, maybe sight of my knowledge and ability made him feel inadequate, in other words, generally bad about himself. It's a very human reaction (but a deeply flawed one) to think that the destruction of a superior rival will elevate you, solve your problems, etc. Often, the reverse will apply; the destruction of a rival can also destroy you – not just by criminalising you but by lowering your self-esteem even further and driving you to depression or worse. Certainly, the effect is always negative – a "lose-lose situation" is the term for it.'

Turning his head, he spoke to his PAC. 'Hi! I hope you're listening to all this! What is your conclusion? Apply to my current situation. Speak out.'

There was a slight hum as the PAC switched to Voice Mode:

'Your general conclusions would appear to be correct. Your assessment of your College situation is accurate. Regarding your current situation, unless unbalanced psychosis is involved – and that is unlikely because you have already thought that several individuals must have participated in the preparation for your sudden departure from the Platform-envy plus imposed inadequacy would seem to be the most likely driver. However, these must have become severe, since most individuals in the normal behaviour range are not driven to murder by envy or personal inadequacy. It is suggested that you must now work through every event that may have contributed to your situation. These are events where you were called to advise on a particular situation or where you offered help and advice voluntarily. The events should be listed and examined to identify who benefitted from your intervention and who might have been covertly offended or disquieted by your actions and presence. When the same names recur, this may suggest instigators. This will be a long and detailed process for you. These are my conclusions and recommendations on the current data you have provided. Recorded, timed, dated.'

The machine clicked as the sound circuit was switched off. Mayn lay back in his seat. 'I think that should be a useful approach. I will apply it and see what progress I can make.'

4

Day 199

After many months of painstaking, meticulous work, Mayn had finally achieved something of a breakthrough. As the days, weeks and months flew by, the number of control units removed from the external bays had proliferated on work benches around the Control Cabin. As he dismantled and tested each component in the units, he had recorded their function along with the power they required and generated. At first, he could see no way of linking up the individual components to begin to build a local control system but gradually his skill and knowledge began to make some difference; he began to make some headway. Eventually, he had linked a range of components together in such a way that his module had the potential to carry out some of the functions he wanted. However, he was missing a very vital part and, in the end, he decided that he would have to design a completely new unit and build it from whatever materials were available to him.

Of course, he had done this sort of work before and he was soon hard at work designing the new master control unit which would interface with his earlier progress. Three-dimensional displays were made and checked carefully. Materials were chosen – here, Mayn had to be extremely inventive, sometimes obtaining the materials he required from integral parts of the escape pod itself. 'As long as I don't remove anything that's vital for the flight of the vehicle,' he said to himself, 'it doesn't matter what I use.' So panels and casework from the structure of the escape pod began to appear in Mayn's new inventions! Finally, the new system was ready for final assembly and Mayn plugged the various parts together, carefully testing the combined functions as he went along.

At last, it was time to connect up his newly-built interface system and he installed this with great care and not a little trepidation. 'I'll be so disappointed if this doesn't work,' he said, 'I've really put my whole self into it and it has taken me months, working on it every day.' He had examined his chances of success through a series of detailed PAC discussions and evaluations. Everything had checked out. However, when he directed the PAC to calculate the success rating of his new system in its entirety, the result had not been particularly uplifting. Clicking the PAC to "receive voice command", he had instructed: 'Calculate success rating of top level control unit. Speak out result.'

The machine was silent for a few seconds, then it clicked into Voice Mode:

"Success rating on data provided is 55%.
Calculations recorded this date/time."

Mayn had felt rather depressed when he heard the rating. 'I had hoped for over 65%,' he thought. '55% is hardly encouraging.'

By this time it was evening and Mayn had been working constantly on his equipment since early in the morning. He looked around at his assembled equipment, now piled on various benches and desks around the Control Cabin, strung together with many electrical leads. 'I must stop now before I fall asleep on the job,' he told himself. 'Time for my evening meal and maybe some thinking, if I'm not too tired. I need to keep making progress on the motivation front. That's got to be key to my understanding of what happened on Yggdrasil and why it happened. Tomorrow, I'll plug my new combined system into the pod's main function controls. I hope I'll be successful; I've certainly worked hard enough on all this – but then, it's all for my own good. Just think how wonderful it would be if I could get this vehicle going! How amazing it would be to feel myself flying out of here!' He felt vastly uplifted as he thought of that. Throughout his life, Mayn had always been an optimist!

After he had eaten and relaxed for a while, he thought it might be useful to return to some of his earlier thoughts on what could have motivated his unknown adversaries on Yggdrasil – the people who had sent him off on his lonely one-way journey. Shortly after he had made the decision to retrace his life on the Platform and examine carefully all occasions when he had provided help and advice, his very first memory was concerned not with his scientific or technical work but with a more social event. Many involved with this important event insisted that he, Maynard Gorton, had "saved the day". He had been widely acclaimed for it at the time.

Mayn was a youthful and energetic twenty-seven when he arrived on SSP Yggdrasil – easily the most famous and important platform in the whole Space Fleet. To be stationed there was considered an honour. Of course everyone knew the famous Maynard Gorton. Since graduating from Space-side College with the very highest honours and awards for his research work, he had worked on the concept and design of Space vehicles and their control systems and many of the Space vehicles used by Command were largely Gorton-designed. When it was decided that his skill and knowledge would be valuable aboard the Command flagship SSP Yggdrasil, Mayn had been promoted to the senior rank of Commander, becoming the youngest person in Space-side history to hold such a high rank.

When he eventually landed on the Platform, after a long journey from Planet Earth, Mayn was greeted as quite a celebrity by many of the reception staff who were there to process his arrival.

'The Chief Commanding Officer wishes to meet you as soon as we finish our reception processing,' they told him. It was obvious this was regarded as a great honour. In fact, it was extremely unusual; CCO1 normally held himself aloof from the officers under his command. Of course Mayn's high rank would have assisted him in this situation. As a Commander, he was only two ranks below CCO1 himself. As he recalled the events after his arrival, he remembered being conducted to the stateroom of the "Great Man" and finding him seated behind a huge desk.

'Come in, Commander Gorton, sit down there. You are most welcome aboard my Platform.' (Mayn had supressed a smile at the term "*my* Platform.") 'I'm Admiral Feltham Sarfeld, CCO1 here. I'm sure you've heard of me. And, by the way, it's customary for all my officers to address me as "Sir" at all times.' Then, in rather supercilious tones, he added, 'of course I am expecting great things of you, Mr Gorton. Command seems to think you will be able to head up the Science and Technical work here as STC1. This is an extremely important post on the Platform – you have 1000 men under your command and a huge range of responsibilities. Definitely not the easiest of tasks, I should say. The last man coped for a while but then made a mistake that resulted in some inconvenience to me, so I had him moved out to a less-demanding post on a smaller platform.' He paused and looked quizzically at Mayn.

'Thank you for that information, Sir,' Mayn responded (I suppose I'd better comply with his "Sir" demand!) 'I will of course do my best.'

Mayn studied CCO1 as the man continued to speak in a distinctly pompous and overbearing manner, pointing out how important the Platform was to Space Command and how its work, under his command, had always been judged to be of the highest quality. 'Command knows that we always operate at maximum efficiency here. You will wish to know that I will tolerate no less. I always expect the very best from my men and that's what they give me.' He smiled thinly. 'Because, if they don't, it isn't long before they are removed.'

After a moments' silence, CCO1 sat back and examined Mayn closely. 'I see from your records that you are extremely young to be a Commander. Twenty-seven?'

'That's right, Sir.'

'Hmm,' the older man said, 'Far too young. I was sixty-two before I became a Commander. I think that's about the right age, don't you? You know, it meant I could act with the authority of knowledge and experience. That's a problem you are going to have, you know. No-one will respect you. You're far too young to be properly effective, don't you agree?'

'Well, Sir, I've been working in command positions for the last four years and, frankly, I've never found my age to be a problem.'

CCO1 smiled sourly. 'Ah, yes. Working Earth-side, weren't you? Things are different Earth-side. More casual, sloppy, you know. It's different here on Space-side and especially in Yggdrasil. Everything is done properly here. Anyway, you were certainly not my choice for this job. I have technical people here who would be superb in the post. However, Command insisted you have all the qualities and experience you need to take on STC1 here. Although I must say I don't believe them, I decided to go along with it. Give them rope to hang themselves, you know?' He guffawed rather unpleasantly. Mayn said nothing but continued to look at CCO1 with a neutral expression.

'Right, Mr Gorton,' the older man said, 'I'm afraid I don't have any more time to waste. I'm always busy with important matters, you know. I don't expect I'll be seeing a great deal of you. My workload is almost exclusively at the highest strategic level, not messing about with meters, screwdrivers and spanners. However, I have one other very important thing to say to you. All officers have been invited to my birthday party tomorrow evening and I expect everyone to attend, including you. Full formal dress, of course, with all medals, honours and awards. You'll find all the details in the bulletin log in your quarters.' After a pause, CCO1 added: 'It is my ninetieth birthday, so it's a very special occasion. There will be a special banquet. The highlight will be the drinking of my special CCO1 wine; this is made for me by the Platform's Master Vintner and it is only drunk on the most important of occasions. You may already know that the CCO1 wine of Yggdrasil is known throughout the Command as the very finest available.'

Now he dropped his head and began to read some papers. 'You are dismissed, Mr Gorton,' he said, without looking up.

'Good day to you, Sir,' Mayn murmured and left.

As a senior ranking officer, Mayn's accommodation was excellent, comprising spacious living quarters with every available amenity and, nearby, a comprehensive office suite with all the facilities he needed to do his work. He had already found a message on the internal communicator that all Science and Technology Division (STD) staff were standing by to be called to a meeting of introduction, except for those on essential duty. Obviously, the STD staff were an extremely important group on the SSP Yggdrasil, being responsible for the smooth running of all the higher-level technical aspects of the whole Platform, not only in terms of maintenance and repair of equipment but also for implementing development and carrying out scientific and technical research. Low-level technical maintenance was carried out by another engineering division.

Mayn peeled off his uniform top and sat down in an extremely comfortable chair. As he closed his eyes, the communicator trilled. He clicked its receive switch. 'Hello,' he said.

'Is that Commander Gorton?' a harsh, impatient voice barked.

'Yes, it is,' Mayn replied equably.

'This is Sub-Commander Grafton Fitch – you've probably heard of me – I've been running the show since poor old Paulo Marzine was kicked out. He was a good man, Paulo and...'

Mayn interrupted. 'What can I do for you, Mr Fitch. I've just arrived in my quarters after seeing CCO1, so I'm not very orientated as yet.'

'Yeah, well, I thought you might want to meet me sooner rather than later. You know, I've been running the show for the last two months and everybody seems to think I've done a pretty good job of it...'

'Why don't you come now and tell me what's on your mind,' Mayn said.

'OK, I'm on my way. Thanks,' the voice added perfunctorily.

Ten minutes later, Mayn's door chime sounded and he operated the control to open the door. A large, bulky and distinctly scruffy individual entered and threw himself into a seat without invitation. 'Hi, Maynard, I'm Grafton. I don't want to waste too much time on this. My idea is that you can take over from me gradually, you know, maybe over a few months. All the boys are used to my command, so I think it will be a good way to keep things going smoothly. I'm fully aware that you're very young and completely inexperienced at this level of authority. I've given a lot of thought to this and I'm sure it's best for me to continue my command for as long as you want – the rest of this year for instance. And listen, Maynard, could you make sure I keep my command allowances? That's only fair, I think you will agree. Whatever happens later on, I really think you should keep me on in a top command position, well, really as your equal, you know. I'm sure you can see the strength in that. The boys will always take orders from me without question while I think it's quite likely you will have authority problems. It's a difficult thing to do, Maynard, commanding technical staff who are highly intelligent and totally dedicated. There are some really bright boys here. You'll see how they all look up to me – and rightly so, too.' The man finally stopped and looked at Mayn expectantly.

Mayn said nothing for several moments while he continued to look at his visitor without expression. Finally, he said quietly, 'I'm glad you came by, Mr Fitch, because I want to ask your advice...'

Fitch interrupted. 'Why, sure, Maynard. Just ask away. I think you'll find my advice invaluable.'

Mayn continued after a pause. 'You're right to say that I have no Space-side command experience. I have headed up several Earth-side research centres and, although everyone held military ranks, these sort of research places are usually quite informal. Are you telling me that the situation here is different?'

'Different?' Fitch was derisive. 'I should say so. Here, we all need to be very disciplined. We can't be informal here or everything will fall apart! If my men don't treat me with formal respect, they'll certainly be in trouble. When you meet them, you'll see how they address me with great respect. I know how to lead my men, you see. I've been doing it for so many years and I'm reckoned to be highly skilled at it.'

Mayn put another question. 'And what about your relationship with the previous STC1, Commander Marzine? Was that formal? How did you get along with him?'

'Of course it was formal, Maynard. I mean, I may not have agreed with everything he said and did – he certainly got things wrong at times – but, he was the boss, he was STC1, so of course I did what he wanted me too, that is, unless I really disagreed with him; then, I just talked him out of it. I'm pretty skilled at that, too.' He grinned at Mayn then became serious. 'Listen, Maynard. Let me lay it out strong and plain for you. It's all about the rank you carry on your shoulder. If you meet someone with a higher rank, you call him "Sir", you treat him with respect and you do what you're told. That's the way the whole thing works and, Space-side, that's the way it works best.'

Mayn looked down at the floor and appeared to be deep in thought. A full minute passed. Then he stood up and put on his uniform top, his Commander rank badges prominent on each shoulder. Then he smiled placidly at the other man. 'Thank you, Mr Fitch, for your advice. I will certainly apply it to my situation here.'

Fitch grinned back. 'You're very wise, M...' Suddenly he stopped, his face a picture of consternation. Silence filled the room. Mayn waited.

'... Sir.' Fitch whispered.

After another pause, Mayn became brisk. 'OK, Mr Fitch, I would like to call a meeting of the staff for this afternoon. Could you see to that, please? Where do we meet? The large Conference Room 1034, Level-8? Yes, I'll find it OK. Shall we say 1500?'

Fitch was visibly deflated as he rose to go. 'Ah, listen... Sir, maybe you could tell the men that I'm continuing to command...'

Mayn interrupted him. 'We'll talk about that later, Mr Fitch,' he said quietly.

There were over 800 men in the Conference Room when Mayn arrived at 1500. Voices hushed as he walked through the seating to the dais at the front. Sub-Commander Fitch was already standing behind a large lectern and made a great show of welcoming Mayn. 'Stand up, everyone. This is Commander Gorton who is taking over from me as STC1 when he's ready. I think most of you will have heard of Commander Gorton, most probably as the youngest Commander the Service has ever had. He's quite a well-known as a Space designer, too, I have heard. Let's all give him a really good welcome and, when he eventually comes around to visit us all in our workplaces, let's show him just how good Fitch's ST Division really is!'

A dutiful round of applause followed as Mayn mounted the dais. Fitch did not move but extended his hand. Mayn shook it perfunctorily. When Fitch still did not move, Mayn said: 'Thank you, Mr Fitch, please take your seat.' He pointed to the front row of seats, largely empty, as front rows of seats so often are. A startled and disquieted Fitch stepped down and lowered himself into a seat. Meanwhile, a low buzz of conversation had filled the room. Mayn held up a hand and waited until silence was re-imposed. Then he spoke in a friendly tone. 'I thank you all for your welcome and I look forward to meeting each one of you and getting to know you, personally. I am told that all aspects of the Division work extremely efficiently and I look forward to seeing that for myself. You may be sure I will always be ready to listen to your ideas for development in your local area when we meet one-to-one. Meanwhile, I thank you once again for your presence here this afternoon. I am aware that a number of staff on essential duty are absent; how many would that be, Mr Fitch?'

Fitch flushed. 'Well, Sir, it's rather hard to tell. But I think it's probably around 120 or 150 or so – there's always so much going on...'

Mayn interrupted quietly. 'Mr Fitch, I would appreciate it if you would send me detailed numbers and a list of all those who were not able to be present here this afternoon, along with their duty locations.'

He returned his attention to the audience. 'This afternoon, I will send out a bulletin to all STD staff. It will include a welcome for all the staff who were unable to be here this afternoon. Meanwhile, thank you again. You may all return to your work.'

'Just one minute, Sir.' Fitch had jumped to his feet and spoke in a loud voice. 'Could you look at this please?' The audience gasped as the large display behind the lectern showed a very long and complex mathematical calculation.

Mayn turned round and looked at it briefly. Then he looked back at Fitch. 'Why am I looking at this, Mr Fitch?'

'Well, Sir, it's something that our previous STC1, Commander Marzine, had been working on for some time. It's the most complicated thing any of us has ever seen. Quite a few of our best mathematicians worked on it with Commander Marzine but the solution has never been discovered. Now, I just thought as you're such an expert, Sir, you would be able to work it out right away...' Fitch sank back into his seat with a smirk of satisfaction as absolute silence filled the room.

Mayn continued to look deep into the eyes of Fitch. As the seconds ticked by the smirk faded from Fitch's face, to be replaced by a look of flushed confusion. At last, Mayn turned around and glanced briefly at the display. 'Is Mr Ivan Gorth, the Senior Mathematician, present in the room?' he asked.

The audience gasped again and a startled man stood up slowly in the middle of the room. Mayn gestured to him. 'Come and join me here, Mr Gorth.' The man came forward nervously and mounted the dais. Mayn smiled at him and shook his hand before leading him to the display, saying: 'I see at least two errors at a glance. For instance this term is wrong – it does not describe its intention – and there are two incorrect signs here, and here. Finally, there is another wrong assumption here.' As he pointed out the errors, Mayn circled each with an electronic marker. 'Would you take a copy of this and make these corrections. I think you will find that this calculation then balances out and meets its intention. Let me know how you get on with it. Just give me a call, anytime.'

'Yes, Sir, I will start work on it right away. Thank you, Sir.'

'Thank you, Mr Gorth.'

Mayn now raised his voice and addressed everyone in the room. 'The meeting is finished, you may now return to your work. Thank you for coming.'

Exchanging awed whispers, everyone shuffled out, leaving Grafton Fitch sitting alone in the front row of seats. As Mayn stepped from the dais and approached him, Fitch began to speak. 'Ah, Sir, about the matter of my command...'

Mayn spoke quietly. 'Before I came here, I studied the records of all staff who are now under my command, including yours, Sub-Commander Fitch. I note that you have served Space Command for many years and that you are very experienced in the work you do. You have long been judged as an effective officer, although, as you know, there have been a certain number of problems recently and the record shows an unfortunate tendency to arrogance. Your command here on Yggdrasil is Area Head, ST maintenance and I'm happy to have you there as one of my senior officers. Thank you for filling the STC1 role on a temporary basis until I arrived. I will visit you in your office at 0900 tomorrow and make an initial inspection of the central servicing bays. Please inform your men. I would like to meet as many of them as possible.'

It was the evening of the following day and the time of CCO1's BIRTHDAY BANQUET had come. Apart from those on essential duty, all of Yggdrasil's officers had filled the large hall in their splendid formal uniforms, many adorned with a glittering array of medals and awards. As a high-ranking officer, Mayn was seated at the raised top table, commanded, of course, by CCO1 himself, who was in high good humour after such good food and wine. Although Mayn could not compete with the many gallantry medals on display (many given for acts of extreme courage in past situations of conflict or dire emergency), the decorations on his uniform reflected his many academic achievements and awards for research and development work and these were as impressive as any in the hall – and much rarer, too.

As a newcomer, Mayn had found the banquet most useful. He was able to meet almost all of the senior officers on Yggdrasil – most were seated at the top table – and he had also taken the opportunity to meet some of the lower-ranking officers who were under his command. After the lavish meal, a number of speeches had been made, all lionising CCO1, who clearly expected that such speeches should be made! Many toasts were drunk and the time for the climax of the evening was approaching. Mayn was sitting beside another Commander who had introduced himself earlier as PPN1. 'It stands for "Principal Pilot and Navigator". My team fly and navigate Yggdrasil when we're on the move and keep it stable when we're not.'

Now the man leaned across and said to Mayn: 'I think you'll really appreciate CCO1's wine. I've only ever tasted once before – he doesn't field it very often! – And I must say it was easily the best wine I have ever tasted. So I'm really looking forward to this.'

CCO1 was on his feet making a speech, which emphasised his very high status and how well-regarded he was within the Command. He concluded by reminding his officers that they were very fortunate to have such an effective CCO1 to command them. 'And now to the high-point of the evening,' he intoned. 'I command that six containers of my special CCO1 wine be brought to the table and served to all. When all have been served, we will drink together in special comradeship and celebration for my 90th birthday.'

As he spoke, curtains behind him were drawn back to reveal a large ornate cabinet. CCO1 turned around to face the cabinet and issued the traditional command. 'Wine Robot, open the cabinet and reveal the finest wine in the world.'

The doors opened smoothly to reveal six wine containers. CCO1 looked around with approval and anticipation as he prepared to give the order to fill the large wine glasses and distribute them to every officer in the hall. Suddenly, he froze. The invisible miasma of silence that exploded from his transfixed body engulfed the room like the orb of a transparent shock wave. Its silencing effect spread relentlessly through the hall, finally stifling the thin sounds of residual merriment in its farthest corners. The effect was as heart-stopping as the sight of a gigantic tsunami rolling ashore, majestically and serially obliterating huge volumes of everyday human activity. Everywhere in the hall, appalled eyes were now fixed upon CCO1 and the scene behind him.

Each of the six wine containers in the cabinet were marked with the red figure "2".

With a great effort, CCO1 came to life. 'Wine Robot, approach,' he barked and the machine glided forward smoothly. 'Where are the CCO1 wine containers? Why has this mistake been made? My orders were unambiguous. Replace these wine containers with the CCO1 wine immediately. I shall require a full investigation to be made into this very grave error.'

The wine robot spoke clearly enough to be heard throughout the silent hall. 'I am sorry, Sir. I have been told to communicate to you that there is no CCO1 wine on the Platform. This is the highest grade of wine available, so it has been substituted. It is hoped that this wine will be satisfactory for your purposes.'

CCO1 fell back against the table with astonishment. Officers throughout the hall looked at each other, wide-eyed with dismay.

'Where is the Master Vintner? I want him here immediately!' CCO1 was now bawling.

The robot replied. 'The Master Vintner is here, Sir. He is waiting outside the entrance door.'

The Master Vintner, a small elderly man, was soon standing in front of CCO1. 'What is your explanation for this outrage?' CCO1 yelled at the unfortunate man. 'Whatever it is, you may be sure you will pay for this.'

The man's voice was trembling. 'Sir, I had prepared the wine for you but there was an unfortunate contamination...'

CCO1 now became purple with rage. 'A contamination! A contamination in my winery! Now you are finished on Yggdrasil! I will see to it that you spend the rest of your miserable life on a prison planet – the very worst I can find.

I will make sure that you suffer...' Now CCO1 was foaming at the mouth.

The Master Vintner fell on his knees and started to weep piteously. 'Please Sir, I have served you long and well. For more than forty years. Please don't...'

'Call for the guards to take this criminal away,' CCO1 screamed. 'Put him in the heaviest irons and throw him into a Category 9 punishment cell...'

A quiet but authoritative voice interrupted. 'Excuse me, Sir. I think there is a solution...' Mayn stood beside the kneeling man.

CCO1 wheeled around and glared at the interrupter with unfocussed eyes. 'You! Who are you, anyway?' He peered at Mayn more closely. 'Gorton, isn't it? How can you possibly be of any help? Return to your seat immediately!'

Mayn spoke quietly again. 'There are six containers of CCO1 wine in Store 4D/574.'

The Master Vintner looked up at him, slack-jawed with astonishment. Then he shook his head. 'No, Sir, it cannot be. There is no CCO1 wine on the Platform.'

Mayn smiled at him gently. 'Yes there is. It is in Store 4D/574.'

The wine robot now spoke, addressing Mayn. 'Sir, I am afraid you are mistaken. There is no CCO1 wine in Store 4D/574. I have just checked my records.'

Mayn pointed to the wine containers in the cabinet. 'Containers like these but marked with gold lettering showing a large figure "1"?'

'Yes, Sir, that is the appearance of CCO1 wine containers. But there is no CCO1 wine on the Platform. I have just checked my records. My records are always accurate, Sir.'

'Go and look in Store 4D/574,' Mayn commanded in a quiet firm tone.

The robot left. The hall remained silent and still; no coughing, shuffling, whispering. Almost no breathing. Everyone held in a sort of rigid suspension, each desperate for resolution and release but filled with increasing hopelessness.

All eyes continued to be focussed on the trio of figures that formed a motionless sculpture at the front of the hall. CCO1 glaring furiously at the Master Vintner, who was slumped forward in despair partially supported by Mayn's hand grasping his shoulder. The minutes passed. Then, almost noiselessly, a new cabinet glided into place and the doors opened to reveal six wine containers, each marked clearly with the gold figure "1".

A blessed life force swept through the hall, a fresh wind of release. A corporate "deep breath" was drawn and the audience flexed and swayed like a field of tall daffodils set in momentary motion by a sudden gust of wind arcing across a field. An intensely grateful sense of normality began to return to the hall. Even CCO1 relaxed his furious pose and his expression softened as he looked at the gold lettering on the wine containers.

Mayn gave the Master Vintner's shoulder a gentle squeeze. 'Leave the hall and return to your quarters. Everything will be all right,' he said quietly.

'Wine Robot, serve the CCO1 wine!' The command was given in a normal voice. Then, before he sat down, the older man turned around and looked quizzically at Mayn. 'How did you know?'

'I saw the wine in the store when I was exploring the Platform earlier today,' Mayn answered gravely.

CCO1 looked thoughtful as he continued to look at Mayn. 'Thanks,' he said finally, 'I won't forget this.'

Mayn stretched leisurely and looked around the escape pod which had now been his lonely home for nearly seven months. He had to admit it looked completely different from the vehicle that had flown off with its hapless passenger. Then, everything was neat and tidy; now, the Control Cabin was a mass of open panels with many wires and cables snaking across the benches and floor. He shook his fist amiably. 'I'll get you going if it's the last thing I do,' he grinned. Then the grin faded from his face as he recalled the devastating truth. If he didn't "get it going", he would die in this vehicle; he knew that. Even if he was clever and skilled enough to bring the vehicle to life, there was still no guarantee that he would establish enough control over it to reach habitation.

He sighed. 'Time for sleep,' he said out loud, 'big day tomorrow. Tomorrow, I throw the switches. Metaphorically, anyway!' He grinned again and retired to his sleeping quarters.

He woke at 0800 with rising excitement. Breakfast was eaten abstractedly and it was not long before he was in the Control Cabin, meticulously checking on the logic of his work and testing each mechanical and electronic connection. Finally, he stood back, smiled wanly and thought: 'I suppose I can't put it off any longer. I've got to switch all this on and see whether the system I've built will work. If it does, the outside cameras will show the flaps, nozzles and control surfaces moving at my command. That's the very first thing I need to see working, because getting the engines to start would be pointless if I can't control the vehicle.'

Mayn decided he should prepare himself for this awesome event. He stood in the very centre of the Control Cabin, closed his eyes and was completely and utterly still for several minutes. It was as if he was drawing power into himself; power from the vehicle, power from the asteroid, power from the void of Space all around him. In his total isolation, he recognised himself as the merest speck of matter in the vast universes of Space. Yet, he knew he was filled with unique life; he knew he had done his very best and applied his considerable knowledge, ability and power to the extreme situation in which he found himself. Minutes had passed. At last, he was ready.

Now he moved, deftly flicking on banks of switches in various places around the Control Cabin. As he did so, a new cacophony of sound began to swell. New lights illuminated, meters swung their indicators across calibrated dials and many display screens flashed into life. Mayn moved swiftly around the Control Cabin with movements almost like a ballet master, checking, adjusting, setting control after control in the precise sequence he had worked out in agonisingly careful detail. Finally, all was ready. Mayn sat down at Control P1 and moved the manual control yokes cautiously, straining his eyes at the outside camera displays before him. His concentration was absolute...

An ear piercing whoop of delight reverberated around the Control Cabin! Outside in the harsh, burning light, Mayn could see clearly that all the jet nozzles of the escape pod moved smoothly to replicate the movements of the control yokes; and all the other control surfaces pivoted and flexed perfectly!

'I'VE DONE IT!' Words of absolute delight yelled at maximum volume. 'The manual control now works perfectly and I can easily hook this system back into the vehicle's automatic system!' Mayn was beside himself with joy. He continued to shout: 'It certainly took me a long time and I needed all my knowledge and skill to make a successful job of it – but – I'VE DONE IT!'

He began to dance energetically around the Control Cabin. He just couldn't help it!

5

Day 230

Starting with the glorious day of his success, Mayn had spent the following two weeks tidying up the many components of his newly-constructed control system. Each unit had been mounted carefully in an appropriate equipment cabinet and the wiring had been rationalised. Some of the units needed to be mounted in the external equipment bays and he had spent many days outside the vehicle, working for hours in his suit. These days were particularly exhausting and he was very glad when all the external work was completed and the external bays could be locked securely and resealed. Back inside the control room with everything completed, Mayn looked around with great satisfaction. Everything had been returned to a neat and tidy condition.

'It almost looks as if this vehicle could be powered up right now and be flown off this asteroid!' he thought. 'Wouldn't that be the most marvellous thing that could happen?'

However, he knew he must never rush things. Firstly, his local control system had to be connected into the vehicle's automatic systems – but, this time, the automatic systems would be programmed under his local control and not by some other person remote from the vehicle!

'That's the next task. Get the system fully connected and then test it fully.' Mayn knew that this next phase of the work would take some time. 'I mustn't be impatient, tempting though it is to get everything done and ready. Everything must be done meticulously. One small slip could be disastrous and completely ruin my chances. So – slowly, slowly and carefully, carefully!'

As he leaned back, he suddenly realised just how tired he felt. 'I've been working on this task for months and months, so it's hardly surprising that I feel washed out.' He looked around again at his progress. 'You know,' he told himself, 'I really think I need a break from all this – a holiday!' At this, Mayn laughed out loud. 'A holiday,' he chortled, 'a wonderful holiday in the worst place in the Universe. That's just what I need!'

However, Mayn knew he was lucky to be alive and especially fortunate that he had been able to achieve all that he had. He also knew that he would benefit from a break from all the meticulous technical work he had carried out. 'I'm firmly on track to be successful and get out of here. I've rebuilt all the control units my murdering friends took out;' he paused and then added, 'well, I should say, I have actually designed a completely new system of manual control – perhaps one that will be superior to the original.' That surprising thought amused him and he smiled. 'I'll just relax this evening and start my thinking tomorrow. I'll spend the next week or two on holiday, recalling my life on Yggdrasil. I'll record and process it all with my PAC and we'll see if any pattern begins to emerge. After all, when (he grinned wryly at the word) I get out of here, I'll need all my thoughts sorted out. The people who did this to me need to be stopped. They could easily do the same to others...' He paused and his eyes widened. 'Perhaps they already have!' This thought increased his resolution to solve the mystery of it all.

The next morning after breakfast, Mayn sat on a comfortable couch, PAC beside him, switched on and ready. 'PAC speak out, review recorded life on SSP Yggdrasil from arrival. '

After a short pause, the PAC began to speak:

"Most staff on Yggdrasil welcomed you and you were given a very friendly reception. Your

reputation preceded you. You met CCO1, Admiral
Feltham Sarfeld. He was superficially quite
pleasant but turned sneering and pompous about
your age. He opined that you were too young
to be a Commander. Also, he minimised your
achievements. He emphasised how important,
efficient and well-regarded he was; also how
he was an excellent disciplinarian. You were
generally unimpressed. Finally, he invited
you (and all other officers) to a special
dinner to celebrate his 90th birthday. You
then met Sub-Commander Grafton Fitch who had been
standing in as STC1. He was casual, rude and
overbearing and clearly suggested you were not
competent to do the job; therefore he proposed
that he should maintain his current elevated
position. Without unpleasantness, you refused.
Fitch then attempted to humiliate you at a staff
meeting by producing an "insoluble" mathematical
problem which you solved immediately. At the CCO1
dinner, there was a very unpleasant incident when
the Admiral's special CCO1 wine could not be
served. There had been a contamination in the
winery. You saved the day by locating a stock of
the wine that no-one appeared to know about. You
also saved the Master Vintner from severe and
unreasonable punishment. The record ends at
this point."

Mayn sat back and thought for a while. 'The next
twelve months were very important. I spent a good deal of
my time visiting all the areas under my command and
meeting every single person who worked in the various
functions – everyone from the top to the bottom. I
think I must make a comprehensive record of all that I
discovered and the actions I took to make the whole
organisation run more smoothly.'

He rose from the couch and went to sit in front of a large
screen. 'I'll recreate the structure of my organisation here,'
he thought, 'and then I can detail the significant events I
can remember and make a record on my PAC.' The man sat

for a considerable time, constructing a complex diagram on the screen; then he made a large number of notes in various areas of the diagram – these identified particular events that he wished to record. Finally, he sat back in his seat and began to recall his series of actions.

He remembered he thought it appropriate to start at the "top" so he began by calling a meeting with the three Sub-Commanders who headed up the Maintenance, Construction and Development Areas of his organisation. He had already met all three men and briefly visited their areas of operation. Although each man had boasted of the quality and efficiency of his Area, he had seen clear signs that this was far from the case. As they sat around a large table in his office, Mayn served coffee and invited each one to outline his responsibility and workload.

The bellicose Fitch immediately jumped in and began to speak in a loud arrogant voice. 'Well, as the senior Sub-Commander in STD, I'm perfectly happy to start the ball rolling while the others are working out what to say. As you know, Sir, I am responsible for all maintenance on the Platform and I command over 500 skilled engineers. Over the years, I have made my organisation extremely efficient and it now operates like it was mounted on finely balanced anti-gravity bearings – virtually frictionless, as you know, Sir.' He smirked knowingly at Mayn. 'All my staff are kept extremely busy and I make sure that they are operating at maximum efficiency at all times. In short, Sir, I run an extremely happy ship. Everyone knows that I am invariably fair and demand a high standard. Anyone who lets me down can expect a very rough ride indeed. You may place your full trust and confidence in me,' he concluded with a winning smile.

'You are responsible for *all* maintenance on the Platform, Mr Fitch?' Mayn asked.

'That's right, Sir – and I guarantee that every item of equipment is kept in top condition.'

'So if I had a defective door lock, your engineers would deal with it?'

Fitch's face fell. 'Well, no, Sir. Not exactly.'

'What do you mean by "not exactly", Mr Fitch?'

'Well, my Area deals with Scientific and Technical maintenance, Sir. Routine, simple equipment is the responsibility of the Utilities Division.'

'Yes, that's what I thought, Mr Fitch. Perhaps you should be more precise?'

Fitch flushed. 'Ah, yes, Sir,' he mumbled.

Mayn now turned a level gaze on the other two men who were smiling derisively at Fitch. 'Is something amusing you, Gentlemen?' he asked softly, without expression.

'No, Sir,' they responded, immediately resuming serious expressions.

Mayn addressed a second officer. 'Tell me about the Construction area,' he said.

Sub-Commander Wilfred Glassford was a smallish, rather portly man who looked rather uneasy and spoke in a high voice. 'I have over 300 specialised construction engineers in my area. As you know, Sir, most equipment is delivered to the Platform in component form. We build all the new equipment received by the Platform, install and test it. Occasionally we are required to construct new equipment designed here on the Platform. That means we need to make all the parts and build all the units from scratch. Then, of course we install and test it just like the component items. Finally, we rebuild all defective and broken items of equipment and machinery, constructing new parts as required. We receive this unserviceable equipment from other Divisions. All my workshops have the very latest high-tech equipment. It is all high-level precision work, Sir, requiring a great deal of skill and training.'

'Does all this work keep your staff 100% busy, Mr Glassford?'

'Yes, of course, Sir. My Area is always extremely busy (Mayn noted that the other Sub-Commanders snorted silently at this statement!) and I need to apply for increased staff numbers from time to time.'

'I imagine your need for experienced construction engineers is difficult to meet, is it not?'

'Yes, Sir, you're absolutely right.'

'So from where are these highly-skilled people obtained?'

'Well, periodically, we do get new specialised engineers from Earth-side.' He paused and then added in a lower voice: 'Sometimes it is necessary to make internal transfers-in.' Mayn noticed the other two Sub-Commanders stiffened and, for a moment, Fitch looked as if he was about to interrupt with a comment.

'Who assesses your personnel requirements, Mr Glassford?'

There was a rather embarrassed silence. Finally: 'Ah, Sir, my personnel needs are recognised as valid and approved by Resources; they then carry out the necessary actions.'

'Do such requests pass through STC1, Mr Glassford?'

Another silence. Then the man replied in an uncertain tone: 'not usually, Sir. Commander Marzine did not wish to see them – nor did his predecessor.'

'In future, I would like to see them – and perhaps discuss them with you, Mr Glassford. I shall send you a directive to that effect.'

Mayn now turned to the final Sub-Commander, a younger bearded man who gave the appearance of wishing he was elsewhere. 'And what of Development, Mr Glinche?'

Sub-Commander Zachariah Glinche spoke very quietly. 'Over 150 research scientists and engineers work in my area, Sir. We assess development ideas our own people come up with, as well as those received from other parts of the Platform. We also work on major research and development programs usually suggested by our own teams. We build the prototypes and, if the systems are assessed as viable, we help to convert the prototypes into operational models. We also pass details of our research to Command for distribution to all other platforms and vehicles as appropriate.'

'How do you make your workload decisions, Mr Glinche?' Mayn asked.

'We meet informally and discuss things often.' The answer was hesitant.

'And who are "We", Mr Glinche?'

The man cast his eyes towards the table. 'Ah, everyone in my area, really,' he said. 'We find informality works best.'

'You mean meetings of up to 150 people in one room?'

'Ah, yes, Sir.'

'Well, Mr Glinche, I agree that informality can be very useful but I think you should have regular research and development meetings with smaller numbers of appropriate staff,' Mayn said in a friendly tone, 'and I would like to be there.'

'Yes, Sir.'

Mayn now rose and poured a fresh cup of coffee for each officer. 'Now I have a question for all three of you. How often do you three meet together?'

Silence greeted his question. Finally, Fitch spoke. 'Sir, we meet each other when there is something to discuss.'

'So when was the last time the three of you met?'

Finally, Fitch spoke again. 'Sir, each Area operates independently and there is usually no need for contact between us. That is the way it always has been on the Platform. Therefore, the direct answer to your question is: "We never meet formally." Occasionally, we may speak to each other but this is unlikely to be about work.'

'So, Mr Fitch, what do you do when a new piece of equipment needs to be built in your Area?'

Fitch smirked. 'We build it ourselves, of course! I just put my best men on to it.'

Mayn looked at him. 'And what do you do when a member of your staff comes up with a development idea?'

'I take that on myself,' Fitch said proudly. 'I can soon tell whether it's viable or not. Most of the ideas that are passed up to me are not worth considering. I usually tell my people to get on with their own jobs and forget about areas they are not qualified to operate in. In any case, I don't believe in change, Sir. It just complicates the issue – that's what I always say. It's one of my "famous" sayings. I have many of these and they're well known!' He grinned.

Mayn turned to the other two officers. 'Do you wish to comment on what Mr Fitch has just said?'

'Yes, I certainly do!' Glassford was indignant. 'Of course I have long known that this was going on and I wish to object strongly. My Area should carry out all construction work. It's set out in our Work Specification and we are the experts.'

'I thought you might say that, Mr Glassford,' Mayn mused. 'What do you do when you wish to propose a development for a piece of equipment? Also, how do you deal with the maintenance of your own equipment?'

'Well, I have excellent procedures for these,' Mr Glassford's eyes gleamed enthusiastically. 'I have some really bright people in my Area and I pass the ideas to them. They come up with some really good proposals and decisions. You will be very impressed, Sir, when you see the sort of thing we do – and, of course, we maintain our own equipment,' he added.

Mayn turned to the third officer. 'What of you, Mr Glinche? What do you do when your prototypes become operational equipment and require formal building? And what do you do about the maintenance of your own development equipment?'

'We do both these things ourselves, Sir,' the man said proudly. 'My scientists and engineers are superb and always do a wonderful job for me.'

Mayn was silent for a few minutes. Finally he looked up and addressed them all calmly. 'Well, Gentlemen, it seems I have a Maintenance Area who does construction and development work as well as maintenance, a Construction Area that does construction, development and maintenance, too and a Development Area that is proud of its construction and maintenance as well as its development work.' The three officers looked at each other with uncertain smiles and waited.

'Is it your recommendation to me that all these working practices should continue or do we need to rationalise the system?' Mayn looked at each officer in turn.

All three nodded vigorously and, inevitably, Fitch burst into speech. 'Well, Sir, everything works so smoothly and efficiently – especially in my own Area. Surely there is no need to change anything?'

Mayn looked at the other two. 'Do you agree with Mr Fitch? No changes?'

'Yes, Sir, we should definitely keep operations as they are,' they both said.

'Fine, then,' Mayn said decisively, 'so the only alteration I need to make is to the top management structure. The current structure is designed for fully coordinated working across the Division and, in reality, we have the opposite. In the new structure, I will assume a more direct management role and I am appointing one of you to a new post as STC2; that officer will be responsible to me for the day-to-day running of the whole Division's work as well as leading the work of his own Area. The other two officers will assume a more subordinate role as Leaders of their Areas, although personally you will of course retain your current rank until you are replaced. At that time, the rank level will be reviewed.'

Fitch burst forth. 'Sir, what an inspired idea. I will be more than happy to...'

'Just one moment, Mr Fitch, permit me to finish. I will appoint Mr Glassford to the new post of STC2.' Mayn looked at Glassford. 'You and I will need to work together very closely, Mr Glassford. By which I mean, every day. There will be a considerable amount of work for us to do.' Mayn then turned to Fitch. 'I am of course aware that you are the senior Sub-Commander, Mr Fitch, but you currently have a very large Area to command and I am sure you would not have the capacity to carry out this additional role. I need you to continue where you are.'

Glassford was pale and looked blank. Fitch looked bewildered and furious. Glinche looked stricken and crushed.

After a moment or two, Mayn stood up. 'Would you please excuse me for a moment,' he said, 'I have an urgent matter I must attend to.' He left the office and disappeared into his living suite next door, closing the door firmly behind him. Here, he sat down on a comfortable couch and picked up some papers from a side table. After five minutes or so, he rose to his feet and returned to the office. As he approached the table, his three senior officers stopped whispering to each other and sat motionless.

As soon as Mayn sat down, Fitch addressed him in an uncharacteristically quiet voice. 'Ah, Sir, the three of us have been discussing your proposal and we would like to make a suggestion. May I detail it to you?'

'Of course, Mr Fitch.'

'Sir, while we recognise the strength of your new proposal, we think it would cause a considerable amount of disruption and we think it would be wise and efficient to try an easier alternative system for a trial period – probably an extended trial period to ensure we can evaluate it properly.'

'What easier alternative system is that, Mr Fitch?'

'Well, it's not really alternative or even new, Sir. It's actually the current system, worked in accordance with the Work Specifications of each Area.' Fitch became silent. Everyone looked at Mayn nervously.

'I see.' Mayn paused to ponder the proposal gravely. 'So we retain the current Area and management structure but Maintenance just does maintenance, Construction just does construction and Development just does development? Is that it?'

'Yes, Sir!' Relieved voices in unison.

Mayn smiled. 'Well, Gentlemen, I'm very pleased to see all three of you working together and thinking so clearly. I think I can agree to your proposal, which means we need not reorganise management at this stage. So here is my instruction for the record:

"From this day, each ST Area will attend ONLY to its designated function, in accordance with its Work Specification. Any other work is to be referred to the appropriate ST Area for their action and this will be carried out with maximum efficiency. There will be active liaison between all three senior Area managers. In addition, there will be a formal Report and Planning Meeting each month here in my office and each of you will attend. Instruction ends."

Mayn continued: 'Would all three of you note that I will be reviewing each of your Areas in detail during the next few months, seeking efficiency in all aspects of your operations.

Meanwhile, I wish to thank you all for coming and for the clarity we have been able to bring to the situation.

Mayn then showed his senior officers out and stretched out on a comfortable couch with a slight smile on his lips.

With all the details of his meeting with the Sub-Commanders now fresh in his memory, Mayn clicked on his PAC and recorded a succinct précis of the key events. He concluded: 'Of course there was never any further discussion of reorganisation from the three senior officers and the three ST Areas worked together with proper coordination from that day. Record ends.'

Now he turned his attention to his detailed review of the three ST Areas, during which he had visited every part of every Area and spoken to all the men employed there. Eventually, he was ready to make a record of the results of these visits and turned back to his PAC:

"Record begins. As promised, I visited every part of my command and spoke to every staff member. The following is a record of what I found and how various problems were resolved:

1. Maintenance Area carried out routine work effectively, although some record-keeping was rather casual. However, staff tended to be bullied and were not allowed to express their ideas to improve equipment, procedures, efficiency or work practices. Management at lower levels was often poor. It took some time but all these faults were gradually corrected by appropriate training and redistribution of staff.

2. Construction Area was better in general management terms but there was often a harsh attitude from superior staff which did not engender cooperation between the various functions. This was corrected with management training. The individual work of the Area was done generally efficiently and mostly with pride. Over a period of time, good quality

staff were identified, encouraged and trained, often achieving supervisory or management posts to the benefit of the Area.

3. Development Area was of course more of a scientific environment. Here, there were many excellent minds although, often, they were not sufficiently coordinated. Informality was so rife that workload was adversely affected. Management and coordination training gradually solved these issues and work output became much more efficient.

4. Within one year, all issues had been solved in the three Areas and I was satisfied that near maximum efficiency and cooperation was being achieved. Record ends."

Mayn lay back and mused. 'I've worked really hard on that record today. Time to stop now. I'm really tired and it's time for sleep. Tomorrow I'll make a start on hooking up my manual control system to the vehicle control system.' He stretched leisurely. 'One more step to get this vehicle ready to begin my very own rescue mission!'

Minutes later, Mayn was in his bunk and sound asleep.

6

Day 247

'My holiday is over!'

Mayn had woken up with a sense of purpose. 'Time to return to the technical tasks.' Lying comfortably in his bunk, he decided he would start this morning to establish a new schedule that would keep him busy on technical work for most of every day, without over-intensity. Now he deliberately put his intentions into spoken words: 'For this part of the task, I need to be relaxed and meticulous – thinking clearly all the time. Because, when I've completed all the reconnecting work and tested the circuits separately as much as I can, it will be time to fire everything up and begin to work towards my departure from this asteroid. Everything has got to work perfectly, so there's absolutely no room for error. I'll plan two, maybe three hours each morning, then a leisurely break for a midday meal, followed by another two or three hours in the afternoon. After that, it will be time to think about my Yggdrasil events and record them for continued analysis.'

Although he had now been marooned on the asteroid for eight long months, Mayn knew that this patient, meticulous approach was the right one – the one most likely to bring him success. So, although he was of course desperate to leave, he was absolutely certain that he should take everything very slowly. 'After all,' he mused, 'it is very important that I can get back to civilisation to report. If my "friends" on the Platform can do this to me – a high-profile senior officer – I am sure they can do it to anyone. All this must be stopped and the only way that's going to happen is for my escape from this asteroid to be a success. I need to get back to civilisation as quickly as possible.'

Filled with energy and purpose, Mayn rose, washed, dressed and was soon eating his breakfast in the rest area. As he did so, he reviewed a three-dimensional model of the vehicle's control systems on a large projection system; this included all the modified equipment he had made and installed, so the visual model before him was a correct representation of the vehicle in its current state. Here, every detail of the original and new equipment were displayed, along with the many connections that were now required. He studied the large model with satisfaction. 'It's a good thing I took the time to record everything I did here in the vehicle's spatial models,' he thought. 'It was a time consuming task when I did it but I knew the work would pay dividends if I ever arrived at this situation. Now I will be able to double-check everything I do.'

Within an hour, Mayn was hard at work in the Control Room, tackling the connections that would join the first element of his new local control system to the vehicle's main control. Most of these were complex plug interfaces with many tiny connections but some required heavier power cables to be connected directly. Of course, he used the highly precise automatic tools that he found in the engineering kits to make these connections. Such equipment was highly reliable and carried out its own checks after a connection had been made. Even so, it was extremely demanding work which required his whole attention and he found he was very tired after two continuous hours of work.

'Time to stop,' he said to himself after the first multiple connection of the very first element had been made and tested. 'It's just as I thought. All this is meticulous work and that's bound to be pretty tiring.' Before starting on his midday rest period, he made a careful record of his progress and made sure that full details were added to the large control model. Then he settled down on a comfortable couch to rest.

After some food, Mayn returned to his technical work in the afternoon and carried out several more hours of careful work. Finally, tired out once again, he recorded his progress on the special model and sat back to review his progress. 'This will take a long time – but I expected that,' he concluded. 'However, I'm sure this is the right approach, applied at the right speed. Any faster than this means that mistakes could creep in and that could mean disaster. So, it's slowly, slowly, once again!'

So began many days and weeks of the careful work which would restore the vehicle to a fully operating Space vehicle fully under internal pilot control. Mayn knew that the sophisticated navigation systems should still be in perfect working order – for they had guided him precisely to this particular asteroid, as they had been programmed to do. 'This time,' he thought with satisfaction, 'the navigation systems will guide my escape and conduct me back to civilisation.'

Meanwhile, in the evening periods after his technical work, he sat down with his PAC and continued to record what had happened during his years aboard Yggdrasil. He had decided that it would be impossible to record everything serially – there was a myriad of events where he had been in contact with numerous groups of staff on the Platform, providing each with informal help. In the end, he decided that he should group all these contacts (those he could recall) into three categories, noting that, within each category, there was a general similarity of action. Mayn was of the opinion that these events were unlikely to be major contributors to his current plight; nevertheless, he wanted his record to be as complete as possible.

He started off with the most obvious category, which he designated Category One – those events where he had provided a useful technical input to a situation. Of course he had helped to solve problems many times in his own Science and Technical Division. These included times when his own managers had asked for his help but, often, his interventions had been much more informal; on visits to his ST Areas, he would contribute helpful suggestions during discussions with staff who were having difficulty with particular technical or scientific aspects of their tasks.

His interventions were always gratefully received, since it meant that the work could then be completed with efficiency and accuracy. 'The Boss suggested we do this,' his staff would say admiringly, 'and now the equipment works like a dream! It does exactly what it was designed to do.' Mayn decided that these interventions need not appear in his PAC record, since he considered such activities to be part of his function on the Platform.

There were, however, many occasions when he was able to help other Yggdrasil staff with technical problems. These were often very informal. Mayn would come upon a situation where there was a problem and, ever ready to help, would stop and join in the discussion of the difficulty. Often, these were very simple matters – a minor malfunction in a simple piece of equipment, for instance. At that moment he recalled an occasion where he came upon a team of mechanics from Utilities Division engaged in replacing a large door hinge. The mechanics were looking puzzled because the new part would not fit. Mayn had stopped briefly and examined the problem: 'The connection strut is the wrong length,' he had said to the man in charge of the team, 'I suggest you measure it against the old strut and bore a new hole where it is required. I think you will then have no further trouble fitting it.'

The Utilities Division supervisor had acted upon Mayn's suggestion and the hinge was soon fitted and working perfectly. He had been most grateful and impressed. For weeks afterwards, he had told everyone the story: 'You know what Stores are like! They had sent us out with wrong components and we were baffled. Then Commander Gorton was walking past and stopped to solve our problem in about ten seconds! And he was really nice about it, too. I think he's a wonderful guy even if he is a senior officer!'

Remembering this, Mayn could recall many other instances over the years, involving people from other Divisions who had problems with particular aspects of the work they had been instructed to do. He could not recall any occasions where he had ignored someone in trouble; he had always stopped to see if he could help – and, normally, he could! He decided he would make a note of all the occasions he could remember and then consolidate these into a fairly brief report for his PAC record.

Category Two was rather more complex. This concerned all the occasions where he had contributed to the solution of organisational problems on the Platform. Obviously, he was responsible for the efficient operation of his own complex Division, its overall structure and the detailed organisation of each sub-structure down to the lowest levels. This was a very important element of his job as STC1 and part of the reason why his function carried such a senior rank. However, he had not been working on the Platform very long before his exceptional talents of problem-solving had been noted. Within a year of his arrival, he was often approached by the management of other Divisions for advice on structural problems in their own areas.

'We've had this problem in our Area for some time now,' they would tell Mayn, 'and it's getting worse and worse. We've tried to solve it a number of times but our solutions never seem to work and we usually need to withdraw them. Is there any chance you could have look at this? We know you are particularly talented in problem-solving and we would be most grateful.'

As time went on, these informal requests came from staff of increasingly high rank. On one occasion, the request had actually come from CCO1 himself! Mayn had been called to see CCO1 and they sat together in his office:

'Listen, Maynard...'

Mayn sighed inwardly. 'Oh dear, first name terms; he wants something!'

'We've got an unfortunate situation between Utilities and Facilities Divisions. It's been building up for a while and various people have tried to solve the problem. Even I have been involved but, of course, I don't want to come into the situation with too heavy a hand...' Mayn smiled inwardly. He had heard about this problem. In the past months, CCO1 had issued a series of dictatorial instructions that had largely been ignored by the staff of the two Divisions! '... so, I am aware that you are quite good with people and I wondered if you could take a look at the problem? Of course there's no doubt I could solve it myself but I'd rather it was solved at a level much lower than mine. In any case, I'm so very busy with strategic matters that I really haven't the time to give to such unimportant matters...' CCO1 stopped and looked encouragingly at Mayn.

'Yes, Sir, I'll do what I can, of course. Could you give me your files on it, please? This will get me up to speed quite quickly. I don't have a great deal of spare time myself but I'm certainly willing to have a look.'

CCO1 looked uneasy. 'Ah... Ah...' he spluttered. 'You want my files? That's a bit of a problem, Maynard. My files are highly confidential, you know. For my eyes only, you know?'

Mayn looked at him calmly. 'Well, it's up to you, Sir. But the more information I have, the better chance I have of analysing and solving the problem, whatever it is.' He waited.

CCO1 was silent. At last he said. 'Actually, Maynard, there isn't much of a formal record of the problem. I had hoped it could be solved without making it into a big issue...'

Mayn understood. CCO1 was trying to sweep a serious problem under the carpet so that it would not reflect upon him! 'Just let me have what notes you have, Sir,' he said quietly.

'I want you to have a free hand, Maynard. You can act with my authority – though just for this, you understand? I want the problem to be solved, without it needing to come up to my level.'

So Mayn found himself back in his own office with a slim envelope of loose papers. Sitting down at his desk, he studied the few sheets the envelope contained. It seemed that this was some sort of work dispute concerning basic operations within the two Divisions. Utilities Division carried out simple routine maintenance and repair tasks across the many levels of the Platform (lighting, heating, cooling, etc.), while Facilities were responsible for cleaning and replacement of worn-out items (wall and floor coverings, décor, furniture, etc.). He could see immediately that the teams carrying out these functions would often be present in the same place. Also, there were bound to be some areas of overlap in the work itself.

After scanning through the sparse paperwork, Mayn identified the problem as obstructive practices between the Facilities cleaning teams and the Utilities maintenance teams. It seemed that there were daily occurrences of obstruction in the many Zones and Levels of the Platform The situation had now deteriorated so much that the essential work of both Divisions could not be carried out. As a result, Platform operations were being increasingly disrupted.

The notes showed that these problems had been tackled at many management levels. There had been intense discussions between managers and supervisors, with multiple staff directives issued. The failure of these initiatives was followed by many more meetings and instructions from higher and higher management levels until (Mayn smiled) CCO1 had somehow become involved; his aggressive edicts had also been unsuccessful! When he had finished reading, he knew there was a serious problem – but he still did not know precisely what it was or what had caused it.

The following day, Mayn asked the Heads of the Utilities Division and the Facilities Division to meet him in his office. Both were relatively young men (though not as young as Mayn) at the Sub-Commander level. They sat around Mayn's table and he apprised them of his role in the situation, after which he asked: 'Could you tell me precisely what the problem is?'

Head Utilities spoke first. 'Well, Sir, basically, Facilities' cleaners obstruct my maintenance engineers from doing their routine work. They place their equipment or themselves exactly where my men have to work.'

Mayn looked at the other man. 'Do you agree with this?'

'Yes I do,' Head Facilities answered, 'but the other way round, of course.'

'So what have you both done about it?'

The men explained how the problem was first identified at the lowest Supervisor level in both their Divisions. When it could not be solved at that level, it had been referred upwards through the various management levels above and, after some months, had eventually reached the most senior officers in the Divisions, by which time the problem was totally ingrained.

'What happened at each level? Why was the problem not sorted out?' Mayn's next question.

It seemed that each management level had studied the problem and liaised with their "opposite numbers" in the other Division. However, their actions, usually taken in concert with the manager of the other Division, had been unsuccessful.

'What did you two gentlemen do when it finally reached you?'

'Well we got together and went through the whole problem in detail,' Head Utilities answered. 'We actually went to some of the sites that were experiencing the problem, saw what was happening for ourselves and talked to our men there. Eventually, we issued identical directives to our staff and tasked our managers to ensure that these directives were carried out.'

'What happened?' Mayn wanted to know.

'It didn't work,' Head Facilities answered. 'The men said they couldn't obey the directives because of the obstructive actions of the other Division's staff. They had said that about every directive they received, right from the beginning.'

'Then CCO1 heard about it and got personally involved – but that did no good either,' Head Utilities added, rather sadly.

Mayn was thoughtful for a while. At last he spoke. 'Gentlemen, I understand the problem but you haven't told me who is actually "calling the shots" here. In my experience, things like this do not happen spontaneously – or, if they do, they are not sustained. They need a continuation of impetus. Who is the person or people behind this?'

The two men looked at each other with puzzlement. 'Sorry, Sir, we don't understand your question. No-one is behind it. It just happens because workload is obstructed. The problem conceived itself and then developed a virulent life of its own.'

Mayn looked from one to the other and then sat with his eyes closed for a few moments. Eventually, he stirred and opened his eyes. 'Gentlemen, thank you for this meeting. I trust you are aware that I am acting with the full authority of CCO1? Obviously, I will keep you informed of my actions but I will not be seeking your permissions before taking command action in your Divisions, if I think it is appropriate.'

The two men looked distinctly unhappy. 'We understand that, Sir, but could you not consult us when...'

Mayn interrupted gently: 'I'm sorry, Gentlemen. If you think about it you will see that I must be totally free to act. Would you issue a directive to all your staff to inform them that I will be visiting them with your authority? It's only fair that they should know who I am when I turn up. Also, I need you to send me the structure and personnel lists of your Divisions, as soon as possible.'

Within an hour, Mayn had the data he had requested from both Divisions. That evening, after completing his own work, he had turned to the Utilities and Facilities data and studied them carefully.

The next afternoon, Mayn travelled to LEVEL-1 and visited a very large communal rest area for general staff. Here, men who had finished their work could relax, eat, drink and access a range of entertainment systems. It was here that men from different Divisions met and socialised. The room was also used to communicate staff directives from supervisory and management staff and there were large data screens placed around the walls. He noticed that the data screens were densely packed with information and instructions. After drinking a leisurely coffee there, he consulted his PAC and instructed it to direct him to the supervisory offices of Facilities Division. This proved to be on LEVEL-2 and he instructed his buggy to take him there.

On arrival at a long corridor, he was surprised to see that the Facilities Division offices were located on one side of the corridor while similar function Utilities Division offices lined the other. He wished to visit a particular office and his PAC had shown it to be some distance along this corridor. Some minutes later, the buggy came to a stop beside a door marked:

"Facilities Division. StRep Office. Orvan Miig".

Mayn stepped down from his buggy and looked at the offices on the other side of the corridor. Not seeing what he was looking for, he walked a little way along the corridor, first one way and then the other. Finally he stopped: 'Ah,' he said under his breath, 'Now that's interesting.' He was standing near an office door identified as:

"Utilities Division. StRep Office. Ricardo Banz."

He walked back to his buggy, collected his files, and walked up to the Facilities Division door, where he pushed the communication button. The screen flicked on and a face peered out, speaking in impatient tones. 'Yes, who are you? What do you want? Do you have an appointment? Mr Miig (it was pronounced *Meeg*) only sees people by appointment and his diary is full for the next two weeks.' The face was unfriendly and aggressive.

Mayn spoke calmly. 'Look at your identifier, please.'

There was a long pause, then the door clicked open. 'Enter, please, Sir.' Mayn did so and found himself face-to-face with the office receptionist.

'Sir, I'm sorry, we didn't know you were coming. In fact we never see senior officers on this floor. How may I help you?' The man had become very obsequious.

'I would like to speak to Mr Miig right away, please.'

The receptionist's face fell. 'I'm sorry, Sir. He is not here. I'm not expecting him back in the office today.'

'Where is he?' Mayn asked.

'Well, Sir, I'm not supposed to say... but... he is in a meeting with Mr Banz.'

Mayn ears pricked up. 'Mr Banz? StRep Utilities? In his office down the corridor?'

The receptionist was dumbfounded. 'How did you know that, Sir?' he faltered.

Mayn smiled. 'It's just one of the things I know. Would you call them, please, and ask them if I could join them for a little while?'

'Sir, I'm not supposed to...'

'You may say to them that I have instructed you to call. Tell them I would like to come straight away.' The receptionist made the call and, moments later, Mayn was pressing the communication button at Mr Banz' door.

'Come in, Commander Gorton! I'm Ricardo Banz.' Mr Banz was a jovial, rotund man, although Mayn noted that the joviality did not extend to his eyes. 'This is a great honour. It must be the first time any senior officer has visited this part of the Platform – except when there are formal inspections, of course.' He led the way into his inner office where another man sat. 'This is Orvan Miig,' Banz continued effusively. 'He is my opposite number in the Facilities Division. We've known each other for many years, we're firm friends and we meet regularly.'

Mayn looked around the room and it was obvious that the two men had been engaged in playing a game of 3D Chess; a current game had been hurriedly pushed aside. 'I see that white was on the point of "checkmate",' Mayn said quietly, inclining his head towards the chess equipment.

Mr Banz flushed. 'Ah... ah... we sometimes play after work,' he said finally. 'It's some time since we had a game, isn't it, Orvan?'

Miig, a thin-faced, pale youngish man, agreed uneasily.

They all sat down. 'What can we do for you, Sir?' Banz enquired. 'Our Heads of Division have informed us that you are visiting our organisations; however, we never expected to see you at such a junior level.' The man smiled, rather derisively Mayn thought.

'I want your help with some information,' Mayn said pleasantly. 'Firstly, I would like to check if my understanding of your functions is correct. You are the Staff Representatives of your respective Divisions?' Both men nodded. 'This means that your responsibility is towards the staff and not the management. Is that correct?'

'Well, Sir, it isn't quite correct,' Miig interjected in thin, sharp-edged tones. 'Of course we are always loyal to the organisation and our superiors but someone must look after the welfare and rights of the staff and that's what we do. That is the purpose of our jobs here on the Platform.'

'I see,' Mayn pondered, 'I think in the distant past you would have been called Trade Union Representatives? In my Ancient History lessons, I seem to remember there were people called "Shop Stewards"?' The two men blenched visibly. 'Well,' Banz said smoothly, 'I would hope we are a good deal more advanced than they were! This job involves careful selection and the training is very thorough and highly sensitive.'

'Thank you,' said Mayn. 'Now, you know that my focus is the problem you have between the workers of your Divisions, don't you?'

'That's right, Sir,' Banz said, 'you're the last in a long line of officers who have come to sort it all out.' He smirked towards Miig. 'We're certainly looking forward to that day!'

'Would you know whether there a manifestation of the problem going on right at this moment?' Mayn asked.

Banz turned towards a screen. 'Yes, Sir, it seems that routine cleaning has just come to a total standstill at LEVEL-5, ZONE 16.'

'Could we go there now and would you be able to explain to me what is happening?'

'Why, of course, Sir. Let's go right now.'

The three men soon arrived at LEVEL-5 ZONE 16. A large group of Utilities Division cleaning staff were crowded against one wall, talking to each other and looking angrily at several maintenance trolleys parked along the opposite wall. Banz went to talk to the cleaning staff while Miig walked across to the maintenance men who were standing around the trolleys, talking quietly. A small group of supervisory staff were deep in discussion in the middle of the floor; at times, raised voices were heard, accompanied by aggressive gesticulations.

Banz returned. 'Another typical stand-off,' he said with *faux* weariness. 'My cleaners cannot access the floor area they are scheduled to clean because the Facilities engineers refuse to move their trolleys.'

Now Miig rejoined Mayn and Banz. 'Yes, as usual it's impossible. The engineers can't do the job on their work schedule unless the trolleys are there to support their lifting equipment.'

'And,' Banz added, 'the supervisors and managers just take the side of their own staff. So these situations are completely insoluble.' As he looked around, Mayn noticed that his eyes were bright with perverse pleasure.

'Thank you, Gentlemen. Could we return to your office now, Mr Banz?'

Back in Banz' office, the three men sat down around a table.

'Would you just give me a few moments, please,' Mayn said and proceeded to work busily with his PAC. While Mayn's attention was apparently elsewhere, Banz and Miig took the opportunity to smile at each other with conspiratorial satisfaction while making covert "thumbs down" signs to each other beneath the table. After a few minutes, Mayn closed down his PAC and looked up at the two men with a smile.

'Progress?' Banz asked brightly.

'Why, yes, thank you. I now know how this problem may be solved.'

Banz and Miig were dumbstruck. This was the last thing they expected!

'What... How?' Banz spluttered. 'Surely there is no simple way...'

Mayn continued calmly. 'Yes, Gentlemen, I have the solution and I am confident that it will work quickly. I have identified a unique team of negotiators who will solve this problem expertly and with great efficiency. I have arranged for this Unique Negotiation Team to be given special powers that will accelerate the process...'

'Just a minute, Sir.' Banz' voice had suddenly acquired an unpleasant rasp. 'As StReps of the two Divisions involved, Staff Ordinances, Standing Instructions, Orders and Directives require that Miig and I must be formally consulted about this. A series of meetings must be set up at the appropriate management levels and we need to consult the workforces over a significant period of time before we can discuss the principle of the process you are suggesting. Furthermore, I would expect that we would want to make amendments to the proposals – and there will be many details to sort out, too. This is likely to take many, many months...'

Mayn held up a hand. 'None of that will need to happen, Mr Banz. I have just authorised an "Emergency Management Situation" in your two Divisions. As I'm sure you know, this means that all your Staff Ordinances, Standing Instructions, Orders and Directives have been suspended until further notice.'

A stunned silence descended upon the office. Banz and Miig were frozen in disbelief. Mayn continued smoothly: 'The Unique Negotiation Team will consult freely with the workers...'

Miig exploded into virulent life. 'No!' he spat venomously. 'We won't allow it! We'll tell the workforce not to cooperate with these negotiators, no matter who they are or how powerful and high-ranking they are. We will make it perfectly clear to everyone that these strangers have no right to barge into our area and take over...' His voice faded away as Mayn focussed impassive unwavering eyes upon his.

'Mr Miig, you would be wise to listen to what I have to say, before you object any more.' He paused for a moment and then addressed both men. 'The Unique Negotiation Team to which I refer will consist of just two specially selected people; namely, you and Mr Banz.' He paused and then added, 'this very important negotiation team will come into being right now – that is, unless you wish to refuse...'

Mayn's words drained all manifestations of life and power from the volume of the office. The room became an inert capsule where time had juddered to a stop. Banz and Miig were incapable of movement, unaware of breath, pulse or heartbeat, now gazing wide-eyed and sightless at each other.

It is a universal fact that total stillness cannot be sustained; movement, however miniscule, is always reborn. As timeless moments passed, eyes of total consternation and bewilderment began to adjust to eyes of comprehension, acceptance, calculation and manipulation... and normal life began anew.

At last, Banz stirred and spoke in a hoarse whisper: 'Ah, Sir... I'm sure Orvan and I will, ah, do our best...'

Mayn smiled at them gently. 'I have one final thing to say. This is an opportunity of a lifetime for both of you. If the problem is solved quickly and I can report to CCO1 how you have been at the centre of the solution, he will be very grateful; so grateful in fact that I think he will wish to reward you both in very significant ways. So I wish you all success in your endeavours, Gentlemen.'

'How did you do it, Mr Gorton?' CCO1 asked in a tone of grudging admiration.

'Well, it was just a matter of identifying where effective pressure could be applied, Sir. Once I had identified Banz and Miig as the lynchpins of the solution, it was just a matter of priming them for the task. I don't know what you have in mind for them, Sir, but their skills with people would merit a move to Resources Division in Middle Management positions where they should deal directly with people. I think you will agree that they both deserve it and I am sure they would work for you with constant and intense loyalty.'

CCO1 made a note of the two names, then turned back to Mayn. 'You know, Mr Gorton, although I never mentioned it, I had already worked out that the solution lay in the direct involvement of the lower ranks. I just never had the time to think it through to its conclusion. I'm kept so busy with strategic matters, you know.' After a pause, he said in a mechanical tone: 'Anyway, thanks for your contribution.'

'Always glad to be of help, Sir.'

7

Day 302

Mayn was becoming more and more exhausted. In recent weeks, he had reached the stage in his reinstallation work that meant he had to work outside the vehicle, dealing with connections between his new modules and the existing control and navigation units that were located in the vehicle's external bays. Unlike the work inside the Control Room, which required absolute concentration in a pleasant, comfortable environment, the outside work was brutal. Although the suits were made to be as flexible, articulated and sensitive as possible, it was often a struggle to produce the absolute precision needed to make the many minute connections that were required. Because of this, progress was extremely slow and connections often had to be remade when earlier attempts were found to be defective. Mayn had found that he could work only for a maximum of around one hour in such an environment; even then, he was mentally and physically spent when he lumbered back to the airlock and dragged himself back inside the vehicle.

Earlier in the process, he had tried to complete two periods of outside working per day. Despite all the pressure to succeed at quickly as possible, he soon had to capitulate and reduce this to one session per day, that lasting no more than an hour. He had found it best to complete these exhausting sessions in the morning, when he was most fresh; his afternoon session was then spent inside the vehicle but he was often disappointed to find that he could not make meaningful progress during these times; technical work often needs to be carried out in a precise sequence and, on many occasions, elements of outside work still needed to be completed before the next phase of inside work could be started.

Mayn tried his best to conquer his disappointment with the application of reason. 'I know very well what the technical rules are. However, I can't help being disappointed when I want to make progress but am unable to do so because the sequence of work must be strictly observed. However, nothing would please me more to get all this finished and...' he punched his fist in the air... 'I WILL DO IT!' The last words were a determined but lonely roar of defiance!

His truncated technical schedule meant that he could spend more time recalling his life on the Platform and identifying events that needed to be placed on record for analysis. Having completed the record of his first two categories, he now turned to Category Three. He had decided this was where personal, individual help would be recorded. Mayn was aware that these were the events that had earned him his nickname of the "Yggdrasil Healer" on the Platform.

Helping people with their suffering was nothing new to Mayn. Even as a small child, Mayn had always been keenly aware of the presence of pain in others. Early in his life, he had discovered that, somehow, he could help to assuage suffering in others, whether this was caused by psychological trauma of some kind or was the result of physical injury or illness. From a very early age, he would appear at occasions of suffering and, by his words and actions, appear to apply an invisible balm that would bring healing and restoration to the situation, whatever it was.

He was, of course, fully aware of this "power" and considered it his duty in life to help where he could. As he grew older, he concluded that the power came somehow from his love and deep compassion for others. He had looked carefully at other people and concluded that most people did not seem to have this power. 'That makes it all the more important that I should apply my power to every situation where it is needed,' he thought, 'because there is no doubt this is a power for good.' This was his implacable conviction.

Many years before, as a young teenager, he had been greatly moved by a particular spiritual story. A travelling man arrived at a village and was attacked, robbed, beaten and left for dead. He was left lying on the ground broken and bleeding – but no-one helped him. As the hours passed, a number of village people saw his plight but they all ignored him; they passed by on the other side of the road, with their gaze averted. Then, after a long time, a man of love and compassion came. He attended to the injured man with tenderness, treated his wounds and then took him to a nearby inn, where he arranged for the man to stay until fully recovered. Before leaving, the rescuer paid all the money needed for the man's care. 'And – I'll pay for as long as it takes,' he had stressed to the innkeeper.

Mayn remembered thinking: 'I must never walk by on the other side'. From that moment, he resolved to make this a rule of his life that he would never break.

'I suppose Category Three contains a few sub-categories,' Mayn mused. 'The first and most obvious (Category 3A, I suppose) concerns action to protect the weak and those who suffer because of the cruelty of others. Psychology and sociology often calls this "bullying".

From his schooldays, Mayn had often seen bullying taking place. However, like many young people, he assumed that there would be no bullying in the adult world. 'When people grow up and become men and women, they know bullying is wrong, so it stops happening,' he had thought. When he reached adulthood, he found that his assumption was wrong! Admittedly, the bullying was different, often less physical and more psychological – but it was still there. Furthermore, he discovered that it could be more of a problem in the enclosed microcosm that was SSP Yggdrasil!

When he came to work on the Platform, it was not long before he became aware of occasions of bullying. While most of the events could be described as "low-level" bullying, he occasionally came upon situation that was more serious and required action. He remembered one occasion when he came upon a slim young worker being seriously bullied by a group of much stronger, older men. Inevitably, there was one member of the bullying group who was in the lead. In a quiet corridor, Mayn saw this large powerful man physically attacking the young man, first grasping him by the throat and repeatedly slapping his face hard, then throwing him violently to the floor and kicking him cruelly in various parts of his body, all the while making insulting, derisive comments. Meanwhile, the others in the group greatly enjoyed this violent spectacle as they spurred on their muscular friend with salacious glee. Such is the evil side of humanity.

When the bullies had gone, Mayn went to the distressed young man and helped him to sit up. 'What's your name,' he asked gently.

'Garrold,' the boy sobbed.

'What is your job here?'

'I'm a Personal Servant, Class 3'.

'Does this happen to you often?'

'All the time,' the young man whispered, 'I don't know why these men should hate me so much. We don't work together, or operate in the same location. Their leader has attacked me many times and they force me to buy them food and drinks. I'm cut and bruised and I ache all the time.'

'Who is the man who attacks you? Do you know his name?'

'His name is A'Fhagro. These men are a Utilities Labour Squad and he is their Overseer.'

'Don't worry, Garrold,' Mayn said, 'I'll help you.'

The young man looked at him tearfully, recognising a very senior officer for the first time. 'Sir, there's nothing you can do. You'll only make things worse if you report them.'

'I won't report them. You are going to solve this problem yourself.'

The young man was flabbergasted. 'Sir, I can't stop them. They'll just hurt me even more – injure me even more, maybe even kill me!'

'Listen,' Mayn said, 'Sit down over here and listen carefully to me...'

The young man walked into the hubbub of the rest area that was filled with workers sitting at tables, eating and drinking. In the centre, the bullying overseer and his team sprawled around a large circular table, laughing loudly and causing considerable disruption in the area. Workers at other tables often looked at the men with distaste but were quick to turn their gaze away if any member of the aggressive group looked towards them. Seeing the young man approaching, one of the group nudged their leader and inclined his head towards the approaching young man: 'we could do with some more coffee, couldn't we, Sol? And why should we pay for it when we've got him, eh?'

As soon as he came within reach, the muscular Sol seized the young man's arm in a painful grasp: 'Five coffees, boy, and make it quick.'

The young man turned to face him and looked straight into his eyes. 'No.' A quiet, resolute voice.

The man's jaw dropped open. 'What?' he yelled incredulously, instantly silencing everyone in the room with the animal violence of his tone.

'No,' the boy repeated.

Sol sprang to his feet, grasped the young man's throat with a large hand and shook him violently. 'Get the coffees, boy, or I'll break your neck,' he rasped menacingly.

Still looking straight into the man's eyes, the boy raised a hand slowly and touched the middle of Sol's barrel-like chest with one slim finger. Everyone in the room gasped in astonishment as a soundless explosion propelled the large muscular figure backwards over his chair to land on his back with an almighty crash several metres away. Dazed, he struggled to sit up. The young man continued to look straight into his eyes and the bewilderment on the man's face turned slowly to abject fear. At last, the young man dropped his gaze and walked away slowly. By the doorway, Mayn smiled and turned away.

Back on the asteroid, Mayn remembered many more occasions where he had to step in and help the weak. He made a list of all those he could bring to mind and made a record for the PAC. Then he turned his mind towards the next sub-category, which he had decided was concerned with psychological illness or breakdown. 'Obviously, there are many reasons why the human mind becomes overloaded and begins to malfunction or shut down. Modern medical procedures are very good at repairing and re-growing body parts – what they can do now is really sophisticated – but their progress in the equivalent psychological areas has been much slower.'

In an environment like Yggdrasil, psychological problems were not infrequent. The staff were subject to a range of stresses and strains in their daily life and work. In addition, being apart from their families for extended periods was another strain. It had long been known that the human mind can be remarkably fragile in these circumstances. The 57th Century psychiatrists and psychologists did their very best to understand the totality of human brain operations. They had long studied the way people's brains responded in all situations but, even now, there was still much to learn, partly because the brain and its aberrations were subject to constant change and mutations.

From his many years of experience, Mayn knew that his "power" was able to help in some of these psychological cases. Although many he had helped had been staff members in his own Division (and therefore were clearly his responsibility, he thought), he did not confine his efforts solely to his own staff; the principles of "never walking by" always held good for Mayn.

Now he remembered a typical example. Major Gunard Klaasj was a highly intelligent logistics expert, a senior officer in the Logistics Division. From the time of his arrival on the Platform a number of years before, he was recognised as an extremely hard-working and gifted officer, who took his responsibilities very seriously. He was very good with people and highly respected by his staff, who were completely dedicated to doing a good job for him. His superior officers were extremely pleased with the results he achieved.

Then, to the concern of all, the quality of Gunard's work began to decrease, imperceptibly at first and then with increasing effect. He made more and more mistakes and issued incorrect instructions to his staff. Furthermore, he became unapproachable and intolerant of criticism; where in the past he would have listened carefully to the comments of his staff, he now dismissed their contributions angrily. In consequence, the quality of the work in his department went steadily downhill. Eventually, his superior officers had to act and, despite his vehement protests, suspended him from his duties and referred him to Medical for examination and assessment. Here, Gunard continued to deteriorate and he became more and more withdrawn and uncooperative. The PsychoMed Team worked intensively on him, subjecting him to batteries of tests and using their most sophisticated machines and techniques.

Brain scans showed progressive deterioration of that organ and this of course began to affect a whole range of his physical and mental capacities. Weeks went by and Gunard gradually lost control, first of his body, then of his senses and finally of his mind. After that, his autonomic functions began to switch off and it became necessary to connect his body to a range of machines to keep him "alive".

The PsychoMed Team continued to study and test Gunard and there were many high-level medical conferences about him. The Senior PsychoMed (Lead Surgeon Ferd Kolber) had conducted these meetings many times and finally concluded: 'I am afraid we have been unable to ascertain what catastrophic disorder triggered Gunard's condition. I cannot remember an occasion of such complete collapse where our analysis efforts have been such a complete failure. We have seen a number of severe cases of collapse in the past but, by using the deepest physical and psychological analysis techniques, we have been able to recover the situation for the patient – although, inevitably, it has not always been possible to completely restore the damage caused by the trauma. I think we have to accept that as inevitable.

'However, this does not help us in this case. Obviously, we can keep Gunard "alive" indefinitely but, if his brain keeps deteriorating at the speed it has done, he will not only need artificial equipment to carry out all his autonomic functions but will need an artificial brain as well. If we reach that state of affairs, we shall need to consider viability – there are procedures for this eventuality but I cannot recall them ever being used.'

Ferd Kolber looked around his colleagues. 'Does anyone wish to comment or make any further suggestions before we move on?'

A youngish doctor near the foot of the table raised a reluctant hand.

'Yes, Ben?'

'Ah... Sir... should we speak to Commander Gorton?' A soft, hesitant voice.

The room suddenly became still. Ferd frowned and, down the table, Ben blenched and hunched lower in his seat, beginning to wish that he could slide under the table!

Finally, after a pause of several endless seconds, Ferd spoke: 'You know, that may be a good idea, Ben. After all, we've got nothing to lose now, have we? We've tried everything and we've come to a complete stop. Meanwhile, our patient continues to disappear.' He looked along the table. 'I'll contact Commander Gorton later today. Good bit of lateral thinking, Ben!'

'So that's the situation we are in, Commander Gorton,' Ferd Kolber concluded. 'I'm speaking to you because I know you have taken an interest in difficult medical cases before. Furthermore, I believe you have been able to contribute positively. We discussed your involvement at our Case Conference today and I promised to discuss it with you, hence my call to you now... You could meet me tomorrow evening at Medical? That's excellent, I'll look forward to that... You would like to look at the complete patient record and discuss it with me and whoever else I think should be there? Yes, of course that will be possible. I'll round up some of my staff who have been involved with this case and we can go into everything in whatever depth you require.'

Mayn sat around a large table with Ferd Kolber and several of his medical staff. Reports, schedules and charts had been displayed on the large screens and there had been an intense discussion about all aspect of Major Gunard Klaasj's condition. Knowing that Mayn had not been trained in medicine, the staff had been most impressed by the depth of his knowledge and questioning. Finally, Mayn sat back in his chair and addressed everyone:

'Thank you for all the detailed information you have given me. It seems that Major Klaasj is now in a completely dependent state – that is, he could not possibly live without the medical support you are giving him here.'

'That is absolutely correct, Mr Gorton,' Ferd replied, 'do you need my staff for anything else now?'

'No, thank you. You have all been most kind,' Mayn smiled. The medical staff left the room, leaving Mayn and Ferd alone.

'Do you mind if I ask you some questions now, Mr Gorton?'

'Not at all.'

'Now that you have all the background, what are your intentions? I am aware that you have been able to help with some difficult medical conditions in the past. As you know, you have something of a reputation for that on the Platform. I was wondering whether you are able to tell me how you might be able to make progress when we, the medical experts, can't.'

Mayn was silent for a moment or two, then he spoke quietly and introspectively: 'I'll answer that as best as I can, Ferd. Of course you're absolutely right that I am not a medical man, although I have always taken a keen interest in medical and psychological matters... anything to do with the function of the human race interests me very much. I think maybe I can explain what happens like this. As a medical and psychological expert, no-one better than you knows that the healing of a person is not carried out by you or any other human being, no matter how well-trained they may be. What the human medical expert does is create the best conditions for healing and recovery to occur and the mystery of the body and the life-force within it carries out the healing. Of course, I accept that some human interventions need to be quite heroic – like replacing a diseased organ or rebuilding shattered bones. Once that expert work is done, however, the body takes over and carries out the healing. I take it you have no problem with any of that?'

Ferd nodded silently and Mayn continued: 'However, there are some injuries or diseases that are too severe or too advanced for the body's healing processes to deal with, even with the assistance of the most modern and sophisticated medical techniques. There are also some cases where the body's own healing processes turn against themselves. Finally, particular injuries or diseases can prove to be beyond current expert knowledge. It would seem to me that Major Klaasj is a sad example of this last category. This is no-one's fault. It is just a manifestation of the fact that humanity, despite all the progress we have made over the millennia, will never know everything.' He paused and looked at Ferd. 'That is my assessment, Ferd. Do you agree?'

'Yes, Mr Gorton, I do. We all know this to be a fact in the medical profession, although, I must say, you do express it succinctly.'

'Thank you, Ferd. Now I'll try to answer the actual question you asked me! Despite all that I have said about the reality of disease, injury and recovery, we all know that there are cases – not many, probably only a few – where spontaneous recovery occurs after an illness or injury has been judged to be terminal. That's right, isn't it?'

Ferd nodded in agreement. 'Yes, I have seen the occasional miracle in my career!'

Mayn smiled. 'There, Ferd, you have just said the key word. Miracle! Totally unexplained recovery!' He paused and then continued. 'You see, Ferd, I am sure we all take part in miracles. However, most people, it would seem, don't recognise their role in a miracle. They think that the good thing that has happened is coincidence, good luck or maybe someone else's doing. So what about me? That's the question you asked. Well, I regard myself as no different from anyone else – except for one thing – I believe I am more sensitive to the role of miracles or, to put it into a medical context, more sensitive to spontaneous healing. And that's why I can sometimes help in what are judged to be difficult or hopeless situations. Of course it's not me who solves the problems, causes the healing or whatever but sometimes it seems that I am privileged to be the channel, or perhaps the catalyst. Have I answered your question, Ferd?'

Ferd was silent and thoughtful. 'Thank you. Yes, you've answered my question but no, I don't understand, not fully, anyway. However, I do accept everything you have just said. I can only sit here in hope that we can somehow get a positive outcome for Gunard.'

Mayn rose to his feet. 'That is why, Ferd, with your permission, I will go and spend some time with Major Klaasj. I need to be alone, please. And I hope that it will do some good.'

The door glided open and admitted Mayn into a totally controlled volume of pleasant warm freshness and reassuring shadowless lighting. Behind him, the door closed noiselessly.

The body lay supine on the bed, pathetically small and almost naked, penetrated by tubes and electronic cables in many places and festooned all around with bundles of brightly coloured wires leading to connectors adhered to or embedded in skin and flesh. Many complex units of medical equipment stood guard in serried ranks around the bed; other smaller instruments hung on spindly stands or clung to nearby walls. Electronic displays in a myriad of colours flickered their changing values constantly. The principal noise in the room was that of a vacuum pump, its bellows extending and contracting as it pretended to replicate human breathing. Several underlying deep electrical tones provided a boring sub-musical baseline as the interference beats of their frequencies cycled around each other in a repetitive sonic dance.

Mayn stepped towards the bed and threaded his way between the equipment, carrying a small chair behind him. Eventually, he was able to sit down beside the bed, quite close to the almost inert figure of the man Gunard, his regular chest movement mimicking life. For more than half an hour, Mayn did nothing, sitting completely motionless with his eyes closed and hands palm upwards in his lap. Then he stood up and spread the fingertips of both hands upon the large transparent globe that completely encased Gunard's head. When he finally lifted his hands away, the perfect imprints of his fingertips glowed gold on the surface of the globe; then, very slowly, the whorled imprints faded away. After sitting down again, Mayn placed his hands on top of Gunard's, experiencing a surprising contact with warm flesh. After another ten minutes, he removed his hands from Gunard's and rose to his feet, to gaze intensely for a few minutes into the lifeless face within the globe. Then, slowly, he left the room, exhausted.

Five days later, Mayn received a call. An excited voice said: 'Commander Gorton? It's Ferd Kolber. He's improved! The scans show reconstruction of the brain and he's beginning to respond to stimuli! You've done it! It's a mir...' he stopped.

'Yes, you're absolutely right, Ferd. That's exactly what it is... a miracle! It just shows us once again – the construction and operation of the human body is awesome. And although, down the millennia, we have been allowed to know many things, we still have a huge amount to learn. In this case, Gunard's recovery will make a very good bit of medical research for you to publish? I'm sure he will continue to make progress and may well become fully fit again.'

'You, know, Mr Gorton, you're clearly right about that. I certainly should publish this.'

'There's just one thing, Ferd...'

'What's that, Mr Gorton?'

'When you're publishing the case – you'll leave me out of it, won't you?'

There was a pause. 'Well,' Ferd said slowly, 'I will if that's what you really want but it was you who...'

'No, Ferd. You're wrong about that. I just happened to be around and maybe I was used as the catalyst, I don't know. It's perfectly possible that the spontaneous recovery might have taken place without my involvement...'

'I'm sorry, Mr Gorton, I don't believe that! But I will of course respect your wishes. However, I think I might use the word "miracle" in the write-up! That should stir up the traditionalists quite a lot, don't you think?'

Mayn laughed. 'Well, why not? It was a miracle, wasn't it?'

And, in time, Gunard Klaasj made a full and complete recovery.

8

Day 329

Mayn had sat back in his comfortable couch on the evening of the day before and spoke to his PAC. 'PAC, take record. I think I've now covered all the occasions of help I gave to people on Yggdrasil during my five years there, with the exception of what I think of as the two "big ones"!' I've certainly covered Category One and Two by recording notes on all the events I can remember. I found it appropriate to split up Category Three. "3A" was helping the weak with their problems – and there were quite a few of these. "3B" dealt with psychological illness or breakdown – again, there were many of these, of which the most dramatic was Gunard Klaasj. It was a great joy to see him returned to full health and strength. I have also recorded a few events in Category 3C. This was concerned with alleviating suffering associated with physical accidents and minimising their effects. Review record ends.'

As he worked on Yggdrasil, Mayn was always aware of suffering caused by physical accident. There were always many mechanical operations being carried out on the Platform and many of these involved large, heavy pieces of equipment. Although the safely of staff was always taken extremely seriously, supervisory or equipment failure occasionally put staff in danger. Then, if someone was unlucky, injury would occur. Most of these injuries were slight and could be dealt with easily by normal first aid practices but occasionally, more serious injury was caused. Mayn's sensitivity to such events took him to the site of the injury where he could apply his "powers" to reduce immediate suffering and minimise the injury. Thus, a crushed worker would be found in a trapped situation but (miraculously) was released with minor injuries only. Likewise, an accident which appeared to have caused serious physical injury to someone would (luckily) be revealed to be surprisingly superficial when the person was rescued. At such events, Mayn tried his best to keep a "low profile" and, many times, staff did not realise that he had been present. Mayn had recalled as many of these events as he could and made a record for his analysis.

Now, after another exhausting day working outside the vehicle in his suit, he was ready to detail the first of two important events where his input had not only been significant but obvious to all. This incident had occurred about one year before his unexpected departure from the Platform. There had been a flurry of worried activity when Space Monitoring reported that a vast magnetic flux had been generated by a cataclysmic universe event not many light years away. The data from this event had been profiled and the results indicated that the Sector in which Yggdrasil was operating would be seriously affected by this very dangerous flux. Of course, SSP Yggdrasil was constructed to withstand the effects of such fluxes but the Space Monitoring staff warned that this was a very extreme event that was well outside the ranges of their monitoring equipment. It was predicted that this magnetic flux had the potential to cause considerable damage to the millions of electronic systems in the Platform. Their initial calculations suggested that most systems on Yggdrasil would be disabled by the flux; there was even a danger to the operation of life support systems, the report concluded.

The report of this forthcoming event had migrated upwards through the Yggdrasil management levels and eventually reached CCO1 himself. Predictably, he was furious. He immediately called an emergency meeting in his office that included all his top-level staff. The Space Monitoring Team were instructed to attend and explain all their data. Of course, as the Commander of Science and Technology

Division, Mayn was present and he had brought some of his best electro-nuclear physicists along with him.

The Head of Space Monitoring (Major Klee-wan) presented his report, showing all the data on large screens. The magnetic flux was of unprecedented power and was travelling towards Yggdrasil in such a way as to maximise its disruptive electronic effect. It would arrive in three weeks. He was aware that Yggdrasil was fitted with the full range of magnetic shields but he had looked into this and thought that the standard shields that were the normal fitment to Space vehicles would not provide the necessary protection. In fact, they would be totally swamped. Therefore, Yggdrasil was in a situation of real danger.

'So what do you intend to do about this?' CCO1 roared at the unfortunate man.

The man was totally taken aback by this vehement attack. His face paled. 'Sir,' he faltered, 'of course there is nothing I can do about it.'

CCO1 became purple with rage and fixed the man with an apoplectic eye. 'You come here before this meeting to warn us that an extremely dangerous event is going to affect my Platform. You tell us that this is going to be the worst event we have ever experienced on Yggdrasil and that our lives are in real danger. Then you inform us that, despite your detailed investigations into the matter, you can do nothing about it!' CCO1 was shouting at the top of his voice. 'I judge this to be incompetence on your part and I will make sure that this display of incompetence is included in your records. Furthermore, I will...'

'Excuse me, Sir.' Mayn's quiet tones. 'May I have your permission to say something?'

'No, Mr Gorton, you may not,' CCO1 yelled rudely, 'I don't want to be interrupted when I...'

'But I think you are absolutely right about incompetence, Sir,' Mayn interjected smoothly.

Everybody in the room gasped and CCO1 was stopped in his tracks. Completely surprised, he turned to look directly at Mayn. 'Well,' he said in a much lower tone, 'it's good to hear that at least one person here recognises the truth of what I'm saying – recognises that this intolerable situation needs to be dealt with extreme vigour. You may speak, Mr Gorton.'

'Thank you, Sir.' Mayn paused. 'This officer before you is Head, Space Monitoring. He is an expert in that field and his staff have been very assiduous in assessing the dangers associated with this severe and dangerous magnetic flux. Furthermore, I have followed the calculations he has displayed to us today and can see that they are correct in every respect. Also, I agree fully with his conclusions, which I think are well-balanced and very clearly expressed. Now of course you are completely right when you say he is incompetent to advise you further, because his specialism does not extend his knowledge into areas of high-level decision making where damage, destruction and danger to life are involved. Also, it would of course be inappropriate to expect someone of his rank to make recommendations directly to you on the course of action you should take. This officer's responsibility is to inform you about the flux and I think he has done that in an exemplary fashion. In fact I think he and his team are to be congratulated for their assiduous work.'

CCO1 was quiet as he looked down at his papers. 'Well, Mr Gorton, of course I accept the logic of what you are saying and I agree that our Space Monitoring staff, under my efficient command, always provides us with an effective service.' He looked up at Head, Space Monitoring. 'You may sit down. However we may wish to ask you questions about the data and conclusions you have submitted to us.'

Now CCO1 addressed all those present. 'Does anyone have questions for our Space Monitoring expert, on the subject of this magnetic flux report?'

'Yes, Sir, I have.'

CCO1 squinted along the table. 'Yes, who are you?'

'Commander Norton Wood, Sir, PPN1. (Principal Pilot and Navigator).' He looked along the table to Major Klee-wan. 'Could we just move away from this flux? I mean, could we just outrun it?'

CCO1 was impressed! 'Are you able to answer that right now?' He fixed a forceful eye on the Major.

The man stood up. 'Yes, Sir, I can,' he said in a distinctly relieved voice. 'Running from it will certainly result in some reduction of its effect. However, I am afraid the reduction effect is not particularly large. For instance, if the platform transported at maximum speed away from the approaching magnetic flux, I have calculated that this would reduce the flux energy effect by 7%. There is certainly no way that movement of the platform could nullify the effect of the flux completely.'

'Thank you.' PPN1 made a note.

'Any more questions?' CCO1 looked around.

'Yes, Sir, Major Lancing, TechProtect3.' (One of Mayn's officers) 'If we stayed put in the position we are now, how much more strength would we need to put in the shields to protect ourselves? For instance, if we modified all our shields to 185% of their current power, which I think might be possible, would this be enough?'

The major consulted his papers. 'In my report, I have suggested that the platform shield system must be upgraded urgently to a maximum protection level. 185% would of course be helpful and have some effect but I am afraid there would still be significant damage at that level of protection.'

Mayn asked: 'How much would we need to boost the shields to gain full protection?'

'This is very difficult to quantify, Sir. I did some work on this and the ratio suggested was at least 800% of current protection levels.'

'Could we do it?' CCO1's question was to Mayn.

'I very much doubt it, Sir. What is your opinion Mr Lancing?'

'I think impossible, Sir. However, I'll get my team on to this right away and I'll get a maximum figure to you as soon as possible.'

'Thank you, Mr Lancing. As soon as you can, please.'

CCO1 looked around. 'Is there any reason why we could not move the platform?'

'Sir, Major Bramsgur, Survey Systems. We would need 8-10 days to discontinue the deep survey operations that are in progress. Once this is done, we will have no problems.'

PPN1 spoke again. 'Sir, I'll need to check with Platform Propulsion. There may be engineering works in progress. When we have a major stop, such as we have now, their schedule will specify a major overhaul, replacement or upgrading of systems. I will need to check this and find out if the main propulsion is currently fully operational. There may be a delay for that reason.'

'Right,' CCO1 was decisive and began disseminating his responsibilities as quickly as he could. 'PPN1, take charge of movement operations. Liaise with engineers immediately and report. Plan a move at maximum speed from this Sector as soon as possible. STC1, take charge of shield operations and set shield strengthening in motion as soon as possible. Report progress. This meeting is ended. You may all return to your duties.'

Within hours, Mayn had set up a meeting in his office with his Shield Engineering and Control Unit: 'Gentlemen, I take it that you have all heard about the severe magnetic flux we will experience in three weeks? This flux will be stronger than anything we have experienced before and we need to boost our shield strength as much as possible. Now, Mr Lancing, you suggested at CCO1's meeting that a shield boost to 185% was achievable?'

'That's right, Sir.'

'Is this a boost using all existing components?'

'Yes, Sir, we can just increase...'

'No need to go into the technical details, now. We know that 185% is insufficient to deal with the problem. The important question is – how can we boost the shields considerably beyond that? Or could we redesign them, re-engineer them, using more powerful components?'

'Well, Sir, I have a number of ideas but I need to get the team together to work on it...'

'As you know, Mr Lancing, time is very much against us in this, so would you please go to work right away? If there are serious problems or if you have anything important to show me, I can always be contacted and can come to your laboratories.'

Three days later and TechProtect3 was exultant. 'Sir, we've worked on this day and night and we've come up with a much stronger shield design. We've used... (there followed a detailed technical description of the new equipment). Mayn listened carefully and asked a few pertinent questions about the robustness of the design. Then he asked: 'So, Mr Lancing, what's the bottom line, how much does this boost our shield protection compared to the existing fitment?

'Well, Sir, we've tested this as 420% better that the standard shield we have fitted to the Platform right now. That's using all the components at maximum stretch. We think the life of the components will be much reduced but, I assume we'll only need to use this level of protection for a short time; I hope that's correct? I mean, just while the flux passes through?'

Mayn agreed. 'I think that's correct – it would certainly seem to be logical. Anyway, I can report to CCO1 that we have achieved +420% protection. However, I recall HSM was calculating +800% but imagine there was a good deal of estimation in there. Anyway,' he smiled, 'this is very good work you have done here. If you come up with any more ideas that would boost protection even more, go ahead and see if you can build it. The stronger protection we can build, the happier everyone will be.'

'Thank you, Sir. We'll give the whole thing some more thought and I report to you if we make any further progress.'

On that same day, PPN1 stood in the headquarters of Drive Control in Platform Propulsion. 'You mean the principal propulsion unit is totally dismantled? Yes, I do recall seeing the schedule for your maintenance and upgrading work – that was about two weeks ago, wasn't it? As far as I remember, the upgrade on the schedule was to take 17 days, isn't that right? So this work should now be nearing completion, shouldn't it?

What's that? It isn't? Why is that? Do you think I can't read a work schedule?'

Head, Main Engineering (Sub-Commander Alwin Borg), sighed. It seemed that he frequently had conversations with people about engineering schedules. His section took great care to be meticulous about the schedules but people seemed to read into them what they wanted to see.

'Listen, Sir,' he said patiently, 'you are of course right that the upgrade to the Platform Propulsion System was scheduled to take 17 days to complete – and that's exactly the number of days it will take. However, that upgrade is on a periphery of the system; to do this work only involves a Class 3 dismantle. The point is... that's just a small part of the maintenance and repair work we're doing on the whole propulsion system. It's one year since we carried out a major strip-down and complete check – and that's exactly what we are engaged upon now. All this is on the work schedule; as you know, Sir, the schedule is quite a long document and, although I'm always careful to include a summary at the top, that often doesn't get read either. So people become convinced that we will be back to full operation long before the schedule specifies that we will.'

'So, Mr Borg,' PPN1 said in a taut but resigned voice (he heard excuses every day!), 'just tell me what the timescale is here. I take it you know we are entering an emergency situation, don't you? There's a severe magnetic flux coming our way and it might wipe us out.'

Borg sighed again (it seemed he was always sighing!). He had heard so much about emergencies before. 'Well, Sir, what the schedule says is that Platform Propulsion will be fully repaired, serviced and upgraded in exactly one month from now. This outage timescale was agreed with Platform Workload Operations last month. I understand that Survey Systems have a major program under way and they need all that time to complete it.'

'Look!' PPN1 was becoming irritated. 'One month is no good. In fact one month is a disaster – no it's not, it's a catastrophe. This is an emergency! We are in danger of being wiped out! We need to move the Platform to the next Sector and we need to do it now. This is an order from CCO1 himself. Am I making myself clear?' Despite himself, he was now shouting!

Borg said nothing. He manipulated a few controls and pointed to an image projector which gave a wide three-dimensional view of Yggdrasil's Propulsion Hall. The huge propulsion units that dominated the volume of this hall lay dismantled in many pieces, temporarily fastened to huge cranes and large frames. Hundreds of engineers were swarming over all the parts. It was a scene of frenetic activity.

Finally, he murmured: 'As you see, we are working at full speed. We always do. The Platform Propulsion will be ready to operate in one month's time. Before that, there is no question of moving the Platform under main power.'

CCO1 was striding about the room in an extremely agitated state. Predictably, the news about the unavailability of the Platform Propulsion had been badly received and he was now incandescent with rage. 'I'll find out who was responsible for this and I will destroy him,' he was bawling. 'This is totally unacceptable. I would never have agreed to such extensive engineering works. Someone has acted without authority and I will make sure they are punished with utmost severity for placing us all in so much danger.'

All his officers, including PPN1, who had been compelled to break the bad news, cowered around the table, heads down, unmoving, hoping that CCO1 would not find a reason to turn on them personally.

'Sir,' Mayn's calm voice, 'you will know that the major rebuild of the Platform Propulsion System is something that takes place every year. This is essential work but it is, of course, routine. We, your loyal officers, are all aware that you cannot possibly deal with routine matters yourself and that you delegate low-level work to your subordinate staff. We, all of us here, carry out your routine orders meticulously. If you look in the records you will find many years of routine matters that you have delegated; I have here the records referring to the annual Platform Propulsion work which confirms what I say. Your signature of delegation is here for this rebuild to take place during this period of time.'

'However,' he continued, 'I have a proposal to make which may be of assistance. My scientific and technical staff have been working hard to upgrade the shields which protect us from magnetic fluxes. Without a great deal of modification, they can upgrade all existing shields to be twice as effective as they are now. As you know, Sir, we have shields all over the exterior of the Platform. In addition, they have already succeeded in making completely new shields that are over four times more effective than existing units and we may be able to improve them further. Now that we know it to be impossible to transit away from the flux, I propose we should concentrate our new powerful shields on the front of the Platform, siting as many as possible there. Although we cannot move the Platform under its main power, our manoeuvring power systems will allow us to turn the Platform around to face the direction of greatest danger and hold that position until the danger has passed. This strategy will give us the greatest chance of emerging unharmed from the magnetic flux onslaught.'

An almost physical tide of relief swept through the office and many voices murmured: "Good idea", "brilliant suggestion", "that should work", etc.

CCO1 stopped his violent pacing and looked at Mayn. 'Mr Gorton, are you convinced that this proposal will work?'

'Yes, Sir, certainly it will work. But its effectiveness will depend on the strength of the magnetic flux. We will build our shields to be as strong as possible and deploy them as effectively as we can.

'Does anyone wish to comment on Mr Gorton's suggestion?' Suddenly, CCO1 was sounding much more cheerful!

An enthusiastic chorus of agreement was the response of all in the room.

'Then, Mr Gorton, we will adopt your solution and I authorise you to mastermind the details, using whatever Platform facilities you need for the purpose. The meeting is ended.'

Mayn co-opted many engineers from other parts of the Platform. Some were set the task of upgrading the existing shields to 200% of their current effectiveness while many others set about constructing the new, more powerful shields. Further design improvements had boosted the effectiveness of these from 420% to 490%. Many hundreds of units were produced and Space teams began to fasten the equipment to all parts of the front of the Platform. Everything was connected up so that it could be controlled from the Flight Deck, the area on Level-10 where PPN1 and his team operated the Platform while it was in transit. It was decided that PPN1 himself should take control of the system when the magnetic flux passed over them.

As the days reeled by, counting down to what had been entitled "Day Zero", the manoeuvring system was energised and the Platform was turned around slowly to the correct orientation to meet the worst of the flux. The system was tested exhaustively and it worked superbly.

Finally, all was ready. Optimism was rife. And time ticked steadily by.

Day Zero dawned. The magnetic flux was forecast to arrive at 1129. Tension built steadily through the morning. All staff had been instructed to assemble in their workplaces and power usage throughout the Platform was to be minimised from 1100 until further instructions were broadcast. Everyone was instructed to strap themselves in because the prediction included the likelihood of buffeting, especially when the flux struck at its most powerful. On Level-10, engineers had tested the shield power again and again and reported that all was in readiness and fully operational.

By 1030, almost all Senior and Control Staff had assembled on the Level-10 Flight Deck. CCO1 arrived at 1045, taking his seat in the High Command seat and strapping himself in tightly. At 1100, PPN1 (Commander Norton Wood) entered "Command Position A", fastened his body straps and placed his hands and feet on the sensitive multi-control pads. Immediately behind him, Mayn entered "Command Position B" and did the same. To his right, Head, Space Monitoring entered the Countdown Position and set the equipment to broadcast the Standard Countdown Procedure all over the

Platform. The clear beat of ticking seconds was now heard throughout the Platform, interspersed with periodic voice confirmation of the countdown progress. Soon, everyone else in the Flight Deck room had assumed their designated seats. All seat straps were fastened tightly, checked and tightened again. Gradually, the shuffling, coughing and muttered comments died down as if the ticking seconds were somehow linked to a progressive fader control. The fear of the unknown was manifested by trembling hands and pale faces everywhere. Eyes were blanked and breathing bated so that hearing and sensation could be attuned to the maximum.

At 1123 they all heard it; felt it. A progressive, increasing tremor was beginning to pass through all parts of the Platform. By 1125, no-one could be unaware. This was no longer a tremor but an increasingly vicious vibration, seeking out construction movement and weaknesses in all parts of the Platform. Lights began to flicker in distress and some equipment began to trip out and give up their functions. 1127 brought a sudden deafening cacophony of noise and clamour, augmented by screaming and cries of distress, as large fixed items on many levels were torn from their mountings. These began to slide and tumble around uncontrollably as if alive, wreaking havoc on everything in their path. The rattle of major relay switches operating to cut power to fundamental machinery brought additional terror as many systems powered down and withdrew their essential functions. Lighting was largely extinguished and acrid smoke began to creep into many areas. Loud and frightening warning horns sounded but the automatic fire equipment failed to respond to the command of its sensors.

1129 arrived. At Control Position A, Norton Wood was thrown violently against his retaining straps as he struggled to respond to the myriad of events lighting up his screen and displays, his hands and feet racing across the control pads. Behind him, Mayn contributed with similar actions but it was clear that the Platform was beginning to sustain considerable damage; worse still, essential life support systems were being closed down or destroyed. As he scanned the information before him, Mayn knew he was witnessing the forthcoming death of many people and the absolute destruction of key Platform equipment.

Suddenly, a display in front of Norton Wood exploded violently in his face and he gave a terrible cry before slumping unconscious or dead across the controls. Immediately, Mayn unstrapped himself from Control Position B, negotiated the plunging, heaving floor of the Flight Deck to move Wood's body from Control Position A. Quickly taking his place, Mayn removed gloves, boots and socks and placed his uncovered hands and feet on the control pads. Havoc continued and the effects were now so serious that the Platform sensors indicated a danger of total breakup. Banks of warning klaxons began to sound stridently.

Mayn spread his fingers wide on the control pad and pressed his bare feet firmly down on the foot controls and held his body rigid and motionless. All present saw his body beginning to glow. As the seconds ticked by, the glow became incandescent and the heat from his body could be felt by those many metres away. Suddenly, the clamour and motion stopped abruptly. Warning klaxons ceased to sound. The Platform began to power up again and restoration repair systems became energised and started their work. On all levels, staff unfastened their straps and stood up on unsteady legs to embrace those nearest to them. Apart from many breakages around them, everything was returning to normal, with the restoration and cleaning robots already hard at work.

Mayn was slumped over the controls of Control Position A and many in the room feared that he was dead. Everyone was delighted when his still figure began to move. They rushed forward and helped him up, awed to see that his face, hands and feet were burned to a charcoal black. However, as they watched, his flesh was restored to its normal colour.

'Must have been a trick of the light,' they said to each other. 'He looked like he had been burned to a cinder. We thought he wouldn't survive but then we saw his skin was OK. And, soon, remarkably soon, he was back to his usual self. He's a wonderful guy, you know. He saved the whole Platform. He saved all our lives.'

'So how is Commander Norton West?' Mayn sat with CCO1.

'He's recovering in Medical. They say he will recover fully but it will take some weeks to restore him back to normal.'

'That's good,' Mayn smiled. 'He did a really brave job at Control Position A, Sir.'

CCO1 was silent and looked at Mayn introspectively. 'How about you, Mr Gorton? How are you after that ordeal?'

'I'm fine, Sir. Fully recovered. Norton had already done most of the work and taken most of the injury before I got there.'

'You know, Mr Gorton, I don't think that's right. I think the Platform would have been destroyed or, at least, catastrophically damaged, if you hadn't taken control.'

'Well, Sir, I just did what needed to be done, that's all.' Mayn said quietly.

9

Day 348

It was sheer perseverance and backbreaking hard work that finally did it. Mayn had continued his daily schedule of connections, checking and testing without a break and, at last, he was near the completion of the job. Looking into the external bays, he could now see only a few connections that needed to be made for his local control system to be complete. 'Unless anything goes wrong, I should have that done in just a few days and then I'll need to start my schedule of engine and flight control testing. At the same time, the whole navigation system will need to be completely checked and I'll have to confirm exactly where I am and where I should go when I lift this vehicle off this asteroid.' Mayn sat back and indulged in some imaginative thoughts. 'I can just see it! The roar of the engines under my control, the vehicle lifting off smoothly, then turning to my set course. Then the smooth, weightless flight across Space before the Navigation System brings my destination into focus!' Mayn felt absolutely wonderful as his mind reeled through this reverie.

His thoughts now turned to his evening tasks. Now that the end was in sight he recognised the absolute importance of his Yggdrasil record – especially those items he had identified as the last "major events". These were the ones that he thought were most likely to have triggered the violent response that had cast him away in an uncontrollable space pod almost a year before. Having completed his electronic workload for the day, Mayn was ready to recall the second of his major events.

'This was a really complex and tricky one,' he thought. 'There are many elements to it and I'll need to make sure that I don't miss anything.' He stretched out comfortably on his couch and pondered for a while, placing the events in the right order before bringing all the fine details back to mind. 'It's all about Mr Gorth's young friend who had suffered a mental breakdown.'

It had started about six months before his unexpected departure from the Platform. One evening, he was called by Mr Ivan Gorth, the Senior Mathematician who he had first met in the Conference Room on the day of his arrival.

'I'm really sorry to come to you directly, Sir, but there is a matter that is worrying me very much. Do you recall meeting Lt. Bik Hatrige? He is one of the mathematicians who work for me. Last year he became seriously ill and he has now been with Medical for some time. I understand that you and he worked together Earth-side. He was always talking about you, Sir, saying how wonderful it had been to work for you.'

'Why, yes, I do remember meeting Mr Hatrige at your department – just once, I think. And, yes, we did work together Earth-side for a short time. I was aware that he was on the Med Patient Roll. I hope he is now recovering well. Is he? I haven't seen a recent report.'

'Well, Sir, that's the problem. Hatrige has been in the medical bays for several months. I visited him regularly but, in the last weeks, they will no longer allow me to see him. They say he is too ill. And now I've heard something else. Something that worries me very much, Sir. Something I don't want to speak about on the communicator.'

'Could I just ask you one question, Mr Gorth? Is your concern something you should discuss with your manager? I only ask this because I don't want to unnecessarily bypass the normal chain of command.'

There was silence at the other end. Then Gorth spoke very softly. 'Sir, I would not be calling you directly if I thought this was something normal.' He paused again, then added in an even softer voice, 'Something bad is happening, Sir.'

'You had better come to my office, Mr Gorth.'

Gorth was soon sitting opposite Mayn in his office. He looked extremely nervous.

'Relax, Mr Gorth, have some of this coffee. Tell me exactly what is worrying you so much?'

The man gratefully accepted the cup of coffee from Mayn and sipped it before speaking. 'Sir, Bik Hatrige had some sort of mental breakdown. One moment he was working normally in the office and the next he had gone unstable and was running around the office screaming and throwing his equipment into the air. The first time it happened, we were able to calm him down but he couldn't tell us what the problem was. I spoke to him in my office for a long time, trying to find out what was troubling him but he wasn't able to tell me. He insisted it had nothing to do with his work or his family back Earth-side. I did check on both these things but I could see nothing wrong with his work and the report from Earth on his family was completely normal. Anyway, the attacks continued to happen and eventually I had to refer him to Medical.'

Gorth, sipped some more coffee and then continued. 'They took him away and ran all sorts of tests. After many weeks a Psych Medic spoke to me. He told me that none of the tests had showed them what the problem was. Furthermore, he said the problem was getting worse and that Bik was now confined and had to be restrained. He said it would not be possible for me to visit him any more. I protested about this, saying that Bik had never been violent with me but the medic insisted that he was very much worse and it would not be safe for me to visit him. Of course, he said their investigations would proceed until they found out what the problem was and cured him. I had to leave it at that and the weeks passed by without any further word. Several times, I did raise it with my manager and he reported back that he had checked with Medical and the situation was unchanged. So I had to leave it. Somehow I felt uneasy. Then I received a note. This is it. I don't know who it's from. As you see, it's just a few words scribbled on a paper.'

Gorth held out a crumpled piece of paper and Mayn took it, smoothing it out on his desk. Scrawled on the paper, in very rough uneven letters, it said:

"Ur friend Bik in danger. He transfrd for TP. No-one ever come back frm TP."

Mayn looked up and raised his eyebrows quizzically.

'I have a good friend in Medical,' Gorth responded, 'and I asked him about TP. He said he knew nothing about it but would make enquiries. Eventually he came back to me, his face white. Taking me aside, he whispered, 'It was difficult to find out but I have been told that TP is the place you go to die. I think the TP Unit is located somewhere way down on LEVEL-O. That's all I know. My informant told me to keep very quiet about what he had told me. He said I should forget all about Bik. The implication was clear. I would never see Bik again.'

Mayn was silent as he continued to look impassively at the man.

'Sir,' Gorth said, tears running down his face, 'Bik is a good man. Why isn't he being transferred Earth-side if he's terminal? Why can't they cure him? No-one dies of mental breakdowns now.'

Mayn finally spoke. 'OK, Mr Gorth. Leave this with me. Don't speak to anyone else about this. I'll get back to you on this. Thank you for coming.'

After Gorth had left, Mayn brought up a comprehensive diagram of Yggdrasil on a large screen and studied it for a considerable time. Then he looked up the servicing responsibilities of his maintenance teams and established which team dealt with LEVEL-O equipment.

The following morning, Mayn called one of his Class 3 routine servicing bays and asked to speak to the person-in-charge.

'Master Tech Wha-su', a clipped voice responded, 'I'm i/c and I'm very busy. So I hope this is important. What do you want?'

'Commander Gorton here, Mr Wha-su.'

'Yeh, yeh. And I'm the Queen of Sheba, whatever that is! Come off it, Jed!'

'Mr Wha-su, look at your identifier, please. This is Commander Gorton.'

There was a brief pause followed by a gasp. 'Sorry, Sir, I...'

'Never mind that, Mr Wha-su. Will you come to my office right away, please?'

Ten minutes later, a shamefaced, worried man arrived at Mayn's office.

'Sit down, Mr Wha-su, I have something to ask you.'

'Sir, I'm really sorry about...'

Mayn smiled. 'Always look at your call identifier, Mr Wha-su. It can save you a lot of trouble!' He held up a hand. 'Let's just forget that. I believe your team deal with the servicing of the equipment on Level-o Area 684B? Is that correct?'

The man still looked confused. 'Ah, LEVEL-O 684B? That's Medical Disposal, isn't it? Yes, Sir, we service their equipment.' He thought for a bit. 'Although there's one area we're not allowed to go to. They say they have a special team to service that themselves. "Fine by us", I always say.'

'Where is the area you are not allowed to enter?' Mayn displayed the image of the appropriate area of LEVEL-O.

'Ah, let's see,' the man examined it carefully. 'Yes, here it is. It's these rooms here – 684B/32-34. We go everywhere else in the area. The routine is every six months. When I return to my bay, I can tell you when we last did it.'

'Thank you very much, Mr Wha-su. I don't think I need that information at the moment. I'm just building up my knowledge of Platform operations.'

'Thank you, Sir.' The man looked worried. 'Ah, about the mistake I made on the communicator, will you...' Mayn interrupted. 'Forgotten, Mr Wha-su – this time,' he added with a twinkle, 'you may return to work.'

Mayn waited until late that evening and then, in casual sports clothes, he climbed onto his buggy and made his way to the nearest ILT (Inter-Level Transporter). It was here he found his first surprise. There was no LEVEL-0 selector on the ILT control pad! This was something he had never noticed before. Mayn selected LEVEL-1 and, once there, asked a number of passing staff how he could access LEVEL-0.

The first four groups of men could not help him. 'LEVEL-0? Sorry, Sir' they replied, 'can't help you there. No-one here ever goes to Level-0.' One man added: 'We've been told there's nothing down there except automatic equipment, emergency storage and the like.' Finally, an older man directed him to the far end of LEVEL-1. 'As far as I know, there's an access there. I've never been down there myself. I think the access is controlled, you know, there's a guard unit there. Anyway, you could try that, Sir.'

Mayn thanked the man and travelled along the corridors towards one end of LEVEL-1. Gradually, all signs of normal life diminished and soon he was alone in blank, grey corridors. The man was right. Mayn eventually reached the end of the corridor and, sure enough, there was a small well-lit room with two uniformed men ensconced behind a high desk. A third man, also in uniform, was approaching the desk. Mayn stopped his buggy nearby. One of the men behind the desk was speaking to the man who had just approached:

'Hi, Marty, you'll never guess! You've just come up on the Identifier as "Commander Maynard Gorton! I had no idea you had become such an important person! I'll need to switch to the backup machine. This unit has obviously gone u/s. That'll be the day when we get the top brass down here, eh?' The man smiled broadly before he swivelled around and noticed Mayn standing at the far end of the desk. The smile faded from his face. Seeing this, the others turned around, too. They all stiffened.

'Ah... ah, Commander Gorton,' the man spluttered eventually, 'what can we do for you, Sir? We don't see many senior officers down here,' he added, smiling deprecatingly, 'are you lost, by any chance, Sir?'

Mayn smiled briefly. 'No, I'm not, thanks. Can I get to LEVEL-0 from here?'

'You want to go to LEVEL-0? Very few people go there, Sir. We are required to record the purpose of your visit. That's why we're here.'

'My maintenance crew work down there. I am reviewing all maintenance areas under my command.'

'Thank you, Sir, we have recorded that. Is there anything else we can help you with right now?'

'Yes. Are there many staff down in LEVEL-0?'

'No, Sir. Very few.'

'OK, how do I go down?' The man pointed to a large door that had opened at the end of the corridor. 'That's the Number 43W ILT to LEVEL-0. It will take you down automatically.'

A few moments later, Mayn had reached LEVEL-0. Though brightly lit, it was completely deserted. He examined the direction signs on the walls as the buggy began to take him towards Area 684B. Even travelling at top speed (possible due to the empty corridors), his buggy took around twenty minutes to reach the boundary of the Area. At this point, it reduced speed and continued to drive forward until it arrived at a large roughly circular central area, which had a number of corridors radiating from it. Bringing the buggy to a halt, Mayn now studied a small map he had brought with him, locating himself positively by referring to the various room number direction signs mounted on the walls. After careful comparison, he established exactly where he was.

As he was about to start the buggy moving again, Mayn suddenly became aware of the strange and oppressive atmosphere in this area. The Platform was a constantly busy place, with activity taking place at all hours. On all other levels, the rooms and corridors were filled with the familiar sound of humanity, the bustle and clamour of movement and the distinctive sound of conversation, often blended with laughter, everything imposed on the reassuring sub-hum of life-giving mechanical and electronic systems. Here on LEVEL-0, so much was eerily missing. Subdued machinery was still present, though ears had to strain to hear it; apart from that very low sound, it was completely quiet; dead, even.

Mayn felt strongly that he was the only person on the whole of LEVEL-O.

He shook himself. 'Come on,' he said to himself, 'snap out of it. I can't be the only person on this level. There must be other staff down here. There's always a need to keep some sort of watch over machinery and equipment.' Even so, he could not supress his feeling of unease as his buggy began to glide towards Rooms 32-34, the goal of his mission. Counting the room numbers as he passed, he had checked off the twenties and had just passed Room 30. Ahead of him, the door of Room 31 was on the left of the corridor and then there was a large heavy door that stopped any further progress along the corridor. The buggy stopped at this door and Mayn stepped off to examine the door more closely. A very small black sign announced "TP Facility" and a small red light was illuminated above it.

'HALT!' the shouted command was a deafening pistol-shot in the confines of the corridor and Mayn started violently. Wheeling around, he found himself facing two uniformed men, both fully helmeted and pointing their weapons at him. One of the men focussed a remote identifier on him. Instantly, both men lowered their weapons and approached him, saluting him deferentially. The one with the remote identifier spoke. 'Commander Gorton. What can we do for you? We were not advised of your coming. You are not on the visitor list. Can we help you with anything?'

Mayn looked squarely at the man and spoke with quiet authority. 'Yes, you can. What does TP stand for?'

The man's face fell. 'Ah, Sir, I'm sorry. I'm not supposed to answer...'

Mayn interrupted. 'In that case, would you call Head Medical, Surgeon-Commander Jomo Sangyar? When you get him, tell him Commander Maynard Gorton wants to speak to him on a very urgent matter.'

'Sir, I'm very sorry, I'm not authorised to do that. I can only call my immediate superior, the Guard Leader, if there is a genuine emergency – and my orders are that he must not be called in any other circumstances.'

Mayn produced his PAC and spoke to it: 'Set up a voice call to Head Medical.'

The guard paled. 'Sir, please don't...' he paused; 'TP is 'Termination Procedure,' he blurted. 'Sir, please don't tell anyone...'

'I wish to enter the TP area. Open the door.' Mayn spoke again with firm authority.

The man's face was stricken. 'Sir, you cannot enter. There is a Procedure in progress and it is not allowed for anyone to enter...'

Mayn produced his PAC again and began to set up a voice call.

'Sir,' the guard's voice was now filled with panic, 'please don't do that. Entering the TP area during a Procedure is absolutely forbidden. We would be severely disciplined...'

'Open the door. Now!' A soft but forceful command.

The guard's resistance crumbled. He stepped over to a control unit mounted beside the door. There was a loud "click" and the heavy door swung open. As Mayn stepped forward, the guard made one final attempt to dissuade him from entering. 'Sir, please, listen to me. It is very dangerous to enter while a Procedure is...' the man's voice faded out of earshot as Mayn walked quickly into the darkness beyond the door.

He soon found the light controls and ascertained that Rooms 32 and 33 were empty and silent. Room 34 was different. Here, all the lights were on. Machinery hummed and indicator lights were illuminated on control panels around the room. The centre of the room was taken up by a large plinth topped by a long black rectangular box, its top panel closed and clamped down. There was a transparent viewing panel in its side and Mayn stepped close to it. Through this, illuminated by a pulsating light of an unpleasant bilious hue, he could see the motionless form of a naked man, lying supine on a long metal tray. Many electrodes were attached to his head and body, each one connected to thick black electrical leads that snaked away to a battery of connectors on the inner walls of the box. Mayn turned his attention to a large control desk nearby. Every indicator light glowed red and every readout indicated "zero". Mayn looked through the glass panel again and recognised the face of Lt Bik Hatrige, set in an unmistakable mask of death.

The Intruder Alarm had been activated. Reinforcements from other areas of Level-0 had been summoned and had arrived with great clamour at top speed. The Guard Leader had been called from his rest. Even the Guard Officer had been roused from his sleep (an unprecedented event) and, when he arrived at Area 684B in an extremely foul mood, mouthing threats, he had judged the situation so serious that he had called Major Hicks, Senior Security Officer for backup and support. In addition, he had called Major Bannerman, the Senior TP Facility Officer, who commanded the unit. As each new individual or group arrived, they received a comprehensive briefing on the situation. Thus, a considerable amount of time passed while a large security force built up in the corridor outside the door of the TP Facility. No-one wished to act without the proper safeguards!

Finally, Major Hicks, the Senior Security Officer approached the Senior TP Officer. 'Although I am the more senior officer here,' he said pompously, 'I am putting you in change, Major Bannerman. After all, this is your facility and you should lead us in our search for the intruder, who has been identified as Commander Gorton. He must be found and extracted as soon as possible. Once we have done that, I will assess the situation further.'

The large security force moved slowly and cautiously into the TP Facility area, commanded (but not physically led) by Major Bannerman, who was closely followed by Major Hicks. Curt orders were given. Rooms 32 and 33 were swept, declared uninhabited and in powered-down standby mode. Gradually, the heavily-armed security force gathered outside the brightly-lit Room 34. Listening equipment was deployed and a low buzz of conversation was heard. Signs of human life were detected and pinpointed within the room. Habitation levels were checked and found to be safe. Preparations were then made to blow open the substantial door with explosives until Major Bannerman intervened to point out that the door was unlocked and could be opened in the normal way without damage.

A spearhead consisting of a comprehensively armed security squad was assembled and ordered to thrust its way into Room 34 with great speed. In battle formation, eight heavily armed guards charged into the room with a great clatter of boots and then stopped in considerable confusion. Moments later, judging that the greatest danger had passed and not wishing to miss any of the drama within, most of the others in the corridor crowded in behind them. Finally, the two officers deemed it safe to enter. Everyone had now become still and all eyes were fixed on two men who sat beside the large machine in the centre of the room, whose top cover was now gaping wide. One of the men was dressed in casual sportswear while the other was covered only by a crumpled white sheet. The men were deep in quiet conversation. Neither paid any attention to the crowd of newcomers in the room.

After an extended pause, Major Hicks realised it was his duty to take charge of the situation and barged his way through the crowd to the front. 'I am the Senior Security Officer. What is the meaning of this trespass?' he said, intending to sound confident and authoritative; however, his voice let him down, coming out pathetically shrill and squeaky. The two men stopped talking and looked at him quizzically.

After a brief pause, the fully-dressed man stood up and spoke quietly. 'I am Commander Gorton.' He indicated the man beside him. 'This is Lt. Hatrige. He requires to be taken immediately to Medical on Level-6. Is there anyone from Medical here?'

The Senior TP Officer stepped forward somewhat unsteadily. 'I command this facility, Sir,' he said in a quavering voice. 'I am Major Bannerman. This facility is a sub-branch of Medical.'

'Would you arrange for a medical transport to come to this room immediately, so that Lt. Hatrige may be transported to the Medical Bays on Level-6 and handed over to the doctors.

I am sure he is completely well now but all his vital signs need to be checked and assessed before he is released to return to his work in the Science and Technical Division.'

Major Bannerman stepped close to Mayn and spoke in a hoarse whisper. 'But Sir,' he said, bulging eyes fixed on Bik Hatrige, 'this man cannot possibly be alive. He has been processed in this facility. I supervised the Procedure personally. I can assure you he was d...'

Mayn held up a hand and smiled pleasantly at him. 'Thank you for that report, Major Bannerman. However, as you can see, Lt. Hatrige is alive and well. He needs to go to Medical to be checked. Now, please.'

Despite the presence of so many, the room was completely still and silent, with no sound of shuffling or coughing. As Mayn and Lt. Hatrige began to walk towards the door, the crowd parted respectfully to let them through. They hadn't taken many steps when there was the sound of a single pair of clapping hands from someone near the back of the crowd. Immediately, others joined in and, within seconds, the room reverberated to deafening applause as everyone (apart from the two officers) joined in. The applause continued for at least a minute before a smiling Mayn held up a hand for silence.

'Thank you, Gentlemen. I think everything is now in order here. Your officers will direct you back to work.' Mayn took the arm of Lt. Hatrige and they walked through a corridor of smiling faces and applauding hands.

There was an introspective silence in the office. 'So how did you do it?' The older man spoke across his broad desk.

'I don't really know.' Mayn's voice was soft. 'I think I recognised a spark of life there...'

The older man nodded. After some moments, he spoke again. 'The TP Facility is kept a secret, you know. Knowledge of it would be bad for the men. Few people, a very few people, know about it. And the staff who work there are sworn to absolute secrecy. Even someone as high up as you, Mr Gorton, would not normally know about it.'

Mayn said nothing but his active mind recalled that euthanasia aboard Space vehicles was strictly forbidden by Command. The silence lengthened. Finally CCO1 stirred. 'So now you must keep it secret too,' he added.

Mayn thought about this. Finally he said. 'Yes, Sir.'

CCO1 rose, indicating that their meeting was over and accompanied Mayn to the door. 'Ah, Maynard... Just one final thing... We're saying that you were visiting Hatrige in a Medical Bay on Level-6. Could you just remember that?'

A moment of rising tension, then: 'Yes, Sir.'

'End of this record.' Mayn lay still and thought for a while. At last he spoke again. 'PAC, take event data from last record. Analyse personal risk to me. Allocate risk percentages to all personnel involved and report significant values. Speak out when ready to report.' Then he went to the kitchen to fetch a drink. When he returned, the PAC was ready to report. 'PAC, speak out report.'

"Data indicates that several risk points arise. No risk is envisaged from the general staff present in Level-0, including the guards whom you ordered to give you access to the TP Facility. However, there may a slight risk associated with the two officers who attended, the Senior TP Officer and the Senior Security Officer. Because of their rank level, the risk is held at 20%. Other more senior staff in Medical may present risk, even if they were not directly involved. Head, Medical is placed in this category. He and other senior Medical staff are complicit in the operation of the TP Facility. Therefore the risk is assessed at 34%. CCO1 presents the greatest threat. You have identified that he is organising or condoning illegal activity. He is also in overall charge of the Platform. There may also be a question of diminished personal status in his mind because of you. The risk is assessed at 46%. Analysis ends."

Mayn was quiet and thoughtful as he switched the PAC to "standby".

Ten minutes later he was sound asleep in his bunk.

10

Day 355

Mayn had spent every day of the previous week working in the external bays. He had made the final connections between his local control units and the standard vehicle control system and all the circuits had been tested. Everything looked fine. At last, he had closed and resealed the bays, ready for departure! After this, he had spent some time making a very careful visual inspection of the vehicle and, while he admitted it had lost a certain amount of its pristine sparkle, everything seemed to be in good serviceable shape and the vehicle looked more than ready to take to Space once again.

'Now I'd better examine and service all the exterior parts of the landing gear,' he thought, 'because they will need to work perfectly once I unclamp from the asteroid.' After take-off, the four struts of the landing gear would retract into the body of the vehicle and be covered by smooth sealed panels. After working through the servicing schedules for all the struts and joints of the landing gear, Mayn turned his attention to the four substantial foot clamps, satisfying himself that they would unclamp quite easily from the rugged surface of the asteroid when the time came to operate the disconnect control. Finally, he had deployed a ladder and climbed carefully over the top surface of the vehicle, knowing that his light weight would not cause any damage. This reassured him that the outer skin of the vehicle was intact and in good condition.

'While I'm here, I'd better spend a little time servicing these external sensors,' he thought, 'because I'm certainly going to need these working at full capacity.' After completing the sensor servicing tasks, he returned to the Control Cabin and ran the external sensor viability testing routines and was pleased to find reports of 100% sensitivity.

At last, Mayn looked around him. 'I think I have done it! I think I'm ready!' He punched the air in pure joy! It just seemed the right thing to do!

Not long after his arrival on the asteroid, he had been able to establish positively where he was located in Space. He had been surprised but very grateful to find that he was still able to access the standard database of Space maps on his vehicle systems. Admittedly, his lack of communications equipment meant that the maps would not be updated; the Command updates always showed the latest positions of all the vehicles, platforms and outposts. Of course, his own vehicle was not identified on the display, either. However, the maps had allowed him to establish where he was in Space, and he thought he had identified the asteroid, too. As he displayed the three-dimensional mapping image, he thought: 'I'm delighted that my murdering friends were not sharp enough to remove this basic navigation aid. Presumably, they were sure I would never be able to transit away from here – but' he smiled with grim satisfaction, 'I think I'm going to prove them wrong about that!' He had already noted the location of a medium-sized Command outpost that was near the periphery of the Sector and checked its exact coordinates. 'Good,' he said out loud, 'I intend that my Command friends will have a visitor soon!'

His next task was to check the planning of his route to the Command outpost. 'Once I have detached from here and stabilised the vehicle – that might take me some time, because I know this asteroid tumbles irregularly – I will be able to input the Command outpost coordinates into Navigator Control and then my system should take me there.' Mayn smiled happily at this thought! He could begin to envisage the golden moment when his vehicle would be transiting smoothly through Space towards his freedom and the resumption of his life.

He knew he would have a problem when he approached the Command outpost. He would be unable to respond to all normal identification calls. However, he knew their auto-sensors would be able to identify his vehicle and they would certainly allow him to approach and land without delay. 'They'll just have to bring me into their bay manually! It'll give them some useful practice in the technique!' He smiled happily and continued his thought. 'I can just imagine the Command staff being really puzzled. I can see them trawling through their records and scratching their heads: "Hi, Carver (a random name plucked joyfully from nowhere!), that vehicle is a standard escape pod registered to SPP Yggdrasil but we have no records of flight-plan or transit details. It's really weird! What's going on here?" Again Mayn smiled. 'They won't be puzzled for very long after I arrive and debrief!'

Mayn lay back and stretched his arms upwards. 'Enough for today. Time to eat and rest.'

That evening, Mayn turned his thoughts to the record of the Yggdrasil events he had assembled on his PAC. Now that he was coming very close to the time of his Command debrief, he decided that he must carry out a final review. PAC in hand, he examined once again the complete list of events carefully and considered whether he had missed anything of significance. Starting at the time of his arrival on Yggdrasil, he took each month serially, listened to his PAC record for that time and tried to recall any other occasions where he had been able to provide special help, no matter how minor this had been. These concerned situations where his help was sought by others as well as the events he had come upon inadvertently – those to which he had applied his "never passing by" philosophy. By the end of the evening he had managed to recall a very few other minor events that had slipped his mind on the "first pass". He fitted them neatly into the record.

At last, tired, he lay back in a glow of satisfaction. He felt he had made a very comprehensive record of his "special" activities on the Platform and was now able to go ahead and order a complete PAC risk analysis based on the whole five-year range of his data. This analysis would be similar in scope to the one he had ordered on his final major event, when he had helped Lt Bik Hatrige to "recover". The new analysis would provide a logical assessment of his personal risk and suggest those most likely to be responsible for his current predicament.

'I wonder if the PAC will confirm the results it gave me before,' he said to himself, recalling that the machine had identified CCO1 as the person who had the highest risk rating. 'That time, the analysis only covered the TP staff and CCO1 as the overall commanding Officer. I must say I can think of other people who might not have been very fond of me, too. It will be interesting to see who comes up when the complete dataset is used for the risk analysis. I'll set that running tomorrow. And while it's doing its work, I will work on a qualitative process of analysis and see if I can come up with any particular theories. Then, I'll be more than ready to assemble my debrief to Command and will be able to present all the supporting evidence.'

It was late evening. Mayn lay comfortably in his bunk in the sleeping compartment. He had been drifting off to gentle sleep when a sudden thought catapulted him back to full wakefulness: 'WHEN SHOULD I GO?'

The words leapt into his mind and became emblazoned there as scrolling pneumatic letters. Large, jolly, portly letters, full of iridescent colour, full of joy, full of optimism, full of success. Eyes now wide open, he repeated the amazing words out loud: 'When should I go?' They sounded wonderful, awesome. In some respects, almost an incomprehensible foreign language.

Surprisingly, he had never thought about the timing of his departure. 'That's incredible,' he murmured. Yet, deep in himself, he knew why. When, almost a year ago, he had discovered the range of the task in front of him, he knew he could not possibly set a temporal goal – that would have been ridiculous! His malefactors back at the Platform had so disabled the vehicle that his initial assessments had produced unbelief, then deep despair. It had taken time for his natural optimism to well up from that turgid soup of desolation.

But things were different now and he did not allow the letters, the four words, to disappear or even be dimmed in his mind. He captured them, kept them there – they were his – he was entitled to these letters, these wonderful words! But he couldn't help remembering the disbelief, the despair, the enormity of the task – no, not *the* task – the lots of tasks, the many tasks, an awesome myriad of tasks! But now, today, he had won through. He hadn't given up, had he? He had just plugged on and on – and on, until – he had won. And *they* had lost!

In the bunk, he turned over. "When should I go?" Yes, the words were still there. He would keep them there. They were his. He closed his eyes and fell into a serene, but not dreamless, sleep.

Perched at Control P1, his hands and feet danced purposefully over fully-known controls, adjusting, manipulating... caressing. In response, life flickered obediently into circuits, chambers and tubes, precisely as it had been designed to do. Forces were born, flowed and expanded, feeding each other. Arrays of indifferent indicators around him could not stop themselves confirming the onset of burgeoning, meaningful life in long-dead components and systems. Tremors grew rapidly from conception to adulthood, manifesting as powerful vibrations, full of life and virility. Heat became fire and fire became incandescence. Joyful noise built exponentially.

All was well... Very well!

Though with reluctance, the grasp of the asteroid was defeated as the forces of detachment won the battle; untethered distance between rock and metal grew steadily from metres to decametres and beyond. A final act was played out as purposeful metal feet recoiled into the comfort of their metallic wombs above.

All was well... Very well!

Inexorable thrust impelled the vehicle ever further from the influence of the asteroid while auxiliary control systems entered the fray to rebalance movement from the asteroid's tumbling motion to the blessed stillness of empty Space. Slowly, gradually, unwanted movement was tamed. Peace reigned.

In unhurried time, expert hands added essential coordinates; numbers and letters of apparent mystery, carried to the bowels of machinery and metamorphosed into instructions that blossomed into electronic thought and action. New power flowed and the mystery of acceleration thrust reassuringly against his body. Unmeasured minutes cumulated to bring the vehicle's speed to its maximum, now transiting along a set course; arrow-straight towards freedom and justice.

All was well... Very well!

And the man in the bunk smiled in his sleep, his lips silently forming the words:

"When should I go?"

Of course Mayn remembered his vivid dream the next day. 'That was a wonderful dream and I think it may be a good omen for the future. In my dream, everything worked as it should. The departure from the asteroid was perfect. I was able to stabilise the movement quite quickly and it wasn't long before we were underway at full speed towards the Command outpost.'

As he ate his breakfast in the rest area, he focussed his mind on the sudden appearance of the four words that had preceded his wonderful dream. 'That was really strange,' he thought. 'Isn't it funny that I had never given any thought to the time of my departure – even when all the work had been completed. I have been wanting to leave ever since I got here and now – suddenly – it seems that I can!'

With a sharp pang of pure pleasure, Mayn now realised that this was the truth. He had done all the work. He had tested everything he had done and he knew that everything worked as it should. He had examined the vehicle inside and out; he had serviced all the equipment so that everything would operate correctly. There was nothing else to do. He had done everything and now there was nothing to stop him.

However, the human mind can act peculiarly in such situations. Suddenly, Mayn felt a strange reluctance to take the final decision – the decision that would part him from this dreadful asteroid for ever! Throughout the many months that he had been marooned here, his mind had been fixed upon repairing the damage that had been done. It was an extremely complex process with a very clear goal – to give him control of the vehicle and make it possible for him to leave. Yet, now that he had achieved his goal in every way, he felt a strange reluctance to act!

'Perhaps it's the devil you know,' he said wryly, 'but this is one devil I wish I had never known!' He paused. 'Clearly, what I need to do is set a date for my departure. I want to run the complete PAC risk analysis today and do my own manual analysis as well. I'll do that after lunch today and then I'll establish a departure date this evening.

'PAC, take total SSP Yggdrasil event data recorded. Analyse personal risk to me. Allocate risk percentages to personnel and report significant values. Explain the logic behind suggested numerical values. Record result and indicate when voice report is available.' Mayn set the PAC aside and settled down to think about his own analysis.

Mayn had long concluded that the perpetrators of the crime against him had to include figures of considerable authority plus people who were extremely talented in technical matters. He was sure that the technical challenge would have been well beyond any technician of normal ability. The redesign and modification that he had seen in the vehicle was of the highest standard. 'So I need to be looking for at least one excellent technician,' he concluded.

First of all, there was the planning. Who was the instigator? And why? How had the decisions been made? Who was involved? Who decided on this particular course of action? Who chose this asteroid? That was an expert decision. And who was the pilot who controlled the vehicle remotely? Only a very small number of staff could have carried out this task.

Then there was the question of how the technical modifications had actually been carried out. It must have been done with great secrecy – only a very few people must have known what was really going on. He knew that the work had been done in a very remote part of the Platform but, in normal times, even that sort of area would still be visited routinely by many people over a period of time. The most likely solution was to designate the whole area "out-of-bounds" for all but those concerned with the work. However, this had its dangers because people are always curious – especially those who may have worked there formerly and were now prohibited from entering.

Also, he knew that the actual work would need quite a large workforce. All must have been sworn to secrecy though, of course, most of the "deeply secret" information (what the project was really about) would be known by only a few – and these would be the most senior people, those who made the fateful decisions.

Thirdly, there was the aftermath. How was his sudden and total disappearance explained? This was not something that could be ignored. Staff do not disappear; even if they are killed, there are strict procedures to deal with the remains. Even if someone dies in a Space accident, their body is always recovered. All bodies are returned to Command. Also, how was the disappearance of the escape pod explained on Yggdrasil? All personnel knew that a broken-down Space vehicle, no matter how or where it was adrift, would always be recovered.

Fourthly, there was the Command cover-up. The "loss" of a senior officer and the disappearance of an escape pod vehicle should, of course, have been reported to Command. Obviously, it hadn't been. If it had, there would have been an immediate Command response; at least one rescue vehicle would have come to the area and searched until the situation was resolved and fully explained.

Lastly, Mayn's knowledge of Command procedures meant that someone (or a group of people) must be impersonating him on Yggdrasil. Not, of course, in physical terms (the staff on Yggdrasil must know that he had "gone" and accepted whatever explanation that had been offered) but in terms of Command contact. Command would still be communicating with him as normal and someone must be answering in his name. Surely this was not a situation that could be sustained indefinitely? He shook his head disbelievingly.

He sat in complete stillness and thought for a while. Finally, he shook his head and spoke: 'Now it's time for me to review the people individually.

He knew he had to start with CCO1, Admiral Feltham Sarfeld. 'In any case, he was one of the first people I met on arrival on Yggdrasil – and certainly the most powerful!' As CCO1, Mayn knew the man had almost unlimited power. Of course he was legally and morally bound by Command instructions but, like so many commanders in remote locations, paid scant attention to them. Clearly, he was autocratic and addicted to aggrandisement – a very dangerous combination. It is unlikely that CCO1 would know about all of Mayn's "special help" events – although he may well have had a network of spies who kept him quite fully informed. Certainly he was aware of the CCO1 wine episode, the Utilities/Facilities staff dispute, the amazing recovery of Major Klaasj, the magnetic flux near-destruction and the dramatic "rescue" of Lt Hatrige. On several occasions, Mayn had been aware that CCO1 had no great love for him – there was probably an element of jealousy involved. However he now concluded that the Hatrige event would have changed CCO1's view of him rather more fundamentally, because it was then he had discovered that euthanasia was applied routinely on the Platform. 'This would certainly make me a very dangerous man in his eyes,' Mayn concluded.

The next candidate was also very interesting – Sub-Commander Grafton Fitch. Mayn knew Fitch had attempted to bully him at first and then, when that had not worked, tried to humiliate him in front of the ST Division staff. Although he had been relatively gentle with Fitch, he knew that the man was bound to dislike him and that he would be a likely ally in any plot against his Commander. Furthermore, he must be something of a "friend" of CCO1, because he had been selected to command ST Division when CCO1 fired the previous occupant. 'Fitch has plenty of negative energy – but certainly insufficient technical knowledge to do the job on the escape pod,' Mayn thought. But would he be able to recruit someone who has the necessary knowledge? Probably, he thought.

Now Mayn turned his attention to his Sub-Commanders Glassford and Glinche. After their little skirmish about working practices, Mayn had detected no further trouble from either, although subsequently both their Areas required significant reorganisation and better leadership. 'In a way, Glassford is a bit of an unknown to me,' Mayn thought. 'He seems to be efficient and knowledgeable enough and I suppose he is quite a good technician. Glinche is more of the boffin scientist – I'm familiar with the type, being one myself,' he smiled. 'However, I don't think I'd regard either as a threat to me.' Then he thought about the rest of the ST Division. 'None of Glassford's or Glinche's subordinates suggest any danger for me. And Mr Gorth the Mathematician and Bik Hatrige are friends of mine, I think!'

Now he turned his mind to other Divisions. 'I had very little contact with the Utilities and Facilities bosses. I was tasked to solve their staff problem and I did precisely that. So I don't think they can have too much problem with me, although they didn't like me "taking over" temporarily; however, they knew that was with CCO1's authority. Then there was the two Staff Reps, Miig and Banz, a couple of tricky characters, these. Once I had identified them as the key people, I got them on-side, let them solve the dispute and then arranged for them to be promoted. There should be no problem there, I think.'

'I can completely discount the bullied young man event, I think. That was solved by empowerment and there is only a very tenuous link back to me. I imagine the young man was very pleased! On the other hand, the Klaasj case was much more complicated and involved direct contact with PsychoMed and the patient himself.' Mayn recalled this had been an occasion of approach by Lead Surgeon Ferd Kolber. Happily, Mayn's intervention had been successful and, in the following discussion with Kolber, he thought he had been able to shift the responsibility away from himself. 'Ferd was already convinced of miracles and accepted that the body heals itself – sometimes with a little bit of medical or other intervention! And I managed to get myself written out from the account that he published, so I cannot see anything negative for me there.'

Mayn frowned as he recalled the magnetic flux event. That had been extremely dangerous. He knew that his powers had been tested to the limit and that his input had managed to recover the situation for Yggdrasil, just in the nick of time. Of course his personal involvement in the whole situation had been ordered by CCO1 himself since many of the key staff (e.g. Shield Engineering and Control) were commanded by him. After the event, he was sure CCO1 was glad to be alive and grateful that "his" Platform had been saved. Unfortunately the power that Mayn had needed to use was obvious for all to see and it was possible that CCO1 was jealous of that power – and worried about the diminution of his own authority. Mayn remembered that CCO1 had hardly spoken to him after the event, while others had been fulsome in their praise and congratulations. 'It's difficult to assess that one, I think.' he concluded, 'there are positives and negatives there.'

What about the others? He had saved Commander Norton West's life by detaching him from Control Position A and taking his place. West had thanked him for that but were there other factors to consider? Subsequently, someone must have remotely piloted the escape pod. If not West, who? All the others on the Flight Deck had been enthusiastic in their congratulations; he couldn't think of any reason why anyone should join in a plot to murder him.

Then, finally, there was the Gorth/Hatrige event. Although perhaps more than 100 staff had been involved in the drama of Level-0, Mayn felt sure that the vast majority posed no threat to him. However, he thought the danger increased when higher rank was involved. Although the Senior Security Officer (Major Hicks) was the most senior rank in the "guard group", Mayn felt he posed very little danger. 'Contact with him was quite minimal,' he thought. Then he paused. 'On the other hand, they would need security, guards, etc., when the escape pod was being worked upon, wouldn't they? So maybe he cannot be discounted.' He now turned his attention to the other officer, Major Bannerman, Senior TP Facility Officer. Here, the illegality of the TP Facility was a factor. Major Bannerman must know that his work was totally illegal. So Mayn's knowledge presented a personal threat. 'I suppose he must be a suspect,' he thought.

Finally, Mayn trawled through the many other staff he had known on the Platform. In the end, he could think of no one else who might want to do him such vicious harm.

'So that's it,' he said, 'that's the analysis from my memories. Now I'll see how this ties up with the PAC results.'

Mayn collected the PAC and noted that it had completed its work. He clicked in on:

'PAC, speak out report. Report first on PAC process and execution.'

"Analysis assessed as very complex.
Considerable processing and manipulating
power was required. There was a very large
data input to correlate and many pathways to
explore and assimilate. Process very time-
consuming, execution 6.632 minutes, note PAC
Category Extreme. All requested parameters
are calculated. Report details only those
individuals who acquired risk factors of
significance. Process Execution Report ends.
Permission to speak out analysis report?"

'Display Analysis Report'

Executive Summary:	Total staff reviewed 8358, equals total complement SSP Yggdrasil.
Group 1	assessed 8253 (98.744%) unin-volved in task. Calculated Risk Factor 0-1%.

Group 2	identified 80 (0.957%) staff involved in task as security or general non-specialised workers. Calculated Risk Factor 2-8%.
Group 3	identified 25 (0.299%) staff involved more deeply in planning, technical work or implementation. Calculated Risk Factor range 6-49.9%. (Note: 49.9% is maximum possible)
Main Report:	Detailed analysis of Group 2 and Group 3 staff; Risk Factor 2-49.9%.
1. Security staff acting as guards.	Number estimated at 30. These individuals do not know you personally. Not involved with project detail. Possible acquisition of minor information about project. Senior Security Officer (Major Hicks) had minor contact with you. His risk factor upper end of this range. Calculated Risk factor 2-8% (low).

2. General engineering workforce involved in non-specific supervised work.

Total number estimated at 50. Some physically within the project on general construction or simple modification tasks. Others employed in their normal workplaces, engaged in unidentifiable unit construction for the project. These may know you as senior officer, no/minimum contact. Some may be under your command. Calculated Risk factor 5-12% (low).

3. Space Control staff involved in transit of escape pod.

Total number estimated at 4. Would be working under schedule from elsewhere. Probably given false reason for transit and non-return. Possible peripheral involvement or knowledge of project. Calculated Risk factor 7-16% (low/medium) with the more senior staff at higher end of risk.

4. Sub-Commanders Glassford and Glinche and their senior staff.

Total 7. Knew you well. May have been offended in the past by your actions within their areas. Other motivations unknown. May have participated in project but unaware of central intent. Calculated Risk Factor 15-20% (medium).

5. Senior TP Facility Staff.

Total number estimated 3. Had contact with you. Knew that you recognised illegal activity. Would follow orders from superiors in Medical. Calculated Risk Factor 19-27% (medium). Senior TP Facility Officer Major Bannerman at highest end of Risk Factor.

6. Head Medical (Surgeon-Commander Jomo Sangyar) and immediate subordinates.

Estimate at 3. These senior people know you. They know you have discovered illegal TP Facility and that they are individually involved. Calculated Risk Factor 25-38% (moderate-high).

7. Remote Pilot.

Total 2 involved. Possible PPN1 (Commander Norton West) but your action to save his life reduces this likelihood. Other pilots under his command (unknown identities) may have been persuaded or ordered to act. The pilot must know some details of the plot. Calculated Risk factor 34-40% (high).

8. Sub-Commander Fitch and his senior staff (Confidants).

Total number 5. Uneasy relationship with you. Friend of CCO1. Probably would gain promotion if you were disposed of. Calculated Risk Factor 39-47% (high).

| 9. CCO1 | Admiral Feltham Sarfeld has difficult relationship with you. Jealous of your powers. Worried about his personal status being reduced. Now knows that seriously illegal activity has been discovered by you and that he is directly responsible. Calculated Risk Factor 49.99% (Note: This percentage is highest available Risk Factor). |

{Analysis Report ends}

Mayn was grave as he switched the PAC to "standby". He reviewed what he had heard:

'Even although the PAC and I approached the analysis from a different basis, the result was very similar. The biggest difference was its comments about the piloting and the Space controllers. Apart from Norton Wood (who I discounted), I don't know any of the pilots or the controllers, so I cannot imagine any of them would wish to murder me. Anyway, the pilot and the controllers need not be told the truth. They could just have had it logged as a training flight or something experimental. So now I've been through it all and I'm more than ready to debrief to Command.'

He sat silently for a moment or two. 'And now... I'm ready to answer that wonderful question: When should I go?' He looked up at his time record. It said "Day 356". He shook his head. 'I've been here on this asteroid for 356 days, just 9 days short of a complete year. No wonder it feels like I've been here for a long time. On the other hand,' he looked around, 'I have achieved wonders. And now, it's coming to an end.' He consulted the wall calendar which displayed "Day98, UY5665".

'So I could leave on Day99 of UY5665.' He considered this. 'Tomorrow? A bit rushed, I think.' He felt a little relieved as he said this. He looked at the calendar display again.

'How about Day100? That's a nice round number?' However, somehow he felt little enthusiasm for that particular day. 'Calendar Day100 is my Day 358?' Again no lift of enthusiasm.

Now he thought for a little. 'I know! I'll leave early on Day 360. 360 degrees – the full circle! A complete revolution! Now that really is meaningful and it makes me feel good. That's absolutely the right day to leave, I feel sure. I'll just relax over the next couple of days, do what I like, keep thinking the whole thing over again and then I will be more than ready to leap off this asteroid and head for my Command debrief on the glorious Day 360! Just think – I should be having my evening meal in the Command outpost!'

Human beings always know when they have reached a right decision. They are suddenly suffused with happiness, positivity and optimism! All the doubt and agonies they had been feeling while they were grappling with alternatives had been swept away miraculously by the dramatic cleansing that accompanies the "Right Decision".

That was exactly how Mayn felt at that memorable moment, on that memorable day, in that memorable place.

All was well... Very well!

11

Day 360

After a restful night, Mayn had wakened early. Now he was having a leisurely breakfast in the rest area. 'Just think! My last breakfast on this vehicle!' He felt wonderful. He finished his breakfast and purposefully made his way to the Control Cabin, a quiet, familiar area, yet charged this morning with drama and anticipation. The vehicle was ready. He was ready.

Then it started. It was just like his wonderful, amazing dream. He had gone through the check list meticulously and noted that all was in readiness. He had activated his PAC:

'PAC take record. This is Commander Maynard Gorton about to depart from asteroid AT56G7/89 where I have been marooned for the last 360 days. The escape pod vehicle was disabled so that there was no local control or communication facilities. I have spent the last 360 days restoring control. I will now depart this asteroid to transit to Command outpost KVX749B where I will debrief. The time is 0907, Day102, UY5665. Record ends.'

Now he was settled alertly at Control P1, his hands and feet dancing purposefully over fully-known controls, adjusting, manipulating... caressing. In response, life was flickering obediently into circuits, chambers and tubes, precisely as it had been designed to do. Forces were being born, flowing and expanding, feeding each other. Arrays of indifferent indicators were confirming the onset of burgeoning, meaningful life in many components and systems. Tremors were growing rapidly from conception to adulthood, manifesting as powerful vibrations, full of life and virility. Heat was becoming fire and fire was becoming incandescence. Joyful noise was building exponentially.

All was well... Very well!

Though with reluctance, the jealous grasp of the asteroid weakened as the vehicle's forces of detachment began to prevail... and then there was blossoming orange, so very bright... heat, so very intense... then sound so loud it instantly became silence. Everything flowed effortlessly into oblivion...

And then time arrested.

Mayn regained some degree of consciousness. There was light. Sound was returning. Strident klaxons? Why so loud? Eyes daring to open. Why was he looking at a tangled ceiling through a large transparent dome? His body had a knowledge, a memory of intense cold but now heat was returning. He closed his eyes, body drifting away... returning... drifting away... returning... how many times?

He had no idea how long he had lain on the floor. Minutes? Hours? He did not know. He tried to make his mind work, to make some sense of what he saw, heard, felt. Then, a first glimmer of understanding. Something had gone wrong. Something catastrophic. At last he recognised the dome around his head as a Crawler Helmet and with this identification came more realisation. When the disaster happened, he must have been blown unconscious from Command P1 as the vehicle was torn asunder. Then the destruction of the cabin life systems would have triggered the Crawler Helmets to deploy. They were the very last line of defence against death.

One of the helmets must have fallen close to him and immediately carried out its designated function. It had powered to his unconscious, dying body on the floor and moulded itself to him to preserve his life. He turned a pounding head slowly and saw the Control Room full of chaos. At the same time he heard the unmistakable sound of the automatic repair systems working at maximum speed to restore the integrity of the cabin and bring it back to a habitable condition. Mayn recalled the details of the restoration systems he had designed and remembered testing them with catastrophic hull disruption. Instantly, he knew what had happened.

Tentatively, reluctantly, he began to test out the operation of his body; after some time, he thought everything seemed to work to some degree. Gingerly, he levered himself up. His clothes were burned and in rags around him but his body, apart from some scratches, bruises and minor burns, seemed to be intact. He crawled painfully to a display panel and was able to check the life parameters in the cabin; they showed values rising to near-normal after a catastrophic cabin disruption. Seeing this, he was able to detach the large Crawler Helmet from his head and shoulders, laying it aside carefully, knowing with certainty that it had saved his life. Now he began to investigate and assess his situation.

One glance out of a vision port confirmed that he was still on the asteroid. In addition, he saw that the vehicle was still firmly clamped to the rocky surface. As he looked towards the rear of the vehicle, it was obvious that an explosion had happened in the main engine bay. He was able to use his internal cameras to make a quick visual check of that area of the vehicle. The damage he saw there confirmed his suspicions; there had been a very powerful explosion and, by zooming in, he could see that all the central parts of his propulsion system had been totally destroyed, ripped apart and reduced to jagged shards. Now he slumped down to the floor in the ruins of the Control Cabin.

After a long silence, he spoke out loud in an incredulous, shocked tone. 'So they installed a potent explosive device in the engine bay, in the unlikely event that I was able to achieve local control. The device must have been heat-detonated when I boosted the engines to full power.' He bowed his head and continued in a whisper: 'I recognise I will never be able to make this vehicle Space-worthy again. The hull has been completely ruptured.' He lowered his head on to his cupped hands. 'They've beaten me... I've lost...' for the first time in 360 days, Mayn wept bitterly.

There followed four days of despair. Mayn discovered that the vehicle's airlock was still operational and had been outside the vehicle in his suit to inspect the damage further. He found that a large area of the hull had been blown into Space; some of the shattered pieces could be seen orbiting the asteroid. Inside the totally-destroyed engine bay, the huge explosion had blown the engine apart. However a careful search showed traces of a very powerful plastic explosive that had been moulded around the main engine beneath its protective covers. A further search yielded the remains of the control mechanism, just recognisable as a heat-activated detonator capable of being armed remotely.

'Just as I thought,' Mayn muttered, 'activated from Yggdrasil after I arrived here. None of my lower-level engine test runs would have achieved the temperature needed to set the device off. Only full power activated the detonation – exactly as planned.' Disconsolately, he returned to the Control Cabin of the shattered vehicle.

Next morning, the ever-practical Mayn had started to clear the Control Cabin of debris and begin to restore what systems he could. Crucially, the vehicle's automatic repair system had been able to restore the integrity of the living spaces and all the necessary life support systems within them, so his life was preserved and could continue. However, all the work on his local control system was negated – there was now no vehicle transit system to control. Also, he found that he had lost the standard database of Space maps that had enabled him to establish his position, so now he was more isolated than ever!

That evening, he sat down with his PAC. 'PAC take record. My attempt to leave asteroid AT56G7/89 and transit to Command outpost KVX749B has failed due to the detonation of a concealed heat-activated explosive device in the engine bay. I stress this was deliberate sabotage and intention to murder. I was rendered unconscious by the blast and all control and living quarters were breached, causing complete depressurisation and exposure to external conditions. My life was saved by a Crawler Helmet and then by the automatic repair systems of the vehicle which restored the cabin to viable life conditions. However, the vehicle is now totally disabled and I can no longer leave the asteroid.' At this point, Mayn paused for a while to review his situation. Then, shaking his head in despair, he ended the record. 'Report ends. Scientist-Commander Dr Maynard Gorton.'

'What do I do now?' he asked himself. 'Just wait to die? Because that is what must happen in due course. At some point, a key system will break down or wear out and the repair system will be unable to restore its function. Then the vehicle will stop supporting life – my life. I think that my chances of ever leaving here are now very slim. And there's absolutely nothing I can do about it.' His voice faded and he sat silent and impassive for a long time.

After his evening meal, a very despondent Mayn climbed into his bunk, where he eventually drifted off to sleep after he had managed to slow his racing mind.

'Mayn?' A little girl's voice. Lucy's voice!

'Lucy? Is that you?' In his dream, a delighted Mayn responded.

'Yes, it is.'

'Lucy, where are you? I can't see you.'

'No, Mayn, you won't see me. I haven't come to play, you know. I've come to remind you of the Key.'

'The Key, Lucy? What Key? What are you talking about?'

'I've come to remind you of the Key,' Lucy repeated.

Mayn smiled serenely. 'You better remind me of it, then!'

'OK. Are you listening?'

'Yes.'

'The Key is "Conversion without Loss".'

'Sorry, Lucy. Why "Conversion without Loss"? I don't understand.'

'Don't you remember, Mayn? That day we were extremely naughty and went swimming in the forest pool? That was when you said it. You said: "The Key is 'Conversion without Loss'. Never forget it".'

Mayn's mind reeled back at lightning speed. He remembered! Both he and Lucy were around ten years old. There they were, sitting on the grass in her garden, just out of sight in the trees. It was an extremely hot summer's day and, despite being very lightly dressed, both were very overheated and sweaty.

'I wish I could find somewhere to cool down,' Lucy said.

'I've got a wonderful idea, Lucy. Let's go and have a swim in the pool in the woods. The water there is always really refreshing. I've been there with my parents a couple of times.'

Lucy had looked at him sadly. 'You know, Mayn, I wish we could. There's nothing I'd like better. But we can't. We're not allowed to go to that pool.'

'Well, I know that! But I've arranged we can go!' Mayn replied with a conspiratorial grin.

'Arranged we can go?' Lucy was incredulous. 'Have you gone mad? You know we aren't allowed to go to that pool on our own. And we're not allowed to go swimming unsupervised. In fact, we aren't allowed to go to the woods, either. Listen, Mayn, have you forgotten that we're monitored? Our parents know exactly where we are and can always keep an eye on us. And if we stray into off-limits areas, they'll hear the warning tone.'

Mayn smiled at her. 'Well... I've changed the system a little bit, Lucy. I've been doing a little bit of work. I don't like this "Level Two Monitoring" we children have to put up with, so I've... eh... modified it a bit...' He smiled. 'The Key is "Conversion without Loss", you know. Never forget it.'

Mayn had been fascinated when he was taught about the ancient electronic equipment that had been designed to protect children. Tens of thousands of years before, the earliest monitoring systems had been very crude, often involving nothing more than noise amplifiers linked by very simple radio circuits. Mayn remembered that one of the most basic pieces of equipment had been called "baby alarms". This had caused a great deal of mirth in his classroom when an example was displayed and dismantled. The pupils were astonished at the simplicity, crude design and unreliability of these ancient artefacts. Then, as the centuries and millennia passed, the history lesson showed them how protection and monitoring developed to become extremely sophisticated and efficient. The tutor had reviewed the current arrangements for them, showing the pupils how all the babies and young children of their days were fitted with tiny life monitors, which not only kept their parents and guardians fully aware of their condition at all times but could apply corrective action, if required. Thus, the child's problem or other requirements could be dealt with safely and effectively at all times, using sophisticated bio-electronics. This was known as "Level One Monitoring".

The pupils were also reminded that there came a time in their lives when it was deemed inappropriate to monitor their bodies in such detailed way. This was part of the edicts in the Charter of Human Freedoms and Rights enshrined in Modern Galactic Law. Mankind had always been greatly concerned with the concept of personal freedom. This did not mean that child monitoring was completely removed when children became a little older, because parents and guardians have always been concerned to keep their children safe from any kind of harm. However, from around the age of six, it was decreed that the monitoring should be reduced to routine location-finding and, if necessary, activity identification. This reduced "Level Two Monitoring" was applied to children until their early teenage years, after which it was considered legally and morally inappropriate to interfere with their approaching adult status.

The vast majority of the older children accepted Level Two Monitoring with equanimity. In any case, they thought, there was nothing they could do about it, was there? The equipment was completely tamper-proof and highly sensitive to any attempt at interference with its functions. Inevitably, there were always a few individuals who had the motivation, intelligence and skill to baulk against such interference in their lives. Of course, Mayn was one of these! It had not been easy but he had found a way to alter the operation of the Level Two Monitors.

Lucy was looking at him with alarm. 'A Key? Conversion without Loss? Whatever do you mean, Mayn? What have you done?'

'Nothing much, Lucy. I've just built this little converter unit here. When I switch it on, it changes our monitors. It converts the monitoring system without losing any of their normal functions. The result is that we are free to go where we like and do what we like!'

'What!' Lucy was beginning to understand – beginning to appreciate how such a modification might be useful! 'Does it really work? You would certainly get into a lot of trouble if it doesn't!'

'It works very well, Lucy. I've tested it a number of times and it works brilliantly!' He moved to switch the unit on.

'Don't!' Lucy's voice was frightened. 'Will this affect me, too?'

'Yes, it affects anyone close to me.'

'Just a minute, Mayn. What do our parents see on their monitoring displays?'

'Oh, it sees us located somewhere safe, somewhere we're allowed to go.'

Lucy was thoughtful. 'But, Mayn, isn't there a flaw in that? What happens if they go to where we are indicated to be, only to find that we're not there?'

'That's a really good question, Lucy! Congratulations! But it's OK, I've thought of that. They won't find us there and their portable monitor display will tell them we've gone somewhere else – another safe place. If they're desperate to contact us they can always make a personal voice call and then we'll come back quietly and secretly. It's OK, the whole system works like a dream.'

Mayn remembered the absolutely wonderful time they had in the cool, clear water of the pool. Slim, pale bodies cleaving through the water, leaping from the bank, cavorting and splashing; afterwards, drying themselves in the bushes, exchanging delighted, conspiratorial grins of pure pleasure. Then, refreshed, they returned to a "safe" place where Mayn switched off his converter unit and they replaced their virtual identities with their real selves!

Mayn rolled over in his bunk and spoke in his sleep: 'It's just a bit of conversion, Lucy. "Conversion without Loss". Nothing to worry about.'

Then he woke up, eyes wide. 'Conversion without Loss,' he yelled. 'That's it! I need to think converters. Lucy has been sent to me in a dream to take my mind along the converter path. The message is that I need to convert something to produce a powerful Distress Signal! If I can't go to them (and now I certainly can't), they'll need to come to me. And they *will* come if I can transmit a Distress Signal!'

As he washed, dressed and ate a distracted breakfast, he couldn't help his mind tumbling with many thoughts: 'You know, maybe I got this whole thing wrong. Maybe I applied the wrong approach to my predicament. I was so fixated on making the vehicle work again, totally concentrated on restoring local control. Because I designed this vehicle I thought it was something I could do.' He paused, introspectively. 'And I actually did it, too. I would have succeeded if they hadn't planted explosives in the engine bay.' He sighed. 'Anyway, that's all over now. I need to think. I need to switch my mind to transmitters. I need to construct a powerful Distress Signal from the electronics I have here. I need to think conversion units. That's why Lucy was here.'

Now he sat down in the Control Cabin. 'What electronic transmitter/receiver equipment do I have? Well, they removed all the standard communications gear and all the emergency communications. They left absolutely nothing. OK, I've always had my PAC and that contains a transmitter/ receiver but it's relatively low power. Designed only for short range, no use at all for a Distress Signal.' Suddenly he was silent and still. 'That's it,' he whispered, 'when I wanted to change the Level Two Monitor, I modified the system by building an external converter unit! That converted the monitoring system without loss of its normal functions. What I now need is an external converter unit that will massively boost the output signal from my PAC without losing any of the normal PAC functions! Because I need the normal modes of the PAC to continue the record of my progress here.'

With renewed vigour, Mayn spent the rest of the day examining electronics. Using an electronics analyser (part of the standard engineering kit on the vehicle), he started by scanning as many of the electronic components he could find in the vehicle and cross-referenced his findings with the technical information stored in the engineering databases. Then he worked to understand what function each unit carried out and determined how it was constructed physically. Finally, he considered whether such a unit could find a place in a converter booster that could broadcast a powerful signal on the Space Distress Frequency.

Once again, the weeks passed as Mayn spent part of each day on his quest to build a converter that would communicate with his PAC and boost its modest transmission signal in the appropriate frequency range. Eventually, he came to the conclusion that he could not build a booster of sufficient power to transmit a 360 degree signal in all planes; of course all Space Distress Equipment did just that, so that the powerful signal could be picked up from any direction at considerable range. In the end, by combining and modifying a large number of components, Mayn was able to produce a signal booster that sent a Distress Signal in a narrow beam.

'This will work,' he concluded as he looked at the modified range of components he had strung together, 'but it can only achieve a limited beam. If anyone senses my narrow radio beam as they pass through it, they should recognise a Distress Signal. So this gives me a chance of being found and rescued, all thanks to Lucy and "Conversion without Loss".'

At last, Mayn felt very much better! He knew there was a significant amount of Space traffic in the Sector, although standard routes did not bring transiting vehicles close to the asteroid.

'Anyway, it's a chance – and it's the only one I've got!' he concluded.

12

Day 896

He had a routine. It had been refined over the weeks, months and years. Like all routines, it was repetitive and Mayn had grown resigned to its recurring nature, because it undoubtedly represented the only remaining hope he had. The routine consisted of a simple procedure to rotate his narrow Distress Frequency transmission beam through 360 degrees, with each successive rotation tilted in a slightly different plane. He had constructed a crude manual machine to do this. The whole sequence took around two hours to complete and the object was to replicate, to a small degree, an omni-directional distress transmission. He carried out this routine two to four times a day.

Each time, he thought: 'Some wonderful day, someone is going to transit through my narrow little beam and their scanning equipment will register a Distress Transmission. Then they will pinpoint where I am and rescue will follow.' Mayn did his very best to stay optimistic but, inevitably, the passage of years had taken toll of his morale.

Until now, the general condition of his vehicle had held up well and he had been pleased with its resilience. The automatic repair system that he had engineered into the vehicle had been very effective in dealing with the explosion; the extensive damage caused to the living space had been repaired with quite remarkable efficiently. Since then, all the support systems needed to keep its human occupant alive, fit and well had performed as designed. They kept themselves powered up from external radiation sources. In addition, any breakdown or malfunction had been repaired or corrected without problem. However, the GTN67UV escape pod had not been designed to be self-sufficient for years. Indeed, in most cases, its expected use was in the order of days, if not hours; anyone who was forced to occupy an escape pod would expect to be rescued very quickly.

Of course, Mayn had thought about the "final" emergency. He knew there could be no optimism here. He knew that if any of the prime life systems of the vehicle failed, his lifespan would be reduced to days from that point. Then, he would need to live in a suit to preserve his life. He knew that modern suits were constructions of great sophistication. They were cleverly designed to meet all the needs of the human body for respiration, nourishment, effluent and cleanliness. However, it was assumed that the wearer of a suit would return to a habitable environment within hours, where he would remove it and return it to its docking rack. There, the suit would connect automatically to systems that would restore it to complete sterility and indistinguishability from new. A suit was never designed for extended habitation; it could never become a pseudo Space vehicle that sustained an occupant for a long time.

After arrival on the asteroid, he had found two suits in the vehicle, both new and of the latest model at that time. In the last years, he had used a suit many times for trips outside the vehicle. Since the catastrophic explosion, he had not ventured outside very often; there was no reason to go, apart from a "change of scenery". All this time, he had been careful to use only one suit, deliberately retaining the other for the time when the vehicle may no longer be able to support him. However, he knew that the onset of an uninhabitable cabin meant he would have just a few days to live.

And so the distress beam was rotated... and rotated... and rotated...

And nothing happened.

After the explosion and the wreckage of his chances to leave the asteroid, Mayn had found his incarceration particularly difficult. Then there was that glorious moment when Lucy came to him in a dream and gave him a new direction for his energies. He was immensely grateful to the Universal Power that had done this and assumed this was the same power that used him as a channel or catalyst for goodness throughout his life. When he finally managed to start his Distress Transmission – albeit a pale shadow of the real thing – he had been elated and felt that the intervention to direct his activities should lead to the one thing he wished for so much – rescue! However, in the weeks and months that followed, nothing happened, despite his enthusiastic and energetic daily attempts. Eventually, he had to settle for the routine of his activity and accept whatever happened.

In this new and very calm frame of mind, he decided to "open" himself.

'The ancients used to call this meditation,' he said to himself, 'I think I'll call it "communing". That seems to be the right word for it.'

So, from then, in the times in between his periods of mechanical beam rotation, Mayn lay on a couch and opened his mind. At first, nothing happened. He found that his brain was still too active, darting here and there, gambolling with a myriad of thoughts. Gradually, over the weeks, however, he found his racing thoughts were quieting. It was then he felt surrounded, pervaded with power and love. He found he could "commune" – but, afterwards, he had no clear memory of what precisely had happened. He just felt an incredible sense of power and fulfilment; a sense of serenity – more real than he had ever experienced.

'I must be doing something right,' he often smiled on his return to "normal" life.

13

Day 1,519

Then one awful day in UY5668, he heard it starting. He knew it had to come; bio-mechanical, electronic failure was inevitable, designed in. The warning tones, the flashing lights, the whine and clink of loyal repair and replacement systems. Activity and events becoming more frenetic and extreme. The persistence of warning tones, increasing in stridency, now being joined by their fellows calling out from other vital systems.

Immediately, he had gone to scan the control panels and it was clear that a catastrophic malfunction was developing. He did his best to intervene but the equipment was now old and tired, arthritic and fragile, well past its scheduled restoration or replacement timespans. He observed the progressive physical fractures, components now groaning and grinding in protest as desperate relays struggled to isolate damaged circuits. Then the *coup de grace* of bright, crackling arcs of fire igniting flickering flames of various hues, to feed acrid smoke plumes that rose ominously to the ceilings above. He saw that the atmosphere was beginning to fail and the temperature was falling rapidly. Lights were flickering and dimming as system death took hold.

Now the final chapter opened. With small puffs of explosion, the Crawler Helmets deployed. Mayn knew it was time for him to flee. Hand clamped across nose and mouth, he stumbled, retching, to the suit cabinet and chose the unworn suit, fitting the helmet over his head. Automatically, the helmet restored his immediate life requirements. Moving as quickly as possible, he donned the rest of the suit, closing and fastening it securely. Within ten seconds, the main fire system recognised a catastrophic emergency and blanketed everything with glutinous chemicals. Everything, including the man in the suit, disappeared beneath a deep layer of clinging, toxic foam.

Time had passed in unknown units and a new unwelcome reality gradually emerged, accompanied by a sterile, cloying silence. The fire foam dissolved, progressively revealing a blackened, wrecked structure devoid of motion, light or heat. After a while, the man in the suit stood up and began to move slowly around what had been the Control Cabin, now an awesomely bleak alien void with no possibility of life. He knew everything was inert, dead... yet... what was that gleam under the blackened control desk? He moved closer then stood stock still.

'My PAC,' he whispered, 'still working, still attached to my signal booster unit, also still working.'

So the hours had reeled past, counting down to the third of three pointless days. The suit worked perfectly for more than two of them. On the third day, it began to generate polite advisory notices: "Certain elements of functionality will need external attention soon"... "100% functionality cannot be maintained without a base station recharge"... "life functions may be adversely affected within 4.76 hours"... etc.

As the minutes and hours counted on relentlessly, the advisory messages became increasingly urgent, demanding attention. Musical warning tones began to sound and stark messages were flashed on the internal helmet screen – if remedial action was not taken soon, there would be irredeemable damage to the occupant – it had been necessary for the suit to switch to its emergency backup system – it should be noted this has a limited capacity only and is not designed for extended use.

Then: "FINAL WARNING... FINAL WARNING... This suit will be power-drained in 30 minutes... Danger of death... Danger of death... *Danger of death...*" A mind-numbing repetition.

Mayn walked slowly from the Control Cabin, entered the sleeping compartment and closed the door firmly. Bulky in his suit, it proved difficult to manoeuvre himself on to the remains of his bunk but, slowly and carefully, he was finally able to lie comfortably supine. He obscured his helmet, closed his eyes and, with a slight smile on his lips, reviewed the 33 short years of his life. That done, he waited, stilling his final conscious thoughts.

At the predicted second, the suit began to power down in a muted chorus of falling tones akin to embarrassed murmurings. Then there was only the gentle sound of human breathing. The build-up of toxicity is not associated with any sound of its own; it is a stealthy, silent killer.

In due course, the sounds inside the suit became those of a human physiology trying despairingly to gain access to an inadequate and steadily dwindling supply of oxygen, tantalisingly held within the volume of an increasingly toxic gas.

'Con... vsn... wout... loss...' Four final polluted gasps.

Then silence.

Part Two

Leo and Cy

14

The First Day

Entropy continued to increase, as it always does. It was clear that the escape pod was gradually being subsumed by the asteroid. Thirty years before, the vehicle had arrived gently enough, sinking neatly into a hollow in the jagged rock strata, touching down on deceptive spindly legs with elegant precision, then locking itself to the surface with cleverly designed clamping feet. Then, it was an alien object of bright orange and silver which contrasted cheerfully with the primeval black and grey of the tortured asteroid rock. Now, it was no longer bright orange and silver. The years had taken their toll on its brightness, on its existence, on its life. In time, it would become a largely indistinguishable excrescence on its host.

Leo and Cy were stretched out on their rest couches, as they usually were at this time of day. They sometimes laughed at their usage of the word "day", because, although their journeys took them through uneven periods of light and darkness, these were certainly not patterned as "days" or "nights". However, their training (now many years before) had impressed on them that the human body functions best when it works to some sort of regular regime; therefore all Space workers were instructed to adopt a "day-night" structure into their working lives and to cumulate this into weeks, months and years, in the approximate pattern that history had provided for them. Of course, Universe Command determined the exact passage of months and years. After all, it was important that the huge number of Space workers used the same timescale across all the universes. This was why a large panel in the Control Room displayed: "Day147, UY5694".

Although their space vehicle was large and capacious, Leo and Cy were the only human staff on board. All the essential functions of the vehicle were controlled by complex and highly sophisticated bio-electronic systems. When particular work came their way, the men had access to a large number of robots and sub-vehicles, each one perfectly designed for its range of purposes.

'Fourteen years since we scanned this Region,' Cy murmured, checking records on a large display, 'and we didn't find anything to do the last time.'

'Well, it keeps it more relaxed that way,' his partner responded easily, 'after all, we're not looking for work, are we?' Good naturedly, they agreed they weren't.

'I must say, when I volunteered for IRS (Intergalactic Rescue and Salvage), I thought it would be a more exciting life,' Leo smiled.

'True, it's generally been quite quiet but we've had a few interesting moments, haven't we? I suppose the most exciting time was that large cargo ship rescue three years ago.'

'Sure, they were certainly very pleased to see us. We had no problem with it, did we? All our systems worked like a dream and we had all sixteen crew on board in just a few hours. And we got the salvage credits, didn't we? That was a pretty good outcome for us. I must say, the people who designed these IRS J87Vs did a really good job of it. Even though that ruptured cargo ship was much bigger than we are, we were able to take it into our capture field and hold it stable until we delivered it to the salvage facility, remember? That was really a high-point for us, wasn't it?'

'Sure was,' Cy agreed, 'but we don't want too much excitement in our lives, do we?'

They smiled at each other. They were always comfortable and relaxed in each other's company. Anyway, if either of them wanted to take themselves elsewhere for a bit, there was always the Entertainment Unit, wasn't there? You could set up anything you wanted there; absolutely anything you fancied. And there was also the occasional Home Leave to look forward to as well. That came every five years or so.

In fact, in all the years that Leo (Leonardo Granvic) and Cy (Cyrus Funte) had been together in the J87V rescue vehicle, there had never been any problem between them; never any friction or strife. This was not because their personalities were similar; far from it! Leo's relaxed, rather gentle disposition concealed his devastatingly powerful intellect, totally dedicated to the tasks in hand, while Cy's distinctly more mercurial temperament constantly drove a scintillating matrix of energy and totally focussed intelligence. Alone in the vehicle, the disparate temperaments of these two men combined seamlessly to create an immensely strong psychological and intellectual bond of comradeship, as well as making them exceptionally effective in the complex and hugely important roles they played in the vast expanses of Space.

Their formation into an extraordinarily talented team was a tribute to the meticulous selection procedure that chose only the very best for space-side posts and to the arduous training that followed. Both these procedures had been developed and honed over many years to produce near perfect results. Then, the most exceptional candidates were formed into RPs (Rescue Pairs); these were destined to become the IRS Operatives who took command of the latest IRS vehicles that patrolled a huge volume of Space in accordance with the RS Command Rescue and Salvage Plan.

The RS Command Resource Leaders had long known that the quality of selection and training processes was of great importance for all space-side staff; however, it was recognised that the RPs, with their unique rescue roles and only each other to depend upon, had to be of the very highest and most reliable quality. Crew lives and the recovery of extremely valuable equipment depended upon the constant effectiveness of these operational RPs.

As all human beings do, the two men sometimes reminisced about their past lives and quite often this covered their time of selection and training, the time that they came together for the first time. They had both graduated from College graded "X1s" (essential if you had ambition to go space-side) and had gone on post-grad to achieve a whole range of "PG1s" in technical, psychological and physical areas of knowledge. The culmination of all this activity was an invitation to join the prestigious Space College for assessment. They often told each other hilarious stories of their struggles with the enormously difficult tests they were required to pass. First, there were the "Knowledge Drains" using DT (Direct Thought) techniques, which first had to be learned. Here, no physical processes were involved, just the reception and transmission of knowledge and decision at blinding speed. Then there was the psychological and physiological coordination required to control hugely complex simulators and finally, the constant and relentless monitoring of their physical and mental state day and night. The candidates were never allowed to relax.

Cy laughed as he described some earlier parts of the training courses. 'We all thought it was incredibly hard when we carried out all the exercises individually, didn't we? I thought my brain was going to explode with some of the DT procedures – but there's no doubt you got better at it. After a while, I decided that maybe my brain wouldn't explode, just malfunction and die! And I used to think: "I bet they would soon get me back up again – they wouldn't want to lose all the time and effort they had put into me!" Even then, in the middle of it, that made me smile.'

Leo agreed. 'It was the same with the simulators. You were always doing about twenty control operations at a time and they kept throwing events and problems at you constantly. Fortunately, most of the controls were set for DT; this left your hands and feet free to deal effectively with the unexpected – usually!' He smiled at the memory.

'And then they began to assemble the Pairs,' Cy prompted. 'You thought it was bad when you were coping with it all individually but then you had this other stupid guy linked in dual control with you and the whole thing went belly-up – big-time! Quite often, the simulated vehicle went out of control and terminated, remember? Do you remember the ear-splitting horns? The monitors were absolutely furious when that happened!' After some reflection, he continued enthusiastically. 'They paired me up with that guy Hansi – you remember him? It didn't work, big time! It was a disaster. We were in DT conflict – though I heard later that that's not uncommon. The monitors soon realised the impossibility of it and broke the link between us. Hansi disappeared real quick; I wonder what happened to him?'

'Yes, I had a few guys paired up with me,' Leo mused, 'some weren't too bad but when you arrived we clicked in right away. We started acting like a proper team right away, didn't we? The monitors recognised it immediately and formed us into a Pair within a very short time.'

'Yes,' Cy smiled teasingly, 'I found I could always carry you along pretty well!'

'Yes, my boy, you were always pretty wonderful at that!' They both grinned.

Although the two men were "tuned" to each other and could have conducted all their conversations in DT mode, they always spoke out loud (Voice Mode) when they were together, face to face. Years before, they had agreed they would adopt this routinely. They would use DT when they were apart; this made sense, since they wouldn't need to bother with clumsy communication equipment and convert their thoughts into words. However, when they were together informally, face to face, they would use traditional physical speech unless they were dealing with operational matters that required increased speed and efficiency. 'Using speech is much more relaxed and social,' Cy had said, 'we're in no tearing hurry when we're in Voice Mode, so why use high-speed voiceless transmission? Also, it's a good discipline – it keeps us in practice. When we go home, nobody would be tuned to our DT wave so we need to use our voices.' Leo had agreed and that had become their rule.

The sensation of a low tone made them sit up and look at each other meaningfully. A DT transmission from the vehicle's Central Coordinator had registered in their minds.

> Sensors have picked up a very
> weak and highly intermittent
> Distress Signal.

'Pinpoint'

Cy's DT instruction. They both turned their attention to the large display as a signal indication flashed on a small asteroid some distance away.

'Identify.'   AT56G7/89

'Data.'

{Instantly, information was displayed}

Exact Universal position shown relative to
nearby objects

Details:	Orbit displayed. Spin/ movement measured.
Dimensions:	Displayed...
Composition of rock and minerals:	Displayed...
Record of condition variations:	Displayed...
Visits:	One recorded. Survey by SSP Yggdrasil. Survey Crew 874. UY5607

Report Summary: Life zero. Mineral
                    assessment Zero. Atmos-
                    phere Zero. Usage score
                    Zero."

Leo looked at Cy, his face wrinkled in puzzlement. Then he spoke out loud: 'That survey was 87 years ago. No Distress Signal works for 87 years. In any event, the SSP would soon send out a vehicle to search for the origin of a Distress Signal. And under the Law, they would need to initiate a Universe Call for an IRS vehicle.' He turned back to the screen and DT instructed.

'Analyse Distress Signal.'

                    {Data appears}

Signal: very weak, less than S0.14.
                    Pulse weak, intermittent trans-
                    mission.

Signal
Equipment: non-standard.   Likely match:
                    Modified PAC Type D4467/B.

Operational   PAC Type D4467/B in use
span: UY5661 to UY5665

Leo whistled softly. 'So if that date range is true, it's unlikely that the vehicle (or whatever it is) will be much older than UY5661; that's only 33 years ago. We should do a distress scan on a year range around then.'

Cy instructed:

'Distress scan UY5656–UY5671. Current Sector.'

          No distress reports UY5656/UY5671
          this Sector.

'Distress scan all years this location asteroid AT56G7/89'

          No distress reports asteroid
          AT56G7/89 all years.

The men looked at each other. Cy spoke crisply. 'OK Leo, Local Command Decision. We go to Condition C. We need to investigate what has happened on AT56G7/89'

Automatically, both men assumed full DT Mode as they settled into their vehicle command roles.

'Activity power up. Propulsion set 8. Advise all systems of impending flight.'

'Set course: Coordinates AT56G7/89.
Compute distance/time.'

'Report activity and decision to RS Command'

'Initiate.'

A slight tremor ran through the vehicle. There was no dramatic sensation of movement but, on the large screen, the white spot identified by their serial number began to move steadily towards asteroid AT56G7/89.

On the 3-D visual scanner, the two men saw the asteroid grow from a tiny spot to fill most of the display. The vehicle began to decrease speed. Commands were issued.

'Compute asteroid AT56G7/89 movement and lock on.'

'Search for origin Distress Signal and display.'

At first they could see nothing as their systems began to search the asteroid surface below after matching its movement at an optimum distance. Then, precise quartering began. When nothing had been located on the current scan of the asteroid surface below, the vehicle manoeuvred to the next scan section. After some hours, the system reported:

System report: Signal pinpointed

Automatically the scan zoomed in close and the visual display showed a dull metallic object, its shape vaguely familiar as a small Space vehicle.

'Identify.'

> Standard Escape Pod Type GTN67UV.
> Serial GTN36716XT

'Origin?'

> Production Xenos Facility UY5659.
> Deployed SSP Yggdrasil UY5660

'Current factors?'

Vehicle condition:	Not operational. Seriously damaged. Possible breach of hull indicated. General condition poor. Many components missing, cannot identify. No operational power.
Signal indications:	Weak narrow signal beam broadcast on Distress Frequency. Intermittent.
Origin of signal:	Modified PAC Type D4467/B. Signal boosted by unknown equipment.
Lifescan report:	All scans indicate no life present.

Cy and Leo turned to face each other.

Cy (in DT): 'We could send a robot in. Your thoughts?'

'In normal circumstances, I would say "yes" but this isn't normal.'

'We could seek advice from RS Command.'

'That would waste time. I think they would want an RP investigation.'

'I think so too.'

They paused, then Cy spoke: 'It's pretty late in the day. I think it would be best if we started our investigation tomorrow morning. After all, it's pretty certain that we aren't rescuing anyone here, are we? We could sit down and make some provisional plans this evening so that we're ready to go in the morning.'

'That's a good idea, Cy. Let's do that. It would be appropriate to give this whole scenario some serious thought, anyway. What has gone on here is extremely strange.'

Firstly, the two men sketched out their plan of action for the following day.

'I propose that I go down physically. I'll take you with me on virtual, of course,' Leo said.

'Yes, agreed, Leo.'

The special virtual technology that they would use had been developed many decades earlier. In the past, it was recognised to be very dangerous to leave an IRS vehicle totally unmanned while its RP crew carried out essential two-person operations outside; in earlier days, there had been a number of serious incidents when investigating technicians suffered malfunctions that prevented them from returning to their rescue vehicle. This required major rescue operations to be mounted and there had even been a few fatalities connected with this problem. Then the Space Innovation Laboratory had developed a completely new technology to solve this perennial problem. A new "virtual buddy" technology allowed an investigating technician to be accompanied and supported by a virtual colleague who did not physically leave the IRS vehicle. Thus, vehicles need never be left unmanned. If required, the "virtual buddy" could immediately "return" to the vehicle at any time and reoccupy his physical body. Once the new technology had been fully proven, it was installed in all IRS vehicles and, from that time, RS Command instructed that IRS vehicles should never be left totally unmanned for any reason.

'I think Lander Pod A4 will be the most suitable vehicle for the terrain of this asteroid, so I'll use that,' Leo continued. 'I'll just specify a check through the preparation records to make sure it is 100% operational. Tomorrow morning I'll get the surveyor scope to identify the best landing spot that's nearest to the escape pod.'

'OK, Leo, I think we're now prelim-ready for the operation. Could we just spend some time discussing what we know about this situation and what the possibilities might be?'

'Well, Cy, I get a feeling this one might prove to be a major puzzle. I mean, there's no doubt that Command controls all vehicle Space movements meticulously. Even more so, they control the movements of personnel – and they always have done so. Of course I suppose this escape pod could have been remotely controlled from SSP Yggdrasil – but why send an empty escape pod on a Space transit to a small valueless asteroid? Why lose a valuable Space vehicle?'

'Yes, I agree with all that, Leo, but that doesn't fit all the facts either, does it. The transit path of the escape pod would still need a planned record to be submitted and I think we can assume that no record was made of this transit. That is absolutely forbidden by Command Law.'

'I suppose it might be useful to establish where SSP Yggdrasil was when this pod transit took place. I mean, was it close enough for this to be a remote control transit? If it wasn't, if it was pilot-controlled, then that's an even greater mystery. Who was the pilot, what was he doing and why was he doing it? It just makes no sense at all.'

'Well, Leo, I'm going to go for the first option, because I can just about imagine that one. It was a remote controlled transit, made for an unknown reason. Don't you think that's the most likely option?'

'But what about the damage to the vehicle? Our systems reported severe damage, didn't they? Hull breach – there's nothing worse than that. Why would a remotely-controlled pod transit to a small asteroid, land and then suffer severe damage? It's incomprehensible.'

'Could it have been damaged on landing?'

'Well, I suppose that's remotely possible, but Space vehicles have several safety systems built-in to ensure that can't happen, don't they?'

'OK, Leo, here's the only scenario that fits that. While it was docked at Yggdrasil, the pod somehow had an explosive device planted on board that no-one could defuse. So they decided on the SSP to jettison the pod and send it to an asteroid where the device would explode harmlessly.'

The two men looked at each other gravely, then burst out laughing.

'That's a really good one, Cy. It sounds like the sort of logical game we were forced to play while we were under training. It fits all the facts but, taken within the reality of logical existence, it's absolute rubbish!'

'Well, Leo, I agree with you, it simply doesn't make sense. Even if that crazy logic was right, it still doesn't explain why the transit was made without a Command Report – or, indeed, why there was no Command Report about the mysterious pod fitted with an explosive device that no-one could defuse!'

'Anyway, Cy, let's find out about the position of Yggdrasil around that time. That's something that might be useful to us after we've established the situation on the asteroid.'

The two men turned to their information displays and made the necessary interrogations.

'Look, Cy, this is where it's located now, at the opposite end of this Sector. Now let's check where it was 30 years ago. Ah, yes, SSP Yggdrasil was certainly in this part of the Sector during these years. They had a very big survey job to do around here and, although they moved around a little from time to time to meet the needs of the survey, basically they were always within easy reach of this asteroid. Certainly an escape pod of this type would have been able to transit from the Platform to this asteroid within half a day – easily within range. Also, it's within the range of remote piloting.'

'We'll just note that for future reference, Leo. It will be relevant to our conclusions after the investigative visits we're going to start tomorrow. I think we've done really all we can for the time being, so let's call it a day.'

Leo was reflective. 'I was just thinking. Funny name, isn't it? Yggdrasil? What do you think? Did someone throw a bunch of letters into a bucket and tip them out? And it came out as Yggdrasil?'

'Actually, I raised a query about it,' Cy said. 'Believe it or not, it's actually one of these names from an ancient Earth myth. Northern Europa, I think. It was supposed to be a sort of tree-God or a tree-spirit thing that had its roots in the Earth and its branches in the heavens! These ancient guys had very good imaginations, don't you think?'

'Good question for a team quiz, Cy!'

Laughing, the two men retired to their bunks for the night.

15

The Second Day

Following their usual breakfast, Leo and Cy were soon back in Main Control.

'I'll start the system preparation of Lander Pod A4,' Leo said, settling down at his control position.

Cy nodded. 'And I'll start the sensor sweep to identify the best landing spot for A4. By the look of the terrain we can see, I don't think there will be too much trouble.' He turned to his control console:

'Sensor system activate.'

'Commence sweep scan of facing surface Asteroid AT56G7/89. Identify best landing location for Lander Pod A4 close to escape pod GTN67UV and report.'

Reply: Sweep scan indicates closest
                      suitable landing location for
                      Lander Pod A4 is 54 metres
                      from GTN67UV. Coordinates are
                      transmitted to Lander Pod A4.

'Right, Leo, your landing co-ordinates are input to A4. We're only 54 metres away.'

'Wow, that's close, Cy! Thanks for that. I'll go down to the launch bay to prepare for the transit. I'll DT call you when I'm ready to go and you can join me.'

'Acknowledge.' Cy's DT reply.

Leo left Main Control and made his way to the Launch Bays. Here he carefully donned the equipment he would require, including the special "virtual buddy" sensor equipment that would enable him to take Cy with him. After meticulous checks, he boarded Lander Vehicle A4, which was powered up and ready for the short journey to the asteroid's surface.

Meanwhile, in Main Control, Cy set all systems to automatic and set the Instantaneous Problem Warning. He then entered the virtual pod and plugged himself in. Instantly he was a virtual buddy in the lander with Leo and was ready to accompany him wherever he went on the asteroid.

Within thirty minutes, the Lander Pod, a small, highly efficient vehicle of advanced design, landed smoothly on the asteroid surface, close to the forlorn hulk of the escape pod. Leo looked across the twisted rock of the asteroid towards the escape pod.

'Look at that, Cy, the hatch ladder is down. That answers one of the questions we were discussing last night. This vehicle arrived with personnel inside. It must have been piloted here from SSP Yggdrasil. Then the personnel who were in here must have suited up and disembarked. This means that either they are outside the vehicle and lying around here someplace, or they're back inside the vehicle. I think we need to establish that right away. Either way, it's difficult to say how much of them will be left but the suits should be pretty intact. They're very robust.'

'Can you remember, Leo? How many people are the GTN67UV escape pods designed to carry? That will be useful to know.'

'Just a minute, Cy. I'll check my PAC – the answer is two. There are two bunks on board and it carries two suits.'

'Right. So we're looking for one or two bodies, aren't we?'

'I guess we are.' Leo was sombre. He suited up and left the lander by its air-lock. Soon, he and the virtual Cy stood beside the derelict vehicle. 'This is in really bad condition,' Leo said, touching the eroded metal hull with a heavily gloved hand, 'but it's still upright, standing stable in its landing position. There's no damage to the legs and the ship has adjusted itself to be level. So I think we can say this was a proper and routine landing.'

The ladder was still intact and Leo began climbing. Soon he was beside the outer hatch. 'Obviously there's no power in the vehicle. I'll use my suit power to open this.' With a grating sigh, the hatch opened hesitantly. Leo and Cy entered the lock and closed the outer hatch.

Cy checked some dials. 'No atmosphere, Leo. Gone long ago, obviously. You'll need to stay in suit.'

The inner hatch opened slowly and they entered the inside of the vehicle which was dark, still and freezing. Leo shone a powerful light around. 'There it is, Cy, the origin of the Distress Signal. It does look like an obsolete PAC with some sort of hand-built signal booster connected to it. Why didn't they just use the standard Distress Signal equipment?'

'Maybe it's non-operational, Leo. Let's check it.' He opened a panel. 'Leo – the Distress Signal equipment is gone! Removed! That's why they didn't use it.'

'And look at this, Cy, the personnel who were on this flight tried to fix the vehicle. You see how a number of panels are open and equipment dismantled. I wonder what they were trying to do.'

'Make it work again, I should imagine,' Cy replied laconically.

'Very clever!' Leo smiled, 'but I reckon you're right. It seems to be the vehicle control panels that are dismantled.' He looked again. 'Furthermore, a lot of what is inside is non-standard. I don't recognise these control units – and, I see they have been working on the communications packs, too.' He examined some more panels and gave a low whistle. 'Hey Cy, look at this! This fits with your Distress Signal discovery. All the essential communication units are missing.'

'Maybe you should do a viability scan and check whether there have been other modifications made to the control systems,' Cy said. 'I recall that a lot of equipment has to be reached from external bays. We can do a comprehensive viability scan on all that without going outside.'

They waited while their scanners did their work. 'You're absolutely right, Cy. Most of the control equipment in the externals bays has been completely modified. The scan reports that most equipment is modified or improvised. No details or specification can be given.' He shook his head. 'How strange! I wonder why?'

'Listen, Leo. I've just worked something out. If a lot of the control equipment is completely non-standard – our scan has just told us that – where is all the standard equipment that should be in this vehicle?'

'There doesn't seem to be any,' Leo replied.

'That's exactly right!' Cy was triumphant. 'There never was any! This vehicle was flown on remote control. The personnel inside were just passengers – or should I say, prisoners!'

'Hmm,' Leo was thoughtful as he examined the evidence. 'Looks like someone sent these people on a Space journey without a return ticket,' he said finally. 'And they spiked their communications, too,' he added.

'Do a viability scan on the rest of the vehicle, Leo. We've covered most of it but there may be more to find.'

Their eyes widened when they saw the results of the scan. 'Cy, the scan reports that the engines have blown up and that's what ruptured the hull. The report identifies a heat-detonated explosive device as the reason for the explosion!'

They were both silent as they took in the evidence they had gathered. Finally, Cy said: 'So it seems that these people were sent to this asteroid on a remote control transit, in a vehicle with no local control system – or, should I say – in a vehicle which had had the local control system deliberately removed. Then, it looks like our prisoners attempted to reconstruct the control system. We don't know how successful that was but they were certainly able to start the engines, unaware that they had been booby-trapped. Then the explosive device was activated, ending their attempt to leave here. However, by a miracle, they survived the destruction. Afterwards, they managed to construct a Distress Signal transmitter but the signal was so weak and narrow that it has not been picked up until now.'

Both men became silent again as they assimilated what they had discovered.

Finally, Leo spoke. 'Surely that awful story you have just recounted cannot really have happened, Cy? Surely no-one space-side would ever do such a terrible thing? It's against everything we believe. We are all trained to do everything we can to preserve life, aren't we?'

'Yes, Leo, of course we are. Let's hope there's another explanation. Anyway, I suspect you and I are going to find out. I reckon that is exactly what RS Command will direct us to do, so we better gather as much information as possible while we're here.'

Leo shook himself and looked round. 'OK, Cy, we need to search the pod and the surrounding area to find the bodies of these people, or what little remains of them.'

They soon found what they were looking for in the sleeping compartment of the pod. One body lay supine on a couch inside a fully closed suit. Leo tried to look through the helmet visor but it was impossible to see through; full obscuration had been enabled. Leo straightened up and they both stood silently, their thoughts racing as they tried to imagine the agony that this unfortunate man must have felt as the power that kept him alive leached away and the blackness of unconsciousness and death overcame him.'

Leo gulped and then said: 'What do you think we ought to do, Cy? Should we open up the suit and find out who is inside?' They both pondered this for some time.

'I think not,' Cy said finally. 'There will be all sorts of clues in there and it would be much better if this was handled by a forensic specialist. That could be done on SSP Yggdrasil; they'll have every facility there. There may be a fully intact frozen body in there or it may just be a heap of clothes and bones. It all depends on the conditions in here at the time of death and subsequently. We really need an expert to work on this.'

Leo nodded. 'I agree with that analysis and course of action. You can return to our vehicle, Cy. I'll close up here and join you. We'll report our interim findings to Command and, while they formulate their response, we'll review the situation and see what we have discovered and deduced so far.'

'OK, Leo. I'll exit virtual and prepare to receive you in the dock in due course.'

'Fine, Cy. I just want to do one final thing. I'll switch off the PAC Distress Signal and its booster. It's done its work, hasn't it? It was a really brave attempt.'

'Yes it was. I wish fervently it had got us here earlier. I wish we could have rescued him. How I wish I could get my hands on who did this to him...'

A report of their findings had been sent to RS Command. Now the two men sat side by side in the Control Area. Cy started the review. 'OK, there's no doubt that the rescue pod made a successful landing on the asteroid, arriving without damage. On the evidence we've seen, there was only one person on board and his remains are lying in the suit in the bunk. There could have been another person in the vehicle but I doubt it; had there been anyone else, I would have thought they would have chosen to die together in the vehicle when the power finally ran out. Also, I noticed there was another suit stored in the vehicle and I think the standard fitment is for two.'

Leo agreed. 'Ok. Let's review what we learned about the condition of that vehicle. It had been greatly modified. From our superficial examination by viability scan, it could not be controlled by the occupant. He was just a passenger inside. What appears to have been done is against Intergalactic Law. Regarding the standard Distress Signal Equipment, we noted that the whole system had been totally removed too. That, too, is against Intergalactic Law. Somehow our passenger inside eventually managed to build a system to transmit a low-power Distress Signal with only a narrow beam. I think that explains why we received nothing on our last pass through this sector fourteen years ago. Or, maybe the improvised equipment was still under construction.'

'That's a good summary, Leo, make sure you record it. Now let's think about the escape pod. We know something about it from the records. We know it was allocated to SSP Yggdrasil within a year of its manufacture. We've never visited that particular facility, have we?'

'No we haven't, although we have communicated with it once or twice over the years. It's the principal facility in Delta Region and by far the biggest SSP in the Command. It's usually located in one of the twenty sectors around here. We know that it is a very large and complex facility with a considerable number of staff always on board—thousands, I believe. Its main function is survey coordination.'

'So, Leo, if they lost one of their many escape pods, which they most certainly have, why don't we know about it? Why isn't there a report? And, more important still, how can they have lost one of their crew without anyone knowing about it? Why isn't there a report of that?'

The two men were silent. 'It doesn't add up,' Leo said finally, 'it's against all the Space-side Laws.'

Just then, they both felt the familiar sensation of communication from their Central Coordinator System:

RS Command Message received.
Classification P2b. Encoding XCB.

Cy programmed the decoder and they entered their inputs. After a brief pause, the message was displayed. After the addressee identifiers, it read:

You are required to search asteroid AT56G7/89 and recover any other victims/human remains intact. When search complete, capture derelict vehicle GTN67UV and deceased in current condition. Inform SSP Yggdrasil you are joining. Advise them of situation. Assume command of comprehensive investigation with RS Command authority Level Xray7. Repeat assume RS Command authority Level Xray7. While present on SSP Yggdrasil, you

will wear Xray7 shoulder and chest rank flashes at all times. Rank flashes are obtained from your Secure Store under Authority CX7/134Z. On SSP Yggdrasil, you are to establish facts and report to Command earliest with full details.
This is a Priority One investigation.

Leo and Cy looked at each other. 'So it's the lion's den for us?' said Cy.

'Looks like it! But with Xray7 authority, we should be OK. We'll outrank everybody on the Platform, including the Commanding Officer. We were all briefed on this at the end of our training, weren't we? I never thought we would get to use such an elevated rank!'

'Neither did I. But I suppose we need real authority to be thorough and meticulous. It's really essential we establish the complete truth of all this.'

'That's right, we owe it to Command and we certainly owe it to that poor victim down there. We'll make sure he gets justice, won't we?'

'We will. Unfortunately, that won't get him his life back.' As he spoke, Cy brushed tears of anger and sadness from his eyes.

16

The Fourteenth Day

The previous twelve days had been extremely busy for Cy and Leo. Firstly, they had deployed a number of robots to the surface of the asteroid, each one with a comprehensive battery of sensor systems to search meticulously for any other human remains. They thought it most likely that any such remains would be contained within a spacesuit – although all other possibilities had to be covered, too. Every square metre of the asteroid surface had been investigated. This had been far from easy, because the extremely fissured surface made movement very difficult for the robots.

On a number of occasions, Leo or Cy had to visit the asteroid to help their robots negotiate the most difficult terrain. Indeed, several parts of the asteroid were so steeply ridged and fissured that they had to be examined by portable hand sensors operated manually. However, both agreed that no part of the asteroid should remain unexamined.

The results were consistently negative and, eventually, they accepted that there were no other human remains on the asteroid. Finally, they had conducted a very detailed search of the escape pod, to assure themselves that no other bodies were concealed anywhere in the vehicle. This, too, produced nothing.

Now they were ready to prepare the escape pod for its capture by their ship and its subsequent journey to SSP Yggdrasil. Cy spent several days on the asteroid, strengthening the structure of the escape pod at appropriate points so that there was no chance of a breakup when it came time to capture it. When required, Leo came to join him on the asteroid as his virtual buddy. However, there was plenty of preparation necessary aboard the IRS vehicle and Leo was kept very busy on these tasks, too; capturing a damaged or derelict vehicle is always a tricky affair, even with a relatively small vehicle like an escape pod. Eventually, Cy was able to communicate:

'Attention Leo. I think I've sealed everything here and made all the connections. Request you run full tests on the links. I'll stand by here until all the tests show green.'

'OK Cy, test sequence will be able to start in three minutes.'

Sometime later, Leo was able to report an "all-green" situation and Cy was able to re-board his lander and return to the IRS vehicle. They confirmed to each other that they would start the capture procedure the following day.

'Right now, we should complete a final review of what we've done,' Leo said, 'because once we leave here with the escape pod, we certainly won't be coming back!'

'I think I can agree wholeheartedly with that,' Cy smiled, 'this has been a real slog but, of course, it had to be done. Despite the rather sorry state of the escape pod, I'm confident about the capture. All the contact points I established down there were really firm.'

The two men now turned to the details of the capture plan they had formulated days before. Leo brought up all the details on their displays.

'So let's just go through this one last time, Cy. We know about the dangers of fragility but we plan to apply our capture force very gently. All the strain calculations indicated that the pod should detach without rupture.'

Cy indicated the plan stages on the display. 'First, we plan to move in as close as possible and then ramp up our power in very small increments. Once the escape pod is securely in our field, we should be clear for a departure. The navigator says it is a four day transit to arrive in the SSP Yggdrasil area but that's at maximum speed. I think we should transit at a lower speed so that we don't put too much strain on the escape pod. So maybe we should plan for six days. Obviously we'll advise Yggdrasil before we start and warn them of the facilities we are likely to need. I have a feeling we might have a few authority problems with this. These remote space crews become pretty insular and Command staff rarely visit. So they become "laws unto themselves" as the old saying goes. Also, I reckon they're going to find our questions very difficult to answer. But whatever happens, we'll get to the bottom of this. SP Command will want everything sorted out properly. Incidentally, for the sake of our dead comrade down there, I certainly want that too. I feel very strongly about this.' He paused. 'You know, I feel furious about this. That life wasted – and so cruelly, too.'

Leo nodded. 'I'm totally with you on that but we must stay calm. It's what we have been trained to do. We need to be totally professional.'

Cy smiled gently. 'Aren't we always?' he enquired.

The following day found Leo at the main transit control desk, starting to manoeuvre the vehicle closer to the surface of the asteroid. The altitude indicators decreased steadily until they recorded the vehicle at several hundred metres from the surface, with the escape pod directly below.

Both men were in operational DT mode. 'Cy, We are at minimum altitude and fully stable. The distance from the escape pod is optimal for the start of the capture procedure. Confirm when you are ready to initiate the capture sequence.'

'Check. I am setting minimum extension for the field envelope and will monitor carefully.' The field envelope, a powerful electronic matrix, began to extend very slowly towards the escape pod below. Of course the envelope had no visible entity but its progress could be seen on special monitor screens. The two men were silent as they observed the development of the process, keeping a very close eye on the readings from the strain gauges affixed to the escape pod below. At his control position, Leo constantly made sure that the vehicle was holding its exact position, because they wanted to make sure that the extension of the field envelope was completely smooth. Meanwhile, on several occasions, Cy judged it necessary to slow the progress of the field envelope even further as a strain gauge reading gave him some concern. After several hours, Cy reported on the situation. 'Field envelope nearing completion. Expect 100% formation shortly.'

The passage of more time was interrupted by a soft chime and a voice message.

"Report: Field envelope is 100% complete, stable and locked. Phase Two of the operation may commence."

Cy and Leo agreed on a break from the intensity of their work before they started the capture phase. The escape pod was now completely surrounded by a closed field envelope and this force would be used to detach and lift the pod away from the asteroid; thereafter, the pod would be held secure as the IRS vehicle transited across Space. Placing their vehicle on auto-stable, they both sat down with a steaming coffee.

'Do you remember our capture training, Cy?' Leo had returned to Voice Mode.

'Well, I do remember our trainers arranging that our capture would break free from the field envelope that we had extended around it!'

Leo laughed. 'That's what I remember, too! I hear that they do it to all the trainees. They say it's to prepare you for emergencies but we reckoned they were just being nasty, didn't we?'

'Well, we would've thought that, wouldn't we? You remember how we hated that Chief Trainer?'

'I suppose that's inevitable. We were pretty tense after all they had thrown at us. However, it did work, didn't it? It certainly taught us to be careful – and, by that, I mean really meticulous, don't I?'

'Yes, Leo, they knew what they were doing – but it certainly wasn't pleasant for us!'

The two men sat quietly with their thoughts, always easy and relaxed in each other's company. After ten minutes or so, Cy rose to his feet: 'shall we get started, Leo?'

'Yes, let's.'

They returned to their control areas, refreshed and ready.

(DT Mode) 'Cy, I confirm vehicle is fully stabilised and ready for full capture procedure.'

Cy examined the data on his screens carefully. 'All looks ready here. The field envelope is complete, robust and stable. I am engaging capture power – now.'

A vibration was felt through their vehicle as the beginning of a force was applied to the escape pod below. Their screens confirmed the level of the slowly-increasing power. At first, there was no reaction from below but then their sensors detected the beginning of movement. The delicate procedure continued, every reaction of the escape pod meticulously observed by both men in the IRS vehicle. The procedure to detach the pod from the asteroid took over an hour, because its grasping feet had to be persuaded to loosen their grip. Eventually, the close-focus screen showed all four feet had detached and were lifted just clear of the asteroid surface. Then, still very slowly, the escape pod started to withdraw from its rocky host and move towards the IRS vehicle above. Once the pod was well clear of the asteroid surface, it became possible to increase the lift speed to some degree; however, every metre of lift was still carefully observed. After two patient hours, the escape pod had been brought into the powerful and encompassing capture field of the IRS J87V vehicle. Here, without the necessity of tethers or bindings, it would be held in the firm yet delicate embrace that is an enveloping electronic capture field.

Cy locked the escape pod into position: 'Capture accomplished. Success rate shows 100%. All sensors have parameters within optimum tolerances.'

'Good capture, Cy. After we power down here, let's go and eat. Afterwards, we need to transmit to SSP Yggdrasil and let them know the good news that we'll soon be on our way!'

The transmission to SSP Yggdrasil had been formulated:

Priority:	RS1 Personal for CC01 SSP Yggdrasil: Copy to RS Command
From:	IRS48563 Class J87V crew RP766 Cyrus L Funte / Leonardo J Granvic
Message (encoded VB6):	dated UY5694 Day 161
Heading:	Arrival of IRS Vehicle: Special Investigation Priority One.
Subject:	Faint/intermittent Distress Signal received location asteroid AT56G7/89.Origin derelict escape pod type GTN67UV with one crew deceased inside. The pod and deceased have been captured securely by IRS48563.
Information:	Pod GTN67UV Serial GTN36716XT stationed at SSP Yggdrasil UY5660. No record missing crew or vehicle lost reports in Central Records. Please check your records.

Action:	RS Command has directed IRS crew RP766 to conduct Priority One investigation repeat Priority One investigation. Expect arrive SSP Yggdrasil Day 167. Require secure docking and full secure facilities for immediate start of investigation.
Special Factors:	Investigators (crew RP766) will be operating under Command Authority Xray7 (RS Command directive copied). At all times, Xray7 rank flashes will be worn by investigators. Please brief your staff. Your personal cooperation is required. .

{Ends}

The two men sat back in their seats. 'I reckon that should do the trick,' said Cy.

'Yes, we're looking for maximum cooperation – and we had better get it!' responded Leo.

Cy nodded. 'OK, we're ready. We'll set course first thing tomorrow. Let's call it a day.'

Both men headed for their bunks.

The following morning, they settled down to familiar tasks at their control positions.

'0600. Time to get started on our journey,' Leo said. 'With the escape pod in capture, I'll set us at 60% cruising speed. We don't want too much strain on the pod. We've given ourselves six days to transit to Yggdrasil and the important thing is to arrive with the pod in good condition. By the way, is there any reply from Yggdrasil?'

Cy checked. 'Nothing,' he said shortly. Leo grunted.

Leo's hands moved deftly across the control panel as he locked the navigator on to SSP Yggdrasil. After checking the data carefully, he handed over control to the Auto-Transit System:

{DT Command to ATS} 'Execute transit to SSP Yggdrasil. Build to 60% speed and maintain.'

They felt the familiar acceleration. Cy checked and confirmed that the escape pod was held securely in the capture field and noted that all was well.

As the two men relaxed into their seats, Leo said: 'Cy, we need to get the Yggdrasil personnel lists from Command. Might be an idea to get both the current list and the list from 30 years ago. We need to know who was on the Platform when the escape pod "disappeared". We can run a full analysis on the lists and find out the variations.'

'That's good thinking, Leo. That will be an essential piece of information. It's better we should get it from Command. Then we'll know it's correct. Though I think maybe we will ask CCO1 on Yggdrasil for a personnel list – then we can check if it's the same. If it isn't, we will want to know why! That could be a very useful starting-point for us, couldn't it?'

'Mm,' Leo nodded thoughtfully, 'I like that approach – could be very useful. Meanwhile, on the journey, we can have a good look at the lists – especially the senior staff, eh?'

Cy nodded in agreement.

The personnel lists soon arrived.

'Look at this!' Leo gasped, 'I had no idea that these large platforms carried so many people! There are about 8,500 names here! What can 8,500 men be doing out here in Space!'

'It does seem a lot, Leo, doesn't it? But they must need them. We can have a look at the various functions and maybe it'll start to fit into place – at least to some degree.'

Hours later, after they had pored over the lists and asked their PACs to rationalise the structure on Yggdrasil, it was beginning to become clearer.

'Well, this shows us there is a huge range of functions on the Platform. And, of course, you need a very large supporting infrastructure to look after everyone and everything. I must say, I'm beginning to wonder how they can run the Platform with so few people!' Now Leo was grinning.

'OK,' Cy said, 'we'll make you the personnel structure expert, my friend. You're obviously becoming very knowledgeable about Yggdrasil!'

'Well, I do admit I know quite a lot more about it than I did a few hours ago,' Leo admitted. 'I'll just make sure that these analyses are recorded for our future use. Tomorrow, we can start looking at individuals, starting, of course, at the top – no less than CCO1, the Chief Commanding Officer himself!'

'So, Cy, here we have the CCO1, Admiral Feltham Sarfeld. He's a late middle-aged man of around 120 and he's been in charge of Yggdrasil for nearly 60 years! Gosh! That's a very long time, isn't it?'

'Well, as you know, Yggdrasil is considered to be the Flagship of Survey, easily the biggest and most important platform out here. I suppose after Yggdrasil, you can only "fly a desk" at Command, don't you think? Maybe Admiral Sarfeld doesn't want that. Maybe he wants to be "King Bee" for as long as possible.'

'Yes, that might be useful to keep in mind, Cy.'

'Look, Leo!' Cy's voice was excited. 'They've got Maynard Gorton on the Platform! He's STC1 and a Full Commander. He's in change of all things scientific and technical. Now there's a famous man! He designed many Space vehicles, including most of this ship and the whole of the escape pod. He's really famous. And look, he's been on Yggdrasil for 33 years! That's another strange thing, is it not? Why keep a brilliant man like that out in Space? Shouldn't he be heading up a leading research activity somewhere on Earth?'

'Yes, that does seem a bit peculiar. But maybe we're underestimating the importance of SSP Yggdrasil? Maybe

Gorton is going to take command of Yggdrasil when Sarfeld leaves? After all, I doubt they would want to keep Sarfeld there forever, wouldn't you think?'

'Mm,' Cy was thoughtful. 'I still feel it's a bit peculiar. Gorton is quite young, you know. He's only 60. And Space Commanding Officers are usually conflict-experienced – which Gorton is not. However, I suppose we're running out of battle-scarred people?'

'I think you're right, Cy. Anyway, it will be very interesting to meet Gorton.'

Leo continued to scan the list of senior officers. 'None of the other names mean anything to me, Cy. There are quite a few officers at Commander level (including Gorton) and, of course, even more at Sub-Commander. I think our first focus has to be on the technical people – those who look after and service the escape pods. We know they have definitely lost an escape pod – that's it in our capture field back there – so how have they been able to account for that?'

Cy agreed but added: 'Yes. At the same time we'll need to assemble a forensic team to examine the pod and the deceased in it. So Medical will be an early port of call for us. I see the Head of Medical is a Surgeon-Commander Sangyar. I've never heard of him. He will need to supply a pathologist. At the same time we'll need to get together with the Human Resourcers; they will need to delve into their records and explain what happened to our deceased friend once we know who he is.'

'Then there are all the questions surrounding the modification of the escape pod so that it could not be piloted from the vehicle itself. An electronics Space engineer of considerable skill would be required to do these modifications. We need to know who did it – and why.'

'These are very important questions, Leo. I think we'll need to look towards the more research-orientated scientific and technical people for that.'

'There's something else, too, Cy. When you think about it, these modifications to the escape pod, removing pilot control from that poor man inside, must have been done secretly.

The whole Platform could not have known about it. What was being done was highly illegal, so it must have been done in strict secrecy – and that means security must have been involved. That means guards and their officers.'

They both sat silently for a while. Then Leo began to make notes.

'Right, Cy, here's our plan of action: First we dock, meet CCO1 and make sure the vehicle and the escape pod is secure and properly guarded. I'm not leaving the vehicle until I am absolutely sure about that. Then we set up the forensic work – forensic engineers to ascertain what has been done to the escape pod and medical pathologists to autopsy the deceased. At least one of us must be present when all this is going on. Once all that information has been collected, we need to set up meetings to establish the facts about the deceased and the facts about the lost escape pod. Obviously, the investigation will lead us along other paths and we'll follow them as appropriate. I reckon all this is going to take a great deal of time but we know that we must be completely thorough.'

'OK, Leo, record that as our interim plan of action. We'll start with that and modify it as we go along. It's really difficult to imagine how all this is going to play out, isn't it? I mean, so much of it is incomprehensible.'

Leo nodded gravely. 'Yes, Cy, I agree. We'll just have to see how it goes.'

Six days later, it was obvious they were closing rapidly with SSP Yggdrasil. Starting as a tiny pinpoint of light on their visual screens, the image of the Platform was now growing rapidly.

'Let's hope these guys have paid close attention to our requirements,' Cy said grimly.

'Well, we never got an acknowledgement. But I'm sure they must have got our transmission; otherwise it would have bounced back to us.'

'They're probably chasing around trying to find out what happened,' Cy said. After all, this happened a long time ago. On the other hand, you don't lose a crew member and an escape pod and not notice it!'

Leo nodded. 'Well, that's why we're here – and that's why we're arriving as Xray7s. RS Command obviously wants this investigated fully. There could be incompetence or criminality here. In fact there could be both.' He stood up decisively. 'Time to get these Xray7 rank flashes from the Secure Store. We need to wear these flashes all the time we are on the Platform. They should guarantee maximum cooperation – I certainly hope they do, because we don't want to waste time arguing with people.'

'Now that we're getting close, we need to talk about our general strategy,' Cy said. 'Do you remember the training we received on investigation situations? When we wear the Xray7 flashes it boosts us to very high rank – we become temporary RS Command Directors G1. We need to remember to act like them. Absolute formality at all times. Refusing to take "no" for an answer. Any insoluble problems to be reported immediately to RS Command – though I hope it never comes to that.'

'Yes, I do remember the training. I suppose I thought I'd never need to use it. How wrong was that?' Leo grinned broadly. 'Anyway, we'll do our best. It'll be a big comedown when we're finished, won't it? From Xray7 back to the humble RP776!'

'Not so humble, Leo. Just remember we are the "cream" of Space-side. They told us that often enough!'

'OK, I'll go find the rank flashes in the Secure Store.'

Leo was absent for some time but eventually returned with the rank flashes. 'Wow,' he grinned, 'What a process! I had to identify myself formally, submit all my ID details, present my card and enter the Command Authority Code before the system would even think of delivering them. Here they are, a shoulder and chest set for each of us. Let's put them on and see what we look like!'

They fastened the bright red and gold rank flashes in the shape of the RS Command Logo to each shoulder and to the left breast of their tunics.

'Now then Leo, do you really feel three metres tall?' Cy joked.

'Actually, I do feel a little different. I feel a new pressure. I suppose that's what we're supposed to feel?'

'I imagine so, because I can feel it too.' They looked at each other unsmilingly. Finally, Leo spoke quietly. 'We must get to the bottom of this – and I feel sure we will.' They nodded.

Cy looked at the visual screen. 'We're getting pretty close now, Leo. I think it's time to send an arrival message. We'll ask that we are met by CCO1 himself and state that we want an initial meeting with him and his advisors. We'll also ask for the escape pod to be guarded. We don't want any funny business there.'

'That's right, Cy. We should start as we mean to go on. Anyway, the sooner we start the investigation, the sooner we find out the truth – and I'm pretty keen to find that out.'

'OK, I'll get busy on the message.'

Priority:	RS1. Personal for CCO1 SSP Yggdrasil: Copy RS Command.
From:	IRS48563 Class J87V crew
Message:	(encoded HN9) UY5694 Day 168.
Information:	L.Granvic/C.Funte operating as Command Investigators under Xray7 Authority, repeat Xray7 Authority, arriving with GTN36716XT captured. Arrival in your area estimated lapse time 3.75 hours. Will delay docking until 0600 tomorrow Day 168.

Action: We require to be met personally by CC01 at secure guarded
docking area for immediate
initial meeting on Command
Investigation Priority One. IRS
vehicle and captured Escape Pod
to be put under strict guard
24hours to guarantee subsequent
uncontaminated forensic action.

{Ends}

Three hours later, a message was received from SSP Yggdrasil:

Priority: Routine for IRS48563

From: Navigation Central,
SSP Yggdrasil

Message: We have scanned and identified
your vehicle and note you are
on course for SSP Yggdrasil. We
assume you intend to dock. Can
you confirm your identity and
state your intentions? I remind
you that Command Instructions
require you to communicate
with your destination at least
two hours before arrival. Why
have you not obeyed Command
Instructions? Investigation
will commence when you arrive.
Duty Docking Controller SSP
Yggdrasil.

{Ends}

'OK, Cy, I'll get on to this right away. It seems we're going to
have problems here.' He addressed an immediate

message to the Duty Docking Controller. After headers, the text read:

> For your information I repeat Priority RS1 message sent 3 hours ago.
>
> {Message repeated}
>
> In addition to our mandatory requirements stated above, we will wish to investigate why a Priority RS1 communication from Command Xray7 officers was ignored after reception by SSP Yggdrasil. We will require that expla-nation on arrival. Please comply fully with our orders and com-municate docking procedure as soon as possible. L Granvic Xray7 Officer.
> {Ends}

The reply came almost immediately:

> Set Automatic Docking Channel 39. You will dock in S47B. Duty Docking Controller.
>
> (Ends}

Cy and Leo looked at each other.

'A bit laconic, wouldn't you say,' Leo said with raised eyebrows.

Cy nodded. 'Let's hope they're a bit better on the Platform than this message would imply. Let's go and rest. I suspect tomorrow will be a long and tiring day.'

17

The Twenty-second Day

It was early in the morning when the IRS vehicle started its docking manoeuvre. Leo and Cy were pleased to observe that Dock S47B was remote from the main parts of the Platform.

'So far, so good,' Cy observed, 'at least it looks a remote dock. Just what we want.'

Under automatic control, the vehicle entered the dock smoothly and slipped gently into the docking securing system.

'We'll just maintain the capture field for the time being,' Leo observed, 'until we review what the situation is. The escape pod will require careful handling and we need to ensure that it arrives in the right place for the forensic examinations.'

'OK, Leo. Capture Field maintained.'

Leo gave a number of DT instructions to the Central Coordinator: 'Power down propulsion to idle standby. All systems switch to "Condition Docked". Pick up external power and acquire. Equalise atmospheres and open hatches. Go to full manual mode.'

Both men unstrapped and stood up, instantly feeling the heavier drag of Yggdrasil's gravity field.

'We'll feel the gravity a bit strange at first but we'll soon get used to it,' Cy commented.

They both made their way to the hatch and, rather heavily, climbed down to the deck below. To their surprise, the large dock was completely empty; there was no-one there to greet them.

Leo shouted, 'Anyone here?' No reply. 'Hello!' he shouted again, more loudly. Still no reply, no movement anywhere.

'HELLO!' he shouted as loudly as he could, his voice echoing around the vast volume of the dock.

'OK, OK!' A tinny, petulant voice. 'Give me a break! I can't be everywhere at once, you know. I have to run all the operations of this facility alone. And I've had to come out all this way because, for some unknown reason, you guys want to be remote. So, OK, here I am. What's the big panic? What do you want?' A small man dressed in crumpled overalls had appeared from a small door at the side of the dock. He was carrying a data recorder pad. Leo waited until the man had approached them.

'Who are you?' he asked quietly.

'Who do you think I am? I'm the Duty Receiver, come to collect your data. So how about letting me have it so that I can get on with my work!'

Leo stepped close to the man and read his name badge.

'Listen, Dock-Sgt Rancu, do you not know anything about our arrival?'

The man looked at them both quizzically and then glanced at their vehicle. 'IRS vehicle, nice model, so I guess you are RPs. Pretty cushy job, if you can get it. So what about the data?'

'Mr Rancu, do you recognise our rank badges?' Cy's voice, also quiet.

The man peered at the flashes. 'Well, no. Never seen anything like them. Pretty nice, though. Some new IRS badges, maybe?'

Cy and Leo looked at each other. 'Oh dear,' Cy muttered.

'Mr Rancu, scan the badges, please.'

'OK, if you insist... what's this? Command Xray7s. What's...' the man's voice faded. After a long pause, he stammered, 'Listen, guys, is this a spoof? Are you making a joke, here?'

'No.' Leo said.

Through a long series of increasingly senior staff, eventually the Platform Duty Officer had been called. It was some time before he arrived. He proved to be a young fresh-faced Lieutenant.

'What's all this about, men,' he said crisply, bursting in through the door. 'This had better be good because I was on my rest break on Level-7 and I don't take kindly to being disturbed and dragged all the way here.'

The Duty Receiver stepped forward. 'I'm extremely sorry for disturbing you, Sir, but these men have just arrived...'

'Just a minute, please.' Cy interrupted and addressed the officer crisply, 'Lieutenant, you should have been expecting us.'

The young Lieutenant swung around and spoke in a sneering tone. 'Oh really? Why should I have been...' His voice cut off as he processed Cy's shoulder rank. His eyes bulged and his mouth dropped open.

'Yes, you are right, Lieutenant. We have Xray7 rank and we are Command Investigators.'

The young man was stunned. 'But, Sir,' he stammered, 'As Xray7s you outrank everyone on the Platform, even CCO1 himself!'

'That is correct, Lieutenant.' Cy's voice was crisp. 'Will you please arrange for a communication to CCO1, asking him to join us here in this dock as soon as possible?'

It had taken over an hour and many voice communications, but CCO1 and his entourage of senior officers now stood in docking area S47B. It was a frozen tableau. One group of men standing motionless and rigid, glaring furiously towards another group of men standing some distance away, not far from the docked IRS vehicle. This virtual suspension of time had occurred after CCO1's incredibly bellicose entrance:

'You there! What is the meaning of this outrage?' An apoplectic bellow made at the very top of his voice.

Time was nudged into action again as Leo spoke DT to Cy: 'One to one, I think?'

'Yes.' A motionless Cy's response.

'Admiral Sarfeld?' Leo had glided across the deck and now stood squarely in front of CCO1. 'I am Command Investigator Granvic. I need to speak to you privately, right now, Sir. Here in the dock, where we cannot be overheard. Will you please follow me?'

Leo turned on his heel and walked away towards the IRS vehicle. CCO1 snorted and turned to his entourage. 'Call a guard detachment. Tell them we have two men here who need to be arrested and put in irons. Meanwhile, I'll keep this one talking and hear what he has to say.' Pompously, he strutted after Leo. They stopped near the IRS vehicle, well out of earshot of the others.

'Look, whoever you are, what do you think you are doing?' CCO1's tone was one of pent-up fury – his most intimidating persona. 'I guarantee you will be very sorry about this because I have a guard detachment coming and you will be arrested. I will order your interrogation at the harshest level and we will soon discover what all this is about. I have never been treated so disrespectfully in my...'

Leo interrupted. 'Listen, Sir. My name is Leonardo Granvic. Four days ago, I sent you a personal message, Priority RS1, informing you of our transit to you and telling you why we were coming...'

'You know what, boy? You're an idiot! Do you think I can possibly deal with all the messages the Platform receives? I'm extremely busy with strategic matters and...'

'Sir,' Leo interrupted again. 'There's something you need to understand immediately.'

'Oh yes?' CCO1's tone was bitterly sarcastic, 'What might that be?'

'My colleague and I (he pointed to Cy), we outrank you. As you can see from our rank badges, we are Command Xray7s which, as you know, is a much more senior rank than Admiral. Now, listen to me carefully, please. Although you are a subordinate rank, my colleague and I will address you as "Sir" when other members of your staff are present, acknowledging that you are CCO1 here. You will address us as "Investigator Granvic" and "Investigator Funte".' Before you take any further action, I recommend strongly that you read my RS1 message which contains an initial briefing on our reasons for being here. Then we will be able to discuss the way forward.'

CCO1's face was becoming increasingly white with fury as Leo spoke. Finally, he spoke in a strangled whisper. 'You have no right to speak to me like this. I refuse to comply. I will send a message to Command insisting on your immediate removal.'

Leo sighed. 'If you do that, Sir, I will advise Command of your gross insubordination and recommend your immediate removal from the Platform with Space Court charges to follow. I know that Command will implement my recommendations.'

The silence that followed these exchanges was broken by the commotion of the guard detachment arriving. The guards clattered across the metal deck in their heavy boots but CCO1 held up an imperious hand to stop their progress. Confused, the detachment came to a halt, cannoning into each other as they did so.

As CCO1 opened his mouth to speak, his gaze focussed over Leo's shoulder and he froze immediately, his expression turning to astonishment tinged with fear. Leo glanced around and found that CCO1 was looking at the battered escape pod, still held securely in the IRS vehicle's capture field.

'What is that?' CCO1's voice was barely audible.

'It's the escape pod that we found on a small asteroid at the other end of this Sector. It was transmitting a weak Distress Signal using a boosted PAC.'

CCO1 gulped several times. 'Is there any crew?' he whispered after a long pause.

'One deceased is inside.'

Without a further word, CCO1 turned to walk away, his face a mask of confusion. Leo caught his arm and detained him. 'One moment, Sir, my colleague and I need a Liaison Officer to assist us – someone senior. Someone who will be able to help supply all the requirements for our investigation.'

cco1 looked at him blankly and then nodded before walking off rather unsteadily.

About half an hour later, a large, burly man entered the dock area, approached Leo and Cy and saluted: 'Good morning, Sir,' he said to each in a surprisingly nervous voice, 'cco1 has instructed me to be your Liaison Officer. I'm Commander Grafton Fitch. I'm – ah – in charge of Maintenance here. cco1 says I have to get you anything you want, no matter what or when.'

'Thank you, Mr Fitch. We will be very grateful for your help. I'm Investigator Granvic and this is Investigator Funte.'

'Is there something I can do for you now, Sir?'

'Yes. We want to make an immediate start on the investigation. Would you get us a team of dock engineers? We need to de-capture this escape pod. It can be mounted here in this area and then it needs a Class 1 security fence around it. Will you also organise a security team with a guard detachment always on duty?'

They were surprised when they saw Fitch looking at the escape pod with an odd expression on his face. 'Sir, is this the escape pod you found on the asteroid?' he asked.

'Yes, it is, Mr Fitch.'

'I'll go and organise the engineers and the guards,' Fitch muttered, saluting as he left.

The escape pod had been de-captured and settled on a stout maintenance frame beside the IRS vehicle. Cy had gone on board with several dock engineers who quickly set up bright engineering lighting inside. Then everyone left the pod and Cy placed a series of personal security seals on the hatches. These would signal him if there was any attempt at interference. A Class 1 security fence had been built around the pod with a guard post at the entrance and guards patrolling the exterior of the fence.

'Mr Fitch, will you issue an instruction that no-one, no matter who, is to enter the secure area without the express permission of Investigator Granvic or myself. We will be carrying security monitors at all times and will be in constant touch with the area. We would also like you to be available to us at all times during the day. We will need your help and advice to meet people and make our way around the Platform.'

'Yes, Sir. I will be on standby for you. Meanwhile, I'll see to the security instructions. I will return when that has been done.' Fitch hurried off.

Meanwhile, Leo had been approached by another officer. 'Good morning, Sir,' this man said, saluting smartly. 'I am Major Rathwani. I am responsible for arranging your living accommodation while you are on the Platform and allocating the servants and facilities you need. I assume you will wish to live on the Executive Level with all the other senior officers?'

'What Level is this, Major Rathwani?'

'This is level-3, Sir.'

'And where is the Executive Level?'

'That's on Level-9, Sir.'

'We would like to live on this level, as near to this dock as possible. Is that a problem?'

The man looked slightly worried. 'Er, no, Sir. We can soon install suitable accommodation modules into an appropriate area for you. I shall authorise that to start right away. However, will you eat with the other senior officers in the Executive Dining Room?'

'No, Major, we will eat in our quarters.'

'And servants, Sir?'

'Just robots, please.'

'I'll set all that up for you Sir. It should not take long.'

'Thank you, Major. Will you please ensure we have a link to the Platform Information Database with the highest access clearance?'

'Yes, Sir, I will arrange that with the appropriate authority. If you need other items, please call me. My ID is stored on your PAC. And I am always available.'

A lavish accommodation module had soon been fitted close to the docking area. Leo and Cy had gone to inspect it. It proved to be exceptionally comfortable and spacious. In addition, it contained all the information and communication systems that they needed for their investigative work. Large screens constantly monitored the situation in the dock area, focussed on the escape pod and the security operation around it.

Cy threw himself down on a large couch and poured some coffee for them both.

'We have excellent facilities here, Leo. I think we'll enjoy this. We'll find ourselves quite cramped when we have to return to our IRS vehicle!'

'I suspect we're going to be too busy here to enjoy all this luxury,' Leo retorted, 'but we'll do the best we can, when we can!'

Cy sat forward. 'We've made a good start here, Leo. CCO1 took a bit of sorting out but we half expected that might happen. Anyway, he seems tame enough now and so does our Liaison Officer – but I suspect that, deep down, he's not really the soft cooperative type! However, as long as he performs for us, that's all we need. It might be interesting to check him out on the database.' Cy was silent as he brought up the record. 'Ah, yes. He's been here a long time. Almost as long as Admiral Sarfeld. He came here on promotion to Sub-Commander to be Head of Maintenance in the Science and Technology Division – we know that Gorton's in charge of that. There's no record of further promotion here but I noted he's wearing a Commander's uniform now. Funny that. Because that elevates him to the same level as his boss. That's not usually a good idea, is it?'

Leo finished his coffee. 'Hm. It is odd. We'll just keep an eye on Mr Fitch. Meanwhile, I think our first action is to deal with the body in the escape pod. We can't do any of the engineering investigations until that is dealt with. So I think we need to have a conversation with the top medical man. We need to find out who will do the autopsy.'

Cy turned to the screen. 'Head, Medical. Surgeon-Commander Jomo Sangyar. Let's not waste time and call Fitch to set up an early meeting with this gentleman.'

Several hours had passed. Cy and Leo were meeting with Surgeon-Commander Jomo Sangyar in his office. They had been received respectfully. Cy had given a quick résumé of the events leading to their discovery of the escape pod, their discoveries and the reasons for their presence on the Platform.

'We have a number of linked investigations to make before we report to Command,' Leo continued, 'and the first concerns the circumstances and identity of the unfortunate man who died in the escape pod. The body is in the sleeping compartment of the pod, fully enclosed in a spacesuit. We now require a comprehensive autopsy to establish all the facts about his identity and death. We need your best and most experienced pathologist to carry out the autopsy. Of course, we will be present when it is done.'

'There is no doubt who should carry out the autopsy, Sir,' Head, Medical said. 'Principal-Surgeon Alain Martinez is my lead pathologist. However, there is a problem. He is absent from the Platform at the moment, doing work on an adjacent facility. I will call him and ask him to return as soon as he can.'

Cy and Leo looked at each other. 'That's a little unfortunate,' Cy said, 'but I think we still need to move the body from the escape pod. Can we store it with complete security within your facility, Mr Sangyar?'

'We can certainly do that, Sir. We have a secure room for that purpose. When do you wish the body to be moved?'

'As soon as possible. Today, if we can. We would like to start organising the engineering works as soon as possible.'

'That's fine, Sir. The pod is in Dock S47B on Level-3? I'll send a Retrieval Team down there right away. We will store the body in a hermetically-sealed casket. Would that be satisfactory?'

'Yes, thank you. We will meet your team on Level-3. We need to be present when retrieval is made and we will accompany the body to its storage point in your facility. May I emphasise, Mr Sangyar, that once the body is stored, it is not to be touched without our authorisation. Its storage location will be sealed and not opened again until the time of the autopsy.'

'Yes, Sir, in fact there is only one key to each secure storage unit. I will instruct my staff to give you that key.'

The Retrieval Team of four men arrived in a small truck carrying a capacious lightweight casket. A young man saluted Leo smartly. 'Med-Sgt Staakmni reporting as ordered, Sir.'

Leo and Cy escorted the team through the security entrance. Cy disarmed his seal on the escape pod and operated the release. The hatch grated open slowly. They entered and made their way through the depressing, blackened cabin to the sleeping compartment. Leo slid open the door. The white, Space-suited body lay exactly as they had last seen it on the asteroid. A humanoid form lying in a so-familiar resting pose, seemingly poised for wakefulness yet somehow totally suffused with the finality of death. Here, there was no question, no possibility of life or movement, however slight.

The young man assessed the situation with professionalism. 'I think we had better lift the body still reclining on the sleeping couch mattress,' he said to Cy and Leo. 'That would minimise the possibility of further damage to the deceased. May we proceed, Sir?'

'Please do.' Cy and Leo moved to a corner of the sleeping compartment so that they would not obstruct operations while one member of the Retrieval Team left the room to prepare the large casket to receive the body. Just outside the door, the top of the casket was lifted clear. Then, almost with loving care, the other three men slipped heavily-gloved hands under the crumbling mattress and, on the command of their leader, eased the burden upwards. Within a minute, the body within its spacesuit, still lying on the scorched, ragged mattress, had been fitted snugly into the casket.

'Permission to close up, Sir?'

'Yes, please.'

The lid was refitted and clamped down on soft, airtight seals.

The Retrieval Team had returned to Medical on Level-6. Leo and Cy had followed in their buggy. The truck entered a large door marked "Entrance 6/23B Authorised Personnel Only" and proceeded to drive to the far end of a very long corridor, where it stopped. Here, the Med-Sgt unlocked another, smaller door, identified only by the number 6/307X. Leo and Cy followed closely as the truck moved into a spacious room. The truck stopped and the Sgt alighted, approaching the buggy:

'This is the Category 1 Secure Room of M-facility,' he said. 'I have been instructed to place the casket in Unit MS45C.' He pointed to a matrix of storage units along one wall of the room. 'When I have done so, I will lock the unit and give the sole key to you, Sir.'

'Thank you. Please proceed,' Cy instructed.

A large drawer marked "MS45C" was powered out and the casket slid into it. The press of a button caused the drawer to close smoothly and seal shut. The Med-Sgt turned a key in a small complex lock, withdrew it and handed it to Leo.

'This is the only key, Sir. Only you can open this unit.'

'Thank you, Mr Staakmni.' Leo stored the key in a deep pocket.

The young man smiled gratefully. 'Will you please follow me out, Sir?'

Leo and Cy had returned to their quarters on Level-3 and sat relaxing.

'It's getting rather late,' Cy observed, 'shall I call up Fitch and ask him to arrange a meeting with the top engineers for tomorrow morning. Once we have a team of the right people, we can start the forensic engineering examination of the pod to find out how that vehicle was modified. It might take them quite a while, though. We'll certainly need the best people for this.'

'That's fine, Cy. Let's arrange that for tomorrow.'

A call was made to Fitch. 'I'll arrange a meeting with Head of Construction and Head of Development for tomorrow, Sir. I'll instruct them to bring members of their teams who might be suitable for your purposes.'

'Mr Fitch, could you ask Commander Gorton to attend as well? I think it's about time we met him. He's the Head of Science and Technology, is he not?'

There was silence at the other end. 'Ah... Ah...' Fitch spluttered.

'Is there something wrong, Mr Fitch?'

'Ah, no, Sir... I just choked on something. Sorry. Yes, Sir, I'll ask Commander Gorton to attend.'

'Thanks, Mr Fitch. I think we need not disturb you again today.'

'Meanwhile,' Leo said, 'shall we go along to Equipment Records and ask about our escape pod Serial GTN36716XT. That should produce some interesting information, shouldn't it? I wonder how they will explain its loss.'

They consulted Platform Info and noted that Equipment Records was located on Level-5. They instructed their buggy to take them there.

The Equipment Records room was not large. Data storage does not take up much volume. There was a reception counter with a rather elderly man sitting behind it. His uniform was that of a Sub-Lieutenant. Head down, he was reading intensely and ignored the visitors despite the warning tone that had announced their presence. Leo nudged Cy and pointed to a large display just beside the desk. On it were large pictures of Cy and himself with bold text below explaining that they were Command Investigators of very high rank. Wherever they were encountered, they were to be treated with the utmost respect and nothing was to be withheld from them, no matter the security classification. All staff were to ensure that they were completely familiar with these photographs so that no mistakes could possibly occur. This order was signed by CCO1 and over-marked "Action Priority Red".

After a couple of minutes, Leo said: 'Excuse me...'

Without looking up, the man said: 'Time?'

'1732.' Cy said, after a short pause. 'It says so on the clock on your desk.'

'Just so,' the man said. 'Equipment Records closes at 1730. Pity I can't help you, whatever you want. Come back tomorrow 0930 – we open then – and I'll see if I can fit you in.'

'This is a priority matter.' Leo said calmly. 'We would appreciate your help.'

'Sorry, boys,' the man said, equably enough, 'can't do it. Everyone says it's priority!'

'Yes, but this is Priority Red.'

'Sorry,' the man repeated, still looking down, 'but nothing is Priority Red...' he looked up and looked straight at them with laughing eyes and the widest of grins, '... except for these guys, whoever they are.' He pointed an extended forefinger at the display beside him.

The next moments became a fascinating scene of slow-motion transformation, carried out with impressive precision. First, the broad grin faded very slowly from the man's face, imposing a mask of utter seriousness where there had been high good humour before. At the same time, the extended forefinger was joined slowly by a thumb and three other fingers to form a completely flat hand while, simultaneously, his legs unfurled to lift him to a stiffly standing position, by which time the flat hand had arced upwards to his head, completing a very smart and proper salute.

'Sub-Lieutenant Barnes. How may I help you, Sir,' he said, in a grave, professional tone, as if these were his very first words to them.

Cy and Leo smiled at him. 'We would like to see the record for escape pod Serial GTN36716XT. Sitting down, the man's hands flashed across his control pad. A page of records was displayed in front of Leo and Cy.

'Will you go through this for us, please?'

'Of course Sir.' He pointed to each item on the display:

```
Escape Pod            Model GTN67UV Serial
                      Number GTN36716XT.

Delivered to
SSP Yggdrasil         UY5660 Day97
```

Completed and commissioned	UY5660 Day122
Located	Dock 342E, UY5660 Day125.
Routine and test transits:	{'That's this list here. Sir. Last usage is Day122 this year'}
Last maintenance of escape pod:	Day115 {'Also this year, Sir'}

Leo and Cy looked at each other in surprise.

'You mean this vehicle is still here in the Platform? Still in use?' Leo said.

'Yes, Sir. I agree it is one of our older pods but these vehicles don't get a great deal of usage, so they last a long time. Of course, they are always meticulously maintained.'

'Could we look back the usage when it was new? Say, UY5660-5665?'

'Yes. Sir. Here is the list. There's nothing unusual here. Just test flights and the occasional maintenance use around the perimeter of the Platform.'

'Do you have any more detail on these early usages?' Cy wished to know.

'Not here, Sir. Full details will be stored on the vehicle's log. That's held in the vehicle with a copy in the Dock Office.'

'Well thank you, Mr Barnes. We'll be back if we need more from you.'

'Any time, Sir.' The man saluted. 'Always delighted to help. Here is a screen copy of the data.'

'Thank you.' Then Leo turned back. 'Ah, Mr Barnes – is that vehicle still in Dock 342E?'

'Yes, it is, Sir.'

Leo and Cy sat in their quarters.

'So it's still here!' Leo said quietly.

'But we know it isn't!' Cy exploded.

'I think we should pay a quick visit to "our" escape pod next door. I think we should pick up the log and scan the ID info. Then we can compare it with what we find in the duplicate pod – that's what it is, isn't it? A duplicate. It must be.'

'Yes,' Cy responded, 'but how do you create a completely new escape pod? We'll certainly need to dig into that.'

'Agreed. We'll get on to that tomorrow.'

They picked up the log from the escape pod. Fortunately, it was still possible to interrogate it because the data were recorded in very robust equipment specifically designed to withstand accidents. They also scanned other items of physical evidence in the pod (ID plates, etc.) which gave model and serial number data. Cy recorded all this on his PAC. 'We can compare this carefully with what we find in the duplicate escape pod and see whether we can spot anything,' he said. 'We can get an expert to help us – someone who was NOT on the Platform 30 years ago.'

The two men locked up the escape pod carefully, set the security seals and left.

18

The Twenty-third Day

'Commander Gorton sends his apologies, Sir. Unfortunately, he is already committed elsewhere.' Fitch had drawn them aside and murmured this news to Leo and Cy as the senior ST Division staff gathered in a Meeting Room.

'Thank you, Mr Fitch. 'We'll just have to meet him some other time when he's available,' Leo replied.

'However,' Fitch continued, more loudly, 'all the ST Area Heads are here with their teams, so, hopefully, they will be able to meet all your requirements.'

Leo and Cy sat down side-by-side at the end of the table. 'Shall we all sit down, Gentlemen?' Leo called. The men straggled to fill the seats along the length of the table and the hustle and bustle quieted to a hush of expectation.

'Thank you for coming to this meeting, Gentlemen,' Leo began. 'I am Command Investigator Granvic and my colleague is Command Investigator Funte. We are also members of the IRS. Several weeks ago, while we were transiting through the eastern part of this Sector, we detected a weak and intermittent Distress Signal. We tracked it and found it came from a damaged and derelict escape pod, Type GTN67UV, located on a small asteroid. On investigation, we found that the vehicle contained one deceased. We were able to capture the vehicle intact and, since it was originally registered to SSP Yggdrasil, we have brought it and its contents here for forensic examination. This is a Priority One Command Investigation to be carried out as soon as possible.' He paused for a moment as he scanned the faces up and down the table, noting a wide range of reactions.

'For your information, the deceased has now been removed from the vehicle and will be the subject of a full pathological examination soon. We now require the vehicle to be examined forensically. It is obvious that it has been modified greatly and we wish to know what has been done, for what purpose and by whom. Therefore, we need several highly-qualified engineering specialists who will start work on the vehicle right away. I remind you that this is a Priority One Command Investigation. Do you wish to add anything, Investigator Funte?'

'Thank you,' Cy replied. 'No, I have nothing to say at this time. However, may I suggest that the ST Area Heads comment? Would you like to start the ball rolling, Mr Fitch?'

'Ah, yes, Gentlemen. As you know, I am in charge of Platform-wide maintenance. I have a very large staff, some of whom maintain the hundreds of GTN67UV escape pods we carry. Any of these teams would certainly be able to give you information about the on-board equipment they service. For deeper knowledge, however, I think I would suggest a Construction or a Development scientific engineer.'

Cy noted that the two Sub-Commanders at the table frowned with irritation!

'Thank you, Mr Fitch. Could I hear from Area Head, Construction?' He checked his PAC display. 'Sub-Commander Wilfred Glassford?'

'That right, Sir.' The voice was thin and reedy. 'My ST Area has specific expertise in modular and general construction. We assemble and construct all the units that are transited here and also develop our own equipment as required. I have engineers who know the construction of the GTN67UV pods very well. We complete the final build on the pods and commission them. I would recommend my senior engineer, Scientist-Major Biranco, for your task. He is highly experienced and has worked in my Area for 35 years.' He gestured down the table and a tall slim man stood up. Glassford continued. 'He could bring a small supporting team.'

'Thank you, Mr Glassford. Now Development. Sub-Commander Bruno Leigh, I believe?'

A young man stood up. 'Sir, I have extensive knowledge of the GTN67UV and would be pleased to offer my help, along with appropriate staff from my Area.'

'Thank you, Mr Leigh. May I ask how long you have served on the Platform?'

'17 years, Sir. Before this, I worked in Space Research, Earth-side.'

'Thank you. Does anyone else wish to speak?' Cy looked down the table. 'No? Then would you give us a moment, please?'

Leo and Cy switched to DT mode.

'Leo, I think the Development man should look at the duplicate. As a relative newcomer, we know he couldn't have been involved in whatever went on here 30 years ago.'

'Yes, I agree, Cy. And the Construction expert, the Scientist-Major, can start to look at "our" pod. Head of Construction might want to come too but I have a feeling he's quite happy to pass it on to his subordinate.

'Yes, I thought so too.'

'Regarding Fitch's Maintenance people, I doubt that they could contribute anything the Development people couldn't. We can hold them in reserve. Agree?'

'Yes, Leo, I do. So if you go to our pod and keep a sharp eye on the Construction team, I will take our Development Head and see what he makes of the escape pod in Dock 342E. I've got the data and the visual scans of our pod's IDs, so we should be able to make detailed comparisons. OK?'

'That's fine, Cy. Obviously, well keep in touch.'

'Agreed. I think we should keep the existence of the duplicate a secret for the moment. I'll just invite Mr Leigh to accompany me – alone – and then no-one can get ahead of us to alter evidence!'

'Good thinking, Cy, are we ready break the good news to the happy band?'

'Let's do it!'

Leo rapped on the table and silence descended.

'Right, Gentlemen,' he began, 'Mr Glassford, we accept your offer of Major Biranco and he will shortly accompany me to the damaged escape pod on Level-3. Major Biranco, you are welcome to bring a small team. Of course, you are welcome to come, too, Mr Glassford.'

'I think I will allow Major Biranco to assess the situation before I become involved,' Glassford said. 'Perhaps later...'

'That's fine, Mr Glassford. Major Biranco, what will be the composition of your team?'

'Just Lieutenant Hulse,' Major Blanco said quietly. A very young man stood and saluted.

'Fine. And Investigator Funte has a special task for Sub-Commander Leigh. Thank you, everyone.' Everyone stood and most began to leave the room. The three officers who had been selected gravitated towards Leo and Cy.

Leo turned to Fitch. 'Mr Fitch, we won't need you for a while. We'll call you.'

'Ah, Sir, perhaps I should just come along...'

'That won't be necessary, Mr Fitch. There is very little space in the pod. Thank you for arranging this meeting.'

Leo gestured to the two Construction officers. 'Follow me, Gentlemen. We'll go to the dock in my buggy.' Five minutes later they had entered the dock area and were approaching the heavily guarded escape pod. Before they reached there, Leo stopped the buggy and turned to the two officers. 'I just want to brief you both before we arrive. My colleague gave you the general background of the discovery of this pod. I just want to stress one fact to you. There is no doubt that this escape pod came from this Platform. The records show that it was delivered here 34 years ago in UY5660, that it was commissioned within weeks and used here thereafter.' He turned to the younger man: 'Mr Hulse, were you serving on this Platform in UY5660?'

'No, Sir. I arrived here just 6 years ago as a junior officer. Before that, I was studying Earth-side. I am only 31 years old.'

'Thank you.' He turned to the other man. 'Mr Biranco, from what Mr Glassford said, you were on Yggdrasil in UY5660?'

'Yes, Sir, I was. I arrived in UY5658 after intensive specialised training in Space Construction work. Since then, I have been promoted three times and I have been the Senior Engineer in the Construction Area for the last 14 years. I have extensive knowledge of the GTN67UV escape pod and hope that I can assist you with your important investigation.'

'Thank you, Mr Biranco. So you would have been in a junior position in UY5660?

'Yes, Sir.'

'Can you, by any chance, recall completing and commissioning any GTN67UV escape pods around that time?'

The man smiled faintly. 'Sir, I worked on many. A routine task.'

'Do you recall doing any special reconstruction work on an escape pod?'

'No, Sir. I did nothing except the routine tasks for which I had been trained. Anything non-standard would have been handled by more senior staff.'

'I see. Final questions. I have reason to believe that this vehicle disappeared from the Platform 3 to 6 years after UY8660. Can you recall anything unusual happening over that time? Did anyone disappear from the Platform?'

The man thought for a moment. 'I cannot recall anything unusual, Sir.'

'OK. Now we will enter the escape pod. I want you and your colleague to examine every part of it carefully, give me your assessment and answer my questions.'

Leo conducted them through security and opened up the pod. They climbed the ladder, entered the hatch and switched on the engineering lighting. Both men gasped as they saw the extent of the destruction.

Biranco's voice wavered: 'What could possibly have happened here to cause all this, Sir? I have never seen such extensive damage.'

'That's what I want you to tell me,' Leo replied quietly. 'I shall sit over here and wait.'

A rather puzzled Sub-Commander Leigh joined Cy as all the other staff left the room. 'Here I am, Sir, reporting for duty!' he said, with just a faint tinge of irony.

Cy was grave. 'Come with me, Mr Leigh. You and I have a rather important job to do. With your "extensive knowledge" of the GTN67UV escape pod, you are exactly the man I need.'

'Should I bring anyone else with me, Sir?'

'We shouldn't require anyone else, Mr Leigh. We're going to look at one of the Platform's GTN67UV escape pods. It's in Dock 342E. Can we go in your buggy?'

'Yes, of course.' Leigh's voice was filled with puzzlement. 'Why are we...?'

'I'll tell you when we arrive, Mr Leigh. By the way, as far as anyone else is concerned, you are just showing me the features of a GTN67UV. We need to keep our real purpose secret. You'll soon see why.'

Dock 342E was towards the opposite end of the Platform, so it took some time to get there. At last they disembarked from the buggy and entered the dock.

'Good morning, Sir.' A technician approached them. He addressed Leigh, whom he obviously recognised. 'Can we help you with anything?'

'No thanks, Frank,' Leigh said, 'I'm just showing Investigator Funte an escape pod. I just thought I'd choose a well-maintained dock!'

'Well, Sir, you've come to the right place!'

There were two identical GTN67UV escape pods in Dock 342E, both held securely in their launch bays.

'Two vehicles! That could be useful,' Cy opined.

Leigh looked at him with a slightly puzzled expression but said nothing.

'The vehicle we are interested in has the Serial Number GTN36716XT Can you check this vehicle's ID plate?' He pointed to the nearest escape pod.

'Of course, Sir.'

The main hatch was opened and they boarded. Leigh walked to the front of the Control Cabin and consulted an ID plate mounted on a main spar. 'What was that Serial, Sir?' he called.

'GTN36716XT'

Leigh shook his head. 'This isn't it, Sir. This is a newer pod; probably 7 or 8 years old.

'That's fine, Mr Leigh. Let's go to the other pod. But just leave this one open. We may want to return here.'

Leigh's face revealed puzzlement. Why should they want to re-enter an escape pod in which they had no interest?

Seeing his expression, Cy murmured: 'Don't worry, Mr Leigh, all will be revealed soon.'

The second escape pod was opened up and they climbed in.

'GTN36716XT' Leigh called out, reading the plate. That's your serial, I think, Sir.'

'Correct, Mr Leigh. Now, will you please look at my PAC display? This is a visual of the ID plate of the broken pod in Dock S47B on Level-3.' The fire-blackened plate clearly identified the vehicle as "GTN36716XT".

Leigh's eyes flicked several times from the PAC visual to the ID plate on the spar in front of him. 'Impossible,' he said quietly, 'I know something about the procedure for producing these ID plates. Two identical plates cannot be manufactured. It's impossible,' he repeated.

There was a brief silence as the two men stood motionless beside each other.

Then Cy spoke very quietly. 'So what are your thoughts?'

'Well, Sir, we must establish which vehicle is the original. I'm not sure how we...' his voice faded away. Then: 'Just a moment, though,' his voice rose excitedly, 'you can scan these plates to confirm the serial with an e-tag. A duplicate plate will be blank, I believe.'

'Can you scan this plate?'

'Yes, Sir, with my PAC.' Seconds later, he whistled softly. 'Sir, this plate has no e-tag value. It's completely blank! Let's check the ID plate in the other escape pod over there – that will confirm that my scan system is working.'

They re-entered the first escape pod. 'Yes, Sir, look at this! The Serial is confirmed by the e-tag scan!'

'Fine, Mr Leigh. Just stand by and I will confirm the situation in our recovered pod.' He called Leo's PAC.

'Leo, would you scan the main ID plate and bring up the e-tag, please. It's on the main forward spar.' There was a short delay, then Leo replied. 'Scan confirms "GTN36716XT" – I've just sent the data to your PAC. Is that the information you want?'

'Yes, that's excellent, Leo. We are making progress here, I think. How about your operation?'

'We're going fine, too. But there's a lot to do. It will be a while yet before conclusions can be formulated, I think.'

'Ok, Leo. Talk to you later.'

Cy turned to Leigh, showing him the scan image on the PAC. 'This is absolute confirmation that the recovered vehicle is the genuine escape pod. So, what is your conclusion, Mr Leigh?'

'It can only mean one thing, Sir. It means that this vehicle we are standing in is a duplicate!'

'I agree. Now, would you examine this vehicle carefully to establish how a complete GTN67UV vehicle could be duplicated here on the Platform? I will stand back and let you get to work. Oh, by the way, here is the original Log from the pod on level-3. Could you look at the log in this vehicle and give me your conclusions on that as well?'

Cy sat down and observed Leigh as he began to examine many parts of the structure and the installed components of the vehicle. From time to time, he checked the construction of various items in the other escape pod nearby. After two hours, he approached Cy.

'I have my conclusions, Sir.'

'Go ahead. I'll record what you say.'

'Well, Sir, there is absolutely no doubt that this vehicle has been constructed from a combination of new spare parts from Technical Stores. However, other parts have been manufactured specially – items like the main frames or body panels that are not expected to fail during the life of the vehicle. I would imagine that the spare parts would need to be obtained carefully, to avoid arousing suspicion among the Stores Staff. Regarding the locally-manufactured items, I judge it would have taken a long time to produce them – complex designs, patterns and models would be required – and all this work would need to be done with great secrecy. I can show you a large number of places in this vehicle where the construction is clearly non-standard. Finally, I have examined the two logs and there is no doubt that the log in this duplicate vehicle is a fake, locally produced.'

'Thank you. An excellent piece of work, Mr Leigh. Now, may I have your opinion on something else? Who do you think could have done this?'

Leigh's face paled. 'Sir, I do not think I am competent to make any specific accusations. In any case, I was not here when all this happened.'

Cy raised a placating hand. 'I'm sorry, you misunderstand. I am not asking you to suggest names, I am merely asking what type of people might have been involved – engineers, scientists, etc. Had you been on the Platform 30 years ago, you, yourself, would be a suspect!

There was silence for a couple of minutes as Leigh thought deeply. 'Well, Sir, I suppose this is how I see it. Technical Stores staff must have been involved but not necessarily complicit. However, the planners and constructors must have been fully in the picture. They must have known that they were building a duplicate vehicle. The technical expertise to do this work is considerable. I would doubt whether any Maintenance Area engineer would have had the skill. The best engineers in the Construction Area would certainly have had the skill, knowledge and equipment. The scientist engineers in my own Development Area would certainly be capable of the more subtle work – but not building a major new component – a new mainframe, for example. I cannot think of any other scientific staff on the Platform who could take on such a task. One final point, Sir, because this was a major piece of engineering work that must have been done in significant secrecy – no doubt, professionally guarded, too – it would have required management authorisation, involvement and coordination at a very high level.'

Cy was silent for a few minutes. Finally he said: 'Thank you again, Mr Leigh. I think your assessment is very useful. I have one final question. We know that one man was lost from this Platform around 30 years ago – the dead man in the pod. Do you have any idea who that might have been? Have you ever heard any rumours?

'No, Sir. As you know, there are a lot of people on the Platform, over 8,000. I have personal knowledge and contact with relatively few of these. And, of course, there are frequent staff movements in and out of the Platform. Anyway, the autopsy will soon provide you with an identity, will it not?

'Well, yes, it should, Mr Leigh. Thank you for all your work today. It is very important that you keep all this strictly secret. I may wish you to do further work on the Investigation. Would you deliver me back to Level-3, please?'

'Of course, Sir.'

The buggy came to a halt and Cy climbed out. 'Thank you. Ah, Mr Leigh, something is puzzling me: The three Areas of ST Division are Maintenance, Construction and Development, are they not?'

'Yes, Sir.'

'And they are structurally equivalent, are they not?'

'That's right, Sir.'

'Then why is Commander Fitch a higher rank than you and the same rank as STC1?'

Leigh looked confused. 'I'm sorry, Sir, I don't understand your question. Commander Fitch is STC1. I understand he has been for a long time. Certainly he has been STC1 all the time I have been here and a long time before that.'

Cy concealed his surprise. 'Thank you for that explanation, Mr Leigh.

Major Biranco and Lieutenant Hulse had worked diligently all day. Now the three men sipped coffee together and Leo sought progress reports from them. 'How are things going, Gentlemen?' he asked.

'Well, Sir, Hulse and I are making good progress. I must say, there has been so much to look at and analyse. We want to try and put it all together before we report to you. I think we may be able to do that in a couple of hours.'

'That's fine. Take your time and get it right.'

Shortly after this, Cy returned and he and Leo assumed DT communication. 'We have a result on the vehicle, Leo. There's absolutely no doubt that the escape pod docked in 342E is a duplicate that has been put together here, partly from spare modules and partly from specially manufactured parts – something that would have taken considerable skill, not to mention the problems of doing it all in strict secrecy. Mr Leigh has been most helpful, not only analysing the duplicate but giving me some ideas about the sort of people who might be responsible. I was going to suggest a check of the historical stores records but I don't think that's necessary now, because we know that's how the duplicate was built. However, we don't know who authorised it to be built.'

Leo was thoughtful in his reply. 'You know, Cy. I think we can begin to speculate why. Our vehicle, this one we're sitting in, was used as a means of execution. A man who was stationed on this Platform was sent away in this vehicle to die. Maybe in a little while, when my team report, we'll know a bit more about how they did it. This should take us closer to the murderers.'

They sat thinking for a moment or two, then Cy "spoke" again.

'Listen, Leo, I got something else extremely significant from Leigh. I'll tell you about it later on. It looks like your two investigators are just about to address you with their findings.'

'Sir,' the Major said, 'May I now report to you? We have come to a series of conclusions about what happened here.'

'Yes, please.'

'Well Sir, basically, we think that three things happened to this escape pod:

Firstly, large parts of the original local control system were stripped out and replaced by specially constructed non-standard systems that permitted remote control operation only. This must have been done on the Platform because many new parts have been used.

Secondly, the non-standard remote-control-only systems were removed subsequently and parts were cleverly adapted or re-manufactured to form a completely new local control system for the vehicle – a really remarkable and highly-skilled task that very few people could have done. We think this was done when the vehicle was stranded on the asteroid by the person who was marooned there.

Thirdly, a heat-operated explosive device was detonated in the engine bay. We have identified the explosive material as a variant that was current 30 years ago. This device could be armed remotely so would allow the transit to the asteroid to take place without detonation. When the engines were started on the asteroid, the explosive device detonated and destroyed the vehicle. We think that would have happened when the occupant boosted the engines to full power, while attempting to start the transit.

'Thank you, Gentlemen, for your really excellent work here,' Leo said. 'May I stress to you – all this must be held in absolute secrecy. We may need you for further work or discussion later.'

Leo and Cy returned to their accommodation.

'So what's the exciting news from Leigh, Cy?' Leo's first words. 'I'm really curious!'

'Hold on to your hat, Leo! I asked Leigh why Fitch is a Full Commander, the same rank as STC1. My question puzzled him. He said Fitch is a Commander because he is STC1! That has certainly been the situation for the last 17 years (when Leigh arrived) – and he understood that Fitch had been STC1 for many years before that! But the Command staffing list lists Gorton as STC1 and Fitch as Head, Maintenance!'

Leo digested this information and then added: 'And we know that Fitch wants us to believe that Gorton is here on the Platform! Only this morning he told us that Gorton couldn't attend our meeting and sends his apologies!'

They were silent for several moments.

'So it looks like it's Gorton in the suit.' Cy's voice was a quavering whisper.

Leo's eyes indicated shocked agreement.

19

The Twenty-fourth Day

They sat silently at breakfast, each engrossed in his own thoughts.

Finally Cy spoke. 'What Leigh told me yesterday moves things forward at breakneck speed but the whole thing just makes me feel empty, devastated. A brilliant man like that...'

'What can possibly have happened? It makes no sense at all.' Leo held his head in his hands.

Cy tested a bit of optimism. 'Maybe it isn't him, Leo. Maybe there's another explanation.'

'Well, I can't think of any other scenario that fits the facts we now have. Command thinks Gorton is still here and we know he isn't. Meanwhile Fitch, and others no doubt, want us to believe he is still on the Platform when in fact he hasn't been here for 30 years or so. And we have to conclude they are duping Command about this by responding to Gorton's communications. They must have a "virtual" Gorton here on the Platform.'

'You don't mean that someone is walking around pretending to be Gorton?'

'Sorry, Cy, I didn't mean physically impersonating Gorton. Someone is a virtual Gorton. Receiving his communications and dealing with them as if Gorton were still alive.'

'Mm, I understand. Of course, you're right. Command would soon become suspicious if they sent queries to him and never got an answer.'

The two men sat thinking. Then Cy spoke. 'Well, when the autopsy is done, we'll know who died in the escape pod. If the body is Gorton's, then our job switches to finding out who his murderers are, doesn't it?'

'What if the body isn't Gorton's?'

'We'll have to brainstorm that one when it happens, Leo. I think our investigation has enough loose ends to keep us busy for the moment. But, whoever it is, he has been murdered and we will be investigating that – and we'll be finding out who was responsible and making him pay!'

Leo nodded in agreement. After a moment, he jumped to his feet. 'Listen, Cy. I suddenly have a bad feeling about this. I think we should go and check on our evidence to ensure it's being looked after as we directed. Let's go right away and check the escape pod. And in any case, there's something I think we ought to pick up.'

Soon after, they arrived at the dock, checked through security and entered the pod.

'You know, Cy, I had a dream about this last night. I dreamt there was a message recorded on the victim's PAC and that it had a lot to tell us. Because the PAC was used to generate a distress signal, I had forgotten that it could have evidence recorded on it. I know it's under the control desk where our victim left it, so I'll just detach it from the signal booster and then we can...' His words stopped abruptly.

'What is it, Leo?'

'It's gone! The PAC has been removed from the booster unit.'

'Listen, Leo, actually, it's OK...'

'It's far from OK, Cy,' Leo exploded uncharacteristically, 'we've just lost some absolutely crucial evidence. How can we have been so stupid?' He began looking around the cabin wildly. 'Maybe Biranco detached it and left it lying around here somewhere... I know, I'll call and ask him...'

The communication was brief. 'No joy, Cy. He assures me that PAC was wired up to the signal booster unit. We've lost it! This is a total disaster!'

'Leo, please, calm down and listen to me! It doesn't matter if the PAC has gone. We haven't lost the record it contained.'

Leo froze and looked at Cy with astonishment. 'Of course we have!'

'No, we haven't. On the day we docked and de-captured the pod, I thought it would be a good idea to transfer that PAC's data record to my PAC. I did it just before we locked the pod up and, in the middle of all the turmoil we were in, I forgot to mention it. Now, let me make it quite clear. Whoever stole the PAC will find no data on it! I've got everything here, securely in my PAC.'

Gradually, Leo's expression turned from distress to delight. 'Cy! You've saved the day. You're brilliant! You're a genius! I've always said how clever you are...'

Cy grinned. 'I don't remember that! You must have said it very quietly...'

'You know, Cy, I've just realised when it happened. It was when the body was being moved. There was a time when one member of the Retrieval Team was alone in the Control Cabin, you remember? We were in the sleeping cabin along with the other three members of the team while the fourth man was outside in the Control Cabin, preparing the casket to receive the body. He must have been under orders to steal the PAC. That's the only time that "outsiders" were ever alone in the Control Cabin since we arrived. I'd just love to know who he delivered it to, wouldn't you?'

'I certainly would, Leo. Maybe we'll find out in due course. Right now, we know how it was done but not by whose instructions. It could have been any of the people who were originally involved. Of course, that man's boss is Head, Medical. We'll remember that!'

Hugely relieved, they locked and sealed the pod once more and returned to their quarters.

'Later on today,' Cy said, 'we'll run the data record and see if it has anything to tell us. Meanwhile, there's another very important thing to check upon. The body in the casket. Before we leave to check on that, however, let's call Head, Medical and ask whether there's any news about the return of his pathologist Martinez to do the autopsy.'

'Hello, Mr Sangyar. Investigator Funte here. Have you any information on the return of your pathologist? You expect him to return today? And you suggest tomorrow for the autopsy? Yes, that will be satisfactory, thank you.' Cy ended the call. 'You heard that, didn't you, Leo. Our pathologist friend will do the autopsy tomorrow. That will be one more hurdle cleared, won't it? Now let's go and check on the body, as you suggested.'

'Cy, there's one other thing to check and maybe we should do it now. I would like to confirm that Command messages are still coming in for Commander Gorton; also that they are being answered. We need to check in ComCen – I'm sure these messages will be Cat-S and handled separately. ComCen is on our way to Medical, so shall we make a quick call there?'

'OK, Leo. It will be another bit of the investigation ticked off.'

Leo instructed the buggy to take them to ComCen Reception. As they entered, the clerk at the desk recognised them and looked distinctly alarmed.

'Yes, Sir, how may we help you?' he said as he sprang to his feet and saluted.

'Could we speak to whoever is in charge of the Cat-S Message Centre?'

'Yes, Sir. Will you please wait?' He disappeared and returned with an elderly Lieutenant.

'I am Lieutenant Gonvitch. How may I help you, Gentlemen?'

'Could we speak to you in your office?'

'Yes, please follow me.' The man took them to a very small, cramped room with barely enough room for a desk and three small chairs. 'I'm sorry, there isn't much room,' he murmured.

'Lieutenant, would you display for us the list of Cat-S messages that have been received in the last three months?' Leo asked.

The man looked at them very doubtfully. 'Sir, I am not authorised to do that. Even for you. Cat-S messages have the highest security priority and no-one except the addressees ever see them. Absolutely no-one. I have taken the highest Command Oath on this matter.'

'That's fine, Lieutenant,' Cy interjected, 'we would not want you to breach your oath. We do not want to access any of these messages. All we want to do is glance at the incoming addressees. You can do that for us, surely?'

'Well,' the Lieutenant conceded, 'I suppose if that's all... and in view of who you are...' He turned to a screen and interrogated it briefly. Then he swivelled it towards Leo and Cy.

'Thank you.' They scanned the list. Cy indicated three messages addressed to Commander Gorton M.

'Could we see the outgoing Cat-S list please?' Here, Cy tapped softly on two messages that showed the originator as "Commander Gorton M".

'What do you do with incoming Cat-S messages, Lieutenant?'

'I forward them to the addressee's Secure Mailbox, Sir. Only I know these addresses. There is no record except in my memory.'

'And what happens about the replies?'

'They are securely forwarded to me and I transmit them on special channels, Sir.'

'Thank you for your help, Lieutenant.'

'A pleasure, Sir.'

Leo and Cy rose to leave. 'How long have you worked here, Lieutenant?' he asked.

'35 years, Sir.'

'And have you ever met Commander Gorton?'

'No Sir. Senior Officers never come to ComCen. They are just names to me.'

'Thank you again, Lieutenant.'

Cy and Leo were soon on their way again.

'So your theory is proven absolutely, Cy. They are duping Command about Gorton. And, by tomorrow, we will probably have established that the body in the escape pod is Gorton. Then we'll have to start an investigation into his murder.'

'Well, I'm hoping that the deceased's PAC record will tell us where to look. After all, that poor man had months, maybe years, to work out who sent him off into Space to die and also why they did it. If he has actually left us that sort of record – and I hope fervently that he has – then we will be able to make rapi343d progress with our criminal investigation.'

Leo nodded seriously. 'Yes, the PAC record is our lifeline to the truth.'

Finally they reached Level-6 and headed for the large door marked 6/23B. When they arrived there, they found it blocked by fencing. A prominent notice read:

Medical Facility Entrance 6/23B

NO ENTRY

This entrance is closed
for maintenance

Leo's face darkened. 'I don't like this, Cy. We had better find a way in as soon as possible.'

They drove along the high blank wall of the Medical Facility for some time but there were no other doorways to be found. However, at one point, they heard sounds of heavy machinery at work behind the wall.

'Better try the other way and see if we can find an entrance there,' Cy said. They turned round and drove back, passing the closed entrance and travelling on for some distance. At last they came to a small entrance with a guard post.

Leo addressed the guards behind a counter. 'We are Command Investigators Granvic and Funte. Will you direct us to Room 6/307X please?'

The guards looked at each other. 'Just a moment, Sir,' one said and disappeared. After a pause, a very young officer arrived and said: 'I'm very sorry, Sir. You cannot enter here. It is not permitted. I have been given strict orders by my superiors.'

Leo wasted no time and called Head, Medical. 'Hello, this is Command Investigator Granvic. May I speak to Commander Sangyar immediately, please? He's not there? Who are you, then? His Secretary? Well, do you know who I am? You do? Well, that's good. Investigator Funte and I wish to enter the Medical Facility and go to Room 6/307X. The door we wanted to enter is closed for maintenance. We are now at another entrance where for some reason your guards are refusing us admission. Will you instruct them to let us in and direct us to Room 6/307X? What? You cannot do that? You don't have the authority? Then would you get someone who has the authority? What's that? There's no-one else there? Everyone is at an important CCO1 meeting? It is a Top Security meeting and the doors of the Meeting Room are sealed? You're saying there's no way of contacting anyone inside?' Leo decided that enough time had been wasted and broke the connection.

'Cy, there's something very wrong here. I reckon we're being obstructed deliberately. I'm sorry but I think this is an emergency. We really must get in here immediately.' He turned to the young officer who, clearly, was now trying to hide behind his guards.

'Would you join us out here please?' he commanded firmly.

The young man came forward very reluctantly. 'What is your name?'

'Sub Lieutenant Danzig, Sir.' the young man whispered.

'Do you know who we are and why we are here?'

'Yes, Sir.'

'Listen carefully, please. If you insist on obstructing us, there will be very serious personal consequences for you and for those who gave you these orders. Order your men to open the barrier and let us through.'

The young man's face was ashen as his brain raced: 'Open the barrier, Sergeant Glenn, let the Command Investigators through,' he called in a cracked voice.

'Thank you, Danzig. If you get into any trouble over this, contact me personally and I will deal with the situation. You are doing the right thing. You are obeying the orders of a Command officer.'

Soon Leo and Cy were travelling at maximum speed along a wide corridor, following the directions of the guards at the entrance, who had pointed the way to Room 6/307X. Some five minutes later, as the noise of machinery blossomed ahead of them, they were forced to stop at a large blue screen that filled the corridor completely. From behind this screen, there was the deafening noise of heavy industrial activity.

'Listen Cy, I think Room 6/307X is just the other side of this screen.' They approached the obstacle, finding it made of a thick, rigid plastic material.

'Look here, Leo. I think this is an access.' Cy pointed to the outline of a small door at one side. They pushed it and it gave way slightly before coming up against some sort of bolt or locking mechanism on the other side.

'Stand back, Cy. I'm going to try a kick. It all seems pretty flimsy.' So saying, he took a short run-up to the door and planted a mighty kick at the place where the door had revealed some movement. The flimsy door flew open with a crash and they stepped through into a totally astonishing sight. In front of them, large robot demolition machines were tearing the floor, walls and ceiling into pieces. The area had become a large void filled with heaps of twisted debris. Then Leo grasped Cy's arm and pointed. There, on the floor, lay a broken, splintered door marked "Room 6/307X".

As they looked at the broken door, totally aghast, the demolition machines stopped abruptly, imposing an unlikely, sepulchral silence upon the scene of devastation, transforming it into a dramatic stage-set of jagged detritus and cloying, swirling dust.

'What do you think you're doing? No-one is allowed in here.' A small man in full protective gear had appeared from behind the huge machines and removed his helmet to address them in harsh, arrogant tones. 'Furthermore,' he continued, 'you are disrupting my Mandatory Work Schedules and this will be noted adversely in my report.'

'We are Command Investigators. You should know about us from your orders.'

The man was silent but they could see recognition in his eyes.

'So what do you want?' he said angrily, 'this is an extremely dangerous area and you should not...'

Leo interrupted. 'What is your name?'

'Engineer Blahtson,' the man replied after a pause.

'Do you know who we are?'

'Yes. I saw the order.'

'Do you not call senior officers "Sir"?'

There was a longer pause while the man thought about this. Then, finally, 'Yes... Sir.'

'Right. What is happening here?'

'This area is being reconstructed.'

'What has happened to Room 6/307X?' Cy demanded.

The man smiled thinly. 'Well, as you can see, it isn't here any more! I told you, the area is being reconstructed... Sir.'

Leo stepped close to the man. 'Where are the secure body units that were in Room 6/307X?'

'Don't know anything about that,' the man said laconically. 'The room was stripped out before I started this morning. I just operate the demolition machines, that's all I do... Sir.'

'Who is your senior officer? Who is in charge of this area?'

'There's no senior officer anywhere near here. I'm in charge. I'm the only person here. I told you. I operate the machinery. There's no need for anyone else. I always work alone... Sir.'

'Right,' Leo was firm and decisive. 'You had better help us. Show us where the contents of Room 6/307X might have been taken.'

The man was very reluctant but Leo prevailed upon him forcefully. They started a tour of the immediate area around the "reconstruction zone". There were many large rooms, some still furnished for the various purposes of the Medical Facility. They came across several storerooms but none of these contained any body storage units. Finally, they found a room that was locked.

'What is this room?' Cy asked the man.

The man consulted his PAC: 'Just says "Auxiliary Store" here.' he said.

'Can you open it?'

'I suppose I could,' the man said, slowly producing a master key.

The door opened and there they were – the body storage units from Room 6/307X. They hunted around for Unit M545C. 'Here it is,' Leo called.

Cy produced the key and fitted it into the lock, turning it first one way and then the other. 'The key won't work,' he called.

'Let me try.' Leo's efforts were equally unsuccessful. They stood back, nonplussed.

'Needs to be powered, I should think,' the small man said from behind them. 'Electronic, these locks. Everyone knows that... Sir.'

'Can you power it?' Cy asked.

'Don't know,' he replied, 'I'll have a look.' He disappeared around the back of the storage units. A few moments later he appeared carrying a thick electrical cable. 'Need to power this up from somewhere,' he said, squinting around.

'What about there?' Leo pointed to a power distribution point on the wall.

The man produced a universal tool and removed the power point cover. 'Look,' he said, 'I'll power the cable and you try the key again.' This time the key not only unlocked the unit but the long drawer slid out silently. They looked at it with dismay. The drawer was completely empty. The casket was no longer in the unit.

Cy and Leo had returned to their quarters and were trying to rationalise the situation.

'OK. They're trying to lose the evidence. First, they've stolen the PAC from the pod in case it has evidence on it. Then they are determined that the body should not be autopsied, presumably because it will reveal the identity of the person they sent to their death. These are the two bits of actual physical evidence we have – and both have now disappeared.' In despair, Leo held his head in his hands.

'No, Leo, we've got the PAC record and, of course, we've still got the escape pod! I imagine that's too big to "lose". Anyway, right now, let's do our utmost to find the body, if it still exists. I reckon they must have taken it somewhere very remote, somewhere where very few people go. Logically, I would imagine that medical staff must have been involved.' He examined his PAC. 'Yes, Medical occupies a large area of Level-6. That's where all the Operating and Treatment Rooms are as well as the administration offices. Wait a minute, though, Medical also have an additional complex on Level-0. Look at this, Leo...' his voice rose excitedly, 'there's an area in Level-0 called "Medical Disposal". That must surely be worth a check!' He sprang to his feet.

Leo also jumped up. 'Cy, I've just remembered something! All spacesuits have a powerful tracker built in. It's standard rescue equipment. It's possible that our suit's tracker might still be working, because the power units are self-sustaining. We can scan the appropriate band widths and see if anything comes up.' Quickly, he obtained the appropriate band widths used by 30-year old spacesuits and switched on the scan. Almost immediately, a soft "bleep" started and a location arrow indicated downwards.

'We've got it, Leo! I hope that's the tracker signal from the suit. At first guess, I'd suspect this will be on Level-0, probably in the Medical Disposal area.'

Like Maynard Gorton before them, they soon found that none of the ILTs descended to Level-0.

Finally, an older man directed them down a long corridor and they eventually arrived at a guard post, where they were recognised.

'Yes, Sir. How may we help you?'

'We wish to visit Medical Disposal on Level-0.'

'Sir, I am required to ask: "What is the purpose of your visit"?'

'The purpose is "Command Special Investigation". How do we get there?'

'The Level-0 ILT is over there, Sir. Do you require an escort?'

'No, thank you. What is the room number range of Medical Disposal?'

The man consulted a display. 'It is Area 684B, Rooms 18-34, Sir.'

Soon they had descended to Level-0. Cy punched in the location and the buggy took them along long empty corridors, deserted and disturbingly quiet. Both Cy and Leo felt a disquieting chill in the air, despite the buggy's insistence of normal air temperature levels.

'Is it a bit creepy down here, Cy? I don't know why but I feel distinctly shivery!'

'You're not imagining it, Leo. I feel it, too.'

Meanwhile, the PAC continued to confirm their progress towards the pulsating signal. 'We're getting quite near, now.' Leo said. 'The arrow is pointing down this corridor. Look, here it is.' A sign announced "Medical Disposal" and the buggy turned to move down a side corridor. 'The room range was 18-34,' Leo said. 'Here's Room 18 coming up.'

The PAC continued to point along the corridor, signal indicator flashing. They passed Rooms 19, 20 and 21. As they approached Room 22, the PAC indicator turned to point towards the room. Stopping by the door, they entered quickly.

'Welcome to Medical Disposal, Sirs! I have been expecting you.' the voice was jovial and came from a rather elegant young man sitting at a desk inside the large brightly-lit room full of humming machinery. 'We rarely have visitors to this very important part of Medical.'

Leo and Cy were taken by surprise by this greeting. 'How did you know...?'

'Security told me you were coming and who you were. I am greatly honoured to meet you. 'I am Senior Med-Tech Forbis,' the man said smoothly, 'How can I assist you today?'

Leo started the questioning: 'Are you in charge?'

'Yes, Sir, I am.'

'What happens here?'

'Well, Sir, Medical Level-6 sends us items for disposal and, as you may imagine, we, ah, dispose of them.' The man smiled.

'What sort of items?'

'Everything, Sir. Everything that needs to be disposed of.'

'What do you do with it?'

'I receive it,' the man said with quiet pride, 'I allocate it to a category and authorise it to be processed.'

'Processed?'

'Yes, Sir, "processed" is the official term for "disposed of"'

'Do your items include biological material, body parts, for instance?'

'Yes, Sir, at times. The result of surgical procedures, of course.'

'Whole bodies?'

'Of course not, Sir. Deceased staff are returned to Command in accordance with the Statutes.'

'Right, Mr Forbis, have you received a body casket yesterday or today?'

'Just one moment, Sir, I will check. Ah, yes, here it is. "One damaged unusable body casket. Contents listed as: One torn sleeping mattress and one time-expired obsolete spacesuit." Received first thing this morning, Sir. Are these the items you are looking for?'

'Where is it? Quickly, please!'

'Sent for appropriate disposal, Sir. I sent it off at 1034 hours this morning. It should have been processed by now...' he consulted a display, 'using Disposer 17B. Wait a moment, though, I see there has been a fault in that system and there is a backlog – which is just starting to be cleared, I observe.'

Cy spoke sharply: 'Will you stop that process immediately? We wish to recover that casket and its contents.'

Expertly, the man's hands flashed across several screen. 'The item was just about to be processed, Sir, but I have taken it from the queue and it should be available for you shortly.' As he said this, a hatch opened at the other side of the room and a very battered body casket appeared on an automatic trolley which rolled smoothly towards them.

Leo released the catches and lifted the top away. Inside, the eerie space-suited figure lay inert on the shredded mattress. Cy examined the suit carefully. 'This suit has not been opened,' he said quietly to Leo, 'the exterior material is intact and the fastenings are securely locked from the inside. You cannot open a suit from the outside. If there is a malfunction in the locking system, the suit needs to be cut open with special cutting equipment. I am sure this has not been done.'

'OK, Cy, that's good. We'll take everything back to our quarters and store it until tomorrow.'

'Agreed, Leo.' Cy turned to the man. 'Who referred these items to you for disposal?'

The man referred to his records. 'Duty Medical Clerk Dune, Sir. It was among many other items. The Duty Clerk receives them from many sources and then carries out his instructions to refer them to this facility.'

'Are all these items examined before they are sent to disposal?'

'Yes, Sir, they are carefully scanned.'

'If the remains of a body were inside this suit, would the scan identify this?'

'Yes, Sir. I am sure it would. I can check with Medical, if you wish.'

'Would you do that, please. And would you tell Medical to send a copy of the disposal documentation to you.'

Forbis communicated with Medical and then turned to Leo and Cy. 'They tell me that this Disposal Instruction directed that no scan should be done, Sir. I will receive a copy of the report almost immediately.' As he spoke, several papers scrolled from a print facility beside him. He checked them and handed them to Leo.

Leo handed the paper to Cy. 'Look at this: "Do not scan items listed below",' he said. 'There are a number of authorisation signatures on the instruction but the originator is Surgeon-Commander Sangyar, Head, Medical himself.' They exchanged significant glances.

'Mr Forbis, is it usual for a scan to be cancelled?'

'Very unusual, Sir. I have never received an un-scanned item in this facility. Not in all the years I have been here. A non-scan requires the personal authorisation of Head, Medical, which, of course, this Disposal Instruction has.'

'Thank you, Mr Forbis. We are going to need a truck to transport the casket. Is it possible for you to arrange that for us?'

'Yes, Sir. I'll get you one personally.' The man left the room and arrived a few minutes later in a small truck. 'Will this be suitable, Sir?'

Yes, thanks,' they said, placing the casket in the truck. Then they programmed their buggy to follow them and set off for Level-3 and their accommodation.

Back in their accommodation, there was a message awaiting them:

"Gentlemen Command Investigators, Principal-Surgeon Martinez proposes that the autopsy of the escape pod body will be carried out at PathLab One at 1400 tomorrow. CCO1 and all other senior officers will be in attendance. After the full procedure has been completed there will be a meeting at which the findings will be discussed and recorded. Do these arrangements meet with your approval?'

Leo and Cy sent a return message indicating their agreement.

20

The Twenty-fifth Day

'There has been a catastrophe!'

Fitch's first words to them in the morning, even before he had entered their accommodation.

'Come in, Mr Fitch. What is the problem?' Cy was calm.

'It's the body from the escape pod. It's gone!'

'Gone, Mr Fitch? Surely that is impossible! The body is in very secure storage in the Medical Department; in a special storage unit that has only one key. This one.' Cy held the key up for Fitch to see, 'I was assured that no-one else could gain access.'

'There has been a terrible misunderstanding – a lack of coordination between departments,' Fitch sputtered. 'But don't worry, Sir, CCO1 has said we will find out who is responsible and they will be punished...'

Leo held up a hand. 'Mr Fitch, what precisely are you telling us? If, somehow, the body has been taken from secure storage, where is it now?'

Fitch looked at the floor and spoke in a hoarse whisper. 'The body has been destroyed by mistake, Sir. A grave error that I can assure you will be most severely punished...'

Leo held up his hand again and there was silence for a few moments; then he spoke to Cy. 'Obviously, this is a matter that needs to be discussed at the very highest level.' Cy nodded in agreement. 'Mr Fitch, would you advise CCO1, Mr Martinez and all senior staff of the ST Division who were attending the autopsy that we should still meet in PathLab One at 1400. We will have a great deal to discuss.'

'But, Sir, if there is no body, why...'

'Just do it, please, Mr Fitch. That's an order – for everyone,' he added. 'I want everyone to be there. Will you make that clear?'

After Fitch had gone, Cy and Leo exchanged smiles and settled down to a leisurely breakfast.

'Cy, after breakfast, we have plenty time to check the PAC data record. It may have useful information for us now that we are approaching the endgame.'

'Fine, Leo, I agree.'

Breakfast was over. The two men sat comfortably in the lounge area and were silent as they listened with increasing incredulity to the record set out before them. Firstly, it confirmed that this was the record of Scientist-Commander Dr Maynard Gorton, starting in UY5664. Then there was the account of his imprisonment in the escape pod and its transit to the asteroid. After this, they heard about Gorton's meticulous and agonising creation of a new control system that would permit him to leave the asteroid. They listened very carefully to his analysis of the reasons why anyone should wish to kill him in this way, hearing also the story of his arrival and the details of his life on the Platform, including his description of the many "healings" he carried out, some of which were undoubtedly miraculous. This was followed by his very useful risk analyses and the identification of possible instigators of the crime against him. Finally, they heard about the explosive device that nearly killed him, his struggle to construct a Distress Signal transmitter and, years later, the eventual catastrophic failure of the pod and his final confinement in a suit within which he awaited certain death. The end of his account was dated in UY5668.

Cy and Leo looked at each other aghast, their thoughts racing. Minutes passed before either could speak.

'So he lasted more than four years on that asteroid – and never gave up.' Cy said huskily. 'Well, I'm not leaving here until I nail the people who did this to Gorton. It's completely inhuman murder.'

After a few moments, Leo grasped Cy's arm: 'Listen, Cy. We need a strategic discussion. First, let's just review where we are now, as succinctly as we can.'

'OK,' Cy started, 'We know that the murdered man is Gorton. He was deliberately marooned on an asteroid, inside a totally disabled escape pod with no means of signalling distress. It took him four years to die – and he struggled to survive during every minute of it. Since we arrived here, our adversaries have attempted to destroy our physical evidence but we have been able to thwart them. Meanwhile, we know they have duped Command for 30 years by falsifying Gorton's living presence here. They also created a duplicate escape pod so that no *vehicle missing reports* would be required. At this moment, they think they have succeeded in destroying Gorton's body but they're due to have a shock tomorrow! In any case, Command would expect us to autopsy the body to provide absolute confirmation of identity.

'Yes,' said Leo, 'and the sight of his remains might stir some people here into revealing their involvement and guilt. It also means that the body can have a proper disposal back on Earth.'

'Correct,' Cy sat back grimly. 'We have an interesting day ahead of us. I propose that we present ourselves with the body at 1400 and demand that the autopsy is done. Then we will have a detailed discussion of the results. A very detailed discussion!

Leo sat silently for a moment. 'You know, Cy, I think that for Gorton's sake, we should arrange some protection for ourselves. We know that at least some of Gorton's murderers are here. Even though we hold very high Command rank, we may be in considerable danger when they realise the evidence we have on them.'

Cy agreed. 'That's good thinking, Leo. These people are capable of anything. I know a couple of important things we should do to prepare for our meeting and to protect ourselves effectively.'

The two men spent some time in their IRS vehicle.

'I can't imagine why we're all standing in this pathology lab area.' Inevitably, CCO1 was testy. 'If the investigators want to have a meeting with all of us, it should be in a Committee Room. We know there is no autopsy to carry out.' The last sentence said with a distinct smirk of satisfaction.

'Well, Sir, I did query it with them but they were adamant. You know what they're like!' Fitch was faintly derogatory. 'Anyway, Sir, if we let them have their way, the sooner we will get ri—I mean, the sooner they will leave the Platform.' He finished with an ingratiating smile.

CCO1 did not answer but glared around him aggressively. The other members of the ST and Medical Divisions stood around in uneasy knots, talking quietly. Close by but on the other side of the transparent electronic screen that divided the viewing area from the operational part of the pathology laboratory, an impassive Principal-Surgeon Martinez stood beside the autopsy table, his crisp surgical greens contrasting sharply with the uniforms of everyone else.

Suddenly, the doors at one end of the room whisked open with a pneumatic sigh. Leo and Cy appeared, pushing a trolley upon which rested a very battered and dented casket. A deathly hush immediately replaced the hum of muted conversation. All eyes were fixed upon the approaching trolley.

'Will you assist us, please?' Cy gestured to the laboratory assistants. Leo unfastened the clips and removed the lid. 'Would you be so good as to lift the body very carefully and place it on the autopsy table?' A pleasant voice of authority.

With the experience of many years, the assistants transferred the stiff, bulky spacesuit from the casket to the autopsy table in one smooth, safe movement and made sure it was lying securely before they withdrew.

As this action took place, Leo took the opportunity to scan the faces in the viewing area. Most reflected some degree of mild shock or surprise at the drama of the situation but a few indicated a much deeper level of astonishment. Was there apprehension there also? He certainly thought it possible.

'What is the meaning of this?' CCO1's voice was a strangely cracked tone.

Leo stepped forward. 'All suits have a tracker on them. We were able to track our deceased to Medical Disposal and rescue the casket and its contents before they were destroyed. As you can see, the suit is totally intact. Once we open it, Principal-Surgeon Martinez will carry out his autopsy on the remains inside and we will proceed to identify who this person is. Then we can start to work out how he came to be sent from this Platform to die alone on a small asteroid.'

Cy addressed Martinez. 'You may start the autopsy right away, Mr Martinez. Please commence when you are ready.'

There was utter silence as Martinez stepped close to the autopsy table and walked around it. Then he spoke quietly to his assistants.

'Sir,' Martinez was addressing Cy, 'there is a problem. We have no means here of opening the suit. It is, of course, closed and locked shut from the inside and I think that special cutting tools are required to breach the material safely so that we can reach the locking mechanisms inside. I require advice from an expert to resolve this problem. Any other action risks damage to the deceased inside.'

'What sort of expert, Mr Martinez?'

'Well, we need a suit expert. I assume we must have such a department on the Platform.'

Cy turned to address the observing audience. 'Gentlemen, who commands the function that deals with spacesuits?'

There was a shuffling silence as the officers glanced at each other quizzically. Finally, Fitch stepped forward. 'Sir, the Suit Maintenance Department is within my command... I believe.' He spoke softly and in an uncertain tone. CCO1 glared at him angrily but said nothing.

'Thank you. Would you please go and find an expert who can help us?'

'Yes, Sir.' Looking rather confused, Fitch hurried from the laboratory.

After a short pause, CCO1 approached Leo, looking distinctly flustered and embarrassed. 'I say, Investigator Granvic,' he said with uncharacteristic quietness, 'while Fitch is sorting this out, could I have a word – in private? There is an office over there we could use.'

Leo looked at him neutrally. 'I'll just call my colleague,' he said quietly and waved to Cy to join them. 'Admiral Sarfeld wishes to speak to us in private.' He indicated the office.

'Fine,' Cy said. He addressed the others. 'Please sit down, Gentlemen. We will resume when Mr Fitch returns.'

In the office, they sat down around a small table.

'Ah, fellows, I just wanted to have a little private conversation...'

'Just a moment, Admiral,' Leo was grave and forceful. 'First of all, we are not "fellows", we are Command Investigators with Xray7 rank. You appear to have forgotten that.'

CCO1 blenched, muttering, 'Sorry, I...'

'Furthermore,' Leo continued, 'please be aware that we are recording everything said in this discussion as part of our investigation.'

There was an extended silence as CCO1 digested this fact. At last he spoke again, quietly and hesitantly. 'Listen, Investigators, I just wanted to say that I had nothing to with all of this.'

'All of this? All of what?' Cy's voice was equally soft.

'This escape pod you recovered. This body in the suit.' He waved in the direction of the autopsy table.

Leo and Cy looked at each other. 'Are you suggesting that, although you were in command of this Platform, you knew nothing about the complete loss of an escape pod? And what is more incredible, you knew nothing about the loss, the disappearance, of one of your staff members?' Cy's voice was incisive.

'Well,' CCO1's voice held an edge of bluster, 'there are well over 8,000 staff on this Platform and I can't know everyone. I couldn't possibly notice if a low-ranking staff member disappeared.'

'Of course, Admiral, but their supervisor would notice that they had disappeared, wouldn't they? And they would report the disappearance – and, in due course, a report of the situation would arrive on your desk, would it not?'

CCO1 flushed. 'Investigator, I'm sorry, you do not realise the scope of my function here. I am a very busy man. I cannot possibly deal with trivia. I have so many strategic matters to deal with, you see. I am sure you must understand that.'

'So if you would not be informed, who would deal with the matter?'

'An appropriate member of my senior staff, I expect. Whoever commanded the Division to which the missing man was attached, for instance.'

'I see.' Cy's voice was icy.

After a short pause, Leo moved the focus. 'Admiral, you have been talking about low-ranking staff. What if a member of your managerial staff disappeared?'

CCO1 was increasingly confident. 'I would expect it to be handled in the same way. You should remember that my organisational record is exemplary. I train my subordinates well. I run a tight ship. I am famous throughout the Command for precisely this!'

'So, Admiral, what if the person who disappeared was a senior officer?'

CCO1's face betrayed his dismay. 'What... I don't...' he spluttered.

'We believe the body is that of a senior officer.'

Leo's uninflected words struck CCO1 almost physically. His face crumpled. He leaned across the table and spoke in a hoarse whisper. 'Listen, I tell you, it was nothing to do with me. Just turn your attention to Fitch, that's my recommendation.

I have reason to believe that he was the instigator. I believe he is the guilty man.'

As these words were uttered, the door whisked open and, as if on cue, Fitch appeared, dishevelled and distinctly wild-eyed. He addressed Leo and Cy in loud, panic-stricken tones: 'What has he been saying about me? I demand a private interview with you right away. I deny his accusations categorically. None of this has anything to do with me.'

CCO1 rose to his feet with fury. 'How dare you burst into my private meeting. This is a disciplinary breach of the highest category and I shall...'

Cy interrupted this diatribe with incisive authority. 'Be quiet, please, Admiral. This is our private meeting, not yours. I would ask you to leave us now. We will speak to Mr Fitch.'

As Cy beckoned Fitch to come forward, Leo led a profoundly shocked and unresisting CCO1 to the door. Before he closed it behind him, he addressed everyone outside. 'Would you all please remain where you are.' Then he addressed the pathologist: 'Mr Martinez, What news of the suit specialists?'

'Mr Fitch said a small team will be with us as soon as possible. Probably around thirty minutes or so. They need to consult the design records to find the relevant details of obsolete suits.'

'Thank you. If the suit team arrive, await my further instructions, please. The body is not to be touched at the moment.' Cy closed the office door and resumed his seat at the table. 'Please sit down, Mr Fitch,' he said. 'Would you like to tell us what you were talking about when you burst in? Note that we are recording what you say.'

Fitch held his head in his hands and spoke in despair. 'I knew he would try to blame me, Sir. But he's the one who is to blame for all this, you know. Nothing like this could have happened without him being involved. I bet he said he knew nothing about it and that I was to blame.' His sentence ended as a pathetic wail!

'What situation are you talking about, Mr Fitch?'

'All this. The disappearance of the escape pod. The disposal of its occupant. They were jealous, you know. That was the reason for it. He was too good for them. That's why it happened.'

A few highly charged moments passed. 'Who is "he", Mr Fitch?' Leo's quiet voice.

'Hasn't CCO1 told you? It's typical, that! He's responsible and he won't even speak the man's name. Instead, he'll slough off the blame to everyone else and then go scot free...'

'Who is "he", Mr Fitch?' Leo's voice held a sharper edge. 'Who was "too good" for them?'

Silence. Then: 'Commander Gorton, of course.' The words forced out with great reluctance, a barely audible whisper.

Leo spoke. 'Are you telling us the body is of Commander Gorton?'

'Yes.'

'How do you know?'

'Because they were all jealous of him. Hated him. Decided to get rid of him, dispose of him.' He paused. 'He was the one who went missing 30 years ago. They locked him into the escape pod and sent it away.' A defeated, broken voice.

'But recently you implied to us that he was alive and here on the Platform. When we invited him to our meeting, you reported that he sent his apologies!'

Fitch sagged even more. 'I was instructed to do that. I had to do as I was told.'

'Who by?'

After a hesitation. 'CCO1, of course.'

A pause. Then Cy started a new line of questioning.

'Who sent Commander Gorton to his death, Mr Fitch?'

'Not me!' Fitch's response was immediate and shrill. 'I would never do such a thing to a fellow human being. You can ask anyone. I'm simply not like that. I was not involved in that.'

'So who did?'

'It was them. CCO1 and his favourites. His medical elite. His engineering elite. They were the ones who did it. They were the ones who could do it. I'm a lower-level engineer in their sight. And CCO1 has always had it in for me...'

'But you were the one he promoted, Mr Fitch...'

There was silence as Fitch wrestled desperately to produce a reply. Finally: 'Well, he needed someone to be STC1 and I was the most senior sub-Commander who could do the job,' he said weakly.

There was a pause as Cy and Leo exchanged glances, switching to DT Mode.

(Leo) 'Sounds pretty unlikely. I would have thought Fitch was deeply involved. What do you think?'

(Cy) 'Yes but he wouldn't have the expertise to modify the pod. Someone else must have done that – and certainly not CCO1 either!'

(Leo) 'I agree. Let's persuade Fitch to tell us who it was.'

Leo switched out of DT Mode. 'So, Mr Fitch, to sum up, you are accusing CCO1 of this crime? You claim it was he who instigated it and caused it to be carried out. Is that right?'

'No, no, not at all, you're twisting my words, I never said that.' Fitch's words were now a hysterical torrent.

'Mr Fitch, just a few minutes ago you stated clearly that Admiral Sarfeld was responsible for what happened to Commander Gorton.'

'Responsible, yes. He must have approved it but his friends actually did it. It was Sangyar, you know. He is the guilty man. It was definitely his idea. He was the instigator. He hated Commander Gorton interfering in medical matters and acquiring a reputation as a healer. Everyone on the platform called Commander Gorton "The Yggdrasil Healer" – did you know that? It had been going on for years. Everybody knew him. All the staff. Everybody. He did good things. Solved problems. Healed people.' Fitch was frenetic, gesticulating wildly.

'But Commander Sangyar is not a technical expert. He could not possibly have been involved in the engineering modification of the escape pod.'

'No, no, of course not.' Now Fitch was shouting uncontrollably. 'But it was his idea. He was the "Prime Mover". He was the one that wanted Gorton disposed of. He was obsessively jealous. He showed it many times, always speaking out against him.'

Now Fitch fell silent, his head bowed.

'Sangyar next, I think?' Cy in DT Mode and Leo communicated his agreement.

'You may leave us now, Mr Fitch,' Cy said, 'If your Suit Maintenance team arrive keep them standing by. The body is not to be touched at the moment. Do you hear?'

'Yes, Sir. Ah, Sir, please do not tell...'

'Leave us, Mr Fitch and ask Commander Sangyar to join us.'

'You wished to see me?' Surgeon-Commander Sangyar was brisk and smiling, 'how can I help you? I am, of course, at your complete disposal.'

By contrast, Leo was unsmiling. 'Sit down, Mr Sangyar. You were holding the deceased from the escape pod in a casket that had been placed in special secure storage in your department. A storage unit which, I was told, had only one key.' He held it up. 'Can you explain to us how the casket came to be removed from the unit and sent for destruction to your Medical Disposal facility on Level-o?'

Sangyar's smile disappeared, to be replaced by a look of deep solicitous sorrow. 'A terrible mistake was made, Sir. The area where the secure units were located was unfortunately scheduled for reconstruction. This happens from time to time. The routine procedure in all these cases is to strip out the entire room contents and store them elsewhere. Of course all furniture must be emptied before removal. In this case, someone thought the casket from that unit was to be sent for disposal. This is extremely regrettable and, on behalf of my organisation, I am deeply sorry...'

'"Someone", Mr Sangyar? Who was the "someone" who removed the casket from the storage unit?'

'Well, Sir, the rooms are always stripped by a special team from Utilities Division, so that reconstruction may commence. This is the total responsibility of Utilities Division and my Division is of course not involved in any of these processes. If you wish, I can find out for you the names of the people from Utilities Division who stripped out the room and then you can...'

He stopped as Leo lifted a hand. 'Mr Sangyar, you are not addressing my question. I asked you: "Who removed the casket from the storage unit?" I have no interest in the subsequent removal of the empty storage cabinets.'

There was a brief pause. Looking down at the table, Sangyar replied very quietly:

'I suppose it was someone from Medical, of course.'

'Who was that "someone"?'

'I don't know.'

'Why don't you know, Mr Sangyar?'

'Well, these are routine matters, Sir. I would not normally be involved.'

'Right. So "someone" from Medical was able to open the high security unit, remove the casket which contained the body of the deceased from the rescued escape pod, a very important and crucial piece of evidence for our investigation. How would they do this, since there is only one key?'

'Ah... ah... there is, of course, a master key for all security units.'

'Held by whom?'

The room became still. Finally Sangyar spoke: 'Well, technically, by me.'

'Technically? What does that mean?'

'Well, it hangs on a hook in my office and I issue it when necessary to a member of my staff.'

'And did you do that yesterday?'

'Not that I can recall.'

'Do you not keep records of such an important matter?'

'Ah... no. You see, the master key is used so rarely. Almost never, in fact. I cannot recall another occasion.'

'Well, Mr Sangyar, it was used yesterday, wasn't it? And it must have been used by a member of Medical. You would not give the master key to anyone else, would you?'

'No, certainly not.'

'So a member of your staff removed the key without your permission?'

'Well, I suppose so. But please remember this was necessary because the storage room was to be stripped and reconstructed. It was essential that it should be done before the Utilities Division team arrived. If I was not present in my office, the key still had to be acquired for that reason.'

'But surely you would still expect to be informed?'

'Well, yes, but in all the commotion, perhaps it slipped someone's mind...'

Leo said nothing but looked at Sangyar sharply.

'Right. Once he had removed the casket from the unit, what would your member of staff do with it?'

'Whatever he was instructed to do.'

'By you?'

'No. I have no recollection of issuing any instructions about this.'

Leo sighed. 'I am afraid that none of this is making sense to me, Mr Sangyar.'

Silence. Then Cy spoke sharply. 'How is an item sent to Medical Disposal?'

'A Disposal Instruction is raised. This is then passed through various authorities for verification and eventually it reaches Medical Disposal. If the Disposal Instruction is correctly certificated, my staff on Level-0 will carry out the disposal of the item or items.'

'Who is allowed to raise Disposal Instructions?'

'It depends on the classification of the item. Class 1 Disposal Instructions are raised by senior staff; Heads of Function Units, for instance.'

'Would this item be Class 1?'

Silence, then: 'Yes. Anything concerned with human parts would be.'

'So the "someone" who acquired the secure storage unit master key would have been given a Class 1 Disposal Instruction, verified and certified at the appropriate levels and instructed to send the casket to Medical Disposal?'

'Yes, I imagine so.'

'Mr Sangyar,' Cy's voice was incisive, 'we know that is what happened. My colleague and I had to rescue the casket just as it was about to be destroyed in Medical Disposal on Level-0! Who raised the Disposal Instruction?'

'I'm sorry, Sir, I cannot answer that. I would need to check the records.' This stated in a more confident tone.

Cy sighed and let a few moments pass. Then he spoke very quietly. 'We know that you raised it. This is a copy of your Instruction, signed by you, then fully verified and certified.' He pushed the paper across the table. 'Furthermore, you specified that the items were not to be scanned, which we understand is standard procedure. Why did you wish to omit the scan, Mr Sangyar?'

Several minutes passed as Sangyar looked sightlessly at the paper, his mind racing like a fibrillating heartbeat, frantic but producing no effective output.

'There must be some mistake,' he mumbled finally.

'Is this your signature?' A whiplash of a question.

'Yes.'

'Authorised and accepted by the validation process?'

'Yes.' Barely a whisper.

'So let's not talk about mistakes. There is no mistake. This Instruction was definitely raised by you. Why did you do it?'

Sangyar looked wildly around, as if hoping for a divine intervention. Finally, a stumbling admission in a broken voice: 'He said I had to do it. I didn't want to. I didn't want to be involved in any of it but he said it was necessary. It was just like 30 years ago. Then, all three of them said he was becoming too powerful. Knowing secret things that he shouldn't. They said they couldn't allow that. That it was too dangerous to let him live.' Now the words became a shrill torrent. 'I argued against it, you know, but they threatened me, too. So I had to go along with it. That's the truth. You must believe me.' At last he stopped, deathly pale, sweat dripping from a contorted face.

'Who is "he" and who are "the three of them", Mr Sangyar?'

Sangyar closed his eyes and swayed in his chair. Then he began talking at breakneck speed: 'I can't keep silent any longer. I've had to live with this for 30 years, forced to do what he wanted because he said, if I didn't, he would shift all the blame on to me and I would be imprisoned for the rest of my life on the worst Prison Planet in the Universe. He said he would see to it that my life was made a permanent hell – and I believe him too! He – and the other two, they are capable of anything. I was never in that inner circle, you know. I was always kept outside and just forced to do anything they wanted. I've had a dreadful time all during the last 30 years. You can't imagine how awful it has been...' The man began to weep loudly.

The minutes passed. Cy and Leo waited until he had quieted.

'Who is "he" and who are "the other two", Mr Sangyar? You need to tell us.' Cy's questions penetrated the silence.

More minutes passed as Sangyar sat almost cataleptic. Then he jerked spasmodically and started to talk in an almost dreamlike state: 'The Leader is the worst, you know. Yes, of course the other two are horrible bullies, never allowing me to be happy, always interfering in my work in Medical. But the Leader is the worst. Always so terrifyingly cold and inhuman, so calculating, so very vicious all the time. I was physically beaten up several times on his instructions, you know, just because I didn't carry out his orders quickly enough. Investigators, you must be careful of the Leader, he's a very dangerous man. Do not underestimate him. Just remember, he's been here in that powerful position for many, many years. He wields his power ruthlessly. And he's well-regarded back at Command. They listen to him and go along with anything he says. Listen to me! Please! He's very dangerous, even to you. You need to be careful, vigilant.' He fell silent, panting rapidly.

Leo spoke softly. 'We are afraid of nobody, especially not your Leader, Admiral Sarfeld. So you don't need to worry.'

Sangyar's head jerked up and he looked piercingly at them both. Then he addressed them in a surprisingly loud, incisive tone, though still threaded through with skeins of panic. 'I'm not talking about him. I'm talking about the Leader, the person who arranged that Commander Gorton should die in the most horrible way possible. I'm talking about Sub-Commander Glassford.'

They had returned to the Pathology Laboratory, where the terrifyingly functional autopsy table still displayed the white, Space-suited body, now even more dazzlingly illuminated by pitiless lighting. Principal-Surgeon Martinez and his acolytes stood close by, his team now augmented by several other figures wearing grey overalls and carrying unfamiliar items of equipment.

A short time before, after Leo and Cy had recovered from their surprise at Sangyar's very bewildering revelation, they had agreed (in quick-fire flashes of DT communication) that they would need to spend some time trying to unravel what they had heard from CCO1, Fitch and Sangyar. Meanwhile, it was appropriate that the autopsy should proceed. The Suit Maintenance Team was now in attendance.

Leo stepped forward and addressed everyone. 'Thank you, everyone, for waiting. It seems we have a full team assembled and so the autopsy can begin.' He nodded to Martinez who, in turn, nodded the Suit Maintenance Team. A tall, young man stepped forward.

'Command Investigators,' he said in a pleasant voice, 'I am Lt Ho Chon. I am in charge of the Suit Maintenance Team. I am sorry for the delay in our arrival but I had to consult the unit's historical records to ensure that I can open the suit for you with the minimum of damage. As you know, this is an obsolete suit, designed over 30 years ago. However, I have the correct documentation here. May I explain to you what I am about to do?'

Cy nodded. 'Please do, Mr Ho Chon.'

'Well, Sir, as you know, a closed suit can only be opened from the inside. It would be dangerous to have unlocking controls on the outside because these could be operated inadvertently with fatal consequences. For many years, suits have been made from lightweight semi-rigid panels that are extremely resistant to damage of any type. Special tools have been developed to tackle the eventuality that faces us here – that is, a suit which has been closed and locked from the inside and now requires to be opened. However, before I begin the procedure to open the suit, Principal-Surgeon Martinez has suggested that a gas sample should be taken from inside.'

Martinez stepped forward and added: 'This may give me some information about the condition of the body, Sir, which will help to determine my handling techniques.'

'Thank you, Mr Martinez. Will you be able to have the gas sample analysed immediately?'

Martinez nodded and pointed to a small piece of equipment on a nearby table. 'This equipment will analyse the gas at once, Sir.'

Cy turned towards the suit technician. 'Please proceed, Mr Ho Chon.'

A special vibration-free drill made a small hole in the suit, the gas sample collected and the small hole resealed. Soon, the gas analyser had done its work and Martinez examined the results.

'This is rather remarkable, Sir. The sample is unexpectedly pure. Literally, almost sterile, well-filtered air but with a very low oxygen content and a high carbon dioxide concentration. There is no evidence of other pollutants.'

'How would you interpret this, Mr Martinez?'

Martinez thought for a moment. 'Well, perhaps the body is intact, originally flash frozen and then desiccated over an extended period of time. Even so, it is most unusual to have no contaminants at all.'

'Thank you. Are you happy for Lt Ho Chon to proceed?'

'Yes, Sir.'

The technician's precision cutting tool was applied to the suit panels at several carefully-chosen places. It took some time to cut through the very robust material but, eventually, the suit was breached sufficiently for a hand to slip inside at the appropriate places and release the internal locks. It was extremely shocking to see the suit now gaping wide, as if a giant surgical incision had been made and the flesh retracted by a gigantic tissue spreader. Many of the watchers could not supress a gasp as the opened suit was seen as high-definition 3-dimensional displays around the room. After the solid, white bulk of the spacesuit, the body inside looked so small, flat and insignificant, completely contained in the soft inner body unit that was the internal part of the suit. Finally, the technician released the suit helmet and lifted it away, revealing a smooth, white cloth completely covering the head.

Lt Ho Chon stood back, his job done, and Martinez stepped forward to start his examination of the body. 'I am beginning to think that there are only bones remaining here,' Martinez announced. 'I will now remove the cloth that is covering the head and we shall begin to see what we have here.' As he said this, he carefully lifted the white cloth away to reveal – absolutely nothing!

The surgeon froze for a moment, taken completely by surprise. Then, in one smooth movement, he deftly drew down the slide fastener on the front of the inner body unit, opening it to waist level. Again, there was nothing inside; no bones, no flesh, no body. Examination of the remainder of the body unit, arms, trunk, legs, revealed a similar complete emptiness. There was absolutely no trace of a body anywhere. Completely perplexed, Martinez stood back. There was a stunned silence in the laboratory. Everyone breathed as quietly as they could and hoped that their heartbeats would not violate the silence. Nobody moved. No clothes rustled, no chair creaked. The usually inaudible hum of the air conditioning became a deafening pulsation.

Eventually, Martinez broke the spell. He turned to face Cy and Leo and spoke in a level, professional tone. 'Gentlemen, as you see, there is no autopsy to be done here. There is no body or, indeed, any physical part of a body. Absolutely nothing.'

Eventually, Leo broke the silence. 'Can we examine every part of the inner body unit for evidence of biological traces?'

Martinez paused and then shook his head slowly. 'I don't think so, Sir. I believe that the suits automatically deep-clean and sterilize themselves as soon as they are vacated.'

Lt Ho Chon stepped forward. 'Sir, may I speak?' Leo nodded. 'What Commander Martinez has said is correct, Sir, but the deep-cleaning, sterilisation and restoration process happens only after the suit is returned to its docking rig. In this case, if a person locked himself inside the suit and then somehow disappeared, biological traces could still be present.'

Leo and Cy looked at each other. 'Excellent, Mr Ho Chon, thank you. Mr Martinez, please take the suit and casket into your safekeeping, make your biological tests and let us have your report as soon as it is available.'

'I will, Sir.' Martinez waved to his assistants to return the suit to the casket. 'Take this to our secure mortuary and arrange for a guard to be stationed on the door.' He turned back to Leo and Cy. 'I will proceed on this as quickly as I can, Sir.'

'Just one moment, please.' Cy said. 'I have a final question for Lt Ho Chon.'

'Yes, Sir.' The man came forward.

'Is there any possibility that the body could have been removed recently?'

'Absolutely not, Sir.' The man was adamant. 'The suit was totally undamaged and intact in every way. Furthermore, it was still hermetically sealed and the inner body unit was closed and completely undisturbed.'

'Thank you. Will you submit a report, please?'

'I will, Sir.'

Leo addressed everyone else. 'You may all stand down now. We will certainly need to talk to some of you in the coming days. Please stand by for that.'

They returned to their accommodation.

'We need time to think about this, Cy. A lot of time! Let's eat and relax this evening and start on the evaluation tomorrow. We've gathered all the evidence we need at the moment and come up with some highly surprising results. I need to get it all straight in my mind before talking about it. Is that acceptable to you?'

'Definitely!' Cy was flushed and emphatic. 'All this makes me more determined to get to the bottom of this and make sure we nail the criminals. I've deliberately used the plural here because I feel sure there are more than one for us to identify!'

'Let's eat,' Leo responded quietly.

21

The Twenty-sixth Day

Breakfast had been a very quiet meal. Both men were deep in thought and the food was consumed abstractedly. Even when Cy offered Leo a refill of his coffee cup, no words were spoken; gestures and nods seemed more appropriate. Neither man wished to shatter this silence of deep introspection.

Now they had moved to the lounge. Cy smiled at Leo as a DT transmission registered in his brain. "Permission to speak, Sir?"

Cy nodded. 'Yes. Let's get started.'

'The mysterious absence of the body actually changes nothing.' Leo's first spoken words.

'I agree but let's check through the reasoning.'

Leo leaned forward. 'OK. Here goes. The mysterious absence of the body changes nothing because we already have so much other evidence to establish the truth. We know it was Gorton in the escape pod. We have his complete record of what happened, what he did and how he died. We have a record of his life on the platform, his analysis of his assailants and we have the independent PAC analysis of the same. And we have the destroyed escape pod, full of the physical evidence that backs up and confirms everything.

'That's fine, Leo. We have also added considerably to that evidence since we arrived here just five days ago. Seems a lot longer, Eh?' He smiled briefly. 'Several people, including CCO1, nearly jumped out of their skin when they first saw the recovered pod. They were even more worried when they heard we had the occupant, too. Using experts here on the Platform, we soon had independent confirmation of Gorton's record of technical modifications to recover the situation. We have also established how the murderers duplicated the missing escape pod. And we know they "duplicated" Gorton, too, such that Command still thinks he's here.'

'OK, that's right, but we have yet to establish who the murderers are and what part each played. The one thing we are sure of, however, is that several people were involved, because the complexity of what was done 30 years ago was huge. And the difficulty of keeping up the deception for decades must have been a constant pressure.'

They were both silent for a moment or two, once again deep in thought.

Finally Cy spoke. 'What about the body, Leo. That's really puzzling me. We never expected that, did we? We know with certainty that Gorton was physically in the escape pod. We know that he died in that suit after it powered down – a suit system will only last a few days without recharge. We found him lying in the place he had gone to die, in his bunk. His body must have been there, in the suit. What happened to the body? How could it disappear from a closed and sealed suit? It's impossible!'

'I know that, Cy. It was the last thing I expected.'

'Wait a moment, Leo.' Cy's eyes flashed with enthusiasm. 'I've just had an idea. Gorton had special powers, didn't he? He described some of the things he was able to do here on the Platform. "The Yggdrasil Healer", they called him – you don't get called that for nothing! He was able to do surprising things; impossible things, even miraculous things. He had powers that no-one else had, didn't he? So could the disappearance of his body be another manifestation of these special powers? I think it could,' he concluded triumphantly.

'Um.' Leo looked unconvinced. 'Maybe, Cy. We'll keep it in mind.'

'Well, if you can come up with a better explanation, let me know!'

Leo's PAC chimed. 'Look, Cy! Here's Martinez' report. He scanned it quickly. 'Wow, this is interesting. He found multiple samples of Gorton's DNA inside the inner body unit and the distribution patterns fitted what would be expected if someone occupied the unit for a significant period of time. The report concludes that Commander Maynard Gorton had definitely lived in that suit for several days at least.'

'That's really good, Leo.' Cy was exultant. 'It establishes that a living Commander Gorton occupied that suit in the pod. But it goes no way to explaining how his body subsequently disappeared from the closed, sealed suit without visible trace. So I'm sticking with my theory. It's the only one that even vaguely fits the facts!'

Leo shook his head doubtfully. 'Well, we'll keep thinking about it, Cy. I must say, I don't know how we'll explain it in our report, though! Anyway, now we come to the really difficult bit. Establishing who did what. And, in particular, finding out who was the Prime Mover in all of this. That's our next task. Whew! Let's break for a coffee! We've been at this constantly for hours!'

Half an hour later, they sat down again.

'Right,' Cy began energetically, 'let's remind ourselves of what Gorton thought and what the PAC risk analysis came up with. We'll need to try and fit these together.'

'OK,' Leo nodded. 'Let's start with the easy one. CCO1! Top suspect by Gorton. Highest risk from PAC. We know him to be an unpleasant, arrogant man. I suppose that's what absolute power can do to you. He has commanded Yggdrasil for a very long time. Jealous of Gorton's power and popularity. Probably jealous of his knowledge and achievements, too. And very likely jealous of his youth, too.'

'Absolutely agreed.' Cy nodded vigorously, 'I think that sums up CCO1. He had motivation for wanting to dispose of Gorton and he certainly had the power to do it. With his authority, he would soon recruit others to do the necessary work. He has just got to be our chief suspect for Prime Mover.

Right. Number Two has got to be Fitch. Gorton had a few run-ins with Fitch when they first met. I see Fitch as the old-style bully type. Always trying to boost himself up by trampling people down while ingratiating himself with the big boss – successfully, it would seem, since he got himself promoted to Commander after Gorton was eliminated. And Fitch is identified as Number Two suspect by Gorton.

'That's right,' Leo responded, 'but I can't help thinking that he might be less involved than the others. It's common enough for subordinates not to like their superiors but few actually murder them! Fitch was outranked by Sarfeld and I reckon his intellectual and technical powers would be surpassed by Sangyar and Glassford. So I see Fitch in a relatively weak position within that group. I think he might have exerted the least influence.'

'Hm,' Cy was thoughtful. 'I do see what you mean, Leo. We'll need to keep that idea in mind. He studied his notes. 'Let's continue. Gorton thought that Number Three suspect might be the remote pilot of the escape pod but I'm not so sure about that. I can't think that Commander Wood, PPN1, would be a suspect, because Gorton saved his life in the magnetic flux incident. I think that an unknown pilot, a subordinate of Wood's, could just have been instructed to fly the pod and land it on an asteroid. He would just have obeyed his orders and thought no more about it.'

Leo nodded. 'That certainly is possible, although the PAC risk analysis kept the pilot function assessed on "high". Let's just keep it in mind. Let's pass on to Number Four, which is our clever and loquacious friend, Head, Medical, Surgeon-Commander Sangyar. He certainly had plenty to say for himself, didn't he? I can certainly see how he was assessed as a significant risk to Gorton. He was (and is in charge of an illegal euthanasia unit. A dangerous, secret job, eh?'

'Yes,' Cy nodded, 'and surely Major Bannerman, the boss of the TP Facility must come into this too, because they were the people actually operating the euthanasia function. Of course, they were only doing what they were told, no doubt.

And let us not forget, the orders for all euthanasia events were likely to come from the top, from CCO1 himself.' He consulted his notes once more. 'After that, the PAC lists the Heads of Construction and Development, that's Glinche – who left Yggdrasil a long time ago – and Glassford, whose name came up in yesterday's interviews. Interesting one, that. A big surprise for us, because Gorton judged that neither of these Area Heads were a risk to him, although the PAC did output a moderate risk. We need further thought and discussion on Glassford, I think.'

Leo was thoughtful. 'Yes. Glassford briefed us on the function of his Area during that first meeting, Cy. He seemed very keen to delegate the work to a subordinate "expert", remember? That's when we got Major Biranco and he certainly did a good job for us. Glassford never looked near. However, he didn't strike us as the dangerous type.' Leo consulted his notes once again. 'I think that's it, Cy. Gorton really discounts everyone else.'

Cy set his notes aside. 'Now that we've reminded ourselves of Gorton's PAC evidence, let's get up to date and talk about what happened yesterday – our fascinating interviews with the three people who are firmly at the top of our suspect list! These were three very surprising interviews, were they not?'

'Yes, they were quite amazing, weren't they? Good thing there was that delay at the beginning of the autopsy, eh? That was a bit of luck for us!'

'Right,' Cy began, 'Admiral Sarfeld's motivation is pretty obvious. He just wanted to get in first and assure us that he had nothing to do with any of it. I mean, an important man like him! How could anyone think ill of him? Whiter than white – and the darling of Command back home!'

Leo smiled briefly. 'Of course we don't know how he is regarded back at Command. I can hardly imagine that he is their top favourite, though. On the other hand, they've allowed him to be in charge of their most important platform for 60 odd years, so he must find some favour in their eyes!'

'Well, I think they'll soon change their mind about that when they hear about the fraud he has been running here.

Keeping Gorton "alive" for the last 30 years! And that's before we find out how much he was involved in the murder.'

'Yes, Cy, let's review that. We know that Sarfeld is not a technical man, he's one of the "old school" military fighting men. But we both feel he must have been highly involved. We know that he was jealous of Gorton for various reasons, most probably based on insecurity. However, I think the discovery of the illegal euthanasia unit could have been the final motivator. Gorton would then become highly dangerous in Sarfeld's eyes.'

Cy agreed. 'So was Sarfeld the prime instigator of the plot, which was then discussed, planned and refined with his co-conspirators?' There's no doubt that he would need very skilled technical people within the plot, as well as people who could organise the significant workforce that would be required.'

'Yes.' Leo paused. 'However, Sarfeld wants to blame Fitch for the whole thing. As we've already concluded, we don't see Fitch as the Prime Mover. I'm sure he had the power to set up the infrastructure but it seems inconceivable that Sarfeld would allow him to be in charge.'

Cy nodded in agreement. 'It was interesting to hear what Fitch had to say. He knew that Sarfeld would blame him! He was absolutely right, too! I can't help seeing Fitch as a sort of pathetic scapegoat here, someone to be loaded up with all the crimes while the clever ones go free.'

'Yes, I do think Sarfeld was attempting to shift the blame. I think Fitch was involved but he was certainly not the Prime Mover. However, now we come to the interesting part. You might have thought that Fitch would identify Sarfeld as the instigator of the crime – but he didn't! He accused Sangyar! So let's turn our spotlight on him.'

Cy referred to his notes. 'Well, we know that several of Gorton's "interventions" were in major medical matters and Fitch suggested that Sangyar was highly jealous of Gorton's prowess. We know of occasions when Gorton saved dying people's lives. Furthermore, it would seem that he brought someone back to life after he had been deliberately "terminated" in the TP Facility. We know very little about

Sangyar, although he must be a well-qualified and experienced medical man to be in charge here.'

'Yes, Cy, and there's no doubt that his medical staff were responsible for both of the thefts of our evidence. Firstly, the PAC and then the body in the casket, sent for destruction – all a huge and terrible mistake, of course!'

'I think Sangyar is likely to be a key member of the murder team, don't you?'

'I agree with that. But let's go to the final puzzle now. Out of the blue, Sangyar identifies the prime instigator as Glassford. Glassford, of all people! Even more surprising, he insists on calling him "The Leader". Can this possibly be true? I really don't know what to think about it!' Now Leo sat deep in thought for some time; then he lifted his head and spoke. 'You know, Cy, it must be one of these four. One of them must be the Prime Mover who persuaded or ordered the others to join them. By all accounts, they may not have required much persuasion, since it would seem they all had reason to dislike Gorton and regard him as a danger.'

'I don't quite see it like that, Leo. I see two, possibly three of this group as murderous conspirators, – certainly CCO1 and Sangyar, and possibly Fitch – but surely not Glassford! I haven't seen any reason for Glassford to hate Gorton, have you? However, I feel sure that Glassford masterminded the technical work on the escape pod. He is a top engineer with a huge amount of experience in engineering construction as well as having hundreds of his own engineers to help him build what he needed for all the modifications. And I am sure Glassford could have enlisted Glinche's help; Glinche's staff could then have worked on specific scientific developments and passed their work back to Glassford. So I see Glassford as an absolutely key technical figure here – but definitely not the Prime Mover of a dreadful murder – and certainly NOT the leader of the group! As a mere Sub-Commander, how could he be? You know how highly rank is regarded here.'

'Mm. There certainly is a lot of logic in what you say, Cy. And, since you've raised Glinche, let's send off a query to him and see if he can recall any special work for Glassford around

30 years ago. It's a bit of a long shot but these scientific guys sometimes keep good records.'

They spend the next ten minutes composing a query and despatched it through their own private communication channel.

'You know, my head aches, Leo. Let's break for lunch now and relax for a while. Then we can plan our next move.'

In reply, Leo leant back and closed his eyes gratefully.

They had lunched when the reply came:

```
Priority:        RS1

Routing:         Special

Channel HBF74. Encoding: JV3
Personal for Command Investigator C Funte,
SSP Yggdrasil

From:            Sub-Commander Z Glinche.
                 Scientist 1, Command RSC.

Heading:         Special workload SSP
                 Yggdrasil, T-30 Years


Information:

Reference to personal records from that time
period indicates several periods of special
research work was requested personally by
Sub-Commander Wilfred Glassford, Head, ST
Construction concerned with the conception and
development of several non-standard control
unit functions understood to be installed in
an experimental GTN67UV escape pod. A few
electronic items completed in my Area and
despatched to Construction. Informal note of
thanks subsequently received from Sub-Commander
Glassford. No other information available.
{Message ends}
```

'Very interesting, Cy. Completely in accordance with the theory you were expounding earlier. This is a useful bit of information, isn't it?'

Cy nodded. 'OK, Leo, where do we go from here?' As he said this, the internal communicator chimed. It was CCO1. 'Yes, Admiral, what can we do for you?'

'Investigators, can we come to you for a meeting, please – this afternoon, if possible?'

Cy raised his eyebrows to Leo who nodded in reply.

'Yes, Admiral, that would be possible. You said "we". Who will be attending the meeting?'

'Ah, well, it's just the three of us. Fitch, Sangyar and myself, of course.'

Cy's eyebrows were raised again but this time in surprise. 'Shall we say 1500 hours in our accommodation on Level-3, Admiral?'

'Well, we could meet in my office...'

'Our accommodation on Level-3 will be fine, Admiral. See you then.'

CCO1 had arrived in high good humour, accompanied by Fitch and Sangyar who were less ebullient but smiled with quiet satisfaction as they sat down around a table with Leo and Cy. By contrast, the two Investigators were serious and unsmiling.

Leo began. 'You wished to see us, Gentlemen?'

'Well,' CCO1 bellowed joyfully, 'we thought we may as well wrap this thing up right away and no doubt you gentlemen will want to be on your way as soon as possible. Then we can all get back to normal. I have a great deal of work stacked up, you know. Strategic matters, you know.' He cocked his head invitingly and waited for a reply.

'I'm sorry, Admiral, I don't understand you. Our investigation has progressed well but is far from over. So, would you explain what you mean?'

'Well, Investigators, it's pretty obvious, isn't it? There's no body. We all saw that yesterday. Only an old, empty spacesuit! So, this whole business about a missing staff member from this Platform is proven to be a totally erroneous fabrication. Yes, 30 years ago my ST Division did carry out an experiment when we sent a time-expired escape pod under special external control to land on a nearby asteroid. I'm sure we can find all the reports of that experiment if we look for them. Of course, that modified escape pod carried suits with it as part of its normal equipment. That's why you found an empty suit there in the derelict pod.' He paused and smiled calmly. 'You see, it can all be explained completely rationally! Now, my staff and I are more than willing to assist you with your report to Command. We can include the Yggdrasil experiment report within it. You will be able to assure Command that nothing is amiss here. Absolutely nothing at all. They will be unsurprised, because they know that I am in charge. I have a superb reputation at Command, you know!'

Sarfeld leaned back in his chair and beamed at Leo and Cy. 'It has been a great pleasure to cooperate with you. It has been useful to us, too. It has given my staff a taste of what a Command Investigation is like. I'm sure many of them will be very glad it's over!'

All the time Sarfeld was speaking, Leo's eyes never left his. He continued his gaze for a full minute after the Admiral had finished speaking. Sarfeld did not notice this as he was too busy smirking towards his two subordinates.

'Who is STC1 on SSP Yggdrasil, Admiral?' Leo asked quietly.

'Commander Fi...' he stopped in confusion. 'I mean, Commander Gorton,' he concluded weakly.

'Ask him to join us, please.'

'What... now?' Sarfeld's faced drained of colour.

'Yes, right now. We must speak to him in person right away.'

There were some moments of absolute quiet.

'Ah, Mr Fitch. Call Commander Gorton and ask him to join us.' Sarfeld's voice held an overtone of panic.

Fitch spoke to his PAC. Then: 'I'm sorry, Sir, Commander Gorton isn't answering.'

Cy spoke sharply. 'Send an emergency response call to him. Now!'

Fitch complied. 'There is no response,' he said after a moment.

'I've just remembered!' Sarfeld burst out. 'Commander Gorton is off-platform. He isn't available. He is on one of our survey explorers. He will not return until...'

Cy interrupted. 'Admiral. No matter where he was, Commander Gorton would respond to an emergency response call.'

'Well, sometimes...'

'No, Admiral.' Cy's voice was menacingly quiet. 'Commander Gorton is dead. He was locked into the modified escape pod you described and sent off to an asteroid to die. It took him a whole year to recreate a new local control system and just as he was about to transit away from the asteroid, your explosive device destroyed the movement capability of the vehicle. He lived on for years after that and managed to construct a weak Distress Signal. In the end, his vehicle failed and he had to live his last days in a suit. We know that his living body was definitely in that suit because there is ample evidence of his DNA there.'

Again, there was silence in the room. Sarfeld had turned pale.

'I didn't have anything to do with all of that,' he gasped.

'Yes, Admiral, you did, because we know you have kept Commander Gorton fictitiously alive in the eyes of Command. To this day, Command think that Commander Gorton is here as STC1. He is listed in that position in the Command Directory and messages are regularly received here for Commander Gorton which are answered by you or someone else instructed by you to do so. We have recorded the evidence of this.'

'It wasn't me, I promise you!' Sarfeld's words were loud and plaintive. 'It was them...' he pointed to his subordinates. 'They are the guilty ones. They killed Gorton. They hated him. I always regarded him as one of my most valuable officers...'

'That is nonsense!' Fitch's strident voice cut in. 'I want to place on record that I have had nothing to do with this. I know absolutely nothing about it at all...'

'Neither do I! I am totally innocent...' Now Sangyar had sprung to his feet and was shouting in a high, hysterical voice.

'Be quiet, all of you.' Leo's calm voice carried force and authority, cutting through the hubbub of denial. 'Mr Fitch, what position do you hold on the Platform?'

Fitch looked stricken. 'Ah... I'm Area Head of ST Maintenance,' he muttered finally.

'Why are you listed in the Platform Directory as STC1? Why do you hold the rank of Commander?'

Fitch was silent, now avoiding Leo's eyes. 'Mr Fitch, you are lying to me. I know you have been STC1 on this Platform for many years – in fact, since Commander Gorton disappeared 30 years ago. There is no way you could possibly be unaware of Commander Gorton's departure, since you took over his job.'

'That's right!' Sangyar's voice was shrill. 'Fitch was promoted as soon as Gorton left. I was really puzzled at the time but it had nothing to do with me. I want to reiterate that I had absolutely no part in all of this. I am sure you have the two guilty men before you, Sir.'

'Really, Mr Sangyar?' Cy voice was incisive. 'So why did you instruct one of your men to steal Gorton's PAC from the escape pod? We know that happened when your Recovery Team came to remove the body.' He held up a hand as Sangyar was about to speak. 'And why did you arrange for the body to be removed from your secure storage and order it to be sent for destruction on Level-0 as quickly as possible? You even had to arrange a reconstruction of the rooms, didn't you, to justify opening the storage unit? And then you insisted that the casket was not to be scanned – which is a set routine in the medical disposal procedures. We know that such an exception would require your personal authorisation – and you gave it.'

A loud clamour of voices greeted the end of Cy's statement. All three Yggdrasil staff exploded into strident denial, leaping to their feet and glaring furiously at each other, waving their arms wildly and making threatening gestures. The situation was degenerating towards physical attack.

'QUIET!' Cy's razor-sharp tones sliced through the sonic miasma of severe aggression that had suddenly filled the volume of the room. 'SIT DOWN! As far as we are concerned, all of you are prime suspects. When we establish which of you led this murderous and inhuman act, our investigation will be complete.'

Deflated, all three collapsed into their seats, limp and unresisting, their faces frozen in deep shock and horror as each one comprehended the full meaning of what Cy had just said. Uncounted time passed as brains struggled to cope. Finally, Fitch was the first to surface towards reality.

'OK, Gentlemen. I was ordered not to tell you this no matter what happened. But the time has come when I have to disobey that order. Now the truth must be told.' He leaned forward and spoke forcefully. 'Yes, I participated. I followed the orders I was given. I am a military man and that's what military men do. But I was *NOT* the instigator of this crime. I was not the leader. The Leader is Sub-Commander Glassford. He's the one you need to talk to. If it wasn't for him, Gorton would still be alive today. Now, for the first time, you have the truth. In your report, I hope you will remember that I was the first to give you the truth.'

Sangyar came to frenetic life. 'Fitch is right. Didn't I tell you that yesterday? Yes, I admit I had your evidence stolen – but I was only following the Leader's instructions. I am not the guilty one. I'm a medical man. I save lives, I do not take them. He looked pleadingly at Leo and Cy, who returned his gaze with inscrutable eyes and remained silent.

Leo turned to Fitch. 'So, Mr Fitch, you insist that the Leader is Sub-Commander Glassford?'

'He is, Sir.' Fitch's tone was positive.

'So why did you tell us previously that the Leader was Commander Sangyar?'

Fitch blenched. 'Because that's what the Leader ordered me to do,' he replied weakly.

Moments passed. 'And do you have anything to say about this, Admiral?' Leo asked this gently enough.

At first, Sarfeld did not react as extended seconds ticked by; then he slowly turned his head towards Leo. 'No, I have nothing to say,' he said expressionlessly.

22

The Twenty-seventh Day

Needless to say, Leo and Cy had spent the previous evening discussing all they had discovered during that day. There had been a great deal to discuss! Now they were at the start of a new day, reviewing progress.

'So, Leo, it looks like we now know most of it. Almost all of it, in fact. Let's just check the bottom line of our conclusions on the three we interviewed yesterday. They came to us, thinking that the lack of Gorton's physical body wound up the case and that all three of them were off the hook. We soon disabused them of that idea! Could you give us a quick précis, Leo?'

Leo checked his notes:

'Sarfeld. Our Number One suspect as the Prime Mover. Has not admitted his guilt.'

'Fitch. Admitted subordinate participation. To our surprise, now says Glassford is the Leader, backing up what Sangyar told us two days ago. Fitch is unlikely to be the Prime Mover, we think.'

'Sangyar. On the day of the autopsy, he told us that Glassford is the Leader and reiterated it yesterday. Admitted being responsible for the evidence thefts but we think he is neither the Prime Mover nor an active participant because medical skills were not involved.'

'Thanks Leo, let's turn our minds to Glassford, now identified as the Leader by two of the three accused. Can this possibly be true or are they just trying to shift the blame on to a lower ranking "innocent" party? At present, I must say it their assertions seem pretty unlikely.'

Cy consulted his PAC. 'Let's look into Glassford's staff record, Leo. Here it is. A very good quality technical man. Top grades in training. Successfully held various technical posts on Earth and on smaller platforms. Was promoted to be Area Head, ST Construction 45 years ago. So he was in post for 15 years before Gorton arrived to be STC1. All reports are good and he is described as being a skilled and inventive technician. There's note of a few management problems in his Area when Gorton came but the new boss soon sorted them out, by all accounts. From then on, no evidence of problems and Gorton's reports on Glassford were invariably complimentary. I just cannot believe that Glassford, a mere Sub-Commander, was the Prime Mover or the Leader. He could not possibly have had the authority.'

They sat quietly for a few moments. Then Leo spoke. 'So, are we fairly sure that Sarfeld is the Prime Mover? He certainly had the power to make it happen.'

'I agree, Leo. However, I think we better talk to Glassford. We think he was involved in the technical alterations – ordered to do so by CCO1, I imagine. You never know, he might be able to add something to our records.'

'OK. However, he certainly seems like a minor player in this affair.'

The meeting was arranged for 1100. As that time was indicated on the clock, the entrance chime announced the arrival of their visitor.

'Come in, Mr Glassford.' Cy's voice was quiet and neutral.

Glassford came forward rather hesitantly, looking at both investigators with a tentative smile. The smile was not returned. They all sat down.

Leo began. 'Mr Glassford, you were in attendance at the autopsy two days ago, were you not?'

'Yes, Sir.' A quiet, unsure voice.

'You saw that no body was found within the spacesuit, despite it being clear that the suit had not been opened since it had been sealed shut by its occupant 30 years before?'

'Yes, I observed that.'

'What did you think?'

'Well, Sir, I don't know what to think, really. I mean, you told us that you had recovered the pod and the body from an asteroid and that the suit was in a completely undisturbed condition. Logically, I can only suggest that there never had been a body in the suit. I really don't know, since I have absolutely no knowledge of the whole scenario.'

'There certainly had been a body in the suit, since there was ample DNA evidence to be gathered from the inner body unit.'

'Ah, well, maybe he had worn that suit on a previous occasion and it hadn't been cleaned and sterilized? I think that's probably the explanation, Sir.' Glassford smiled at them encouragingly.

Leo sighed. 'Mr Glassford, everyone knows that a used suit cannot be reused without cleaning and restoration. The suit simply would not function.'

Glassford did not reply. Now his eyes were watchful.

Leo continued. 'You were here 30 years ago, Mr Glassford, in your present post?'

'Yes, Sir.'

'Then tell me, in the knowledge that the escape pod had transited from this platform to the asteroid 30 years ago, whose body do you think it was?'

Glassford thought for a moment. 'No-one's body, Sir. The suit was empty.'

Leo sighed. 'You have just heard about the DNA evidence collected from the suit. Let me ask you the question in a different way. Whose DNA do you think it was?'

'Sir, I really have no idea.'

There was another short pause. Then Cy took up the questioning. '30 years ago, Mr Glassford, did a senior officer not disappear from the Platform?'

'I don't think so, Sir. I cannot recall that happening. I'm sure I would have remembered.'

'Why did Mr Fitch become STC1 at that time? Why was he promoted to Commander?'

'Because STC1, Commander Gorton, was transferred back to Earth, Sir. That's what I was told.'

'Who told you?'

'CCO1, at a Senior Staff Meeting.'

'Let us turn to something else.' Leo resumed his questioning. 'Did you work on modifications to the local control system of an escape pod 30 years ago?'

Glassford became noticeably more relaxed. '30 years ago! I can't even recall what I did one year ago! Just a minute, I'll check my work schedules and see what comes up.' He consulted his PAC. 'Ah, yes,' he said finally, 'there was a scientific experiment set up under CCO1's authority which involved quite a lot of technicians from my Area – and the Development Area, too, I see. Yes, the experiment was to modify an escape pod for remote control transit only. Quite a tricky job, as I recall. Took several months to achieve. I had to do quite a lot of the design work myself and carefully monitor what my technical staff were doing. It took a long time but, in the end we managed to do it. I understand the experiment was a success. CCO1 was very pleased!'

'Is it not always possible to control an escape pod remotely?'

'Yes, that's right, Sir.'

'Then, why should anyone go to all this trouble to achieve what could already be done?'

'I'm afraid I don't know why, Sir. As I say, it was a CCO1 experiment and I just did what I was told to do.'

'Why did you strip out all the communications equipment from the pod?'

'Did we? Let me see. Yes, I believe we did. I imagine they wanted that equipment for spares. After all, the pod wasn't going to need communications equipment, was it? It was going to be unmanned and the communications equipment would have been totally lost. I should imagine that was the reasoning.'

Leo handed over to Cy. 'And what about the explosive device that was installed in the engine bay, Mr Glassford?' Cy looked at him sharply.

'Explosive device? How strange. Of course I know nothing about any of that. I don't deal with explosive devices in my work. We construct. We do not destroy,' he concluded with the hint of a smile.

'What did Commander Gorton, your immediate superior, think of this experiment?'

'He knew nothing about it, Sir. I mean, he knew that I was doing special project work for CCO1 but he didn't know what it was. The experiment was a secret and all who worked on it in the dock area were sworn to absolute secrecy.'

'Really, Mr Glassford. And did you not think that was strange? Strange that your immediate superior should be kept in the dark while so many of his staff were engaged on this "secret" activity?'

'No, Sir, I didn't. I was too busy doing my job.'

'Who else was involved in this, apart from staff from your own Area?'

'Sub-Commander Glinche (he was Head, Development then) and his staff were involved in the concept and construction of several aspects of the highly specialised control facilities. I remember I was told not to divulge their purpose to him, however.'

'Where did all this modification work take place?'

'Well, some in the engineering dock where the escape pod was mounted. But most of the work was done in my Area workshops or, to a lesser extent, in Glinche's Area. I carried out most of the final installation work myself, since I was the only one who really understood how everything worked. Engineering and design skills of a very high order were required,' he added proudly. 'At times, I required assistance and two senior engineers in my team sometimes worked on the pod with me. I used different people – it just depended upon who was available.'

'Was the dock a restricted area?'

'Yes, of course. We couldn't have had everybody wandering in and out all the time. There was a lot of delicate work to be done and I insisted on total privacy.'

'Who organised that for you?'

'CCO1 gave the security task to Commander Fitch. He set up a restricted area and that worked very well.'

Leo looked up from his notes. 'Could we now turn to what happened when the experiment went ahead, Mr Glassford? What happened then?'

'I don't know. I wasn't involved. After my work was done and tested, I was very happy to return to my normal activities and restore my Area back to normal.'

'Are you telling us that you were not there at the launch of the experiment? Surely that is most unusual? Surely you must have had a keen interest in the experiment?'

'Well, not really, Sir. You see, I could see no point in it. As you say, escape pods can always be controlled remotely. I knew that everything I had done would work perfectly, so I just left them to it. I heard they sent it to a nearby asteroid.'

'Do you know who piloted the remote transit?'

Glassford shook his head. 'I have no idea. As I have already told you, I was uninvolved in the launch. My work was done. Obviously, it was someone on PPN1's team. They are the pilots. No doubt he could tell you who it was.'

Cy leaned forward. 'Tell us about the duplicate escape pod, Mr Glassford. You must have been involved in that?'

Glassford looked at him in surprise. 'You know about that? Well, that was done on CCO1's orders. He said that it would cause much less trouble if we just duplicated the pod rather than report it lost. I thought it rather strange but of course I obeyed his orders and arranged for the job to be done. We had most of the parts. A few parts had to be manufactured specially but the result was excellent.'

Leo and Cy sat in contemplation for a minute or so.

'Mr Glassford, were you the Leader?' Leo spoke sharply.

Glassford's body jerked upright and he looked at Leo with narrowed, wary eyes. 'Leader?' he queried in a rather sharp-edged tone, 'what do you mean: "Leader"?'

Leo allowed a few moments to pass, observing Glassford's reaction carefully. Then he expanded his question. 'Were you the Leader of CCO1's experiment with the escape pod?'

'Ah!' Glassford relaxed and sat back. 'Well, I was to some degree, I suppose. Basically, this was a technical experiment, so it was inevitable that I should take the lead in technical matters. But I only followed CCO1's orders, of course.'

'And what were his orders to you?'

'To progress the technical aspects of the experiment he wanted to carry out. I've already told you what that was. I've told you the whole thing.' The final sentence carried a hint of impatience.

Leo and Cy looked at each other. 'Shall we break for lunch at this point?' Leo asked.

Cy nodded. 'Thank you, Mr Glassford, would you please hold yourself available for a further meeting later today? We still have much to discuss. Thank you.'

Immediately after lunch and following a short discussion, Leo and Cy had called PPN1, Commander Norton Wood, inviting him to meet with them. Soon, he was seated before them.

Leo began. 'Commander Wood, would you please cast your mind back 30 years. I know it's a very long time but this was about the time that Commander Gorton departed from the Platform.'

'We were all sorry to see him go, you know. He really was a wonderful influence here, you know. Did you know that everyone called him "The Yggdrasil Healer"?'

'Yes, we do know that. What did you hear about Commander Gorton leaving?'

'CCO1 told us at a Senior Staff Meeting that Mr Gorton had been transferred back to Earth.'

'Do you recall an experiment with an escape pod around that time? Your department would have been involved because the vehicle was to transit by remote pilot only.'

Wood sat silently for a few moments, then spoke slowly. 'Yes, I do recall something. It was an unusual experiment and there seemed to be a lot of secrecy about it. Of course I was not involved with the experiment. However, yes, I remember being asked for a pilot. I decided to treat it as a training exercise for one of my new boys – I mean, it was a very simple job. Young Jones did it. He was a new Sub-Lieutenant just trained on Earth. I think it was one of the first tasks he did for me.'

'Is he still on the Platform, Mr Wood?'

'No he was here for about five years. The last I heard of him he was a Freighter Captain somewhere in Universe G_z. Is there a problem?'

'No there isn't. How much would your pilot know about the experiment?'

'Nothing at all. Same as me! We were just asked to pilot the pod remotely to an asteroid. We were given the coordinates and told to execute an auto-landing and power down. And that's exactly what young Jones did.'

'Were you present when your young pilot carried out the remote transit and landing?'

'Yes, I was. I just wanted to see how young Jones coped with it, because it was his very first job on the Platform. I recall that he did well. No problems at all.'

'Thanks for your time, Mr Wood. You have been very helpful.'

'Well, I think we can rule out the remote pilot,' Cy said after Wood had left. 'The way the system operates, they just take the instructions and do the job. Clearly, Wood turned it into a training exercise for his young pilot.'

'Agreed, Cy. I think we've pretty well refined it to our quartet, don't you agree? Two of them have admitted participation in the escape pod project, thus placing themselves in the murder scene to some degree. Sarfeld is a "no comment" at the moment, though his silence points to guilt, while Glassford freely and cheerfully admits he was the technical man who masterminded the pod modification, etc. He suggests he's whiter than white, just following orders! But who is the Leader? Who is the instigator, the Prime Mover? Sarfeld said it's Fitch. Fitch blamed Sangyar at first. Sangyar blamed Glassford and Glassford says he is just a sweet-tempered, innocent technical worker!'

'You know, Leo, Glassford is the one who really puzzles me. It's possible he could just have been the technical support, as he says. He just turned the modified pod over to them and took no further interest – again, just as he said. Then, one or more of the trio lured Gorton into the escape pod on the pretext that his advice was required, had him locked in and sent off to die. That is exactly what Gorton described in his PAC log. At that stage, Glassford's technical input would not be required. The pod was then piloted remotely by a young man who thought he was undertaking a training exercise. It still seems likely that Glassford was uninvolved in the murder plot. CCO1 just used him to provide the tool that would enable the murderous trio to carry out their inhuman plan.'

Leo looked worried. 'You know, Cy, your argument is perfectly logical. So perfect that it worries me. The only argument against it is the fact that both Sangyar and Fitch have identified Glassford as the Leader. We mustn't forget that – but, I must say, Glassford doesn't look like the Leader to me. He doesn't sound like the Leader, either. And the fact that he's the lowest rank of the four of them makes it even more unlikely. However, there's something that worries me about him. There is a kernel of something else there. I think we need to dig a little deeper.'

'Dig deeper, Leo? OK, but how do we do that? In the last five days we have been able to collect a lot of damning evidence on Sarfeld, Fitch and Sangyar. We think the most likely Prime Mover is Sarfeld, although the other two could be deep in there, too. On the other hand, we have nothing on Glassford, despite the fact that his work made the whole ghastly thing possible. Just an excellent technician following the orders of his superiors – that's his implacable line.'

Leo was deep in thought. 'You know, Cy, something has just occurred to me. Something I want to check with Commander Wood. Just a moment while I give him a call. This might be nothing but I must check it out.'

He made contact with Wood and they talked for some minutes. Having thanked the pilot, he closed the connection and turned to Cy, his eyes blazing. 'What I have just heard is highly significant, Cy. Go DT and just listen to this...'

The two investigators communicated for some time.

A meeting had been scheduled for 1500, to which Sarfeld, Fitch, Sangyar and Glassford had been invited. Glassford was the first to arrive, diffidently taking his seat at the end of the table, the place furthest away from the investigators. Shortly after, the other three appeared together, a rather sheepish group led by CCO1 and took their seats at the sides of the table. CCO1 sat opposite his two subordinates. Leo and Cy sat at the head of the table.

When everyone had settled, Leo began speaking in a quiet but penetrating tone.

'Good afternoon. We have called you four gentlemen to this meeting to hear a summary of the report we intend to submit formally to Command. As you know, our remit was to investigate the circumstances of the clandestine loss of an escape pod from this Platform, along with the member of staff who was found inside it. Investigator Funte and I were the discoverers of the escape pod, which we found stranded and derelict on an asteroid in the eastern part of this sector. We have established the year of its departure from here as UY5664, 30 years ago'

'Our initial enquiries soon revealed that there had been no reported loss of an escape pod from the Platform and, more importantly, no report of a staff loss. The escape pod was quickly identified as a relatively new vehicle that had been delivered and commissioned on the Platform only four years earlier. The deceased was encased in a closed and sealed suit and we were instructed to leave the body undisturbed so that it could be investigated on the Platform under autopsy conditions.' He paused and looked around the table. 'Investigator Funte will now speak about our progress here on the Platform.'

Cy addressed the group: 'We arrived five days ago and our investigation has moved very quickly between then and now.'

'First and most importantly, we know that the person who was despatched in the modified escape pod was Scientist-Commander Dr Maynard Gorton, then STC1 of this Platform. The pod had been modified so that local control was impossible and all communication equipment had been removed. Mr Glassford has told us he was in charge of all this technical work, in which many people were involved. It was all part of a CCO1 experiment, he told us.'

At the end of the table, Glassford looked at the ceiling and smiled slightly.

Cy continued. 'We know precisely what happened to Commander Gorton during his four years of imprisonment on the asteroid until he died, after which his remains lay in the escape pod for a further 26 years. The autopsy performed here revealed no body contained in the closed and sealed spacesuit but ample DNA evidence has proved that his living body had certainly been there. The disappearance of the physical body is inexplicable at present. Meanwhile, Command have been consistently misinformed about the situation; Commander Gorton was kept fictitiously alive here on the Platform. For the last 30 years, all communications sent to him have been responded to in his name.' He paused and looked around the table. 'I would make it clear to you that we have no doubt Commander Gorton was cruelly and callously murdered.'

Sarfeld glared angrily at Fitch and Sangyar, both of whom looked away. Glassford did not react in any way.

'Secondly, we know that the escape pod was subsequently duplicated here on the Platform so that its loss could not be noticed or recorded in inventory checks. We have located the duplicate and established its lack of authenticity. Mr Glassford has told us that he conceived and supervised this work on CCO1's instructions.'

'Thirdly, attempts to sabotage our investigation were made when Gorton's PAC was stolen from the escape pod and his physical remains were removed from secure medical storage and instantly sent for destruction in the Medical Disposal Unit. Fortunately, neither of these events resulted in a loss of evidence because of actions we took. By his own admission, Surgeon-Commander Sangyar is the instigator of both these crimes.'

Sangyar dropped his head so that he would not meet anyone's eyes.

'Fourthly, we have discovered that many months were required to prepare the escape pod for the crime that would be committed within it. As already stated, this has been described to us as an "experiment authorised by CCO1" and it involved many technical staff, undoubtedly led by Sub-Commander Glassford. Mr Glassford used staff from his own Area and involved members of the ST Development Area as well. However, Mr Glassford told us he, himself, did much of the physical disassembly and assembly work on the pod. We have concluded that Mr Glassford was certainly the technical and design leader on this project. He has emphasised to us that it required a great deal of professional expertise to complete it; he has stated categorically that he was following CCO1's orders at all times. We have also ascertained that the other manpower arrangements for logistics, security, etc., were organised and carried out by Commander Fitch. So, the preparation of the escape pod was under the direct control of Messrs Fitch and Glassford.'

'There is one other person who was involved in what happened to Commander Gorton but we have eliminated him from blame. This is the pilot who remotely controlled the transit of the pod from the Platform to the asteroid. We are satisfied that neither he nor his superior Commander Wood were aware of any of the project details. They merely carried out a routine request to pilot the remote transit of an escape pod, under the authority of CCO1.'

Cy turned to Leo. 'I will now hand back to Investigator Granvic for our conclusions on blame and culpability.'

Leo paused as he looked at each of the four Yggdrasil men around the table. 'I imagine it will be obvious to each of you gentlemen why you are present here. Although a large number of staff was involved in this project, perhaps hundreds, our focus is to establish who is culpable. In other words, we seek to identify the person or persons who conceived, proposed and set this cruel and murderous project in motion. At present we regard all four of you as being deeply involved in the project to murder Commander Gorton secretly. We regard you all as culpable.'

These last spoken words became an almost physical presence in the room, an almost palpable entity, a leaden weight to be laid upon the four accused men.

Predictably, CCO1 sprang to his feet, his face deeply flushed. 'I refuse to be silent any longer,' he roared. 'I object in the strongest possible terms to this slander against my name. I have already told you that I had absolutely nothing to do with this dreadful affair, nothing at all. You have absolutely no evidence against me and I will make sure that my objections to this insult will be taken to the highest possible Command authority. Then we will see who is right and who is wrong!' The room was deathly quiet. All eyes were fixed on the two men at the top of the table; every ear finely tuned for the response they knew must come.

It was Cy who spoke in an unusually quiet, dispassionate tone. 'So, Admiral Sarfeld, you are telling us that a very senior officer on your Platform, an officer under your command, suddenly disappeared without trace and that you were unaware that it had happened?'

'Of course not,' Sarfeld responded in a lower voice. 'I... ah... knew he had been transferred back to Earth.'

'You dealt with the transfer arrangements?'

'I suppose so. I cannot recall every transfer over 30 years.' CCO1 looked triumphant.

'So why was Commander Gorton not replaced by another Commander transferred in?'

'Ah, there is often a time gap in these matters.'

'A time gap of 30 years?'

'Well, I had promoted Fitch and I told Command I was satisfied that he should take the post of STC1 permanently.'

'I see. So why does the current Command Staff Directory still list Commander Gorton as STC1 on SSP Yggdrasil?'

'Just a mistake, I assume.'

'A mistake that has lasted 30 years?'

'Yes.'

'So, Admiral, who on the Platform is pretending to be Commander Gorton? Who is receiving all his communications and replying to them as Commander Gorton?'

'I don't know.'

'You don't know? You mean you don't know who or you don't know that it is happening?'

'I'm unaware of this. I suppose it must be Fitch who is answering.'

'WHAT?' Fitch jumped to his feet in fury. 'This is absolute nonsense! Of course CCO1 knows all about this. CCO1 knows all about everything that goes on here. He's got spies all over the Platform and they report to him regularly. And CCO1 knows all about the Gorton Project. He conceived it. He authorised it. How could anyone else do it? He is in charge here.'

'Sit down, Fitch. I shall deal with you later.' CCO1's face was purple with fury. 'You'll...'

'Please be silent, Admiral,' Leo interjected, 'we have questions to ask Mr Fitch.' Sarfeld sank back in his seat with reluctance.

Leo turned to Fitch. 'Mr Fitch, you have already admitted your involvement in this project. Did you know what the project was to achieve?'

Fitch looked embarrassed and eventually answered. 'Yes, I did. But I was not directly involved. As I told you before, I just followed orders to set up the infrastructure they needed to prepare for the project. I was the outsider in all this. Organising manpower and security does not make me a murderer. I am innocent.'

'Mr Fitch, during our conversation yesterday you changed your mind about the identity of this person you call the

Leader. On the day of the autopsy, you told us the Leader was Commander Sangyar, then yesterday you changed your accusation to Sub-Commander Glassford. Do you wish to confirm that accusation?'

'Yes Sir, I do. It is the truth.'

'And I had already told you about Glassford.' The words burst from Sangyar. 'I am totally innocent of Commander Gorton's death. You must believe me!'

Leo turned to Sarfeld. 'Two of your officers wish to blame Mr Glassford, Admiral. Furthermore they identify him as the Leader of the plot to kill Commander Gorton. Would you like to comment?'

Sarfeld sat in silence, eyes down, not acknowledging or responding to Leo's question.

'I think it is time I said something.' A new voice. The soft tones of Glassford broke the silence.

Cy replied. 'Yes, Mr Glassford?'

'Investigators, earlier today, you spoke to me at length. During that meeting, I was completely forthright about my involvement in the technical and engineering side of this project and, indeed, in the aftermath when I was instructed to build a duplicate vehicle. Everything I told you was the absolute truth and you will recall I offered it without hesitation or demur. Should you have any further questions on the details of these matters I will be more than happy to help. I have absolutely nothing to hide. In carrying out these tasks, I was merely following the commands of my superiors. You will, of course, have noticed that all three of these gentlemen are of a higher rank than I am and are thus able to direct my activities. However, despite my total innocence, two of the officers present have levelled serious accusations against me and, in addition to the comprehensive denial that I have just made, I would like to comment further, with a view to assisting your investigation optimally. While I was not aware of the purpose of the project beforehand, I became aware of it afterwards and I can certainly tell you who was responsible.'

All sound left the room. All eyes were fixed on Glassford. Time arrested, waiting for permission to start again.

'All three of them were jointly responsible.' Glassford's voice was calm and filled with sorrow. 'They all wished Commander Gorton dead and they conceived this project to achieve that wish. The project was conceived by Commander Sangyar. He hated Commander Gorton's successful interventions in Medical. Commander Sangyar is, of course, a man who is familiar with life and death and no doubt is more comfortable with both than we mere mortals are. Of course Admiral Sarfeld authorised the project. He was keen to rid himself of Commander Gorton because Gorton knew all about his highly illegal TP Unit. Commander Fitch was more than happy to help them both because of his many previous conflicts with Commander Gorton. I, of course, was totally uninvolved beyond my technical input. I had no idea of its intention. It is my duty to carry out the orders of my superiors.' Serenely, Glassford sat back in his chair.

Pandemonium ensued. The room reverberated with loud expressions of denial and rage. After it had subsided, a strangely shrunken Admiral Sarfeld turned towards the Investigators and began to speak in a low voice, his eyes resolutely downcast.

'Investigators, it is true that this man,' he pointed at Glassford without turning his head towards him, 'is the Leader. He has been the Leader on this Platform for 30 years. He has been blackmailing me and the others here for all that time, threatening to expose what he describes as our crimes to Command. But there is more, a great deal more. Before that time, he was just an insignificant mouse who stayed out of my way; someone of no account. Then, suddenly, he changed radically. He became a different person. He somehow acquired powers that made him shockingly malevolent and invincible. He then used these powers to take over the Platform by making us his subordinates.' Sarfeld paused and then added in a quieter, introspective voice: 'Of course, if there had only been the threat of his blackmail without the personality change, I would have crushed him and disposed of him very easily.'

Now he lifted his head. 'I know all this sounds unbelievable but he really is extremely powerful. We soon found to our cost that none of us could stand against him. In addition to his mysterious power, he soon formed a personal guard detachment of very brutal men who obey his every command. So, I am ashamed and humiliated to say that I have been compelled, physically and psychologically to obey his orders and put up with his considerable abuse for the last 30 years. So let me be absolutely clear about what I am saying: Glassford is the Leader. The murder of Gorton was his idea. The means of achieving it was his idea – that demonstrates the sort of mind he has. He conceived and carried out the whole vile, ghastly project. He forced Sangyar, Fitch and I to join him and we were compelled to obey.'

Sarfeld continued in a voice more like his own. 'Yes, Investigators, you should quell your doubts and believe everything I have just said, because Glassford has the power to do exactly what I have described. He is the cruel and vindictive murderer of Gorton. The rest of us are mere accessories, compelled to follow his orders so that we can survive here. I say again: this is a man filled with evil power. I have now told you the absolute truth and it is a relief to have finally done so.' Sarfeld sat back heavily in his seat. Sangyar and Fitch were pale, still and silent.

'Mr Glassford?' Leo called after a period of absolute silence.

Glassford was relaxed and smiling. 'A complete and utter fabrication, Sir. I am not the Leader. How could I, a humble Sub-Commander, be the leader of an Admiral and two Commanders? It is laughable. Sirs, it is perfectly obvious. Admiral Sarfeld is the Leader, Commander Sangyar is his second-in-command and Commander Fitch the assistant to them both. I have merely been getting on with my job for the last 30 years, working for Commander Fitch. Regarding the murder project, apart from the technical aspects I have described to you fully and in great detail, I stress once again that I was uninvolved. I knew nothing about it. As soon as the escape pod modifications were complete, I returned to my own work.'

Leo allowed some moments to pass, then looked impassively at Glassford.

'Mr Glassford, you certainly make a convincing case. However, I must ask you a question; it is actually a repeat of a question we asked you earlier today.'

'Of course.' Glassford smiled and raised an eyebrow. 'How may I clarify matters further?'

'Were you present in the Remote Transit Control Centre when the escape pod was launched?'

'Certainly not, Sir. I was not in that department during the launch and, furthermore, I never had any occasion to be there.'

There was a short silence before Leo spoke again. 'We know that to be a lie, Mr Glassford. You were there at the launch. Furthermore we know that you returned later that day after the escape pod landed on the asteroid. On that occasion, Commander Sangyar was with you. And we are aware of your actions on both occasions.'

In the silence that followed, the transformation in Glassford was rapid and startling. He seemed to grow in size and stature. His face changed from a calm, satisfied smirk to become a mask of aggression and hatred, teeth bared, eyes narrowed and blazing. The physical atmosphere in the room seemed to change. Heat, light and positive energy seemed to be drained from the air and replaced by a dark, sterile coldness filled somehow with eddying shadows of evil. The other three Yggdrasil officers shrank in their seats, covering their eyes in an attempt to block out the horror of the moment.

'How do you know this?' The words hissed venomously. Each word struck Leo and Cy like a physical blow. Their voices of response were frozen. Neither could speak but remained transfixed by Glassford's incandescent gaze. He repeated his question in a thunderous voice:

'How do you know this? You,' he pointed at Cy, 'may speak.'

Released from his catalepsy, Cy spoke in a strange monotone. 'We realised that the pod's transit had to be started soon after the victim had boarded the vehicle. We knew that someone had to give that start command. We asked PPN1, Commander Wood, if anyone else had been present in his Control Centre when CCO1's experiment started. He reported that you, Sub-Commander Glassford, had been present and that you were there to give the order to commence transit. You gave this order after receiving a brief communication from someone you spoke to in a contemptuous tone; someone you called "Jo". We assume that was Commander Jomo Sangyar who was watching the escape pod in the dock and had observed Commander Gorton boarding. Mr Wood also reported that you laughed very unpleasantly when the transit started; he was further taken aback when he heard you speak – you probably didn't realise your headset microphone was open – "Goodbye, Commander, I hope you suffer for many years before you die!"'

'Then, later that day, you returned to the Control Centre and asked Commander Wood to confirm that the escape pod had landed on the asteroid. Commander Wood was surprised that Commander Sangyar was with you since senior medical staff never visited the Remote Transit Control Centre. When the landing was confirmed, you thrust a small transmitter into Commander Sangyar's hand and brusquely ordered him to "Send the activation code". Commander Wood thought this was a clear case of insubordination and was greatly puzzled when Commander Sangyar obeyed immediately. You then turned on your heel and gestured contemptuously to Commander Sangyar to follow you, leaving the Centre without another word. Commander Wood considered this behaviour was extremely rude and certainly insubordinate.'

As Cy fell silent, both he and Leo found they had been released from the bonds of Glassford's paralysis. They found Glassford looking at them balefully.

'So, Investigators, what are your learned conclusions from this latest development?' Glassford's voice was now harsh, evil and derisive, totally different from his normal soft tones.

Cy spoke again, this time, his tone level and confident. 'We conclude that Admiral Sarfeld and the others have told us the truth. You are the Leader, the perpetrator and executer of this evil, inhuman crime. Clearly, you are the prime criminal here. Thirty years ago, Admiral Sarfeld and Commander Sangyar were happy enough to join you as co-conspirators and they, too, are criminals. Fitch was also involved but not at the same level as the others. These facts, plus the crimes of violence, blackmail and insubordination that you have committed in the last 30 years, are what we will report to Command.'

Glassford cackled raucously. 'Investigators, let me tell you that you will report nothing to Command, because your life will shortly come to an end and I will continue to rule Yggdrasil as I have done for the last 30 years.' As he spoke, the door opened and around a dozen heavily armed security guards entered to surround the table. 'These are my private guards. They are specially selected for their brutality and I have trained them myself. I will enjoy seeing what they will do to you as you are arrested and imprisoned. There is no hurry to kill you, though I am sure you will wish to be dead many times before death finally comes.' He turned to a very large guard dressed in a Sergeant's uniform. 'A'Fhagro! Take them away to maximum security and prepare them for deep interrogation.' The Sergeant waved his men forward.

'Mr Glassford, may I speak?' Leo's voice, strangely calm. 'I would be most grateful if you would answer two questions.'

'A dying man's last request?' Glassford sneered, 'Go on, then, I like a bit of entertainment! I'll give you two minutes, one minute for each.' He held up a hand to stop the guards.

'Why did you kill Gorton in that terrible way?'

Glassford looked at Leo, hatred etched on his face. 'Why do you think, you idiot? I loathed him, that's why. I have known him for a very, very long time and I have always hated him. He was an extremely dangerous man, with his cleverness, love and goodness spreading across the Universe like a dreadful disease. I have constantly made it my mission to destroy him. I have never stopped. And now, I am absolutely delighted that I have succeeded in my quest. No-one has ever been able to stop me and no-one ever will. My power is infinite and eternal. I have won – again! The Universe is mine and it always will be!' The voice was a deafening bellow, unlike anything human.

Leo spoke again, still calm and in control. 'Thank you. Why did you change 30 years ago?'

Glassford smiled cruelly. 'Don't you understand anything, you fool? I didn't change. I knew the pathetic Head of Construction here was beginning to fret about his career. He was beginning to hate Gorton. He was persuading himself that Gorton had insulted him, humiliated him. Gorton had proposed to promote him in a management reorganisation but this never happened because nobody, including the Head of Construction himself, wanted the ST Division structure to be changed. I saw that Glassford was ready for takeover – *and so I arrived!*'

Now the man wiped away flecks of foam from around his mouth. 'Right,' he growled, 'I've answered your questions, you pathetic fool. No-one will ever know the truth about me and Gorton, because that truth will die with you two wretched investigators.' He turned away, contemptuously. 'Guards, take them away. Maximum restraint.'

'Sub-Commander Glassford, you should know that the Command Monitor and the Council have just heard everything you have said. They have also seen everything that has happened here.' Cy spoke in stentorian, authoritative tones.

Glassford froze in surprise, his expression suffused with consternation. Long seconds trailed by. Then, his face twisted in fury, he sprang to his feet and yelled:

'Impossible! You're lying!' The words fired like high-velocity missiles towards Leo and Cy. 'I have blocked all your communications facilities. Do you think I am a fool? I knew you would try to communicate with them – but I closed all your communication channels down! They will have heard nothing from you since you came here!' The last words were a raucous klaxon of triumph.

'Not so.' Cy's voice was quiet and calm. 'You cannot block communications through our IRS vehicle and that is where our communications have been routed.'

As Cy finished speaking, there was a deafening, electronic hum and five shimmering, three-dimensional figures began to appear at the table, solidifying to become recognisable as the Command Monitor and the four Council members.

The Monitor spoke in a thunderous voice. 'The Council and I have been present in this room since this meeting began. We have seen and heard everything. It has been recorded in Command Records. Sub-Commander Glassford, I order you to surrender immediately to my Investigators.'

'Never!' Glassford sprang to his feet, snarling like a wild animal, his hand now holding a Class One destructor weapon which he aimed at the Monitor and energised its lethal beam. The beam passed through the shimmering figure and punched a jagged hole in the wall some way behind him. Seeing the ineffectiveness of his attack, Glassford swung the lethal beam of his weapon towards Leo and Cy, knowing they would die instantly. As he did so, the Monitor extended a single finger towards him, followed by a brief circling motion. Instantly, Glassford collapsed to the floor, rendered semi-conscious, the weapon melting and disintegrating in a flaccid hand; simultaneously, all his security guards were catapulted backwards away from the table and fell unconscious and twitching on the floor.

The others present in the room formed a silent, frozen tableau as the vast forces of crackling energy diminished and quieted. Eventually, Leo was the first to make any movement, turning his eyes to look quizzically at Sarfeld, Sangyar and Fitch. All three responded by raising their hands above their heads in the traditional gesture of defeat.

The four criminal conspirators had been arrested. It had been necessary to shackle a violent Glassford and confine him in a secure medical facility, suitably restrained by drugs and watched over 24 hours a day. Sarfeld, Sangyar and Fitch had been confined to their separate quarters under constant guard. They had capitulated totally, submitting quietly to arrest and saying nothing. Glassford's company of guards had also been arrested and taken away.

The Monitor now turned to Leo and Cy. 'Investigators, please sit with us around the table. We must talk before we return our plasma-physical presences back to Earth. First of all, we would congratulate you on our work. I will ensure that this is fully recorded in Command Records. You have both acted in the best traditions of RPs in the IRS Service. You know that your service is held in the highest regard throughout occupied Space.'

Leo and Cy thanked the Monitor for his kind words.

'However, your work here is not yet finished. These are my instructions to both of you. You will jointly assume command of SSP Yggdrasil until the new CCO1 arrives. I would expect this to take some weeks but I will process it as quickly as possible and keep you informed of progress. You will choose officers to fill the other four vacant posts on a temporary basis; you may authorise their temporary promotion to the appropriate rank. If the new CCO1 is satisfied with their performances, they may be confirmed in their new posts. You may inform them of that. I have issued the necessary directives for your authority throughout the Platform. Do you have any questions?'

'What will happen to Gorton's murderers, Sir?' Cy asked.

'They will be returned to Earth and tried in the Intergalactic Command High Court. Of course I cannot predict the outcome but it is certain that their Space-side careers are over. I would expect them to be transferred back to Earth on the vehicle that brings in the new CCO1.'

'What of other staff who may have been associated with the criminal activities of the last 30 years? For instance, Glassford's security guards and those who helped him to conceal Commander Gorton's death?'

'I would ask you to establish who they are, question them to establish the degree of their involvement and then make recommendations in your Report. Although you have solved the fundamentals of the crime, there is still a great deal of investigative work to be done, is there not?'

'Yes, Sir, there is,' Leo and Cy agreed.

'I have just one question for you, Investigators. We have read your Interim Report and considered it with great care. What do you think happened to Commander Gorton's body?'

Leo replied. 'Sir, there is no doubt that Commander Gorton died aboard the escape pod on the asteroid. He had managed to live in it for four years and very nearly escaped by using his prodigious knowledge and intelligence. We have his full record of what happened. When the vehicle systems finally failed, he lived in his suit for three days; then, inevitably, he died. When we found him, there is no doubt, absolutely no doubt, that the suit was closed and sealed from the inside, as suits are designed to do. The inner body unit gave us many samples of his DNA to prove that his body had been there. As you know, when the suit was opened by an expert under autopsy conditions, there was no body, nor any trace of one, apart from the DNA.'

After a short pause, Cy spoke hesitantly. 'I have a sort of a theory, Sir. Clearly, Commander Gorton was an exceptional man, capable of doing things that normal people could not do. Capable of doing... miracles, even. I think the disappearance of his body could have been another example of his exceptional abilities. However,' he added with a smile, 'I have to say my partner isn't so sure!'

The Monitor was silent for a few minutes, deep in thought. Finally he spoke. 'Investigator Funte, I do not reject your proposal, partly because it is the only explanation offered and partly because inexplicable things still happen – even in the 57th Century. I think it absolutely right for you to include this possibility in your Report, unless, that is, you find something more rational – more rational, that is, to the human mind.'

'I am grateful for your understanding, Sir.' Cy was pleased with this response!

'Do you have any other questions, Investigators?' The Monitor looked from one to the other.

'Yes, Sir, I have one. I hope you will not think it impertinent.'

The Monitor smiled. 'Ask it, Mr Granvic, whatever it is.

'When you saved us from Glassford's intention to murder us, were you sure that you could defeat such a devastating power of evil?'

The Monitor smiled again. 'Ah, the "power of good and evil" question. It isn't asked often; people are so sure that evil is a devastatingly powerful force, even although we teach that good will always win, don't we?' He paused. 'Here is the truth. Evil is NOT a devastatingly powerful force because evil is *not a force at all.*'

Leo's face betrayed his confusion. 'But...'

The Monitor continued. 'Yes, Mr Granvic, many are confused. They think good and evil are opposing forces but actually there is only one force involved, the force of good.'

'Then what is evil? I don't understand.'

'Evil is merely an absence of good, a lack of good. Listen. A good analogy is light and darkness, which many people think are equal opposites. Just think; you switch on the *power* of light – that clearly is a power – but you don't switch on the power of darkness, do you? You switch *off* the power of light and the result is darkness, a lack of light. It's the same with good and evil. Evil is merely a lack of goodness; it is overcome as soon as goodness arrives because it has no power.'

Leo considered this. 'But how can you prove that is right?' he said finally.

'Good question, Mr Granvic, but the answer is simple. If evil had power of its own and was able to defeat good at times (as so many people think it can), then it would have taken over the Universe long ago and our whole civilisation would live in worlds devoid of love, trust, compassion, kindness, generosity and the like. The fact that the Universe is NOT like this proves that good will always exist to lead our worlds.' He paused and added. 'This is why I *knew* I could defeat Glassford.'

Leo thought for some moments. 'Thank you, Sir, he said finally.'

'And now we must leave you now, Investigators, and re-engage our whole selves with our presences on Earth. On behalf of the Intergalactic Command, I thank you once again for your excellent work. I will be in touch with you very soon. Thank you and goodbye.' The Monitor nodded to his four companions and, without a sound, the five shimmering bodies began to fade. Within ten seconds or so, they had disappeared completely, leaving Leo and Cy alone in the room.

Leo had said nothing as he poured two large glasses of wine, handing one to Cy. The two men looked at each other, their faces lit up by the comradely smiles of those who have been close to death together. Then they drank deeply.

23

The Twenty-eighth Day

'We need a plan of action, Leo,' Cy broke the silence of their early morning individual introspection with a smile. 'But, whatever it is, I hope it will result in a day of peace and quiet!'

Leo agreed amicably. 'Well, we certainly don't want another day like yesterday. I'm hoping I won't need my life saved today!'

'Not for a while, Leo! However, to turn to the business of running Yggdrasil, I think we need to discuss the senior staff issues first. Right away, in fact.'

'OK, Cy. Firstly, we need to put an effective STC1 in place. I think the choice here is pretty obvious – but I'll be interested to hear whether you agree. I think the man for STC1 is Bruno Leigh. He already runs the most scientific of the three ST Areas and, now that Fitch and Glassford are gone, he's the only senior officer left in ST Division, isn't he?'

'Yes, Leigh does look like the best bet.' Cy paused. 'It would be sensible for us to look at his Staff Record, though. Shall we do that?'

In a moment, they had accessed the Platform Confidential Staff Area and displayed Leigh's records. 'Look, Cy. Excellent assessments. Very good scientific background and a skilled and inventive technician. Even good reports here from Fitch!

From the comments, Leigh was the man Fitch went to when he needed digging out of technical trouble!'

'Right, Leo. Hopefully, that only leaves us three more to find! If Leigh becomes STC1, we still need to find three Area Heads.' Then, suddenly, Cy stopped and became thoughtful. 'Just a moment, though, we actually need just two. We know that Sub-Commander Maalouf is Head, Maintenance. He has been since Fitch took over STC1 30 years ago. So that post is covered.

Bruno Leigh sat across the table from the Leo and Cy, coffee in hand. Everyone on the Platform was fully aware of the dramatic happenings of the day before and the staff of all departments went about their normal work activities in a strangely silent manner. Staff looked covertly at each other, wondering who may or may not have been associated with, or even tainted by, the disgraced senior staff that had been removed from their posts. Conversations were whispered. Facts were scanty but, of course, rumours abounded. This, the staff felt, was a time to keep quiet. Very quiet!

'Mr Leigh,' Leo started, 'do you know that Admiral Sarfeld, Commanders Fitch and Sangyar and Sub-Commander Glassford have been relieved of their posts and are under arrest, pending transfer back to Earth for trial?' Leigh nodded. 'And that we are in charge of the Platform, with full powers of authority, until the new CCO1 arrives?'

'Yes, Sir, I do.

'Good.' Cy was crisp. 'We have called you here this morning because our first task is to fill the senior posts in ST Division that are now vacant. We would like your advice. Who do you think should be STC1?'

Leigh answered immediately. 'Sub-Commander Maalouf, Sir, Head, Maintenance. He is a very senior Sub-Commander and has a great deal of experience on the Platform.'

'Can you think of any other candidate who could take the post of STC1?'

Leigh screwed up his face in thought. 'Well, Sir, all the other Sub-Commanders concerned with technology tend to work solely on the engineering side of things – like the Heads of Facilities and Utilities – so I can't see that they would be particularly suitable. Of course, you could go up a rank and choose one of the Commanders on the Platform; however, I cannot think that any of these officers has the right knowledge and experience to lead ST Division. You see, it's not only management and administration, there's a lot of science and technology in it, too.' He paused for a moment, then continued. 'I think Vin Maalouf is your best bet.'

Leo smiled. 'We're a bit surprised that you haven't mentioned the most suitable candidate for the job, Mr Leigh.'

'Really? I can't think who else…' Leigh was puzzled.

'You.'

Leigh's jaw dropped open in astonishment. 'Me?' he said faintly. 'As STC1? But am I not too young? I'm only 47, you know.' The words blurted out.

Cy smiled. 'Mr Leigh, may I point out that Mr Gorton was only 27 years old when he came here as a Commander?'

Leigh though about that. Then he looked at Cy candidly. 'That's true, Sir. But there are very few people even half as good as Commander Gorton was! He was an exceptional STC1.'

Cy let a few seconds pass. 'Nevertheless, we are confident that you are the right man to be STC1, Commander Leigh. You are to take up your new post immediately. Your promotion is also effective immediately and you should adopt the higher rank right away. Here are the authorisation papers. Just one thing, Mr Leigh. Technically, the promotion is temporary but it will become permanent if the new CCO1 is satisfied with you as his STC1. Do you understand?

'Yes, Sir.' Leigh's eyes were still wide with incredulity. Then his face relaxed into a wide smile. 'Yes, Sir.' The words repeated with joy! At that moment, he looked as if he might float upwards from his chair!

Leo shook Leigh's hand. 'We will leave you to consider who should be Head, Construction and Head, Development. As STC1, you will have full access to staff records. Let us know your decisions, please. You may authorise the appropriate promotions, designated temporary until the new CCO1 approves them.'

Commander Leigh left them, walking on air!

'Now we need to examine the structure of the Medical Department,' Leo said, 'to identify a replacement for Sangyar. They accessed the Medical Department's Senior Staff list.

'OK, Cy, in this list, "Head, Medical" is followed by "Principal-Surgeon Alain Martinez", our pathologist friend. From this, it looks like he may be Second-in-Command in the Medical Department. If so, he would be the obvious man to take over temporarily, even if he doesn't want the job permanently. I see that he's been here for just 10 years, so he's a relative newcomer!

'... so you see, Mr Martinez, we need someone to take over the job of Head, Medical on a temporary basis, possibly converted to permanent after the new CCO1 arrives. Since you are Second-in-Command at Medical, you are obviously the first person we should approach.' They sat back, regarded Martinez attentively and waited for his reply.

'Well, I will certainly take over Head, Medical if you want me to,' Martinez answered slowly. 'Obviously there is a need for someone to be in charge. I don't know a great deal about the details of the job – I've always been kept busy within my own speciality. I must say I've never seen myself as an administrator but there's no reason why I cannot continue to be a pathologist, too. As the "boss", I suppose I can pick the most interesting cases to work on.' Martinez finished with a brief, impish smile.

'OK, Mr Martinez. So you will be Head, Medical with promotion to Surgeon-Commander.

'Well, I think we've solved the senior staff position for the time being. Now we can turn our attention back to the investigation. Let's have a look at the other prisoners – Glassford's *Praetorian Guard*.' Cy displayed the list of names on the display.

'Hmm,' Leo said, 'it seems there were ten who were designated "guards" commanded by a Guard Sergeant.' He displayed a large image of the guard sergeant, his facing twisted in a leer of hatred. The caption read "Sergeant Sol A'Fhagro.' And his staff record showed he was originally the lowest class of worker in the Utilities Area until he was transferred to the ST Construction Area as a security guard under the command of Sub-Commander Glassford. His early records identified him as a very violent man who enjoyed bullying others. The other ten guards had very similar backgrounds and it seemed they had worked together in the Utilities Area until their transfer.

'I bet Utilities were very glad to get rid of them,' Cy said, 'they look like a bunch of monsters!'

'I suppose we had better interview them so we can make the appropriate recommendations to Command. Also, it's only fair they should know what is happening to them. Do you agree?'

'Yes, Leo, I do.'

They started with Sergeant Sol A'Fhagro. He was brought to the Detention Interview area in full restraint kit. The escort explained. 'This prisoner is extremely violent, Sir. We need to restrain him constantly.'

'OK, have him sit down. You may leave us.'

'Is that wise, Sir? He is a very violent man. He is likely to be a danger to you.' Eventually, the escorts were persuaded to leave, although they stated they would be just outside the door and keeping a watchful eye on the situation.

The three of them were now alone in the bleak room. The prisoner faced them across a wide table, shackled to the chair, which was fixed to the floor. He looked at them balefully, his eyes unblinking. Both Leo and Cy could feel the evil of his presence filling the air.

Finally, he bellowed at them: 'If I could get out of this chair, I'd break both your necks, just like I've broken the necks of Mr Glassford's enemies for many years. You think you are important. You think you're in charge – but you aren't. Mr Glassford will get me out of this. You have no power against Mr Glassford. He's the boss around here and you two are just pathetic little rats.' Within the vile torrent of his words, filled with a plethora of the most insulting swear words, that was the gist of what this dreadful man said.

Cy and Leo looked at each other. 'I think we're wasting our time here,' Leo said quietly.

'Wasting your time?' the prisoner yelled, 'it's my time you're wasting, you pathetic freaks. Glassford will get you for this. I'll let him know how you've treated me. You'll be sorry! Nobody wins against Mr Glassford. NOBODY!' Again, the words were delivered within a torrent of abuse, rising to a scream at the end.

'Sergeant A'Fhagro, we will recommend your transfer to Earth. Your crimes will be investigated there within Command Security.'

It took four strong escorts to remove the violently struggling prisoner from the room. The other ten guards were also interviewed one by one. Although none was as violent as A'Fhagro, all were aggressive and contemptuous. Each warned the investigators that they were protected by "Mr Glassford" and that he would save them. Cy and Leo told each guard that they would be transferred to Earth to have their actions investigated in the Command Security System.

'Phew!' Leo said as the last guard was taken away, 'that was unpleasant! I'm sure Yggdrasil will be a better place without them. These are bad people, turned evil by Glassford, it would seem.'

Over lunch, Leo and Cy discussed the sequence of their investigations.

'We've dealt with all the prisoners, Cy. Now we've got to find out who else was employed within the project, how much they were involved and how much they knew at the time. I'm going to propose that we rule out the remote piloting staff. Do you agree?'

'Yes, I do, Leo. I also think we can rule out the rest of the Level-6 staff in Medical, apart from those associated with the TP Facility, in particular Major Bannerman. I think he should be our next candidate for interview. I see that Major Bannerman has been here for 40 years. We'll call him after lunch.'

Major Bannerman was dressed immaculately in his best uniform as he sat nervously across the table from Leo and Cy.

Cy started the questioning. 'Mr Bannerman, have you been in charge of the TP Facility for 40 years?'

'Yes, Sir. Actually it's 42 years.'

'Have you always been in charge of it, since you came to the Platform?'

'Not at first, Sir. I was in Medical Engineering for the first few years but then I was offered promotion to be put in charge of the Unit.'

'Did you know that this was an illegal activity, Mr Bannerman?'

The man paled. 'Ah, well, yes. But I did point out it wasn't legal.'

'And what happened?'

'I was called to CCO1's office. He was quite nice to me. He said I was quite right to mention that the TP Facility was a non-standard function. However, if I wanted promotion to the rank of Major, I really should accept the post. Of course, if I didn't want the job, CCO1 said, I didn't need to accept. However, I was unlikely to be considered for promotion ever again and he thought I would probably be stuck in a low-level job – probably a minor administrative post, somewhere completely out of the way. He thought I would probably be demoted to Sub-Lieutenant, since my existing rank would be too high for my new post. He thought this would be a pity, since I clearly was a man with potential. But he wouldn't compel me in any way, he said. It was absolutely my choice.' The man paused. 'Sir, I got the message. I said "yes"!'

Leo continued the questioning. 'Mr Bannerman, what happened after Commander Gorton found out about the TP Facility 30 years ago?'

Bannerman was silent for a moment. 'Well, Sir, nothing happened for a few weeks, then I had a brief voice communication from CCO1 to say that Commander Gorton had agreed to preserve the secret of the TP Facility. So there was nothing to worry about and I should just forget the incident. I can't remember his exact words, Sir. Anyway, that's exactly what I did. And then, not long afterwards, Commander Gorton left the Platform and that was the end of the story as far as I was concerned.'

'So, were you involved, in any way, in CCO1's experiment with an escape pod?'

'No, Sir, I know nothing about escape pods. I've hardly even seen one.'

After Bannerman had left, Leo and Cy compared notes.

'Sounds plausible, Leo. The story about seeing CCO1 in his office has the ring of absolute truth about it, don't you think? I can just imagine Sarfeld – "it's your choice – but choose wrongly and you're finished"!'

'Yes, Cy. Obviously Bannerman has to appear in our report – but as someone who was unlikely to have had anything to do with the plot.

'Fine, Leo. What about the other officer, the Senior Security Officer, Major Hicks?'

'There was very little contact there, Cy. I think we can disregard the rest of that group, although we'll mention their presence in the report.

'Fine, Leo, let's call it a day. We'll need to start the Platform-wide investigation tomorrow. I reckon that will take a considerable time but Command will expect us to be absolutely thorough. My proposal is that we should start with a search through the complete personnel list to find out which staff were working on the Platform 30 years ago; we need to examine each one of these people to find out if they had any knowledge or involvement with CCO1's escape pod project.'

'Yes, Cy, agreed. However we mustn't forget the 30 year deception. We need to find out who was involved in that, almost certainly one of the four murderers. We'll need to trace where Gorton's communications were forwarded to. However, the first task is to establish how much responsibility each of the four prisoners had for Gorton's murder.'

'OK, Leo, We start tomorrow.'

24

The Last Day

They awoke, knowing that this was the last full day they would spend on the Platform. Within a few hours, the staff transport vehicle from Earth would arrive, bringing Admiral Joel Arbuthnot, the new CCO1 who would take command of SSP Yggdrasil. Once they had handed the command over to him, they would be free to leave, free to resume their normal duties, to cruise Space in their quiet and ultra-sophisticated vehicle, ready to speed to the assistance of any crippled or distressed vehicle or installation. By tradition, however, they would not leave until early the next day, so that they could attend the new CCO1's Arriving Banquet, an important social occasion that would give all the officers of Yggdrasil their first guarded glimpse of the new Chief Commanding Officer. By the time they were all eating and drinking in relaxed and pleasurable fellowship, the staff transport vehicle would have left the Platform and would be speeding towards Earth, bearing all the Yggdrasil prisoners to the Command Investigations and the trials that awaited them. In its capacious cargo hold, it would be carrying the sad remains of the escape pod and what little remained of its unfortunate occupant.

The previous weeks had been extremely hectic for Cy and Leo. Their investigation had to cover the complete staff complement of the Platform and there had been many interviews to conduct, followed by a recording of each day's activities.

An initial staff scan revealed that 1,126 out of the current complement of 8,479 had been working on Yggdrasil 30 years before. They found that a significant number of these could be eliminated right away – those who had worked in service functions as catering, general cleaning or non-engineering maintenance, for instance. Also, as a result of their previous decisions, they could omit all those who had worked in Medical, apart from TP Facility staff. Interestingly, however, the system alerted them to the fact that two technicians had been moved from Glassford's ST Construction area to other Divisions around the time that CCO1's project was taking place.

'I think this warrants a check,' Cy had said. 'Let's contact these men and ask them to interview. They might have something to tell us about their ST work and why they were moved.

Leo had agreed and soon the men were called to interview. Both were Technician-Lieutenants – the same rank that they had held 30 years before in the ST Construction Area.

'Gentlemen, would you please cast your minds back 30 years to the time you were transferred out of ST Construction. Were you involved with CCO1's escape pod experiment or do you have any knowledge of it?' Leo was surprised when both men laughed out loud.

'Involved?' one man said, 'we certainly were involved! We were both employed on the strip-out work and reinstallations in the escape pod, working directly with Sub-Commander Glassford. One day, I said to my friend here: "You know, this would be a perfect way to murder someone; lock them in here and send the pod off into Space with no way they could control the vehicle. They would die out there – eventually – and no-one would ever know!" Mr Glassford heard me and the next day we were transferred to Propulsion Unit Cleaning. We've been there ever since. It's a real dead-end job.'

The other man joined in. 'We weren't the only ones to be transferred out, you know. There were a number of others who left the project suddenly, although I think most of them have now been transferred elsewhere in Space.'

'Do you feel that this transfer affected your career progression?' Cy asked.

Again the first man laughed. 'Affected it, Sir? Terminated it, I should say! We were both well-regarded in ST Construction. All our contemporaries have long been in higher ranks.'

'Why do think that is?'

The men were silent for a moment. 'Well Sir,' the second man finally said, 'Mr Glassford damned us somehow. There's no other explanation.'

After the men had left, Leo and Cy compared notes.

'I don't think there any doubt what happened here,' Cy said. 'We know Glassford is ruthless and he just isolated anyone who he regarded as posing the slightest danger to him.'

'Agreed, Cy. We'll just note the names of these men so that we can alert the new CCO1 to a likely injustice.'

Doggedly, the investigators reviewed the 200 or so staff who had been involved with the escape pod project in any way. This revealed nothing of significance. Sub-Commander Maalouf (then a First Major) told them that he had been instructed to take over the normal activities of the ST Maintenance Area while Fitch was engaged in a special task for CCO1. He knew nothing about the project and had been kept busy with normal Maintenance matters. He had been aware that Commander Gorton had left the Platform on transfer back to Earth. Soon after, he had taken over the Maintenance area and was promoted when Sub-Commander Fitch became STC1.

Examination of those who had worked in Glinche's Development Area contributed little. They did whatever work was asked of them and had no knowledge of or interest in the project.

'Now we've just got 42 names remaining on the list, Cy. All are engineering or technical staff, some from the general engineering squads that manned the landing bay and the rest are from Glassford's ST Construction Area. These are the people who most likely carried out the actual modification and preparation work on the escape pod. They have the potential to know most about what was going on. I think we had better talk to these people individually.'

During the next four days, they had interviewed all the staff one by one. Virtually all of them had been involved directly in work on the escape pod. Many admitted to puzzlement, because most knew that the standard escape pod could be controlled remotely. Two of the men recounted that they had actually questioned Glassford about the purpose of the experiment. They reported that he had reacted very sharply, taking them aside and pointing out angrily that the purpose of the experiment was secret and that they would be in very serious trouble if they ever raised such queries again. 'Mr Glassford could be a very hard man,' they said, 'it didn't pay to make yourself unpopular with him! We made a bad mistake there.'

Cy and Leo now concluded that they had completed their investigation on the modification of the escape pod from a vehicle of redemption to one of execution.

'As I see it, Cy, we have one final matters to investigate; who impersonated Gorton for 30 years. I'm sure Command will want to know that. My money is on Fitch!'

'OK, Leo, we need to go back to ComCen for that.'

'We would like to see Lieutenant Gonvitch,' they told the clerk at ComCen. A few minutes later, they were seated once again in the very cramped confines of Gonvitch's office.

'Mr Gonvitch,' Leo spoke softly, 'did you know that someone has been impersonating Commander Gorton for the last 30 years? Impersonating him electronically I mean, not physically.'

Gonvitch looked profoundly shocked. 'What do you mean, Sir? I do not understand. I do not see how it is possible, because I forward all Commander Gorton's communications through his personal, unique channel – a channel that only I know and only I can use. The same unique channel is used for his communications to me. It is not possible for someone else to impersonate Commander Gorton on his personal, unique channel.'

'Nevertheless, someone has been doing it for the last 30 years.'

'But, Sir, you do not understand. There is a biological link in this channel. Me! The channel cannot be rerouted without altering me! Even if you stole Mr Gorton's personal device, the machine through which he receives the communications, you still would not receive his communications. As I say, it's not just about machines, it's about my physiology, too. You would need to alter my brain programming.'

Leo and Cy looked at each other, unsure of how to proceed. Then Leo had an idea.

'Mr Gonvitch, could you send a check message through Mr Gorton's personal channel?'

The man looked unhappy. 'Well, Sir, I am not supposed to...'

'You may send the check message with full Command authority, Mr Gonvitch. And,' Leo added with a smile, 'we would be most grateful.'

'Well, Sir, if you say I can, I'll do it. What do you wish me to say?'

'Just "Test Message 0001."'

The man turned to a device and placed his hands upon it. 'Right, Sir, the message is sent.'

Cy was impressed. 'Thank you very much, Mr Gonvitch. You have a great expertise, there.'

'Thank you, Sir,' Gonvitch replied gravely.

Logically, they started in CCO1's Office. There was no message on any of his devices. They checked his quarters, finally finding his personal device. Again, nothing had been received.

'OK, Cy. I didn't expect it to be Sarfeld. He would have suggested that one of the others should deal with this – using him would have been too obvious and dangerous.'

A thorough check of all Glassford's receiving devices drew another blank.

'Not unexpected again, Leo. As the boss, he would have ordered Fitch or Sangyar to do it. Fitch next, I think. That's where you think it will turn up, don't you? I must say, I tend to agree.'

It took some time to locate Fitch's personal receiving device, since it was hidden on a high shelf in a large office cupboard filled with many other items. Although the machine was ready to receive, it displayed no messages.'

They paused and looked at each other significantly.

'Well, Cy, it looks like it must be Sangyar. He's the only one left. I must say I'm surprised. I would have thought Glassford would have chosen Fitch rather than him.'

There were no messages on any of the devices in Sangyar's office. They were unable to find the personal device in his quarters and, after searching for some time, finally found it a drawer.

The personal device sat on a shelf towards the bottom. Leo lifted it out and read from its display "Test Message 0001".

Later, they sat in their quarters.

'So, Leo, Glassford ordered Sangyar to be Gorton's impersonator. I can hardly imagine he would volunteer. All these years, he was dealing Gorton's confidential communications. So, although he may not actually have been much involved in the physical acts that led to Gorton's murder, he has certainly contributed to the subsequent deception in a major way.'

'OK, Cy. We have one final thing to try and find out, if we can. Gonvitch is convinced that he is sending Gorton's messages personally to Gorton and no-one else. So how have our conspirators managed to do it? How do Gorton's communications turn up on the device held by Sangyar? Because of the biological link, Gonvitch says it's impossible.'

'Right, Leo, I've just had an idea. Gonvitch says he would need to have been altered, operated upon. Well, now we know that he must have been altered. Here is the evidence.' He indicated the device display. 'Sangyar is a medical man. Could he have altered Gonvitch? Operated upon him? Let's look into Gonvitch's staff records.'

'Here it is, Cy. 30 years ago: "Surgical operation to repair neck tendon. Operation carried out by Surgeon-Lieutenant Jeff Crowne." No mention of Sangyar but I bet that's when he did it! Let's see what Gonvitch has to say about it.'

'Well, Sir, frankly it's something I would rather not remember. It was all right at first but it became much worse when this second surgeon arrived. I don't know who he was; he never introduced himself but he must have been someone very senior because my young surgeon was treating him with great respect. Then the operation became exceptionally painful, the worst pain I have ever experienced. They said I should have felt nothing but it was dreadful. It felt as if my head would explode. They strapped me to the table, you know. I couldn't move. I thought I was going to die. I remember screaming as loud as I could but this surgeon just ignored me and continued.'

'And you've no idea who this second surgeon was?'

'No. But I heard my young man call him Surgeon-Commander. That's pretty senior, isn't it?'

Leo and Cy exchanged a significant glance. 'Thanks again, Mr Gonvitch. You have been extremely helpful and we're most appreciative.'

'At that time, there was only one Surgeon-Commander on the Platform,' they said to each other afterwards.

It had been some weeks since they had seen Sangyar. He was brought into the room and seated across the table from Leo and Cy.

'You may wait outside,' Leo told the guards.

As soon as the door closed, Sangyar started to speak rapidly. 'Investigators, I know why you have had me brought here. You have completed your investigations and realised that I am not like the other three. Realised that I am innocent of this horrible crime. Sarfeld, Fitch and Glassford planned to kill Gorton and carried out their inhuman plan. I had nothing to do with it. I hope you see that. I am a medical man. I save lives, I don't take lives. It would be against my Medical Oath of Nurture. I hope that you now believe me and are going to set me free. I confess I tried to destroy your evidence. Glassford ordered me to do this and I have already told you that he terrorises everyone. In the past, I have been beaten severely by his guards. He is a very brutal man. I wish you to know that I will be very happy to testify against the other three. They are dreadful and cruel murderers who deserve everything they are going to get from the Command Courts. I want to thank you so much for your understanding of my position. May I now be set free? You will not regret it.' He smiled engagingly.

Neither Leo nor Cy interrupted the diatribe, waiting impassively until Sangyar had finished.

'You have been impersonating Commander Gorton for the last 30 years.' Leo's voice was quiet and flat.

Sangyar's face sagged. 'No, I haven't. They're lying. It was one of them. It wasn't me.'

'It was you, Mr Sangyar. We have the evidence. Any communication for Commander Gorton is forwarded to him through the Category-S Centre in ComCen. As you know, this is a high-security channel that can link only with the actual recipient only. However, all Commander Gorton's communications arrive on your personal device and have been doing so for the last 30 years. Furthermore, we know now that you operated upon the biological link in this system, namely Lieutenant Gonvitch, to switch Commander Gorton's personal channel to you. We know that you operated upon this unfortunate man without anaesthetic, causing him intolerable pain and suffering. What you did – and the way you did it – is totally illegal under Command Medical Law.'

'Listen, Investigators, I had to do it! Glassford insisted. He said the operation had to be done immediately and so there was no time for the usual pre-operative procedures. Surely you must see that none of this was my fault. I am a medical man. I have devoted my whole life to others. I have always obeyed my Medical Oath of Nurture. I have always been a surgeon of the highest quality.'

Leo sighed. 'No, you haven't, Mr Sangyar. You certainly were not in this case. And I am sure if we investigated further, we would find other occasions of your inhumanity and utter selfishness. You may think you can blame everything upon Glassford and Sarfeld, but let me assure you that you cannot. You will be charged with these medical crimes as well as those relating to your involvement in Commander Gorton's murder. We know it was you who gave Glassford the go-ahead for the escape pod transit to start. You and Sarfeld were overlooking the escape pod bay and you were in communication with Glassford, who was with the Remote Pilot who would unwittingly transit Commander Gorton to the asteroid, the place of his death years later. You are, in fact, doubly guilty and that is what we will report.' Both Cy and Leo averted their eyes as Cy summoned the guards.

'Gentlemen, Investigators, please...' Sangyar's voice was a pleading wail as the guards removed him from the room.

Leo handed Cy a glass of wine and they both sat down, sighing wearily. Then Cy laughed wryly. Leo looked at him quizzically. 'What's funny, Cy?'

'Leo, do you remember what our initial thoughts were? We thought the perpetrators of the crime were Admiral Sarfeld and Commander Fitch. That's what Gorton thought, too and that's what his PAC risk analysis advised. In fact, it's the exact opposite! Glassford is the evil genius who dreamed it all up and Sangyar, with his medical skills, became his pathetic, mindless lieutenant. Clearly, the Admiral was happy enough to go along with Glassford's evil scheme. This would solve a serious problem for him, by getting rid of someone who had become a danger to him – or so he thought. Left to himself, Sarfeld could never have attempted anything so complex. Fitch, on the other hand, is certainly an accomplice but he is almost peripheral to the scheme. In many ways, he was just the servant of the other three – the man who did all the odd jobs. In our Final Report, I think that's how we should present the results of our investigation. Do you agree?'

Leo sat deep in thought for a while. Finally he spoke. 'I'm just running the other participants through my mind, Cy. We'll need to mention all the other players in the Report but I don't see any of them as culpable. Even Major Bannerman, running the illegal TP Facility, was blackmailed into it. Of course, that will need to be closed down and he and his staff reassigned. I think the Level-0 security staff are in the clear as well. They were not involved in anything illegal. The piloting and transit control staff were just doing a routine task—a CCO1 experiment, that's all they knew. And all the engineering staff who rebuilt the pod were just doing what they were told. If anyone asked questions, they were quickly shot down or, in extreme cases, transferred and buried somewhere remote within the Platform. Regarding Glassford's brutal guards who are in custody, they can certainly be charged with crimes of violence but, really, they were only doing what they were told to do. To me, they are a case for transfer out and re-education. Have I missed anyone out, Cy?'

'Only the evidence thieves, Leo, the Recovery Team who were acting under Sangyar's direct orders.'

'OK, Cy, we can put our Final Report together now and await the arrival of Sarfeld's replacement, Admiral Joel Arbuthnot. It'll be nice to get back to a bit of peace and quiet, won't it?'

Cy agreed.

The internal communicator chimed. The display offered a message:

To:	Investigator Granvic
	Investigator Funte
From:	Admiral Sarfeld
	Surgeon-Commander Sangyar
	Commander Fitch
	Sub-Commander Glassford
Subject:	Meeting with Admiral Arbuthnot
Text:	We demand a meeting with Admiral Arbuthnot as soon as possible after his arrival.
	{Ends}

Passed/authorised by Chief, Detention Centre.

The reply was sent:

```
To:          Chief, Detention Centre, for:
             Admiral Sarfeld,
             Surgeon-Commander Sangyar
             Commander Fitch,
             Sub-Commander Glassford

From:        Investigator Granvic,
             Investigator Funte

Subject:     Meeting with Admiral Arbuthnot

Text:        Your request will be submitted.

             {Ends}
```

The staff transport vehicle slipped elegantly into Yggdrasil's largest landing bay, coming to a gentle rest on the waiting dock supports that moulded themselves around the contours of its hull. Ramps extended smoothly and hatches were opened. It was a scene of great activity, noise and bustle.

The Duty Receiver boarded. Finally, all appeared to be ready for the formal arrival of the new CCO1. The Yggdrasil band played suitably triumphant music. Leo and Cy stepped forward to the end of the main ramp. Simultaneously, the exceptionally tall, well-made figure of Admiral Joel Arbuthnot appeared in the doorway and strode energetically down the ramp, smiling broadly.

'Good morning, Sir,' Cy said gravely he and Leo extended hands of welcome. 'You are most welcome to the command of SSP Yggdrasil.' (These were the traditional words of welcome to a new CCO1. Such traditions are important.) The official Event Recorder stepped closer with his equipment; his recording of the scene appeared on displays all over the Platform.

'Investigators Funte and Granvic,' the Admiral said in a most pleasant tone, 'I accept your warm welcome with great pleasure.' (The traditional response.) He shook their hands warmly.

Leo swept his arm around in an arc, encompassing the line of Yggdrasil officers who were lined up facing the ramp. 'Sir, may I present your senior officers.'

The senior officers saluted smartly and the Admiral returned their salute, then walked forward to work his way down the line, shaking hands and speaking to each officer. Having reached the end, he then spoke to the assembled officers. 'Thank you, Gentlemen. We will meet again later. I understand we will be dining together this evening. I will look forward to seeing you all then.' The Admiral then turned to Leo and Cy. 'Let us go up to my quarters now.' So saying, he walked out of the bay, into a waiting ILT and, without hesitation, selected Level-9.'

'So you are familiar with SPP Yggdrasil, Sir?' Leo asked.

'Well, yes,' the Admiral responded quietly, 'I do know my way around the Platform.'

A moment later, they arrived at the CCO1 quarters and entered.

'We have one thing we must ask you right away, Sir,' Cy said.

'Yes, Investigator, what is that?'

'Admiral Sarfeld and the three other senior officers who are detained have requested a meeting with you. Of course they will depart for Earth in a few hours when the transport vehicle leaves.'

'Do you know what it is about?'

Cy smiled. 'Knowing them, I imagine they will wish to convince you of their innocence!'

'I see.' The Admiral grimaced. 'I have read your report, so there's not much chance of that. I will see them, though. They are senior officers and have made an official request. However, I would like both of you to be present. You can set the meeting up for 1 hour from now.

Admiral Arbuthnot sat at one side of the desk, with Leo and Cy on either side of him. The four prisoners were brought in by their guards and told to sit down on chairs facing the desk.

Arbuthnot spoke quietly to the guards. 'We will call you when we need you.' The guards saluted and withdrew.

Sarfeld wasted no time. 'Joel,' he trumpeted joyfully, 'welcome to Yggdrasil. I hope you will enjoy it here. It's a wonderful facility. If there's anything I can do...'

Arbuthnot interrupted gently. 'You four gentlemen wished to see me?'

'Ah, yes, Joel,' Sarfeld continued jocularly, 'you see, there has been a terrible mistake and I have been wrongly accused of a dreadful crime. I'm sure you've heard all about it. But I just want to assure you that it's all lies. I would swear my innocence on the Book of Command Law. I've never had anything to do with it – knew nothing about it, in fact. I'm sorry to say that these three gentlemen beside me are the guilty ones and will no doubt pay the penalty. But I have been wrongly associated with the crime just because I was CCO1 here...'

As Sarfeld talked, Fitch and Sangyar began to protest with increasing stridency.

'Sir,' Sangyar pleaded, 'you know I am a medical man, a man who has devoted his life to healing others. I would never harm anyone. I could not possibly do it, because I have taken the Medical Oath of Nurture and I have always followed it. You must believe me, Sir. I should not be here before you. Yes, these others are certainly guilty but I am innocent...'

'That is nonsense,' Fitch cried, 'I am the innocent one. These three are the ones who murdered Commander Gorton. I was never involved. I liked Commander Gorton. He was my superior officer and I respected him. I would never have done anything to hurt him...'

Admiral Arbuthnot held up an imperious hand. 'Be quiet, everyone, please. This matter has been fully investigated by Command Investigators and a Final Report has been submitted. Within three hours, you will leave Yggdrasil and return to Earth where your cases will be tried.'

The hubbub of protest again filled the room. After a minute had passed, Arbuthnot stood up and looked deeply into the eyes of each of the three protesting men. Under the power of his gaze, their vociferous protests died away. Then Arbuthnot turned to address Glassford, who had made neither sound nor movement since he sat down on his chair.

'And you? Do you wish to say anything?'

Glassford's impassive expression did not change. 'Only that I am innocent,' he rejoined.

After a short pause, Arbuthnot walked around the desk to stand motionless in front of the four men. Looking into each face, he spoke just nine words, slowly and dispassionately:

'I know exactly what happened from start to finish.'

Sarfeld, Sangyar and Fitch recoiled physically as these word daggers sliced into their consciousness, razor-sharp blades of incandescent truth that excised all hope. Glassford's reaction was even more dramatic. He held up his arms to shield himself from Arbuthnot's gaze and emitted an inadvertent cry. Then, his face now suffused with disbelief, he uttered just one word:

'You!' A sibilant whisper that somehow reverberated deafeningly in the room.

Many seconds passed seamlessly as if time had become irrelevant. Then Glassford, his eyes blazing with hatred, sprang to his feet, screaming loudly: 'No! It's impossible – impossible!'

The guards were recalled. The four men were propelled unsteadily towards the door.

'Guards, just one moment, please.' Arbuthnot commanded. The prisoners stopped and he walked from the desk to stand before them. He looked at Sarfeld, Sangyar and Fitch, his gaze switching from one to the other. Then he spoke quietly. 'Someday in the future you three may understand that the impossible can become possible. I give you the Key. It is "Conversion without Loss". Never forget it.'

Then he turned to Glassford. 'You have failed once again, as you always will. You have heard what I have just said to the others. However, I know that you will never be able to understand.'

Glassford's eyes flashed with intense evil. 'You are wrong,' he shouted triumphantly. 'This is the moment of your defeat. Your assertion is nonsense. You cannot convert "impossible" to become "possible" without loss. You cannot! You cannot!'

Arbuthnot's voice was calm.

'Yes, I can,' he said.

I'm possible

"And surely I am with you
to the end of the age."

Matthew's Gospel,
Chapter 28, Verse 20b

The Holy Bible,
New International Version
(Biblica, 1973)

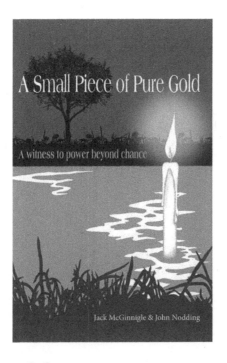

ISBN-13: 9781897913925
RRP: £7.99   Length: 240pp   biography

John Nodding considers his own life from the
angles of family, work, church and travel. More
than most, he had to learn how to abound – or
how to face losses. His experience challenges
readers to become better stewards of God's grace.
Trained as an accountant, Nodding set up his own
computer systems support company for Media
businesses. After selling up, he served as Treas-
urer for various charities and at church. This
often meant having to rein in overenthusiastic
frontline workers! His last fight was with *Motor
Neurone Disease* which affects muscle more than
mind: part of that fight was to write this memoir
in collaboration with Jack McGinnigle.

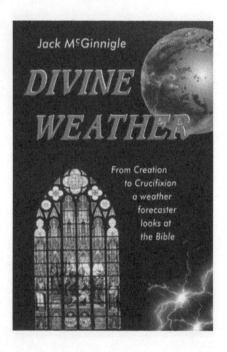

ISBN13: 9781897913611
RRP: £8.99   Length: 256pp   Topical Bible study

A retired meteorologist opens his Bible to help readers reconstruct the surprising number of scenes where weather played a role. He highlights what we can learn about God from weather language in the Bible.

Contains useful illustrations for RE or Sunday School teachers, including a suggested reconstruction of Elija's "cloud like a man's hand"

ISBN13: 9781897913857
RRP: £6.99   Length: 224pp non-fiction

A modern instance akin to the "Wisdom Literature"
of Bible times! In that literary form, the spiritual,
the insightful (and sometimes the painfully obvious)
are subtly blended. Global warming is happening,
and the regions most at risk are often not those who
currently benefit from the consumerist lifestyle. If
individual environmental initiatives seem pointless
because it is too easy for others to cheat, there must
be an opportunity for Christians to show leadership
in community action – remember that *'the earth is
The Lord's.'*

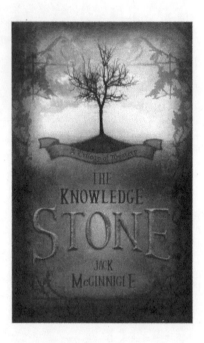

ISBN13: 9781903689820
RRP: £11.99 Length: 414pp Paranormal Fiction

A fascinating trilogy of stories spanning fourteen centuries from the Dark Ages to the 21st Century. Woven around the mysterious Knowledge Stone, each story is a powerful and absorbing account of human actions, emotions and relationships, involving just a handful of finely-drawn characters in tightly-knit, often claustrophobic situations that are filled with acute drama and tragedy. Each story shows that the acquisition of the mysterious Knowledge Stone by one of the characters alters everything in a most fundamental way. The full extent of the mystery is finally revealed in a series of awesome thought provoking explanations linked to powers of cosmic dimensions